Spring's Return

By

Carolyn Tyree Feagans

Carolyn Tyree Feagans
9-27-07

Spring's Return

Library of Congress Catalog Card Number
94-90083

ISBN 0-9634627-2-5

Fourth Printing

Cover photo by the author taken on the
Blue Ridge Mountains

All poems written by the author

Warwick House

Publishing

"A beautiful, heart-wrenching story of the Barrett Family facing personal trials, struggling to grow through volatile societal changes, seeking to find their faith and gaining strength from this great earth. Spanning three generations in time, one is carried from the Blue Ridge Mountains of Virginia to the Black Hills of South Dakota. Wonderful reading for the whole family!"

—Del. Joyce K. Crouch
House of Delegates, Virginia

"It really fills my heart to read such a wonderful book that depicts the Native-American as a loving people. A book that all people should read. It is great to read a book about a loving family and their lives...society needs more books like this!"

—Phyllis Hicks
Director, Monacan Ancestral Museum

"*Spring's Return* captures the turmoil of being half Indian and half white in today's society. The author also shows through her picture in words the real strength of the Native people — the WOMEN!! Beautifully written!"

—George Branham Whitewolf
Monacan Indian Tribal Secretary

"Here are the answers for all the readers who wondered what happened in the lives of Spring and the next generation of Barretts. The author weaves a tapestry of threads gleaned from early days of living in downtown Lynchburg, while maximizing current events over twenty-five years and the awakening of Native-American pride in Amherst County's own Monacan Indians."

—Meg Hibbert
Assistant Editor, *Amherst New Era-Progress*

*Dedicated to the One who looketh on the
heart instead of the outward appearance...*

and

...to one who lived this way...Daddy

Table of Contents

1965

1973

1990

Heath and Emily Barrett

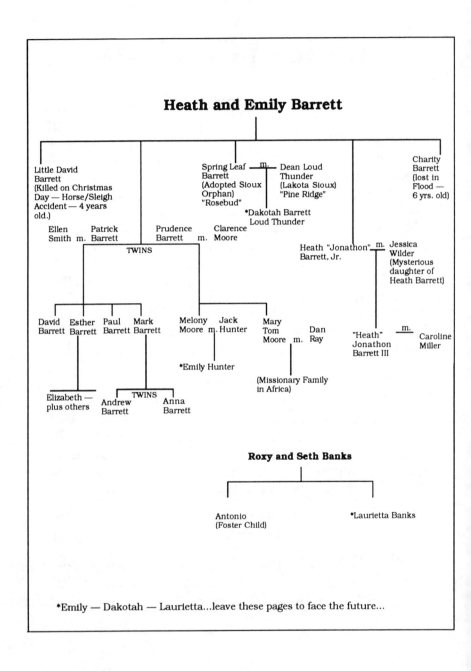

Little David
Barrett
(Killed on Christmas
Day — Horse/Sleigh
Accident — 4 years
old.)

Spring Leaf —m.— Dean Loud
Barrett   Thunder
(Adopted Sioux   (Lakota Sioux)
Orphan)   "Pine Ridge"
"Rosebud"
            *Dakotah Barrett
            Loud Thunder

Charity
Barrett
(lost in
Flood —
6 yrs. old)

Ellen   Patrick   Prudence   Clarence
Smith m. Barrett   Barrett   m. Moore
            TWINS

Heath "Jonathon" —m. Jessica
Barrett, Jr.   Wilder
                       (Mysterious
                       daughter of
                       Heath Barrett)

David   Esther Paul   Mark   Melony   Jack   Mary
Barrett Barrett Barrett Barrett   Moore m. Hunter   Tom   Dan
                                                      Moore m. Ray

                                    *Emily Hunter

                                                      (Missionary Family
                                                      in Africa)

"Heath"   —m.— Caroline
Jonathon   Miller
Barrett III

Elizabeth —   TWINS
plus others   Andrew   Anna
              Barrett   Barrett

Roxy and Seth Banks

Antonio   *Laurietta Banks
(Foster Child)

*Emily — Dakotah — Laurietta...leave these pages to face the future...

Preface

Spring's Return
...to be enjoyed as a novel in its own entity...
...or as a sequel to *The Dogwoods Are Blooming*...

It stands alone, independent, for all to share in the two worlds that Spring Barrett struggles with each day of her life. She bounces back and forth between these worlds — the gentle Blue Ridge Mountains of Virginia and the mysterious Black Hills of South Dakota. She seeks purpose in life, torn between her noble Sioux heritage and her love for her adopted family — the Barrett family of Oak Mountain.

Discover with Spring...her thoughts, her feelings and her revelations. Face with her...joys, trials and regrets. Follow the amazing and inspiring progress of the unique Crazy Horse Memorial in the Black Hills with Spring. Experience life in a small southern town in the sixties and seventies. Feel the trauma of this restless era as the Vietnam saga and racial strife crushed its spirit. Witness the mystery and trial of Heath Jonathon Barrett, III as old and forgotten skeletons tumble out. Through all of this, find comfort in a faith and love shared by the Barrett family...and find comfort in the never changing mountains.

Spring's Return was birthed by one before...*The Dogwoods Are Blooming*. If you have read this book, you must read *Spring's Return* for the rest of the story. However, if you have not, don't miss out on this exciting book!

A brief synopsis of
The Dogwoods Are Blooming...

Its story begins at the turn of the century and follows
a mountain family through three generations. The
main characters, Emily and Heath Barrett, struggle
throughout its pages for purpose, love and strength as
they're faced with incredible tragedies. Emily is the
central pillar of the large family, and her undying love
for Heath overcomes all obstacles including poverty and
infidelity. The loss of two children is a devastating blow
to their marriage. The first, Little David, is tragically
killed at the tender age of four on Christmas Day during
a horse-drawn sleigh wreck. This practically destroys
the marriage as Emily blames Heath for his careless
ways and drinking. Years later their last child, Charity,
who was born severely retarded, is claimed by the
nightmare flood with many others when it hits Oak
Mountain in the night.

Within its pages, the family leaves the comfort of the
Blue Ridge and travels west to the plains of South
Dakota. During this short stay, Emily discovers 'Spring
Leaf' through her work at an Indian mission. Spring (as
her name is shortened) steals her heart along with
Heath's, and they ultimately adopt her, bringing her
back with them to the Blue Ridge Mountains as their
oldest daughter. She grows up on Oak Mountain and
shares the humble mountain cabin with her brothers
and sisters: Patrick and Prudence (twins), Jonathon
and Charity.

The climax of *The Dogwoods Are Blooming* is the
dramatic and traumatic flood at the end of Part I. It is

during this catastrophe that Heath's promiscuous ways with the heartless Betty Lou come to a sudden halt, as she disappears forever. But as fate would have it, the flood abates, the waters subside...however a trickle flows unnoticed...and Betty Lou's seed, the beautiful and intriguing Jessica Wilder appears later in Part II to confound and complicate matters by actually marrying Jonathon!

Meanwhile, Spring deals with her own struggles, delicately walking the fence between her worlds — the white man and the Indian. She seeks understanding. While painting her cherished painting, *The Dogwoods*, at Lover's Leap, she meets him! A Monacan Indian of the Blue Ridge...and falls in love. Disillusioned with their differences, she chooses to leave him...a fateful mistake.

Part III witnesses Heath's death in old age and also Emily's as she quickly follows. Their epitaph symbolizes their entwined lives...' 'Till death us do part... But only for a season...Together again'.

The curtain falls on a pensive scene as Spring sits by the graves of her adoptive parents while tears flow down her high cheekbones. She feels a gentle breeze caress her forehead and senses a presence. She calls out... "Mama, is that you? Is it you, Daddy?" Her voice trails off into the still forest. "Seek and ye shall find...." What? Words spoken so audibly that she expected to turn around and see someone, but there was no one. They had come from within, she realized, from way down within, stashed away many years ago.

We pick up now...to find out what Spring discovers in her search...

Chapter I
The Black Hills

She stomped the brake, bringing the little T-Bird to a screeching halt, and stared in disbelief as the huge buffalo blocked her path with its hostile black eyes upon her.

"Well, just who do you think you are?" Spring demanded, still a bit shaken.

The monstrous creature didn't budge, but stood there defiantly with its tail outstretched, which wasn't a good sign.

"O...kay, so we've come to an impasse! Is it gonna be me or you?"

With a mighty thrust of its enormous head, it thundered off, out of the way and back into the dense Ponderosa Pines. Spring let off the brake, just then realizing how taut and strained her ankles were from the tension. She gassed the little car and sped around the curves that wove their way through the Black Hills.

"An impasse...yes, that's it! That's where I am...even without the buffalo." She laughed aloud. "Why am I here again? Of course...to find myself... remember?" Ironically, a tear escaped her reservoir of strength and momentarily blurred her vision. She blinked and smiled. "Why do you do this to me?" She spoke not to anyone...but to the hills. The old familiar hills...so many times throughout the last twenty odd years she'd visited them, being drawn back time and time again as if by a powerful magnet. She realized there was a kinship here...a kinship with her ancestors whose bones were rotting away throughout these sacred hills. Her thoughts reached back to the first time she'd seen them, when she'd left Virginia to come home to South Dakota. They were beautiful then as they were now. No, they were more beautiful now! Now that she was older...quite a bit older and wiser, she was better able to appreciate them.

As she approached Deadwood, seeing the crowded streets filled with bustling tourists, she felt the old resentment creeping in. She pushed it aside and fought to be objective, determined to be open, to seek...to find. Wasn't that what she'd promised herself? Promised her mama and daddy that last time she'd stood beside their graves?

She whipped into a parking space, feeling a sense of pride in the sleek Thunderbird. It always caught attention, and she liked that. She glanced up to the rearview mirror and noticed the crow's feet deepening. Gosh! That expensive miracle cream wasn't helping either. Oh well, she smoothed back her dark hair. At least, *that* wasn't greying like most of her friends, she thought, while stepping out of the car and locking the door.

"Ma'am, that 'sho' is a fine-looking automobile you got yourself there." The aging man with weathered skin spoke in a distinct southern drawl as he admiringly assessed her vehicle.

"Thank you, Sir. I think so, too."

"You from around these parts?" he asked.

Spring looked up. "Sort of."

"Then maybe you can tell us how to get to Mt. Rushmore. My wife here had the directions written down, but somehow we misplaced them."

Spring looked first at him and then to his overly plump wife, who peered around him with a friendly smile. She began to direct them, but was interrupted.

"You sound like you're from the south? We're all the way from Tennessee, Knoxville, that is."

Spring smiled. "Actually I am — Virginia. Guess we can't hide our southern accents, can we?"

"Don't want to...proud to be from Dixie." The old man swelled with pride.

As Spring waved them off, she felt sort of warm inside. Tourists were people after all...people from all over...even from her beloved Blue Ridge Mountains. Suddenly she felt very hungry and started across the congested street to a restaurant that boasted of Buffalo Buffet and 5¢ Coffee. She could stand a 5¢ Coffee! Once seated in a cozy booth, examining the varied menu, she longed for mountain trout...but the way Mama had cooked it. Not with its head, eyeballs and all staring up at you! Her stomach, feeling just a mite queasy, wasn't quite up to that, and she settled for soup and salad.

Leaning back upon the cushiony red booth, she couldn't help but hear the conversation going on behind her apparently between some couple.

"...but, Honey, I still think it's sad...you know...all of them being herded onto reservations...."

"Now, Katherine, they were a bunch of savages! What else could the government do?"

Spring gripped the cup tightly in her hands, struggling not to turn around. She remembered the many times before when she'd spoken out in anger. To what avail? No, there was a better way, though much slower. Soon the couple got up and strode past her. A young fair-headed fellow with his arm loosely around a petite brunette. Probably on their honeymoon or something, she thought. Her mind skipped ahead. Wonder what Dean was going to think? Would he be surprised? Most likely. Dean Loud Thunder, you can just wait...I'll take my time. Yes, time. That's what I need. Time to think...time to sort through...time to reason.

After half finishing her lunch, she meandered through the busy streets of Deadwood, listening to the western music of another era as it reverberated off the rustic ceilings of the wooden porches that shaded the crowds of hurried tourists. She found herself carried along with the crowd as though caught up in a wave, tossed aside every now and then, to discover another gift shop like all the others displaying western gear and Indian artifacts. She sat down on a crude bench outside one of the shops to watch the parade of faces. This must have resembled that last "gold rush" so many years ago. She smiled while amusing herself with the varied sea of faces. Yes, there was a lot of history here in this little town. The last gold rush in Deadwood! But what did it do to her people? Oh well, she must not look back...but forward. The small T-Bird sped along once again, hugging the narrow curves and inclines of the Black Hills, while Spring's mind raced backwards and forwards, reliving the past and searching the future. Ever since she received his letter, she felt like a school girl all over again. No, not a school girl...at least not her. She never felt that way in school. Guess I'm a late bloomer, she thought to herself with a hint of excitement. Of course, there was another time many years ago. But that was so very far back. It was amazing that she still carried with her those memories so vividly. But *he* was part of a dream. *Dean* is reality. Dean is flesh and blood now...strong and virile...warm and caring. Could they have a chance at happiness? She must not get her hopes up too high...even though he'd begged her forgiveness in the letter. Even though he said he was sorry for all he'd said. But she was too old now and too wise to let her guard down. In spite of these romantic notions, she must be cautious.

The drive from Deadwood to Keystone seemed longer than usual. But finally she rounded the curve and there it was...full of life as always. She needed a stretch plus some gas. After taking care of the latter, she walked through the familiar streets, inhaling the fresh mountain air. Nowhere could compare...except for Oak Mountain. Would she ever choose one over the other? She smiled. They were both old friends of hers. She recalled her last visit to Arizona...to Tucson...and those awesome Rockies. But to her, they were unfriendly. They didn't beckon her to become a part of them.

Instead, one stood in awe and admiration of such a feat. The brave souls that chose to conquer her perilous heights, risked their lives and sometimes gave their lives up to those barren granite peaks. Unlike the famed Rockies, these Black Hills are...well...comfortable. She rested against the Pine fence that separated the busy parking lot and the cold, rushing mountain stream that flowed down from the hills and into Keystone. Her eyes followed the crystal clear water searching for the ever present Rainbow Trout.

"Look Mom...I see a fish!" a lad of about eight yelled into her ear, shattering the tranquillity of the stream.

"I see, Son. Don't fall in." The mother smiled at her as she juggled her packages in order to watch her energetic offspring.

"Hey Mom, why is this place called the Black Hills?" the little fellow asked while tossing stones into the stream.

"Well, because...Brian...I don't really know."

Spring turned to the lad. "You see all those Pine trees up there? There are so many of them in these hills that from a distance, they appear black sometimes."

"Oh." Satisfied with this bit of information, he ran off toward the trail stables. His mom awkwardly followed, only half trotting with the burden of her cumbersome treasures.

Spring slid back into her little car and was glad once more to leave the bustling, busy town of Keystone. But she could never come through without stopping. Its aging charm held a magic all its own, even though Mt. Rushmore had certainly made a boom town out of it. Those famous faces were just up the road now. She wouldn't stop, but looked forward to seeing them as always. They represented one half of her life...her family...her way of life...her America! She wondered what Dean felt when he saw them? Glancing at her watch, she saw that it was almost two o'clock. He would be in class now most likely lost in discussion. She was proud of him. Never had she known anyone so dedicated to teaching. *"There they are!"* she whispered, while feeling the familiar chills as she stared upward into the powerful chiseled faces full of determination emblazoned in stone. Suddenly she felt like standing at attention and singing *America the Beautiful.* Then as suddenly as they appeared, they disappeared. She waited to catch that last glimpse of *George.* Driving around the west side of the memorial, she leaned to see him...and there he was. A stark profile! Her eyes were misty again with such awesome beauty that stirred the artistic emotions within. To think that Borglum didn't start working on it until after he was sixty! Well, there was something to be said for old age...the middle-aged generation, too. Wasn't that what Mary Tom called us? That gal! She smiled as she thought of Mary Tom, and began to feel a twinge of homesickness. She thought of Melony. Poor little Melony. She still couldn't understand it all. Why, Melony was always little Miss Perfect growing up, so sweet and all. Who would ever have guessed it!

Chapter II
The Blue Ridge Mountains

Melony leaned against the open window with its soft, sheer curtains gently blowing in the subtle evening breeze. She inhaled the fresh mountain air as if she couldn't get enough of it. The upstairs window looked out upon a sprawling lawn that boasted of a backdrop like none other. The hazy blue mountains formed a border and a shield from the rest of the world. So glad was she to be away from the rest of the world. So glad was she to be away from Atlanta...with all of its noise and confusion. No place like home, here in the midst of these tranquil mountains...even though Jack could never agree. But then, when did she and Jack ever agree?

Little Emily toddled into the peaceful room, pulling a quacking duck behind her. The wooden toy waddled noisily across the polished hardwood floor and onto the worn braided rug which muffled the quacking to a muted baritone. Little Emily was lost in her own little world of fantasy and didn't even notice her mother watching. Melony's heart filled with love as she watched her young daughter, so precious was she. How could Jack stand being separated from her? At the same moment she thought about these things, reliving the past several months, her parents were also discussing the situation as they drove to church for Wednesday night prayer meeting.

"Now Pru, there's no sense in being put out over all this. You know we can't do anything…but try and help her the best we know how."

"Clarence, you don't understand. We never had a *divorce* in this family in all these years. You can't expect me to just act like it's another…another family crisis that will work itself out. This is final!"

"I know that, Hon, but there's no use gettin' yourself all worked up about it when we can't stop it. I don't know that I would if I could."

"Clarence, how can you say such a thing?"

"Honey, we can't expect Melony to live with infidelity. It just ain't right."

"I know, but divorce! What would Mama say?"

Clarence sighed, "Thank God, she's spared this."

"I'm not so sure."

Clarence turned to look at her, "What do you mean?"

"I just have this feeling that Mama knows."

PRAYER MEETING HAD BEGUN, and the double doors were closed. Clarence and Pru quietly pushed them open and found seats in the back of the small sanctuary. Patrick nodded at them from the pulpit and

continued with his announcements. Prudence noticed
for the first time how grey his hair was getting — a lot
more than hers — but it gave him a mighty distinguished look, even though it was a visible reminder for
both of them. One thing about having a twin, it was like
looking in a mirror as the years slipped by. Oh me, what
is he going to think about the divorce?

This prayer meeting, as well as the last few, was
centered around the on-going violence taking place in
the nation between the Whites and the Negroes. Patrick
was unusually disturbed tonight after the recent violence right in Richmond. He concluded with..."*We don't
know what tomorrow holds, but we do know who holds
tomorrow.*"

After the last Amen and prayer, he made his way
quickly to the front door in order to shake every hand as
he had done year after year...usually the same hands.
But every now and then, there would pop up a strange
one, much to his delight.

"Well, I'm 'askeered' of my shadow these days," Mrs.
Nichols confided to him as she placed her bony hand in
his. "I don't know what this old world's coming to. Used
to be you could walk on the streets and know what to
expect. But a body don't know what to do now."

Patrick gently patted her hand, "Don't worry, Mrs.
Nichols, I don't think it's hit these parts yet. And I'm
sure the good Lord's gonna take care of you."

Prudence smiled warmly at her brother. He always
seemed to have the right words. She stood patiently
beside him while Clarence discussed farm work with a
couple of members in the middle of the aisle.

"Seems ever since that civil rights law was passed

last year, ain't been nothin' but fighting and carrying on ever since," Mr. Abbott added while following Mrs. Nichols out the door. "I knew it was gonna mean trouble." He wiped the perspiration from his brow, folded up the large handkerchief, placed it back in his back trouser pocket and reached for Patrick's hand.

"Good evening, Mr. Abbott. All I can say is our prayers are needed."

"Yes sir, Preacher. You're plumb right!"

Clarence came up behind them, "You ready, Hon. It's a mite hot in here."

"I'll be there directly, Clarence. Go ahead on." She moved closer to Patrick and caught his eye.

"Excuse me, Mr. Abbott."

He hastily joined Prudence, "How's Melony?"

"That's what I need to talk with you about," she began. "She's gonna be gone awhile tomorrow...she and Little Emily. You s'pose you could drop by for a spell?"

"If I get an offer for one of your special desserts, I'll be there right after lunch."

"How about peach cobbler?"

"See you then."

THE NIGHT AIR felt good blowing in the car windows as it passed the recently plowed fields. Clarence noticed Prudence was in deep thought.

"What're you gonna talk to Patrick about?"

"What do you mean?"

"You know, when he comes over tomorrow."

Prudence smiled at him, "I certainly can't keep anything from you, can I?"

"Not after all these years."

"Well, I just thought maybe Patrick, being a preacher and all, might be able to help out the situation."

"Patrick always helps out any situation, but don't go expecting him to perform any miracles."

Prudence frowned, "I won't."

The rest of the trip home was in silence as they each examined their own thoughts about their little girl...their firstborn. But now she faced problems they couldn't mend the way they'd mended a stumped toe when she was small.

Melony lay restlessly upon her childhood bed in the upstairs room she and Little Emily were sharing. Even though the room was dark except for the slight glow of the moon casting its shadows about, she could just about pick out the design on the wallpaper. She had examined it in minute detail many times while growing up, especially when she was forcefully detained there for some mischief she and Mary Tom had gotten into. But she never dreamed of being back here this way...with a young daughter...and no husband. The familiar room that had protected her and comforted her through those years somehow now wasn't the same. What was that old saying? *"You can't go back."* No. She must move on. She must make a new life for herself and Little Emily, and tomorrow, she would begin! It wouldn't be easy. But then, it hadn't been easy the last couple of years. The hurt and humiliation still stung. Why did her marriage have to end up like this? She had certainly tried! She had really wanted it to work...that's why she'd forgiven him over and over again, until that last Sunday. Why did it have to be a Sunday? That troubled scene was again before her, having been eternally etched into her mind. He with his best charcoal suit on, looking as handsome as ever and...she, whoever she was, as pretty as a picture. Arm in arm, they were. The stark realization had hit her like a ton of bricks! She had cried for days, but not anymore...Melony Hunter! She would not look back. She would show him...and everyone else.

Little Emily whimpered in her sleep. Melony pulled her tiny body close to hers and tenderly smoothed her brow while she slept.

PATRICK KNOCKED ON THE SCREEN door promptly at 1:00 the next day. He could smell the peach cobbler already as it warmed in the oven. Nobody fixed peach cobbler like his sister...except for Mama. Mama's had been just as good...maybe just a fraction better.

"Oh, you're here." Pru hurried to the door and unlatched the screen. "Come on in and pull up a chair."

"Melony gone?"

"Oh yes. She and Little Emily left early this morning. Said something about going to visit some old friends over in Lynchburg. Seemed awful anxious to be on her way."

"How is she, Pru?"

Sitting down at the table across from him, she groped for the right words. "Well, Patrick, Melony is... well, she says she's gonna get a divorce!"

He looked up suddenly.

"Yes, that's what she aims to do. Told me so herself just the other day."

Patrick reached over to hold his sister's hand.

"Patrick, you've got to do something!"

"Just what do you have in mind, Sis?"

"Well, I don't know exactly, but you know we've never had a divorce in this family. My gracious, just look what Mama went through."

Patrick sighed, "Mama was one of a kind."

"Certainly you don't condone divorce, Reverend Barrett. I know you don't!"

" 'Course not, Sis. But we can't push Melony back into a marriage that is all wrong. Maybe we need to give it some time...and, of course, this is Melony's decision. Not ours. But I would like to talk with her."

"Yes, that's a good idea. Do you want me to have her call you?"

"No. I'll get in touch with her."

"Thank you, Patrick. I feel better already. How's Ellen feeling today?"

"You know there's nothing worse than a summer cold, and it's certainly been hot here lately...but she's fairing better."

"I was just reading in the paper how this is the worst draught we've had in about ten years. Just think how it must be down in the valley. They tell me old Mr. Martin near about passed out the other day while tending to his chickens. Well, at least we have it a mite cooler 'round Oak Mountain."

"We need to keep on praying for rain. It'll come."

"Have you heard from David lately?"

"Not since the last letter I told you about."

"You know, Patrick, I wish I could be more like you...with an ailing wife, and son in Vietnam. Why, I never hear you complain. And here I am laying my troubles on you, too."

"That's my calling, Sis. To try and help, you know."

"I know. Well, I sent David a care package a couple of days ago. I wanted you to know...filled it with some of my sugar cookies plus some other things. You know, he always liked my sugar cookies so. Don't forget to tell Ellen."

"I won't. That peach cobbler ready yet?"

Prudence busied herself with taking it out of the large oven and serving it piping hot...the way Patrick loved it best. It pleased her immensely to cater to her brother.

"Jonathon been by this week?" he asked in between bites.

"Matter of fact, I haven't seen our baby brother for almost two weeks now. Jessica did call the other day. Said they'd just gotten back from Virginia Beach. Spent a week, I believe."

"I knew they'd gone. Guess Heath went too?"

"Oh yes, although Jessica said he didn't much want to. You know how teenagers are."

"Certainly. I figured he'd gone, too. Hadn't seen him around. You know how close he, Paul and Mark stick."

"I think that's good. Good for cousins to be close... and good for Heath, too...he being the only child and all."

"Heath seems like a mighty fine lad."

"He sure is."

He wiped his mouth with the red and white gingham napkin and stood up. "Guess I'd best be getting on down the road." He pushed the chair back from the table gently. "Have you heard from Spring?"

"No, I haven't. Sent her a letter just last week... and

I told her about Melony. You know how much she thinks of Melony, and of Mary Tom, of course."

"I'm concerned about Spring. She seems so confused and alone. I felt sorry for her when she left. If only she could find peace."

"You know Spring. She's always been confusing. I've never been able to figure her out."

"Yeah, I know. But I hate to think about her all alone way out there...growing old."

"You're right. It's one thing to grow old with a family, and another thing to grow old alone."

"Well, we've gotta keep praying for her. See you later." The screen door slammed behind him, and Prudence smiled as he drove off. There was something special between them.

MELONY SMOOTHED HER dress and put on her best smile while summoning all the confidence she could muster. She pushed open the door to the music store and walked in with her shoulders pulled back the way Mother had always told her to. At first glance, the store appeared vacant, but then she noticed an old, colored man bent over a dust pan trying to scoop up the last remnants of trash. He would sweep the few particles toward the pan, but invariably they sailed through the air, up and over the pan each time, and he patiently repeated the process. He was so absorbed with his task, he didn't seem to notice her at all. She cleared her throat.

" 'Scuse me, Ma'am. Didn't see'ya come in. Wait jest a minute and I go git Mr. Sterlin'."

With that, he disappeared through an open door

leading into a back room. She looked at the worn broom he'd left standing against the counter. It looked out of place there with all the shiny stringed instruments...violins, violas and cellos lining the wall. A beautiful, ornate harp graced the nearby corner, but her eyes were drawn to the other side of the spacious room...to the most elegant piano she'd ever seen. How she'd love to play *it*! Just then a small, wiry man with spectacles resting on his thin, angular nose, rushed forward.

"May I help you, young lady?"

Caught somewhat off guard, Melony forgot her rehearsed opening and could feel herself getting red. "Yes Sir...I would like to...to speak with someone about...about a job?"

"A job?" the serious Mr. Sterling repeated.

"Yes Sir. You see, I play the piano fairly well...and also the guitar somewhat. I thought you might be in need of a teacher...a music teacher...."

"Don't need any teacher now." His abrupt words caused Melony's face to drop. But he quickly followed up, "Know anything about a cash register?"

"Some...and I catch on fast."

"Come on back to meet the wife." He turned and waved her on. "We might be able to use you."

Mrs. Sterling was propped up on several over-stuffed pillows against a Victorian couch that now was faded with age. She looked Melony over from the top of her glasses while still shining what looked like a used trumpet. Her plump hands never ceased their rhythmic motions.

"Molly, this is...what did you say your name was?"

Not mentioning that she hadn't, she quickly replied, "Melony Hunter...Melony Moore Hunter, that is."

"Good morning, Miss Hunter, you kin to any of the Moores around Appomattox way?"

"No Ma'am, I don't think so. My folks are from Oak Mountain."

"I see."

"She's inquiring about a job."

"Do you like serving the public?"

"I don't mind. I like people. You see, I really need a job very badly. It's just my little girl and myself...and I know I could do a good job for you."

"How do you know?" Mrs. Sterling asked inquisitively.

"Because...because I would give it my all!"

"She's also a pianist, Molly, and plays the guitar if we need a teacher sometime."

Mrs. Sterling pushed her glasses back up her nose and dismissed the subject as well. "Put her to work then, Leon."

Melony followed the obedient Mr. Sterling back out to the front, and he gave her further instructions. As she prepared to leave, she turned to him, "You wouldn't by any chance know someone of good character who I might get for a babysitter?"

"Can't say that I do," he replied absently while walking her to the door.

"Jest a minute, Ma'am." The old colored man rose from behind the counter. "I's got a daughter that's lookin' for work...and she 'sho' is a fine character."

"You speaking of Roxy, Jim?"

"Yessum."

"Well, I couldn't think of anyone better." He turned
to Melony. "Jim has a fine family!"

AS MELONY DROVE SLOWLY back to Oak Moun-
tain, she reflected on all the events of the day. Little
Emily was asleep in the back seat. It was hot, and the
evening air felt good blowing in the windows. She felt
excited. She had a job! What was Mother going to think?
She really hoped she could please the Sterlings. That
might be a little hard from what she'd seen. And she
sure hoped this Roxy would work out. One thing for
sure, she couldn't leave her with her friend, Glenda,
again. Little Emily had taken an immediate dislike to
her today. Glenda had changed from when they'd gone
to business school together. Why, she'd been such a
delight to be around at Phillips, but now, she didn't seem
like the same person. You'd think she'd be happy as
anything with a fine husband and two bright children
and such a nice little home. They were buying it, too!
Oh, well, you could never tell about people. She was
anxious to meet this Roxy on Friday...but what was her
mother going to think?

As she neared home, she noticed the masses of bright
yellow Daisies lining the roadside. Mixed among them
every now and then were the striking Black-Eyed Susans.
She smiled. They were her mother's favorite. Even
midst this scorching summer, Oak Mountain protected
its own! She sort of dreaded leaving, but she must. Well,
at least she wouldn't be that far away. Not like Atlanta!
She was torn between Charlottesville and Lynchburg,
but then she thought she had a friend in Lynchburg...
now she didn't know. But she was more familiar with it

having attended the business school briefly. At that
time, however, she'd been sheltered by the aging walls
of the YWCA! Now, she would really be on her own! But
she could do it...she had to!

The roosters crowed and Friday morning dawned
with the promise of another hot day. Prudence busied
herself in the kitchen, frying bacon, but she couldn't
help worrying about Melony. Striking out on her own
like this! Was it safe? What about Little Emily? What
about this person called Roxy?

"Good morning, Mother." The lift in Melony's voice
carried an air of anticipation.

"Good morning, Dear. Is Little Emily up yet?"

"No. She's sleeping soundly. I thought I'd wait a bit
before waking her."

"Good idea. Melony, please be careful about this
situation."

"Situation?"

"I mean — you know — this day and time, things are
different. There's a lot of trouble brewing between...."

"You mean racial trouble?"

"Yes...and you don't know this Roxy person at all...."

"Mother, she comes highly recommended by Mr.
Sterling."

"Well, I'd still feel better if you...."

"What? Had a white girl keeping Little Emily?"

"Well, yes...."

"Mother, you yourself told me that an old Negro
woman raised Grandpa Barrett!"

"I know. But that was different. She lived with the
family. Daddy said Annie was part of the family. That's

the way it was back then."

"Everything will be fine, Mother. Looks like it's gonna be another hot one."

Prudence knew she wanted to change the subject. "Yes, it certainly is, and I know your father's gonna burn up. He didn't put on that cool shirt I laid out for him before going out to the field."

"You know Dad. He's got a mind of his own."

"Amen."

THE SLIGHTLY STOUT colored girl stood in the doorway resting on first one foot, then the other. She appeared nervous but friendly with a broad smile lighting up her smooth, dark face, and her big expressive eyes had a quality of merriment about them. Her simple print dress was pressed and neat, and her freshly polished saddle oxfords stood out as they covered her rather large feet. Obviously, she was young, but how young, Melony couldn't tell.

"Roxy, this here is Melony Hunter," Mr. Sterling began his introductions.

"How do you do, Miss Hunter."

"Please call me Melony."

"And call me Roxy. Everybody calls me Roxy...not Roxanne...I hate Roxanne."

Melony felt warmed already. She liked her!

"Is that the little one?"

Little Emily was quietly sitting on the counter stool where Melony had placed her upon arrival. She appeared drowsy.

"Yes, this is Little Emily...she's still a bit sleepy."

Roxy moved toward her slowly. "Hello baby. My

what a pretty li'l thing you are."

Little Emily smiled up at her.

"Looks like you passed the test," chuckled Mr. Sterling. "Well, here's the apartment ad I told you about." He handed the crumpled paper to her.

"Madison Street," she read aloud.

"Do you know where it is?" Roxy asked.

"Not really."

"I'd be glad to show you. It's not far from our place."

DRIVING ALONG THE COBBLED streets lined with huge Oak trees, Melony stared in awe at the stately old homes from another era. Some were exquisite; others were in a sad state of disrepair.

"Here it is!" Roxy pointed to a large, brown stone house with the most unusual architecture that Melony had ever seen...even in Atlanta.

"It's so big!"

"You can say that again...three floors at least... almost looks like one'a them castles you read about over in England or somewheres," Roxy added.

"Even has a turret...a medieval tower...if you will."

Roxy nodded, "It has class...real class."

"Guess we park on the street?" Melony glanced around.

"Be the only place to." Roxy smiled and Melony looked a bit irritated.

"Well, I'm used to driveways, you know."

Roxy raised her eyebrows and kept quiet as Melony parked the car by the curb in front of the sprawling lawn. She opened the door and got out, looking back at her.

"Think I'll jest sit here with Li'l Emily."
Melony glanced at her already asleep in the back
seat, and proceeded to walk up the wide sidewalk. Roxy
settled back comfortably and stared after her. What a
house! She wondered who might have lived here many
years ago when it was new. Who had all the money to
build such a house? There was a veranda that ran across
the entire length of the front of the house and on around
both sides of it. Above the porch, the house took on its
own personality and divided itself three ways. The right
side was typically an A-roof, but the left side boasted of
its own medieval turret that seemed to leap out of Gothic
pages. The two were distinctly divided by a middle
portion that adorned itself with a solitary dormer that
sat perched atop a midsection, displaying a large oval
opening that was framing a window. At least seventeen
large windows faced the street, including those encir-
cling the turret on all three floors. Graceful shrubs
hugged the house midst traces of flower gardens long
since discarded. The house itself sat atop a knoll with
the back grounds dropping off abruptly. Roxy shifted
her position in order to examine the place more thoroughly. She noticed a smaller house situated behind the
great house, down the hill a ways. It was made of the
same brown stone and the architecture was the same,
only not so grandeur. It must have been the servants'
quarters, she thought...or even the slave quarters. She
wondered what was taking Melony so long.

The realtor marched from one room to the other with
Melony following. She noticed the high ceilings, much
higher than those back home...and the large rooms. The
wallpaper was faded but still pretty. The floors were

wooden with no carpet. She remembered the nice carpeted apartment they'd had back in Atlanta. But she especially liked the immense windows that reached from the high ceilings and spanned the floor, letting in the piercing sunlight. Yes, this could be home. She would make it home...home for her and Little Emily.

As they left, bumping over the cobbled stones, she said to Roxy, "Thanks for everything. One thing for sure, we won't live far apart."

"Nope. You could throw a rock from one to the other, and I'll be able to walk't in no time carrying Laurietta, too."

Melony pulled up in front of Roxy's home. It was very neat but could use a paint job. "Roxy, are you sure you can manage both Little Emily and your little baby, too?"

"Shucks, what you think I am? A weakling? I could handle a dozen if I wanted to." With that, she climbed out and waved good-bye.

"I believe you could," she whispered with a smile and drove off. All the way back to Oak Mountain, she planned and thought about her new life ahead. She'd never lived in a town, except for her brief stay at the YWCA. Even in Atlanta, they'd lived way out in the suburbs which was sort of like country in a way. Not even a place to park your car! She wondered about Roxy. She must have it hard living with her folks and her husband off in Vietnam. Already, she felt drawn to her. She knew Little Emily would be in good hands.

Chapter III
Crazy Horse

Spring stuffed the remaining bundles in the tiny trunk of her car and tried to close it. After several tries, it slammed shut. She turned to look once more at the temporary home she'd enjoyed for the past couple of days. The rustic cabin was nestled among tall Pines and was somewhat private among all the other cabins. It had been nice! Her thoughts were clearer now, and she felt more capable of making the right decisions. She eased under the steering wheel and looked at the unfinished manuscript lying in the seat beside her. Would she ever finish it? She was stuck! She might as well shelve it for now. She was an artist...not a writer anyway. And how could she write her story? She was still living it!

She drove up to the park office to settle up. Dressed in native attire with her hair braided, she walked into the cramped office, receiving more than one curious look. She spoke in her articulate but southern accent, which created more interest. She handed the short, bearded man her American Express card, while feeling the stares, and turned with a smile and walked out. She always enjoyed every opportunity to confound those around her as to who she was.

She headed toward *Crazy Horse*. This was one place she could not pass by. Drawn to it repeatedly throughout the years, she had watched its progress with pride. She remembered feeling a bit skeptic while on her first visit to the Black Hills and also to Crazy Horse. Why, who ever heard of sculpturing an entire mountain! There was a lot of skepticism back then. But down inside, she had secretly yearned for Korczak's dream, too. Wouldn't it be absolutely fantastic to have a whole mountain carved out and sculptured into an Indian. Not just any Indian...but Crazy Horse...a Sioux. Of course, she realized that he would be a symbol of all Indians...a symbol of a past...a symbol of pride. So she had followed its progress for over twenty years, and now she could believe that one day, probably not in her lifetime...but one day, Crazy Horse would sit perched atop that mountain for all the world to see!

As she slowly drove up the long drive, she stared ahead at the massive mountain directly in front of her.

"Yes, I see you, Crazy Horse...you're beginning to emerge from your gigantic tomb of stone."

She pulled up at the visitor center, parked and began walking toward it. Suddenly she jumped! Another dynamited explosion had occurred. Clouds of white smoke billowed out from the top of the mountain, and chills raced up her arms. After the smoke finally disappeared, she sat down on a bench to meditate a while on all the magic around her. The vast cloudless sky, the quietness of the Black Hills, especially after the reverberating blast, and the mountain...that 600 foot mountain that one day would transform into a proud symbol of her people. Then they would look up...yes, they would have to look up. She smiled. And they would feel the greatness...and the greatness of her people! Mt. Rushmore will diminish in size compared to this colossal image. Why, Korczak said that all four of the Presidents' heads will fit into the horse's head. Gazing at the granite mountain, she strained to visualize what it would look like. The white painted outline helped, but still it was difficult. How she'd love to live to see it!

She stood up and started for the visitor center, noticing the large number of tourists, and wondered from where they all hailed. A feeling of gratification filled her soul already bursting with pride. One day there would be ten times this many...maybe a hundred times this many? She just knew it. She walked out on the veranda to get a better view of the mountain that held Crazy Horse a prisoner. "Come on out, Crazy Horse," she whispered with a smile.

A little red-headed girl, with bright yellow bows in her hair, ran over to the large scale model of Crazy Horse. "Look Daddy, here it is!"

"No, Honey." The young father walked past her. "That's what he will look like when he's finished. The real Crazy Horse is still in that big mountain out there."

"Oh."

Spring looked up at the large scale model. With his left hand stretched outward, Crazy Horse pointed...'*My*

lands are where my dead lie buried.'
With mixed emotions, she left.

Dean Loud Thunder tried hard to look interested as
the students debated capitalism versus socialism, but
his mind kept wandering. Where was she? Would she
come? He could see her beautiful, proud look. Each
feature finely drawn as if by an artist's pen...her own
maybe. Her demeanor radiated the nobility of their
race. The proud Sioux. So maybe she was a *Virginian.*
Who would ever know? That was a laugh. She only
looked Sioux. She spoke as the white man...southern at
that. He smiled to himself, then quickly erased it. He
mustn't amuse the class.

"Teacher Dean, what about us?" A promising lad
called Jim interrupted his thoughts.

"What do you mean?"

"Where do we fit in...the Native-American?"

Just then the bell rang, and the students dispersed,
leaving him with that question ringing in his ears. He
still pondered it as he drove home. He must have an
answer for tomorrow...for himself. He thought again of
Spring. *She* would have an answer. She *always* had an
answer! He laughed aloud. Could he handle a woman
that thought like a man...and a white man at that?
Remembering her beauty and her warmth that she
shielded from the world, he concluded that she was
worth it. It may well be a tumultuous relationship...but
what would life be without her?

THE T-BIRD HUGGED the mountain curves like a
glove. Spring looked all around her as the hills dropped

and rose.

"My lands are where my dead lie buried."

The words seemed to echo off the mountain tops. Yes, her dead were buried here. She belonged here. But then she remembered, as always, the silent graves on Oak Mountain far away. They were also her dead. Her ancestors' remains scattered throughout these lands were bonded to her through blood... Sioux blood. But the bond with her Virginia family was "love". Which was greater?

She drove on, nearing her destination...a turning point in her life...a new chapter. What about her job? Who would replace her at the college? That was not her worry. She wouldn't really miss it. Seldom did she get a student that possessed the depth that art demanded...or for that matter, the drive. It just wasn't there. And if she was going to make her home permanently here in South Dakota, she might as well be close to the Black Hills. Sioux Falls was just another city.

Dean pulled into his driveway, still mulling over Jim's question. He checked his empty mailbox and sighed. But as he turned the key in the lock, he could hear the phone ringing. Throwing open the door, he grabbed the phone off the bar.

"Hello!"

"Is this Dean Loud Thunder, the most eligible bachelor on Pine Ridge?"

His countenance transformed into a radiated broad smile.

"It is...if this is that beautiful Sioux Princess from some obscure mountain in the east."

"Oak Mountain?"

"That's it. Oak Mountain. Where are you, Darling?"

"I'm standing here in the midst of pyramids, and I hear the lonely song of the coyote, shadows are everywhere, and I walk beneath the stars."

"Spring, I'll be there in forty-five minutes." He slammed the phone down.

She placed the receiver back on the wall phone and smiled. She walked past the many campsites to where her camping gear lay on the ground, and proceeded to erect her small tent. She was glad now that she didn't buy that nice large tent. This was enough...and she wasn't getting any younger. She wondered again how the Indian women of yesterday erected those large tipis?

She had finally gotten everything functional when she saw a familiar form approaching in the dusk. She rose gracefully, and they embraced.

"I've missed you!"

She lay her head upon his chest. It felt good to be wrapped within his strong arms. He playfully pulled her braid.

"A true Indian today?"

She smiled up at him. "Sometimes I feel the need to look like what I am."

"Which is the most beautiful lady I know."

"Thank you, kind Sir."

"Would you like to take a walk?"

"A walk through the Badlands. I thought you'd never ask."

The two clasped hands and began their walk along the campground trail which led out into the forlorn areas of what looked like *another world* at night.

"You're not afraid to stay here alone tonight?"
She looked at him quickly.
"Excuse me, my lady...let me retract that question.
I'm sure you will enjoy your stay here tonight in the
Badlands."
She smiled. "I will."
"Maybe soon...you won't be alone."
She pretended not to hear, mentally running from
decisions.
They walked on.
"You okay?" he asked.
"Yes," she almost whispered, "The wind is crying
here...crying perhaps for all the injustices committed by
mankind. Listen...it cries and whines like a child
without its mother."
He listened.
The two lone figures stood silently witnessing the
crying wind blowing up through the parched gulches
and sighing through the prairie grass.
Spring knelt down gently upon the hardened sand,
"It's eerie...so desolate...but yet a paradox in the truest
sense. I find it comforting."
"I know. It stirs within me something...that lies
dormant."
"The ancient chants of our ancestors call out to
us...*ho We wah che-pe yu-Sh'KAH-oon dah-KO-tah.*"
Dean looked up surprised.
"Listen, you can hear it...*ho-WE-wah-che-pe, ho-
WE-wah-che-pe...Ghost Dance...Ghost Dance free
Dakotah....*"
The prairie winds continued to whisper the old
Indian chants as the deep shadows vividly defined the

grotesque forms of the Badlands.

Dean sat down beside her and tried to feel what she was feeling. "Makes you wish you could have lived back then...and experienced the great Ghost Dances... the buffalo hunts...and the simple pleasures of their lives...."

"I know," she reached for his hand, "that something that lies dormant within, but stirs at times like this is what makes us different...what makes us Indian. We must not lose it. Our young need to carry it with them into the future. It is too precious to die."

She rose. "*Mako sica...mako sica...*you are truly the Badlands...but you are part of our lands."

Dean remained kneeling. "Spring, my love, will you marry me?"

She looked down at him tenderly as the moon cast its silvery glow upon her displaying all her beauty. She smiled.

"Yes."

Chapter IV
Oak Mountain Homestead

Prudence pulled her shawl tightly around her shoulders as she walked back toward the house. September had certainly brought with it the autumn chill. The few remaining kernels of corn rolled around in the bottom of the feed bucket as she set it down by the well. After having fed the chickens, she set about drawing up some water from the old well. She could hear Melony now. "But Mama, we have water in the house." No matter! It just made her feel good to hear that old bucket go down hitting on the sides of the long wall as it descended and then go "splash" as it hit the bottom.

She listened now as she turned the rickety handle, slowly lowering the bucket. Feeling like a child again, she let go of the handle and watched it fly around as the empty bucket dropped suddenly to its destination. SPLASH! She smiled, waited a second for it to fill up and then feeling the weight of it, she began to wind the creaking wooden handle to draw it up. Her arm tired as it neared the top. She peered down into the darkened well and caught a glimpse of the shiny bucket as it rocked its way to the top again with cold, clear water spilling out of it. She pulled it in, sat it down on the side of the well, and reached for the dipper hanging just above her head. Scooping out a dipper-full, she drank the refreshing water. Times such as this kept her close to her roots. She liked simplicity. She started back again for the house, but couldn't help feeling tired.

She pulled open the screen door to the back porch, and set the bucket down just inside. She opened the kitchen door and welcomed its warmth. After pouring herself a cup of coffee, she sat down at the table to read the morning paper. The headlines read... *"Eisenhower Says Riots, Violence 'Disgraceful'."*

I always did like Ole' Ike. She continued to read... *"Denison, Texas Dwight D. Eisenhower, born the son of a railroad man in this north Texas city almost 75 years ago, returned Wednesday to speak of 'disgraceful riots' and moral deterioration in the United States. The former president said causes of recent rioting and racial violence were not to be found in any one minority group or faction, but rather 'in each of us'."*

"He's right about that," she nodded while sipping her coffee.

Skipping on through a few paragraphs until she found something more to her liking, she read...

"Eisenhower, born in a small white house by the railroad tracks October 14, 1890, came to Denison to take part in the naming of an auditorium in his honor. He previously visited the city in 1946 and 1952. Before making his dedicatory address, Eisenhower visited the house in which he was born. He ran his hand over a bedroom quilt his mother made and said: 'You know my brother and I helped cut the scraps that went into this quilt'."

Prudence wiped her moist eyes with the corner of her apron. She pushed her chair back, closed her eyes and traveled back in time to the little cabin further up Oak Mountain. Mama was busy in the tiny kitchen as always...always doing something for us.

"I miss you, Mama."

She straightened up. I need to put some flowers on her grave...and on Daddy's and Charity's and Little David's. Mama would want me to do that. Maybe I can get Melony to go with me. Melony...all the way in Lynchburg...all alone...she and Little Emily. What is the world coming to? Violence everywhere...in Vietnam...here at home...and young mothers all alone living without a man to take care of them. I just don't know anymore. The shrill ring of the telephone interrupted her thoughts. She made her way to the hallway.

"Hello."
"Pru, is that you?"
"Spring! How are you?"
"I'm fine."

"I can't hear you very well."

"I have some news...."

"Some what?"

"Some news...."

"What news?"

"I just got married!"

There was a long silence on the Oak Mountain end of the wires. But just as there's stillness before the storm, Pru blurted out, "You did *what*?"

"I got married."

"I thought that's what you said. Who?"

"Dean...Dean Loud Thunder. The one I told you about...remember?"

"Well, yes...but I didn't think you'd up and marry him...without even letting your family know!"

"Sorry, Pru, but we wanted it quiet...just the two of us."

"Well...I don't know why I'm shocked. I certainly shouldn't be. You've always been one for surprises."

Spring laughed. "Are you happy for me, Pru?"

She felt her hurt begin to dissipate slowly. "Of course I am, Spring. Of course I am. It's just gonna take a little time to get used to...that's all...a little time."

"Please tell the folks, and I'll call again when we're more settled. We just got back from our honeymoon. A short one."

"Where'd you go?"

"Not far...a cozy little cabin nestled way back in the Black Hills."

"Sounds nice. Sounds like you."

"Like I said, once we get settled, I'll call again. I'll be

moving this weekend."

"You won't be living in Sioux Falls anymore?"

"I'm moving to Dean's home...to Pine Ridge."

"What about your job?"

"I've already resigned. I plan to teach some at Dean's school...where he teaches. It's on the Reservation."

"The Reservation...," Pru repeated.

"Don't worry, Sis. Everything's fine...just fine."

As Pru placed the receiver back on the phone, she began to talk to herself. "But she always said she'd never live on a reservation...and now? And after all this time...all these years...she's married...Spring's married. I gotta call Patrick!" She picked up the receiver again. "Shucks, they're not home. I'll call Jonathon." She dialed the number.

"Nobody's home. I've gotta tell somebody!" She dialed again.

"Melony!"

"Hello, Mom."

"You might want to sit down. You're never gonna believe this."

"What is it?"

"Spring's married!"

"Do what?"

"Spring just up and got married!"

"Aunt Spring?"

"That's right. I just hung up from her."

"Who did she marry?"

"That fellow she told us about. You know, that Indian named Dean Thunder...I mean Loud Thunder...I think. Where in the world do they come up with those names anyway?"

Melony smiled. "Well, how about that. Aunt Spring put one over on us."

"And she's quit her job in Sioux Falls and is moving in with him."

"Well, Mom, that's the logical thing to do."

"And on a reservation, too."

"I see. Mom, it's Aunt Spring's decision, you know. And you know your sister. She's unpredictable."

"You can say that again."

"Well, I think it's great!"

"I just hope she'll be happy. It will certainly be an adjustment...I mean after all these years."

"Just how old is Aunt Spring?"

"Forty-five years old...and a bride!"

Melony laughed. "It's never too late."

Pru grunted. "Guess I'll call Patrick and Jonathon again. Couldn't get them before. You all right?"

"Yes, Mother."

"And Little Emily?"

"We're both fine, Mother."

"And...everything working out all right?"

"Just fine, Mother." She glanced at Roxy, who was staring at her.

When she hung up, she turned to Roxy, "My Aunt Spring got married."

"Aunt Spring?"

"She's my mother's sister. She's an Indian."

Roxy's eyes widened, "She's a what?"

"An Indian. She's adopted into our family."

"Oh!" She continued folding diapers.

"It's hard to believe," Melony thought aloud.

"Why's that?"

"Because she's forty-five years old."

"My goodness...this her first marriage?"

"Certainly is...and we never expected her to get married. She's...well...not into that sort'a thing. She's an artist."

"Everybody's into *that sort of thing*," Roxy remarked.

"Not me! I'll never get married again."

Roxy watched her as she walked over to the window and quietly stared out. "You know, Roxy, this is why I chose this place. This view...you can see over top of the trees and the houses...and way out in the distance. I think I can almost see the top of Oak Mountain."

"That so...where?" Roxy joined her, with a stack of diapers, peering out the tall window.

"You see that row of mountains straight ahead, now look at the last row, the faint, hazy blue one, now look barely to the left of it and you'll see the tip of a distant mountain...I think that's it...Oak Mountain."

"You think so?" Roxy looked at her quizzically.

"I think so...and if it's not, it still makes me feel good to think so."

"How come?"

"Well, this is my home...but Oak Mountain is my *real* home."

"How come you ain't there?"

"Because...because I need to stand on my own feet...be independent...like you, Roxy."

"Me? I don't have no place of my own."

"You would if you could. I know you would."

Roxy went back to folding diapers. "I will when my

man comes home. We gonna get us a little house with a little yard for Laurietta with a picket fence around it. Always wanted one of them."

"I admire you, Roxy," she looked at her sadly, "the way you take your husband being in Vietnam and all. You're a strong person. I can tell."

"I don't take no credit for that. The good Lord takes care of me and Laurietta."

Melony stretched out on the sofa, "Roxy, what in the world are those things?"

Roxy followed her eyes up to the high ceiling. "What things?"

"Those funny-looking things poking through the ceiling...looks like somebody's couch is coming through from upstairs."

Roxy laughed aloud, "Don't you know nothing? They're gas lights...or least what's left of them. Had them before electric lights."

"This *is* an old house."

"Sure is."

" 'Course my home back on Oak Mountain's old, too...but we don't have funny things poking out of our ceiling."

"You must not'uv had gas then."

"Guess they had lanterns or oil lamps or something. Being in the country, things weren't as fancy as in the city. Daddy's told me many times how hard things were back then. It was his folks that built the place, and he being an only child, it was left to him."

"Didn't you ever get scared living back in them mountains...no street lights or nothing?"

She laughed, "Not really. Reckon I was just used to

it."
"I know I'd be...snakes, wild animals...even bears."
"I lived all my life on Oak Mountain, and I never once saw a bear. 'Course, they're there...and folks have seen them, but I never did."
"Just knowing they're there is enough for me."
"Roxy, how would you like to go with me sometime to Oak Mountain?"
She looked up with surprise, "Me?"
"Yes, I'd love to show you my home."
"Maybe...one day."
"In fact, Mom just said the other day that she and Dad are planning a weekend away soon. We could go. You and I, and the girls...and we'd have the place all to ourselves. I could show you my favorite tree and the animals...and we could go hiking...."
"You mean...just us...you and me and Laurietta and Little Emily?"
"That's right. It would be great."
Roxy squirmed in her seat, "I'm not used to any mountains, Melony. I'm fixin' to write my man a letter when I get home. I'll see what he has to say."

"NO JONATHON, I'M NOT TALKING OUT of my head. She got married, I tell you!"
"Lord, have mercy...."
"Now Jonathon, don't go using the Lord's name in vain...."
"Sorry Sis, but the good Lord *will* have to use mercy on the man that Spring marries."
"Well, I know what you mean, but he *is* an Indian. They might understand one another. Leastways, better'n

we did many a time."

"Shucks, Spring's main problem is that she's been by herself too long. Maybe she'll be better now! I mean, maybe she'll be happy and not go running all over the country looking for the rainbow."

"Well, I hope so. You know she's not getting any younger."

"Neither are we, Sis. Have you told Patrick yet?"

"No. I tried calling, but no answer."

"If you get him, tell him to give me a call. Seems there was a little trouble over at the school today."

"What kind of trouble?"

"Some fighting between some of the kids. You know, Whites and Negroes. The boys might have been involved it seems."

"What boys?" Prudence's voice changed.

"Mark, Paul and Heath."

"No!"

"Don't think it's anything to worry about. We just need to talk with the school authorities and get things straightened out."

"Jonathon, that doesn't sound like Heath! Maybe Mark and Paul...but not Heath."

"Well, I think Heath sort of got dragged into it when Mark and Paul jumped the Negro boys over what they were up to."

"What was that?"

"Burning the school flag."

"My soul! Why would they do such a thing?"

"Who knows? Don't forget to tell Patrick."

"I won't. What is this world coming to?"

"THE BARRETT BOYS! THEY STARTED IT!"

"Start from the beginning, fellows," the aged principal prompted the four Negro boys, who were still bristling from the fight.

"It started last week...they been calling us names every time we see'em in the halls," Thomas began hesitantly.

"Who is *they?*"

"All of them...but especially the Barrett boys."

"Which Barrett boys?"

"Paul Barrett...Mark Barrett...."

"Heath Barrett?" the principal prompted again.

"Naw, we didn't hear Heath calling no names, but he sure did throw some mean punches today."

"Thomas, why do you think they were picking on you?"

"Because they don't like us...think they're better'n us...but they ain't."

"Can you boys tell me what on earth you were thinking about when you attempted to burn the flag?"

They all spoke at once making it impossible to understand any one of them.

"One at a time, please. Alfred?"

"Why should we salute a flag, Sir, that doesn't give us the freedom we deserve?"

Thomas added, "And why should we go fight in Vietnam when we ain't treated right back here?"

"I see, boys, but that doesn't give you the right to burn property that doesn't belong to you...especially the United States flag. Now this episode will receive further investigation...and disciplinary action where deemed necessary."

"You gonna punish them White boys?" Duane Davis demanded.

"All who were involved will receive the discipline warranted." He stood up and escorted the boys out. They stopped suddenly at the door. Paul and Mark were waiting just outside. Duane lunged forward, but Patrick quickly stood up blocking the path. Duane halted.

"Why Reverend Barrett, I didn't know you were here." The principal's relief was obvious. "Please come in." Patrick walked by, with Paul and Mark following. Duane stuck out his foot and Mark stumbled, falling onto Paul, who then pushed Patrick into the office. He turned to see the boys scurrying off with grins on their faces.

Once seated, Patrick spoke. "I believe you need to speak with Paul and Mark?"

"That is correct. Can you boys tell me what happened today?"

Mark stood up, "Paul jumped all them colored boys...but he had good reason to...they aimed to burn the flag!"

"How about you, Mark?"

"I jumped in and helped him, of course. We were holdin' our own when things were broke up."

"Sir," Paul began rubbing his bruised arm, "Our brother, David, is fighting over there in that war...and there's no way I'm gonna sit by and see somebody burn that flag...."

A knock on the door interrupted the conversation. In walked Heath and Caroline Miller.

"Heath, I'm glad you're here...Caroline?"

"But, Sir, I'm a witness," argued the pretty young

teenager, "I saw the whole thing!"

"All right. Heath, what do you have to say for yourself?"

Heath looked around the room, at Paul and Mark, then at his Uncle Patrick.

"I'm guilty of fighting along with the rest of them."

Paul and Mark shook their heads. Caroline winced. Patrick smiled.

"I understand you boys have been doing some name-calling?"

"No Sir," Mark answered, "Well, maybe a little... but that's because they're always making remarks about the war and it not being right...and things such as that."

"So that makes it right?"

"Well...no, Sir...." Mark looked around at his father rather sheepishly.

"Boys...Paul, Mark, Heath...I'm going to suspend you from classes for the rest of the week, and I sincerely hope that this action will serve to remind you of the rules of this school hereafter."

"But Mr. Mason," Caroline began, "Heath didn't start anything. He's not to blame...."

Heath stood up quickly, grabbing her hand. "Is that all, Sir?"

"That's all, boys."

THE WHITE '55 FORD sporting its intricate red pinstriping, cruised down the village streets and on out onto the dusty rural roads as fiery rays of the setting sun cast its mystic spell. Heath was deep in thought.

"It just isn't fair!" Caroline repeated. "It wasn't your fault at all!"

"It's okay, Caroline. Chalk it up to experience." He
smiled at her with that winning smile that overflowed
with the Barrett charm.

She snuggled up closer to him, underneath his arm,
feeling like a queen.

"Heath?"

"Yes?"

"Wouldn't it be great if we were married and didn't
have to listen to anyone else?"

"Gee whiz, Caroline. Are you crazy? We're too young
for that heavy stuff. I've got to get my education, and so
do you. But one day when I get ready to take the big step,
you'll be the girl I marry."

She smiled up at him just as the sun dipped out of
sight. And just as suddenly, the rain began to fall in
large, splashing drops that quickly spread over the
windshield in zigzagging waves.

"Guess this must be the tail-end of that hurricane...you know, Hurricane Betsy," Heath remarked
while straining to see.

"The paper said today that over fifty people have
been killed. That's horrible! I'm glad we don't live down
there in Louisiana."

"Years ago, there was a terrible storm here, Caroline.
Dad's little sister was killed in it."

"Really? What was her name?"

"Charity."

"What a pretty name."

"It means love, you know."

"I know." She squeezed his hand.

"Well, here we are, my little protector." They grinned
at one another as he pulled up in front of a stately two-

story house with a new coat of white paint glistening in the rain. It boasted of four large Ionic columns, each graced by its own feathery fern at its base. Caroline's father waved from the backyard as he hurriedly covered his favorite experimental plants. Heath gave her a good-bye kiss and she reluctantly stepped out, ducked her head and ran into the house.

The rain was now beating incessantly upon the window pane as she slid down further beneath the hot, soapy water.

"Caroline?" her mother called upstairs, "Do you need *that* much water? The well will run dry!"

She reached out and turned the shiny, chrome faucet, and the steady stream came to a sudden halt, except for one lone drip. *What was she going to do?* Heath didn't want to get married! He would hate her if she forced him into it. She knew him that well...and she couldn't lose him! Never! She would call Clara after her bath. Clara would know what to do.

"IT'S RAINING CATS AND DOGS out there!" Roxy exclaimed as she burst in the door, throwing water all over the floor while struggling to get Laurietta, her umbrella and the bags all in.

"Good morning, Roxy," Melony called back from the bathroom where she was engrossed in teasing her newly short-cropped hair.

"It's a good one, all right!" She laughed and then wrinkled her nose, "What's that I smell?"

"What?"

"That smell...you know...smells like something

burning."

"Oh."

"What do you mean...Oh?"

"I mean...Oh that smell."

Roxy placed Laurietta on the big quilt in the middle
of the living room floor and walked into the hallway. She
looked at Melony as she sprayed her hair that stood out
in all directions, resembling a cartoon she'd seen once of
a lady with her finger stuck in an electrical socket. But
that wasn't all she saw.

"Melony Hunter...you been smoking!"

Melony laughed, "So? You act like you've never seen
anybody smoke before."

"What's your mama gonna say?"

"My mother need not know *everything*...unless that
is, you wish to inform her."

Roxy shook her head and walked back into the living
room. "None of my business," she muttered.

She pulled the damp newspaper out from under her
coat, slid off the coat and sat down to read.

"What's the news, Roxy?"

"Says here...*Betsy batters Florida Coast*. That's a
mighty terrible thing...that hurricane. Listen to this...
*the onrushing waters were a burial ground for men,
women and children who failed to scramble fast enough
to safety*. I can't read no more of that! New Orleans,
that's where all that happened you know." She laid the
paper down and peeped in on Little Emily who was still
sleeping soundly.

"Roxy, thought anymore about our weekend in the
mountains?"

"I wrote Seth about it last night. Got it in my pocket

to mail today."

"Good. Do you think you could keep Little Emily for me this Friday night?"

"Don't see why not."

"Some of the girls and I are going out. In fact, if you could spend the night, it would be great because I'll probably be late."

Roxy frowned. "Where you goin'?"

"Missy...you know Missy Thomas that works down at the store. Well, she and her cousins are going to a party. They asked me to go along."

She decided not to comment, but commenced to straightening up the kitchen. "You better hurry along, or you gonna be late."

"I'm on my way." She grabbed her raincoat and umbrella, and slammed the door behind her.

SATURDAY MORNING seemed an apparition so brilliant and beautiful as the sun chased away the familiar clouds, along with the saddened tragedy of Hurricane Betsy, and the earth now smiled in its aftermath. Roxy stretched and yawned and quietly got up. She mustn't awaken Laurietta or Little Emily. Creeping stealthily across the living room, the aged planks creaked beneath her weight. She sighed and gently opened the door. She crept down the stairway to the solid front door, opened it and stooped down for the paper, and then stood up, inhaling the crisp autumn air. She couldn't wait for the leaves to change... her favorite time of the year!

Back upstairs, she pulled up comfortably to the kitchen table, sipped the hot coffee and spread out the

paper before her. *'GIs IN VIETNAM EXCEED 125,000.'*
"Yes," she said aloud without thinking, "and one'a them
GIs is my man!" She laid the paper down and leaned
back remembering how proud he'd been the last time
she'd seen him...looking so handsome in his fine uniform. My, how she missed him...but one day he'd be
back, and then they'd start all over.

"Mama," Little Emily called out. Uh-oh, my peace is
over! She went in to get her before she woke Laurietta,
and noticed Melony was certainly sleeping soundly. She
nudged her on the way out, "Time to get up, Sleeping
Beauty."

"Puffed Wheat...Puffed Wheat, Emmy hungry," the
small child chattered as Roxy placed her in the highchair.

"Puffed Wheat again. That all you ever gonna eat?
Little Lady, you gonna turn into a Puffed Wheat!"

Little Emily's merry laugh filled the kitchen along
with the early morning sun thrusting its warm rays
through the tall windows.

"Now cut that fuss out. You gonna wake the dead!"

Just then, Laurietta began to cry. "See, I told you so!"
As she turned to go after her, Little Emily smiled and
tossed the little puffs of wheat high into the air, squealing with delight.

Roxy wondered why Melony hadn't gotten up. She
leaned down close to see if she was actually sleeping or
just teasing.

"Melony Hunter!"

Melony sat straight up, her eyes still closed, grabbing her head with both hands!

"You been drinking! I know that smell. I'd know it
anywhere after my Uncle Walter lived with us. You

can't fool me!"

"Please Roxy...not so loud."

"I know...I know how it is...your head feels big... don't it?"

"Roxy, I'm getting up. I'll be there directly."

Roxy left the room, shaking her head and mumbling to herself, while carrying Laurietta to the kitchen. The plump baby girl stared up at her mother smiling, not understanding a word.

Finally when Melony did appear in the kitchen, Roxy had her things together. "I'll be going now... Laurietta and me. We're gonna enjoy this beautiful day...probably go to the park. I'll see you Monday." She leaned down and kissed Little Emily, and left in a hurry. The door slammed shut.

"Good-bye," Melony whispered.

She sat down feeling depressed. She would like to go to the park, too...and see the beautiful day...but... her head was pounding. She really wanted to go back to bed, now that Roxy was gone. Little Emily began shaking the highchair tray, watching the milk slosh around in her bowl.

"Don't do that, Darling...please." She pulled herself up from the table. She must get herself together. Tomorrow was the big day...the birthday party for Aunt Ellen.

SUNDAY MORNING PROMISED another warm and comfortable autumn day as Melony and Little Emily started out for Oak Mountain. It was 10:30 and they'd skipped church again. She just couldn't bring herself to go. She'd feel like a hypocrite.

As Melony approached Oak Mountain, Reverend Barrett stood before his attentive congregation, but Prudence struggled to keep her mind focused on what he was saying. She hoped the pot roast wouldn't be too done when she returned home. She did so want everything just perfect as it had been a long time since they'd all been together for dinner. She remembered Mama and how she'd enjoyed having the family together. I guess I'm like her after all, she smiled to herself, and jumped as Patrick pounded the pulpit.

" 'Behold, ye have sinned against the Lord, and be sure your sin will find you out', " Patrick's voice rose loud and clear.

Caroline squirmed beside Heath.

Clarence leaned over and pulled his large handkerchief out of his back pocket and got ready to blow. Prudence nudged him with her elbow. He shook his head and returned the handkerchief.

After the last Amen, the Barrett family headed for Pru's, knowing full well what delectables lay in store for them. One at a time, they arrived to find Melony sitting on the front porch watching Little Emily playing in the leaves.

"Hey Mel," Jonathon called out as he climbed out of his new Dodge pickup, "got dinner ready yet?"

"When did you get that?" she called back.

"Got it instead of my new dishwasher!" Jessica teased as she jumped down into Jonathon's arms.

They came up on the porch arm in arm.

"You know, it's great to see older married folk like you still acting like you're on your honeymoon."

"That's because we are, Miss Melony." He reached

over and tousled her hair.

Little Emily laughed aloud as Heath covered her with the crisp, yellow leaves that lay abundantly beneath the old Tulip tree.

"Now just what do you mean 'older folk'?" Jessica demanded, winking at her.

"She means 'old'; that's what she means," Clarence added.

"Think I'll change the subject. Make a pile for her, Heath," she suggested.

"Good idea." He proceeded to heap the large leaves into a nice pile. Just as he scooped up the last armful and tossed them in place...SWOOSH! Mark landed smack dab in the middle!

"Aw come on, Mark...you messed up our pile," Heath chided. Mark stood up and brushed the leaves back in place. "Remember when we used to do this?"

"Sure do. Hasn't been that long ago that we covered Caroline up in them. Could do it again." He grinned mischievously at her as she backed off.

"But things have changed." There was a note of sadness in Mark's voice.

"What do you mean?"

"Well, David's gone. Grandma and Grandpa's gone. Seems like we don't have as much fun anymore. You're always with Caroline. Paul even acts different sometimes. I don't know whether I like this growing up thing!"

Heath laughed. "Well, Cousin, whether you like it or not, it's gonna happen. What's wrong with you anyway?"

"I don't know. Guess the school fight and all...sort of

got me to thinking."

"Oh?"

"Don't you ever think about the future?"

Caroline interrupted, "Heath, come here a minute."

He shrugged his broad shoulders and walked off toward her. Mark kept scooping up the leaves and muttered to himself..."see what I mean!"

Patrick carefully placed his worn Bible on the back seat of his '59 Impala and got out. He started for the house, but noticed Jonathon out back standing at the entrance of the aged shed just staring inside. He was leaning against the corner post that was crumbling with age. Patrick walked up quietly behind him, and although he never turned, Jonathon knew he was there.

"Mama's swing," he said with a sigh.

"I see."

The old swing hung lopsided from a rafter against the side of the shed, its brown paint peeling, exposing the previous coat of white in ragged and twisted designs.

"It's a wonder Pru doesn't clean it up and use it?" Jonathon's voice cracked.

"I don't know. Seems like it ought'a hang there... rest you know."

Jonathon looked into his older brother's thoughtful eyes and smiled. Patrick patted him on the back, and the two walked toward the house.

ONCE SEATED FOR DINNER, Patrick asked grace as they all held hands beneath the table.

"Amen," he concluded, and everyone began talking at the same time.

"Mom, please help Little Emily to some mashed potatoes when they come around. You know she loves them," Melony instructed from across the table. Little Emily was wedged in between Prudence and Ellen, both anxious to assist her.

"Melony, how would you like to play the piano for the church? My pianist is moving away next month," Patrick proposed quite suddenly.

Her head shot up. "Me?"

"Well, I don't know of any other pianist at this table," he kidded.

"Oh Melony, that would be lovely," Ellen added.

"Thank you...thank you for asking, Uncle Patrick... I know it's an honor. But I don't believe so...not just now."

Everyone looked at everyone else.

"Why Mel, I thought that's what you always wanted to do?" her father challenged.

"I did...you're right. But people change...pass me the rolls, please."

He absently complied, but not without a frown.

"That's fine, Melony," Patrick replied. "Maybe later. I just thought I'd give you first chance."

"I appreciate that, Uncle Patrick."

Jonathon intercepted, "Clarence, when you gonna plow up your garden?"

"Oh...I thought about doing it this week."

"You want to borrow my tractor? Understand yours is down right now."

"Yep, got carburetor problems. Can't get to it for a couple of weeks. I appreciate your offer. I'll take you up on it."

"By the way, Prudence, when are you and Clarence taking your trip?" Jessica asked.

"Matter of fact, we're planning on next week. Probably leave sometime Friday."

"Great. I brought you those brochures."

"Mom, would you mind if Roxy and I house-sit for you on the weekend?"

"You...and Roxy?"

"Yes, well...Little Emily and Laurietta too, of course."

"Is that your colored babysitter you're talking about?" her father asked.

"Yes, Roxy is Little Emily's babysitter," she answered defensively.

Paul quit eating for a moment. "You gonna spend the weekend *here*...you and her?"

"And what's wrong with that?" Her face was flushed and growing red.

"Nothing...to each their own." He returned to stuffing himself.

"Well Mel," her father began again, "what do'ya suppose the neighbors will think?"

"What neighbors? We don't even have any within seeing distance! And what if we did? What difference would it make?" Her voice was becoming high-pitched.

"Melony, calm down," Prudence urged gently. "We just want what's best for you...that's all."

"This family's prejudiced!" Melony stood up.

Patrick leaned toward her. "Melony, it's just that Roxy is...different...and it takes some adjusting...."

"What about Spring? She's different!"

"You're right, Melony, but Spring is family. She's

part of this family," Prudence explained patiently.

"What if she weren't?"

"Well...we know Spring...we understand her...to a degree. We love her."

"You see...we love her because we know her and understand her." She sat back down as if to say 'case closed'.

"Melony, of course you're welcome to spend the weekend here...all of you," her mother conceded just before the phone rang. She rose, wiped her hands on her apron and hurried to the hallway.

"SPRING!"

All heads lifted.

"It's Spring, everybody," she called back, although everyone could hear quite well.

"Yes, we're all here." She called again to the dining room, "I told her in my letter we'd all be here today."

"Ask her how's the weather there?"

"Clarence says how's the weather?"

"Right cool, you say. Well, it's beautiful here... Indian Summer...you should be here!"

"Yes, hold on a minute. Ellen, Spring says Happy Birthday!"

"Tell her thank you."

"She says thank you. Do what? Just a minute, Spring. This connection isn't that good. Now what was that?"

"You're PREGNANT?"

All eyes at the dinner table flew wide open!

"Spring, are you sure?"

"You did?"

"Now, Spring, listen to me. I'm a grandmother... and you're older than me. You must be careful and take care of yourself. Who's your doctor?"

"Is he good?"

"That's good."

"Aunt Spring's pregnant!" Melony repeated with a broad smile, laying her fork down, "Wonders *never* cease!"

Caroline left the table.

Everyone was talking at once when Prudence returned. She sat down slowly, and the talking ceased.

"I don't believe it!" she half whispered.

"Why not?" Clarence kidded.

"Clarence, this is nothing to kid about. Spring should be having grandchildren...not children."

"Well, you can't put the cart before the horse!"

Everyone laughed.

"I think it's great," Jessica declared. "Spring needs somebody and now she has a husband and soon a baby." She looked around. "What happened to Caroline?"

"She'll be back soon," Heath answered. "Mom, pass the gravy, please."

"Well, if anybody can pull this thing off, it'll be Spring," Jonathon laughed.

"You're right about that!" Patrick agreed.

Little Emily began to squirm, trying to get down, "Bunny...bunny...I want bunny book."

"What's she talking about, Melony?" Ellen asked while picking her up out of the highchair.

"Oh, she wants her *Alice in Wonderland* book. I'll get it. Did you know that *Alice* turned 100 years old last week?"

"Well, can you believe that! I knew she was old," Prudence remarked. "I remember Mama reading it to us...don't you remember, Jonathon?"

He frowned, "Now come on, Pru. You know I didn't go in for that sort of stuff."

"Oh now, Uncle Jonathon, tell us about *Alice in Wonderland?*" Mark teased, and then ducked as Jonathon threw a roll across the table at him.

"Jonathon Barrett! Will you ever grow up?" scolded Jessica as Mark retrieved the roll, brushed it off and laid it gently on the table with a wink at his adversary.

"Excuse me." Jessica rose from the table and went into the hallway.

"Guess we better straighten up." Jonathon raised his eyebrows.

"Guess *you* better, Dad." Heath laughed while pushing back his chair.

But Jessica had other things on her mind as she stood outside the bathroom door listening to the sobs that escaped the muffled attempt to hide them. "Caroline, are you okay?"

At first there was silence. Then a teary voice answered, "I'm fine, Mrs. Barrett. I'll be out in a minute."

"That's okay. Take your time." Jessica walked off wondering what could be wrong.

"Well, who's ready for dessert?" Prudence asked and was answered by immediate applause.

"Thought so. Melony, you want to help serve?"

"I'll help, too," Jessica volunteered as she returned, still puzzling over Caroline.

"What about Nixon coming to Lynchburg next week!" Clarence addressed the group.

"Understand he's going to be at The Virginian Hotel," Patrick added. "That's where we had that seminar a couple of years ago. You know, for the ministerial group, Ellen?"

"That's right, of course. I can't believe he's coming to Lynchburg!"

"Well, if he'd come a little sooner, he could've celebrated your birthday, Ellen."

She laughed, "Right, Jonathon."

"Now let's not get into politics," Jessica warned while bringing in the first dish of banana pudding. "Ellen, how's Esther doing at college so far?"

"Well, she's adapting, I believe, Jessica. Doesn't seem too homesick. Not like I expected."

"That's wonderful. And how about David? Have you heard from him recently?"

"It's been a while. Sometimes his letters come fairly regularly, and then again, it's a while before we hear anything."

Jessica noticed Caroline quietly seating herself beside Heath. There was only a trace of redness around those beautiful blue eyes. Heath never looked up. "You get lost, Hon?"

"I think so," she replied with an imploring look at Jessica.

Chapter V
Wahanpi

Spring could hear the spirited chants and soulful beat of the drums as she approached the tipi where the prayer meeting was being held in her honor. It was the largest tipi she'd ever seen, and its poles must have reached at least thirty to forty feet. She stood outside a moment, watching the fiery sun making its final descent, casting shadows across the windswept plains. She rubbed her stomach. Even though she couldn't actually tell any difference, it made her feel good just to rub it occasionally. It was time for the meeting to begin at the Native American Church, and she stopped and entered the tipi.

Dean motioned to her, patting the spot beside him while looking at her lovingly. She glanced around as she sat down. Approximately thirty people sat in a large circle with a blazing fire in the midst. She noticed the pipe-drum beaters laying beside the fire.

As the long evening wore on, the singing and chanting became more emotional with many members taking up rattles to accompany their singing — rattles made from gourds and trimmed with beads, braided hide fringe or horsehair plumes. She remembered the plain gourds back home in the Blue Ridge that were used for water dippers. She could see them hanging off the side of the shed at Pru's. She wondered what Clarence would think of these gourds, and smiled to herself. She certainly came from two worlds. The prayers grew more intense, but she was getting sleepy again, even among all this excitement. Why was she always so sleepy? She looked over at her aged father-in-law, who had sponsored the whole thing in her honor. He was swaying back and forth proudly displaying his grand medallion as it shifted with the beat. This striking medallion that hung from his weathered neck boasted hundreds of minute beads, red, blue, white and some yellow. The colorful beads surrounded a white tipi design in the center. The more she watched the medallion move, the sleepier she became. Even sitting up tall and straight and breathing in considerable amounts of oxygen didn't prevent her eyelids from drooping. Her father-in-law nodded at her. He'd told everyone on the reservation that he was finally going to have a grandson! How he knew it was going to be a boy was beyond her.

Prayers were being offered up for her safety, for the baby's safety, for her good health while growing this child within her and for the baby's life ahead. The winds had increased and were whipping the tipi flaps back and forth, but it was warm and cozy inside...and Spring wanted to sleep.

Just as she was about to yield to its overpowering
appeal, Dean nudged her and offered her a cup of Peyote
Tea. She looked up surprised and declined. He frowned
and sipped his own. She glanced over at her father-in-
law again, who smiled at her while chewing on the dried
cactus or peyote. She smiled back, but somehow couldn't
bring herself to partake of the peyote, even knowing it
was the religion of her people...at least some of them. It
was what Dean had grown up with...and what his
father staked his life on. But she felt confused...caught
in the middle again.

"You okay, Honey?" Dean asked softly.

"Yes...I'm fine...just sleepy."

He hugged her to him as the singing continued and
the members partook of the peyote. She knew it was
considered a sacred herb and consumed as a sacrament
just like the bread and wine. Her sleepy eyes followed
the circle around the tipi, taking in her new friends and
relatives...certainly she felt a kinship. It felt good to be
here...but still she felt confused. Oh well, she'd probably always be confused. She pushed her bead-trimmed
moccasins closer to the blazing fire as it popped and
crackled, devouring the Pine logs. Her toes tingled. It
felt so good...so warm.

The next thing she knew, Dean was gently waking
her up.

"What time is it?" she asked, sitting up abruptly.

"Don't worry about the time. You've just had a good
nap, although you did sleep through the entire service,"
he laughed, "but I didn't have the heart to wake you."

She felt ashamed. Here all these people had come
out for her...and she couldn't even stay awake. What

would her father-in-law think? She reluctantly looked
up at him, but much to her relief, he too was in a semi-
sleep. Well, he was eighty something...he had an
excuse. But then, she wasn't used to all night meetings
either. In fact, she wondered if she could ever get used
to them. Brother Patrick's services were too long for her!
The singing and chanting were still going on, and no one
seemed to be paying much attention to her. She stretched
out her legs and noticed the fire had just about died out,
leaving the red hot coals alone to weakly send out a little
heat. The wind still rattled the tipi covering, but its
strength too, had waned. An old man seated beside her
father-in-law rose to put more wood on the fire, and soon
it blazed again.

A willowy creature, slim and light-footed, glided past
her, a beautiful beaded bandolier bag swinging from her
shoulder. It was very old in appearance, but exquisitely
designed. Her appreciation for beauty, especially creative beauty, caused her to marvel at the abundance of
talent bestowed upon this people...*her* people. The
young lady looked down at her and smiled. It was
Dean's cousin, whom she'd already met and taken a
liking to because of her genuine friendly nature. It was
nice acquiring a new family here among her people. Of
course, she'd always felt a part of them. But now she
could actually claim cousins and aunts and uncles
among them...all through Dean. Being an orphan had
robbed her of this satisfying experience. But, of course,
she had her family back in Virginia.

SEVERAL HOURS LATER as the sun climbed upward knocking the chill off the cool autumn day, Spring

delighted in the preparations for the feast that would follow the prayer meeting.

"Is it always like this...such a happy affair?"

Dean was occupied with wrapping up the religious paraphernalia that his father had brought to the prayer meeting. "Usually is, unless it's for some problem or illness or something. Why Spring, here you are a full-blooded Sioux, and you're asking me this? You haven't attended one before?"

"Not exactly. Not this way, anyhow. I've visited for short periods, but not really getting into it this way."

"No, you wouldn't. You have to be a part of it." He grinned at her. "Now you are."

"Dean, can'ya help me with this box?" his father asked while lugging a wooden box behind him.

"Hold on there, Father. You shouldn't be pulling that thing!" Dean picked it up with ease. "I'll be back in a bit, Honey."

She nodded, and watched her agile husband with pride as he strode across the field with the box lifted high upon his broad shoulders, his decrepit father following after.

She looked around at the lively activity surrounding her, and felt quite helpless.

"Is there anything I can do to help?"

One of the two elderly ladies standing beside her looked at her and asked, "You know how to make Pejute Sapa?"

"Of course, I make it every morning...but not in a pot this big." She laughed, wondering why they just didn't call it coffee.

"Guess maybe you can help with the wahanpi." She

turned to her friend, "What'd you put in the wahanpi?"

"What do you mean...what'd I put in the wahanpi? I put the same thing I always put in the wahanpi! Plenty...plenty of vegetables."

"Turnips?" the wiry lady persisted.

"No. I didn't have no turnips. You got turnips?"

"No. I don't have turnips." She turned to Spring, "You got turnips?"

"No Ma'am. You want me to get some?"

"No...no. Take too much time. Cora here was supposed to bring the turnips." She sounded vexed.

"You forgot to remind me. So I forget."

"You always forget."

"I didn't forget the fry bread. I got it. Plenty of it."

"Good. Well, let's add some more onions to the wahanpi. You can do that, little Mother."

Spring looked up surprised. "Certainly. You know, my mother used to fix homemade vegetable soup almost every weekend when we were growing up, and wahanpi always reminds me of that." As soon as she'd said it, she wished she hadn't. Both of them raised their eyebrows.

The wiry one spoke first, "Your mother? She was not Indian?"

"No, she wasn't. I was adopted by a family in the mountains of Virginia...white people...wonderful white people."

"I see."

Now the other spoke. "Virginia? Is it much like our land?"

"Well, not exactly. We don't have these wide open plains. We don't have the prairie grasses blowing in the never-ceasing winds," she looked out now at the tall grass that seemed alive with motion, "but we have mountains, rolling mountains...lots of them."

"Like the Black Hills?"

"Yes...like the Black Hills. Only more of them...lots more."

"I see. The baby...I hear it will be born in 'the moon when leaves are green'."

"That's right. The end of May...the 26th to be exact." The wiry lady grinned at the other. "It is no exact. Baby will come when it is time for baby to come."

Spring smiled. "Guess you're right."

"You are the daughter now of Eli Fire Thunder. This baby will be blessed, for Eli Fire Thunder is a good man," the other lady declared.

"Thank you." Spring went about slicing the onions, feeling the tears flooding her eyes and glad for it. Tears of joy were about to appear also.

The wiry lady shuffled over to her, "You are an artist?"

"That's right."

"Can you paint people?"

"Yes, I would like to paint you."

"ME?" She stepped back suddenly.

"Yes...both of you...here fixing the wahanpi...." Suddenly she felt the strong urge to get out her paints and capture this moment forever.

The other lady spoke, "Why do you want to do this?"

"I wish to paint the customs of our heritage... everyday life. I want to capture the true spirit...in faces like yours."

One looked at the other, "It is good?"

"Yes. I think it is a good thing to do."

"Do we change our clothes?"

"No...no. Please stay just as you are. I will get my things." Spring turned to go and just about bumped into Dean's cousin, Mareen, the lady with the beautiful bandolier bag.

"Spring...." She reached out to her. "I'm so glad you're in our family now."

Spring's reserved nature was taken back a bit by this warm new cousin.

"Thank you, Mareen. So am I. You caught me on my way to the car to get my paints. Please come along."

Mareen quickened her step to keep up with Spring. "Are you enjoying the ceremony?"

"Oh yes, it's different from what I'm used to, but I find it most interesting, exciting and invigorating."

"Well, it's different from what I'm used to, also," the attractive young lady added.

"What do you mean? I figured you'd be used to all this."

"I am used to ceremonies like this, of course. I've certainly attended my share. But I don't belong to the Native American Church like Dean and his father."

"You don't?"

"No. I belong to the Episcopalian Church over in Long Valley."

Spring looked at her suddenly with renewed interest. "How is that?"

"My parents brought us up Episcopalian...and Dean's brought him up in the Native American Church. We differ somewhat, you see."

"I see. Could you elaborate on your differences?"

"Well...I guess you could say I'm not as...well, as

Indian as Dean. Oh, I don't mean I'm not proud to be Indian...for I certainly am. I just mean I am somewhat more understanding of the white man's way of life."

Spring nodded in agreement. "Then you know how tenacious my darling Dean is...and his opinion of the white man in general?"

"Of course. Dean's always been that way...even as a kid. But then, a lot of full bloods are."

"Do you think that makes the difference, Mareen?"

"Well, perhaps it has a great deal to do with it. Mixed bloods like myself often see things differently. Now whether or not it is because we have had more exposure to the white man's world...or whether or not it is because the white man's blood also flows within us...I don't know. I do know we see many things differently."

Spring lifted the trunk lid and began pulling out her canvas and paints. She noticed Father Eli's box was sitting beside the car.

"Here, let me help." Mareen grabbed hold of the large bag.

"Thanks, Mareen." Spring was already feeling a strong friendship bonding between them. The two figures walked back toward the meeting, lugging Spring's equipment.

"I wonder where Dean and his father are?" Spring sounded a bit worried.

"Don't worry. Uncle Eli probably has taken him off on one of his philosophical journeys."

"Philosophical journeys?"

"Oh yes, you'll understand once you get to know your father-in-law a little better. He's quite a character!"

She decided to wait. "Mareen, do you think it is

wrong for Dean to feel the way he does?"

She was silent a moment before answering, as if carefully contemplating her answer, "No, I don't think him wrong, but it is useless. We are like the Jim and the Missouri."

"The Jim?"

"The Jim River...the James River beside the great Missouri."

"Oh, of course. I still have a hard time thinking of the James here in South Dakota. You see, we have a James River in Virginia, also. In fact, it flows very near our home."

"Is that so? Well, you know we call our James 'the Jim'."

"I know."

"And you know what else?" Mareen continued. "The Jim joins the great Missouri just below Yankton."

Spring smiled with understanding. "But, Mareen, can you see the Jim once it joins the Missouri?"

Mareen looked at her sadly. "No, Spring, you can't...they become one."

"Can we become one?" Spring asked.

"Do we want to?" Mareen challenged.

"Only if we don't get lost within its surging waters...if we can keep our heads up high carrying our heritage with us into the future."

"Not only an artist, but a poet. My, I'm glad Cousin Dean married you."

"So am I." She smiled.

BACK AT THE MEETING, Spring set up for work. The two little ladies watched her curiously as they went about their food preparation.

"Don't pay me any mind. Go ahead with your work and act natural. I will paint as you work."

Dubiously, they went back to their tasks, sneaking glances at the mysterious canvas whenever possible. Spring's fleeting brush aptly began capturing this disappearing tradition, but her mind was elsewhere. She could see it already! The painting she'd been waiting for...the noble profile rising out of the surging waters. But she must find the face...the right face.

The two ladies grinned at each other as Spring's skillful hand sought to preserve this minute slice of civilization for future generations.

"Hope she gets my best side!" the one called Cora bantered, while stirring the wahanpi with one hand and smoothing her dress with the other.

After the painting was completed, or at least the basics needed in order for Spring to add her creative final touches later, the orations began. This was what she'd been waiting for from the beginning. What were the people thinking? What was on their minds? Were they in tune with the beat of the ancient drums?

The 'roadman' spoke first. He spoke of the concerns in the schools, and the people nodded in agreement. The schools provided for them on the reservations simply were not going to prepare their children for the white man's world. How could they compete? Why must their children suffer? On and on...the people's real concerns were voiced. Spring listened.

ON THE WAY HOME, Dean chuckled. "That's the first time I've ever seen you quiet...during the orations,

I mean. However, I expected you to speak up at any time."

"It was not the right time."

"I agree. Well, what did you think?"

"Very interesting. A bit strange...but interesting."

"What was strange?"

"Well, the peyote for one thing. Coming from a Southern Baptist background, it's difficult understanding all of this sometimes."

"Don't get hung up on that, Honey. We also believe in the Cross...and the Sacred Pipe."

"How can you believe in all of these?"

"Easy. There's gotta be three ways to the Great Spirit."

Spring looked at him, and for the first time was glad that her mother wasn't there.

"How would you like to go hiking tomorrow...in the Black Hills? Some friends from school are going, and I thought you might enjoy it. Good chance for you to meet them."

"Sounds fine. You know, I really like Mareen."

"Mareen's a good gal."

"Dean?"

"Yes."

"I've decided what to name our little girl."

"Oh, you have, have you. And just how do we know the little bundle will arrive in pink?"

"I know it's a girl. Call it intuition if you like. You know, some of us of the effeminate side possess that. But...it is a girl."

"Whatever you say, Dear."

She smiled at him.

"Well, what's her name?"

"Dakotah."

"Dakota?"

"With an 'h'...Dakotah."

"Very original."

"With the name Dakotah, she will never forget her heritage."

"I see." He contemplated and repeated, "Dakotah."

CLIMBING OVER THE HILLY terrain, Spring breathed laboriously.

"You okay, Hon?" Dean questioned.

"Yes...I'm fine." She inhaled the deep, fresh scent of the Ponderosa Pines.

"Have you ever seen such brilliance in your life? The Aspens have simply outdone themselves this year," Dean's friend's wife, Rosa, exclaimed.

Spring looked around at the shimmering yellow leaves quivering in the slightest breezes that attempted to steal through the forest unnoticed. Then her eyes fell upon Dean's rifle. She moved closer to him. "Dean, I don't see why you brought *that* along?"

"You wouldn't, little one, but I've spent enough time in these hills to come prepared. One never knows."

"I'm with you, Dean. That's why I have ole trusty here." Doug, Rosa's tall, thin husband, patted the pistol hung on his hip.

Spring shook her head, but Rosa laughed.

The one loner in the group, Rich, stopped suddenly up ahead.

"Well, well, look what we have here."

In the distance, a small herd of buffalo grazed contentedly. They all paused reverently, watching the noble beasts as thoughts of their past evoked nostalgia. But a rustling in the nearby brush seized their attention! Unknowingly, an antelope had approached the party, and they turned to stare into the steady gaze of the graceful animal that never flinched as it held its position, then slowly sauntered off.

They sat down for a rest and listened to the sounds of the hills.

"I wonder if they see us?" Rosa spoke softly.

"Who?" asked Rich.

"Our people...our ancestors...."

"They are here," Dean assured authoritatively.

"These hills...they should be ours," Doug sighed.

Spring listened, her heart beating wildly. Yes, the Black Hills...belonged to them...the voices from the past called out....

"Listen!" Rich whispered.

They heard voices.

Coming nearer!

They waited.

It was the voice of the white man. They stood up.

The laughter and youthful kidding broke into the silence of the hills as the four young people appeared in front of them with surprised looks on their innocent faces. The laughter ceased!

Doug moved forward with his hand on his gun.

"What are you doing here? This ain't white man's land!"

Dean moved up beside him with his rifle raised.

The four young people backed off.

"We're sorry...didn't mean any harm...," a frail young fellow choked, "We must'a gotten lost." A charming, petite girl was clinging to his arm, looking like a frightened fawn.

"Dean!" Spring yelled.

He turned to face her frown.

The four young people dashed off.

"What was that for?" she demanded.

"Just a little scare; they'll know who the Black Hills belong to."

On the way home, Dean patted Spring's hand beside him. "You feeling okay, Hon? You're mighty quiet."

She sighed, "Sometimes, I just don't understand you, Dean. Was it necessary what you did today to those young people? Why, they were terrified!"

"Everything we do, Spring, is not necessary...but sometimes it just seems like the thing to do."

She decided against pursuing the subject — one that would prove futile to both of them. Ironically, these same differences that now distanced them had attracted them to each other in the first place.

When they arrived home, there was a telegram waiting for Spring. She scanned it quickly.

"What is it, Dear?"

"It says...it says that my painting...*The Dogwoods* has been selected to receive national honors...an award. Oh, Dean! It says it will be placed in The Sioux Indian Museum in Rapid City...if I so authorize. Can you believe it?"

Her face was flushed, an outward characteristic seldom seen on her proud visage.

"Fantastic!" He grabbed her, hugging her to him. "You have reached great heights, my Dearest!"

She smiled at him calmly, "And I learned how to make *Wahanpi.*"

Chapter VI
The Mysterious Light

"Melony, what's your aunt's name...that Indian aunt?" Roxy called while glued to the morning paper.

"Spring," she replied from the bathroom. "Why?"

"Come here a minute...look at this!"

Melony shuffled out of the bathroom, one hand holding her robe together and the other suspended in mid-air clasping the teasing comb that was stuck somewhere in the beehive she was creating.

Roxy looked up. "This world sure is a crazy place. White folks spending hours tangling their hair all up while we spend hours trying to straighten ours out."

"What is it?"

"Right here." She pointed to the column.

Spring Barrett, local artist, recently received the high honor of having her beloved painting, *The Dogwoods*, placed in the Sioux Indian Museum in Rapid City, South Dakota. The famed work of art was painted right here in Virginia within the Blue Ridge Mountains....

She stopped and ran to the phone. "Mom, have you seen the morning paper? You have? Isn't that great! It's nice having a celebrity in the family. Gotta go...I'll be late for work." She hung up and turned to Roxy.

"Can you keep Little Emily tonight? The girls and I are going out."

Roxy looked up disapprovingly. "Guess so. Where you goin'?"

"Why should I answer that, Roxy? You'll only criticize."

"Must be one'a them dances again. Melony, you gonna...."

"Roxy, I don't have time to listen. Gotta go. See you tonight." She ran in to give Little Emily a quick kiss while she slept. The door slammed behind her, and Roxy listened to her quick, light footsteps descending the stairs.

That night, Roxy lay on the couch in a half doze waiting for Melony. Little Emily and Laurietta had been asleep for hours. A dog was barking incessantly somewhere outside, and she wished he'd shut up. She looked at the clock...*one o'clock!* The wind was beginning to get up, sounding more like a winter night with its little whispers and moans. She decided to look in on the girls, and rose to go into the bedroom. Quietly creeping into the darkened room, she smiled at the two of them, curled up in their respective beds sound asleep, with Little Emily content with her thumb in her mouth and Laurietta's head buried in the pillows as usual. As she started to go out, her eyes automatically turned to the window. The shade was halfway up, and for some reason, she felt drawn toward it. She peered out into the dark...and jerked back!

There was a *light* in the little house that sat down in the lower backyard. She stood there, unable to move for a moment as haunting images passed through her mind. Suddenly, it was gone! She continued to stare at the little house, once again immersed in darkness. It was vacant and had been for many years. In bygone days, it had housed the servants of the big house, and before that, the less fortunate slaves. Roxy sat down with her eyes fixed on the little house, and her imaginative mind conjured up pictures from the forbidden past. Was it a ghost of the past...a ghost of another era...another time...a slave time? Suddenly, something scratched the window screen! She gasped! And then, she felt foolishly timorous as she was made aware of the source...a tree limb had brushed the screen as the wind manipulated its victim. She continued to sit and watch the little house that was barely visible in the quarter moon, with only the swaying trees distinguishable as they twisted and stooped beneath the wind. She anxiously wished Melony would hurry home. What was it the neighbor had said...it hadn't been occupied for over twenty years. But where did the light come from? Time slowed to a snail's pace, and drowsiness was overtaking her, but still she watched. The night wore on...two o'clock. She jumped as the front doorknob turned.

Melony walked in and began pulling off her clothes as she made her way toward the bedroom. Roxy met her halfway.

"Melony, you ain't gonna believe this...but I saw a

light…a light down in the little house. It was there and then it was gone…."

"Roxy, what are you talking about?" Melony pushed past her.

"A light, I tell you. You know, in the little house out back. I saw a light…sort'uv like a candle in the window…I believe it might'uv been a candle because it seemed to be kind'a flickering, you know."

"Well, it would have to be a candle light. That place hasn't had any electricity for years. Now come on, Roxy. I'm sleepy. Let's talk about this in the morning. You sure you didn't dream it?"

Roxy frowned. "No, Ma'am. I didn't dream it. Couldn't have. I ain't been asleep…been waiting for you."

"Well, now I'm here. Let's turn in. Good night."

Roxy stood looking after her, once more taking in the obvious liquor and cigarette odors. 'Course she wasn't interested in any light. Roxy turned and went to bed, soon falling asleep herself. But Melony lay awake for much longer with thoughts racing over the night…but mainly on *him*. He was not like anyone she'd every known…such charm. That's what really captivated her. Whenever he smiled at her, she melted, feeling all warm inside. And those eyes, such intriguing eyes that kept her wondering what he was thinking. And the way he danced, or they danced, as if they were made for each other. She could have danced all night with him…she practically did, much to Diane's irritation. But, who could blame her? She wondered if she'd hear from him? Diane had bets that she wouldn't, but she was just cross because they were so late getting home. She turned over to go to sleep, and saw Little Emily's crib in the semi-darkness. Precious little one! Suddenly, she felt an overwhelming guilt for leaving her. Then all those thoughts and feelings began crowding back into her mind...her broken marriage...her pain...her failure ...her life. What about *her* life?

The next morning Roxy stirred about noiselessly, fixing her coffee and going down for the paper. She'd let the girls sleep as long as they would, and Melony, too. She got ready to sit down and indulge in her paper and coffee, but instead she was drawn to the window, and keenly observing the little house, she noticed it looked the same as always...desolate, forlorn...but normal! Could she have perhaps imagined the light? No! She went back to the table.

The headlines stood out...*"JURY ACQUITS KLAN MEMBER IN SHOOTING."* She read on....

Ku Klux Klansman of Detroit sports a 10-gallon hat as he arrives at session of trial. The Klansman left the courtroom without commenting on the verdict. He smiled broadly and puffed rapidly on a cigarette....

Roxy tossed the paper aside and gulped down her coffee. Would this violence ever end? Oh well, she couldn't let these things bother her. She poured herself another cup of coffee and picked up the paper again...*"KING CALLS FOR MORE MARCHES IN SOUTH TO OBTAIN JUSTICE."* "Amen," she voiced aloud and kept reading....

"Large communities all over the Southern United States are

obeying the civil rights law and showing remarkable good sense," King said. But he added, "We still have a long way to go. We have left the dust of Egypt and have crossed the Red Sea, but there is still the frustrating wilderness before we can reach the Promised Land."

Roxy leaned back in her chair and smiled. He sure did know how to put things. She thought she heard a little movement in the bedroom, and quickly scanned the rest of the paper, knowing she wouldn't get much reading done once the girls came to life.

CHASE IN SPACE READY TO START...Cape Kennedy, Fla. Barring any holds in the numerous countdown, an Atlas rocket will blast off at 1 a.m. EST, hurling an Agena space vehicle into orbit. At 11:41 a.m., a Titan rocket will launch the Gemini spacecraft in blazing pursuit of the Agena. And, if the flight plan is followed smoothly all the way, the two will meet over Hawaii about 5:40 p.m. to accomplish the first link-up of two crafts orbiting at 17,500 miles an hour.

"My...my, what is this world coming to...chasing each other around in space now!"

"What are you mumbling about?" Melony asked while yawning her way into the kitchen.

"Oh nothing. Today's the day they gonna hook-up those space ships in space. Mama said we best be figuring on having some bad weather. Always do when they go fooling around up there. If the good Lord meant for us to be up there...why He would've put us there."

"You're probably right about that, Roxy. Do we have any bacon?"

"On the second shelf. Little Emily and Laurietta still asleep?"

"Yes."

Melony placed the bacon in the frying pan and leaned up against the stove. "Roxy, you should see him."

"See who?"

"Clint."

"Clint?"

"You know, the one I told you about."

"Oh yeah, I forgot. You saw him again?"

"Yes...and I think I'm falling in love." She was poking at the bacon in a dreamy sort of way.

"Why do you say that?"

"It's the way I feel...you know...well, how did you feel when you first met Seth?"

She looked up suddenly. "You can't compare this with my Seth."

"And why not? You were in love...weren't you?"

" 'Course we were. But mine and Seth's...well...it was special."

"What do you mean by that?"

"Seth and me...we were in love always...ever since first grade. We growed up together, you know. I can't put my finger on the time when I actually fell in love with him. I just can't ever remember not loving him."

"I see what you mean. Have you heard from him lately?"

"Oh yes. I always hear from *my man*. His letters come like clock work. They may be a little late sometimes, but that's not his fault."

Roxy had gotten that pensive look that always accompanied her thoughts of Seth.

"But Roxy, Clint is special, too."

"How do you know? You don't even know him!"

"Well, you don't have to grow up with someone to know them. I just know he is. I feel it."

"You better turn that bacon."

She quickly began turning the already crisp bacon that sizzled and popped. "Want some?"

"Maybe one slice. Melony, I just want you to be careful. I don't think much about meeting a man in them dances."

"You ever been to one, Roxy?"

"I should say not! And I don't plan on ever going to one either. My Pa would've pulled me out by my hair if he'd caught me in one'a them places. He told me so."

Melony laughed...and little Emily laughed, too. They turned to see her standing sleepily in the doorway holding her blanket.

THE GOLDEN AUTUMN days passed into winter, and Christmas was quickly approaching. Oak Mountain looked the same, as Melony drove up the barren hillsides. Wintertime had a way of stripping it of all its beauty. Well, almost all of it. An openness pervaded the winter forest that allowed one to feel the magnitude of its breadth, and view the distant ridges as naked Oaks climbed them, shivering in the bitter chill.

She noticed a partial wooden fence still standing midway up one of the nearby ridges. She'd never seen it before, but now it stood exposed representing another time. *Time!* How it kept marching on...not waiting for anyone or anything. She looked at her watch. She better hurry on. Mother wouldn't be too happy if she were late for dinner, and she couldn't wait to see Little Emily. It had been almost a week, and she certainly missed her. But it was good for her to spend time with her folks on Oak Mountain and experience some of the sweet memories that she still carried tucked away in the corners of her mind.

Prudence peered out the kitchen window. "She should be here any minute now." She wiped her hands on her apron and picked up Little Emily. "Yes, Mommy's coming soon." Little Emily clapped her pudgy hands.

"Clarence, did you hang up that Christmas wreath on the door like I asked you?"

"Yes Ma'am, I did," he answered from the living room.

"Thank you, Dear. Melony always likes to see that on the door. You know how sentimental she is."

"You did say that Jonathon and Jessica are coming over later?"

"That's what she said this morning on the phone. Jonathon's feeling better. Think it was just a twenty-four hour thing."

"Good. I need to talk with Jonathon about the alternator on my truck."

After dinner, Prudence and Melony set about the dishes.

"I'll wash and you dry," Prudence offered.

"I don't mind washing, Mom. You washed last time."

"All right. I'll dry." She pulled out a clean dishtowel from the cabinet drawer. "Well, how are things in the city?"

"Fine."

"Are you still seeing the young man?"

"Yes. He's taking me to a Christmas party over in Charlottesville next week."

"I see. When will we get the chance to meet him?"

"Oh, soon I'm sure." Melony rocked on her heels, trying to conceal her own questions. Why *wouldn't* he come to meet her folks?

The back door flew open and in walked Jessica. "Hello!" she gasped underneath her shawl.

"It's not *that* cold, is it?" Prudence asked. "How are you, Jessica?"

"Fine...and yes, it's getting colder by the minute. Hi, Melony."

"Hello, Aunt Jessica. Where's Uncle Jonathon?"

"Out back with your dad. Been a while since we've seen you?"

"I know. Staying busy. How's Heath?"

"He's doing all right, I guess. That is...if he could get away from Caroline."

"I thought you liked Caroline, Jessica." Prudence frowned as she placed the glasses in the cabinet.

"I do. It's just that she can't get an inch away from Heath most of the time. I think she smothers him."

"Don't suppose you're jealous?" Prudence questioned jokingly.

" 'Course not. That's not it. Caroline's so moody these days. I don't know what's gotten into her anyway."

"Does Heath date anyone else?" Melony inquired while finishing up the last of the dishes.

"You kidding? No. He only has eyes for her."

"Melony, look out the window," Prudence prompted. "Look at your father carrying Little Emily around on his shoulders just like he used to carry you and Mary Tom.

My, how time flies. 'Course he'll probably have back troubles tonight."

Melony watched them, sensing a strange longing. "Too bad we can't stay kids."

Prudence and Jessica stared at her questioningly.

"I mean life is so simple when we're little."

"You're right, Melony." Jessica grabbed an apple from the table and wiped it off with the end of Prudence's dishtowel. "By the way, Pru, has Patrick heard from David lately?"

"Oh yes, he finally got a letter the other day. I know this war is hard on Patrick. I just wish it would hurry up and end!"

"Looks like there's no end to it. I told Heath he'd better get into college, or he might end up there like David."

"You're right about that, Aunt Jessica. The paper said the other day that 40,000 more GI's are being sent over. That'll make about 200,000 there. It's hard to believe."

"And just think about all those wives and little children left here behind," Jessica added.

Melony thought of Roxy and Laurietta. "Roxy sure does take it good. But she's so strong."

"Roxy?"

"You know, Jessica. The young girl that keeps Little Emily," Prudence explained.

"Not to mention that she's my best friend," Melony added.

"Oh yes. I'd forgotten." Jessica stole a glance at Prudence. "And her husband is in Vietnam, too?"

"Yes. He's been there for about eight or nine months."

"I heard they're talking about calling a 'truce' for the holidays...have you ever heard of such a thing?" Jessica exclaimed.

"Well, I think it's good. They ought to stop fighting at least for the Lord's birthday," Prudence declared.

Melony couldn't help but notice how attractive Jessica looked. She was quite striking in her middle age with a figure still youthful looking, and thick, dark hair that had only a few grey traces. But it was her skin that held the secret...flawless, smooth and still holding some of its childlike glow.

"Aunt Jessica, how do you keep looking so young all the time?"

"Why, Melony, what a sweet thing to say. Remember, Child, we must never become slack with our appearance. That is if you plan to keep your man... and I plan on keeping mine!"

They laughed as the men entered.

"What's so funny?" Jonathon asked.

"Nothing, Dear." Jessica winked at Melony as Jonathon strode over to give her a big kiss.

Little Emily trudged through the door behind them, carrying Lucy Bell, Pru's big mama cat. It was all she could do to hold onto her, and even then parts of the big tabby were spilling over.

"Put her down, Darling."

"But Mommy...she's my kitty." She backed away holding onto the cat tightly.

"Now Emily, that's Grandma's kitty...remember."

Jessica jumped down off the stool, and stooped to whisper something in Little Emily's ear. Little Emily took the cat to the door and let her out.

"What did you say?" Melony looked puzzled.

"It's my secret. Always worked with Heath," she teased.

Prudence shrugged her shoulders, "Heath was always such a good little boy."

"He still is." Jessica smiled.

"I LOVE YOU, TOO, HEATH." Caroline hung up the phone. She would miss him today, but he'd insisted on studying at the library. He was becoming quite scholarly, she thought. Oh well, she should be proud of him, and she was, but somehow, she felt jealous. She thought about what Clara had said...how she was jealous of anybody or anything that came between she and Heath. Maybe Clara was right. She usually is. In fact, I wonder where she could be? She grabbed her jacket and went outside. The cold air hit her, and she shivered as Clara came running up the road, waving her hand high in the air. Caroline smiled. Clara always made her feel better. They walked around the yard a while, breathing in the cold air and blowing out little circles of smoke.

"You feeling okay, Miss Caroline?" She'd called her Miss Caroline ever since that day in school when old Miss Udley, the substitute teacher, had called her that all day to teach her respect. Caroline had purposely called the teacher by her first name because of a dare.

"Yeah, I'm okay, I guess."

"You're not still having those nightmares, are you?"

"Not much. Sometimes. Guess I always will."

"Nope. You shouldn't think that way. Time heals, they say. We just haven't had enough time yet." Clara always included herself in any of Caroline's problems.

"Clara, you're the greatest. You make it sound like we both had the...the abortion...instead of me."

"Sometimes I feel like I did." She reached out and patted Caroline on the shoulder.

"Well, I don't know what I'd do without you. I have to have someone to talk to. I don't think I could bear it alone."

"That bad, huh?"

"I just can't get it off my mind...especially when I see a baby...like the other day when we were at the store."

Clara remembered. "Like I said, it will take time. Let's make some oatmeal cookies! Will your mother mind?"

"No. She's got one of her headaches...is in bed. Sounds like a good idea to me. That is, if I can lick the bowl?"

"It's a deal." Clara laughed, happy to see Caroline joking.

The day wore on, and Caroline and Clara enjoyed themselves like old times, making cookies, going for a walk and completing picture albums. They'd been friends since third grade when Clara and her folks had moved to Oak Mountain from somewhere in Alabama.

As they placed the last picture in the picture album, Clara said she had to go.

"Well, thanks for helping me with the album. Mother has been after me for some time to finish it. And... thanks for everything else."

"You're most welcome, Miss Caroline. Tell your mother I hope she feels better."

"Sure. I'll talk to you tomorrow."

That night, Caroline lay in bed thinking about Heath and their life together. She wished they could get married, and he would be here beside her, but he had to finish school. He was insistent about it, and it seemed so far away. Finally, she drifted into a troubled sleep. The setting was dreadfully familiar. The walls were bare, a dull green, and it was cold. She was scared and alone...but really not alone. There was a presence there...in the room...but she couldn't see anyone or hear anyone. She felt herself groping around as if blind. The presence was growing stronger. It was a sweet presence...and then she heard it...barely. That tiny, far away little voice. It seemed to be laughing ever so softly as if it floated with the gentle breezes that caressed the fragrant budding trees. She reached out. She wanted to make contact. But then it happened! That sweet presence was being wrenched from her...painfully! NO...PLEASE!

She sat up, perspiration dripping from her forehead as she clutched her pillow. Finally, she lay back down as the tears slowly slid down her pretty face and onto the crisp white pillowcase.

THE SATURDAY BEFORE Christmas dawned clear and cold. Melony rolled over beneath the warm covers. She didn't want to get up. She'd rather lay there, cozy and comfortable, thinking about him. In fact, that's all she did these days...think about Clint. But she was concerned. Why wasn't their relationship moving along faster? She felt they were at a 'stand-still'.

"Mel, you gonna get up today or tomorrow?" Roxy whispered so as not to awaken the girls.

She grunted, and pulled the covers over her head.

"Come on, Mel. I'm gonna go to Peck's this morning. Got to get some Christmas shopping done!"

Reluctantly, Melony pulled herself out of bed and grabbed her robe. She followed Roxy into the warm kitchen. "You mean you aren't finished yet?"

"No Ma'am. I've got to get you something yet."

"Now Roxy, I told you not to bother. You shouldn't spend your money on me."

"Ain't you gonna get me something?"

She laughed.

Roxy reached up and turned on the radio on top of the refrigerator.

"Remember, Gemini 7 is supposed to splash down today!"

"Oh, that's right. I've been waiting all week!"

"Don't be sassy. There are things going on in the world more important than Saturday night dances, you know."

Melony cleared her throat, "You're leaving Laurietta with me?"

"Sure thing. I can get a lot more done that way. I appreciate it."

"Certainly, I owe it to you. You remember Little Emily and I are going home this evening. Mom wants us all to go to Uncle Patrick's church for the Christmas service tomorrow. You gonna stay here tonight?"

"Probably so. When will you be back?"

"Tomorrow night," she replied while walking toward the bathroom to get ready.

Little Emily climbed down out of her bed and peeked into Laurietta's crib. She poked her little finger gently into the little girl's tummy, trying to awaken her. Laurietta let out a cry. Little Emily jumped back, placing her hands demurely behind her back as Roxy appeared in the doorway.

"Lil Emily, did you wake up my girl?" she asked, knowing all along what had happened. Little Emily hung her head. Roxy picked up Laurietta, who ceased her cry instantly, and reached out for Little Emily at the same time. "Come here, little lady, to Roxy." Her tiny face lit up and she ran to her.

She carried them both in her arms into the kitchen. "Let's get some oatmeal this morning...nice warm oatmeal."

Melony followed them with a mouth full of toothpaste, "Good morning, Sweetheart." She leaned down to kiss her, and Little Emily pushed her away giggling. Melony went back to the bathroom to finish brushing.

"Here it comes!" Roxy yelled out.

"What?"

"Gemini...it's splashing down! They just said so on the radio."

"Wonderful." Melony went about applying the last of her make-up.

"Let's see. 9:05...just like they said. Isn't that amazing how they know these things?"

"Who are you talking to?" Melony called out.

"Myself, of course."

"Oh. I thought so. Where did it land?"

"In the ocean...about 565 miles from Bermuda, they say."

"I'm glad it's them."

"Me, too. Somebody's gotta be clean crazy to go up in

one of them things. They don't have no right to be up there."

THAT NIGHT ROXY remembered their conversation about the spacecraft. She wondered if it was gonna rain as she looked out into the night. There was definitely a mist about the moon. She'd just put Laurietta down for the night, and was looking forward to reading a while. She loved to read, especially novels about faraway places where she'd never been nor would ever go. Gothic novels, Melony called them. Whatever they were, she could almost imagine herself being there in one of them dark castles surrounded by moats with the fields in the distance. What were they called? Moors, yes that's it. Why they didn't just call them fields she didn't know. But moors sounded more mysterious. Suddenly everything seemed awfully quiet, and she looked around the spacious living room. Melony always said this place resembled one of those castles in England or somewhere. She guessed maybe it did. Then the quietness was broken by a pelting rain on the windows.

"I knew it!" she said aloud. "They've gone and done it again. We'll probably have rain for several days now. It might even be raining for Christmas! Why they don't just stay down here where they belong...I don't know." She rose and walked softly into the bedroom to check on Laurietta. Yes, she was sound asleep. She started to look out the window at the increasing rain, but had second thoughts. She'd purposed to forget that incident and hadn't mentioned it since, but still the memory was haunting. That's silly, she scolded herself. Grandma always said if there's something that scares you, face up

to it! Briskly, she walked to the window, as little
rivulets of water trickled down the panes on their curvy
courses. She leaned closer, peering through the watery
window panes.

"Oh no...," she whispered, while clutching her gown
to her. *There it was again!* She stood frozen to the
spot...her gaze fixed upon that light. "Oh, Melony, why
did you have to pick tonight?" she whispered. The light
began to move slightly...away from the window. Roxy's
eyes followed. It disappeared for a few minutes, but
Roxy kept her vigil watch. Then it reappeared! She
jumped back. "Oh Lord, you gotta help me. You know
how scared I am!"

The rain was coming down harder, and she had to
struggle to see through the watery waves on the darkened window. She could barely make out the light. It
seemed to move from time to time. What was she gonna
do? The light went out! Roxy stood there in that spot for
another thirty minutes until her legs began to ache.
Finally, she went back to the living room, checked the
night latch and reached for her Bible. No Gothic novel
tonight! She turned to the Psalms, snuggled down
under the quilt and read. Soon she slept.

JUST LIKE ROXY predicted, Sunday morning
brought a cold, misty rain that lasted throughout the
day. Melony sat up straight in church, feeling very
uncomfortable. Why, she didn't know. She had too
many questions, too many unanswered questions...not
to mention a pervading guilt. Her mother looked over at
her and smiled, while Little Emily drew pictures on her
lap, and her father squirmed in the seat beside her

trying to get comfortable. They all turned to the aisle and slid toward the center of the pew as Jessica and Jonathon arrived, with Heath and Caroline following. Caroline looked charming in her soft, furry white jacket. Her hair was tied up with a crimson bow except for a few ringlets that had escaped and hung loosely around her lovely face. Melony smiled at her, and she smiled back. Soon the service was underway, and Patrick began to expound the message he'd spent hours preparing. This was a special message...his Christmas message about 'charity...love...and how mankind should treat his fellow man'.

"My text today is Matthew, chapter eighteen," his strong, but gentle voice flowed from the pulpit, and there was a silence in the pews. "'At the same time came the disciples unto Jesus, saying, "Who is the greatest in the kingdom of heaven?" And Jesus called a little child unto him, and set him in the midst of them. And said, "Verily, I say unto you, Except ye be converted, and become as little children, ye shall not enter into the kingdom of heaven" '."

Melony looked down at little Emily scribbling her pictures...such innocence, honesty and trust.

Patrick continued, " 'Whosoever therefore shall humble himself as this little child, the same is greatest in the kingdom of heaven. And whoso shall receive one such little child in my name receiveth me. But whoso shall offend one of these little ones which believe in me, it were better for him that a millstone were hanged about his neck, and that he were drowned in the depth of the sea'."

Caroline gripped her purse, feeling sick to her stomach. The words reverberating off the corners of her mind...'whoso shall offend one of these little ones...it were better for him that a millstone...a millstone were hanged about his neck...and that he were drowned in the depth of the sea...'.

Melony happened to look her way and noticed how white she'd become. She wondered if she was okay, but saw that she was focused on the sermon. Patrick continued reading the passage as the small congregation followed with their Bibles.

" 'For the Son of man is come to save that which was lost'." He paused, allowing the congregation to digest this important quote. Melony leaned over to read these words herself from her father's Bible..."to save that which was lost." She certainly felt lost.

Suddenly, Caroline stood up and left. Melony followed. When she reached the front steps, Caroline was sitting on the top step and leaning against the railing.

"What is it, Caroline?" she asked as she sat beside her.

She waved her off.

"Are you sick?"

"I'll be okay," she answered weakly.

"Do you want me to get Heath?"

"No...I want to be alone. Please...I'll be fine."

Reluctantly, Melony rose and went back inside. She looked back at the lovely young girl as the door closed between them. How puzzling and mysterious she seemed.

Roxy pushed the old carriage over the uneven stones and up the hill. Laurietta seemed to be enjoying the briskness, the cold. Her bright eyes were looking all around. Roxy was thinking about the silent prayer they'd just had for the boys over there in Vietnam. It was very touching. The whole Christmas service was very touching...almost too much! She fought back the tears. She knew Christmas would be hard...without him, but somehow she thought she was prepared. Suddenly, she felt awfully faint. She breathed in the sharpness of the wintry day, and pushed the carriage forward up the incline. How she missed him! But what about *him*? How must *he* be feeling right now? "One day, Laurietta, one day soon, you gonna see your daddy," she spoke to the little girl that was totally unaware of it all, "and your daddy is gonna be so proud of you!" She began to think of his homecoming. Things would be different. They wouldn't be able to stay with Melony and Little Emily then. No, she and Seth and Laurietta would have to find their own place...and be a real family. 'Course it was mighty nice for her and Melony to live together now and share the expenses and such — even her folks thought so when they made the decision. 'Course there wasn't much room for her and Laurietta after her brother Joel moved back home. She wondered what Melony and Little Emily would do when they moved out? Oh well, maybe she'd be married by then. But she didn't put much faith in this here Clint. Something told her things just won't right with him.

IT WAS CHRISTMAS EVE, in nineteen hundred and sixty-five, and the church bells and chimes could be heard throughout the city of Lynchburg. If one were to stand down by the James River and look up the steep hills that climbed upward towards the darkening sky, he could count at least six church steeples within close proximity. Such was the spirit of Lynchburg...called the city of churches. And now on Christmas Eve, many of them were filled with happy, expectant, but thoughtful and prayerful people. In the midst of such troubling times, it was good to stop everything at least once in the year and renew one's soul.

Bells pealed, candles flickered and sincere prayers were lifted on that night as hearts united in love once again. A lone tear rolled down Roxy's cheek as she held her candle while it fluttered and tried to extinguish itself. She hugged Laurietta tightly and prayed for Seth.

Miles away from the quaint little city, past the scattered villages, up into the wooded Blue Ridge Mountains, another church bell rang out each and every time the heavy rope was pulled, lifting the frail lad with it.

The parishioners filed in slowly, shivering from the cold mountain air, and took their seats quietly. There was that special aura that hung in the frosty air not only on Oak Mountain, but all over, everywhere...*it was Christmas Eve.*

The Barrett family were all seated in their usual pew...all except for Melony. She was restlessly walking the floor of her apartment, waiting for Roxy to return. And finally, she did.

"I thought you'd never come!"

"I took my time. I don't see why you have to go out tonight...it's the Lord's birthday!"

"Little Emily's already fast asleep, and I won't be late tonight. We've got a big day tomorrow. I've got to hurry now. The party starts in twenty minutes." She quickly left.

The music was loud, the festive spirit intense, and Melony danced feverishly to the beating pulse of it all. Between the music, the dance and the drink, she felt thrilled and light-headed.

"Well, if it isn't Miss Melony...straight out'a the pages of *Gone with the Wind!*"

She looked up to see Brock Horton with a sinister smirk across his angular face.

"Just what is that supposed to mean?"

"You know, Sweetheart...Miss Melony...so prim and proper...so untouchable...except that is for a certain Rhett maybe...."

"That's none of your business."

"Oh my, we're feisty tonight! By the way, where *is* your Prince Charming?"

"He's out of town for the holidays."

Throwing back his head, he let out a gusty laugh. "You don't really believe that, do you?"

"He's visiting his sister in Maryland...if it's any concern of yours," she replied, thoroughly vexed by now.

He raised his bushy eyebrows and held her gaze with his leery grin.

"Brock Horton, if you have something on your mind, go ahead and say it. Don't stand there looking like the cat that swallowed the mouse!"

"It's Christmas Eve, Miss Melony. Time for all good married men to be home with their families."

A cold chill slid down her back and up again. "What are you saying?"

"Just what I said." He toyed with his words, enjoying every minute of this. "Clint, ole boy, happens to be at home."

Melony stared at him.

"Don't mean to tell me you really didn't know?"

"Brock, are you telling me the truth?" Her words came out shaky.

"Just as married as he can be!" He smiled.

She lifted her glass to her quivering lips. "I don't believe you."

He laughed again. "Believe what you like."

He lit up a cigarette.

Melony's mind was racing. Slowly, unanswered questions were beginning to fall into place. No...it can't be!

"Prove it to me!" she demanded.

"Be glad to. Come along with me, and I'll show you his car parked beside his house." He continued smiling.

She hated him at that moment, but she must find out. They left the party together, and took off in his new red Mustang. Driving toward the east side of town, and down a quiet residential street lined with young Maples, her heart began to beat faster. The street boasted of attractive white cottages, each with neatly trimmed shrubbery. Before he could speak, she saw it!

"There it is."

Melony's heart stopped! Parked beside one of those neat little cottages was Clint's car. Lying beside it, was a child's small bike. A sick feeling way down in her stomach was making her nauseous. She felt angry. She felt sad.

Christmas morning arrived. The first rays of light fell upon the regal lines of the Moorish architecture of the house on Madison Street. Those welcomed rays found their way into the upstairs kitchen where Roxy was pouring herself coffee. Picking up her cup and carefully balancing it, she tiptoed into the living room to revel in the magic of the moment! Inhaling the strong cedar scent and proudly surveying the brightly wrapped gifts, she felt contented and returned to the kitchen. She stepped over to the window and scanned the little house out back. Everything looked normal. She hadn't seen *it* again since that night when Melony was gone. Maybe it *was* her imagination! But somehow, she couldn't believe it. She sat down at the table to wait for the girls and Melony to waken. She simply couldn't wait to see their little faces! "What's this?" she asked aloud while picking up the paper lying in the center of the table. Melony must have left it last night. She looked puzzled as she read...

What's it all about...this life we live?
Full of confusion from year to year
I cannot figure it out...this life we live
Oh how I wish it would come clear

How can so much beauty survive
In a world of such ugliness?
How can happy moments stay alive
In a world full of sadness?

Where can one put his trust
When all seems to deceive?
But isn't it a must
To have something to believe?

How can temptation be so sweet?
And yet the results be so sour
Why must the innocent suffer defeat?
Why must it be so unfair?

How can a life full of anticipation
Continually end in disappointment?
And midst the crowds, we daily run
Yet alone our lives are spent

What's it all about...this life we live?
Full of confusion wherever we go
I cannot figure it out no matter how I live
So it must not be for me to know!

Roxy laid the poem down thoughtfully. Poor
Melony...poor Melony, she thought, and then looked up
to see her standing in the doorway, her eyes swollen and
distant.

"Mel, what happened?"

"You were right," she answered weakly.

"You mean...."

"Clint."

"I'm sorry, Mel...."

She sat down opposite her, "He's married, Roxy."

"NO! You mean to tell me that low-down, good-for-
nothing scoundrel that's been leading you on...is married?" Her voice grew louder with each word.

"Sh-h-h-h. You gonna wake the girls."

Roxy got up to pour herself another cup of coffee.

"Want one?"

"No. Thank you."

"I knew something was wrong. I felt it in my bones." She turned to Melony and handed her the poem. "You gonna be all right?"

"Oh yes. Life goes on…and I have no more tears to shed," she answered sadly.

Roxy reached out and gave her a big hug, "Mel, it's Christmas morning, and we got'a whole lot of goodies in yonder under that tree. Let's go get the girls up."

Melony smiled weakly. "Let's."

Chapter VII
Dakotah

The shrill ring of the telephone woke Prudence from her peaceful sleep, and she stumbled to get it. Switching on the light, she noticed it was only 4:00 a.m.!

"Hello."

"*It's a Girl!*" the voice on the other end yelled.

"A girl? Dean, is that you?"

"Yes. Spring had a baby girl...we have a daughter!"

"Why Dean, that's wonderful...how's Spring?"

"She's doing great...like a trooper."

"As I would expect...how much did the baby weigh?"

"Seven pounds and two ounces...and she's twenty inches long...and beautiful...just beautiful...just like her mother."

"Oh Dean, I'm so happy for both of you...and I'm so happy it's a girl. Tell Spring I said so, and tell her I'll be making my flight arrangements today like I promised."

"That's great. I'll call later."

"Dean...what's her name?"

"Dakotah."

"Dakota...like the state...you mean?"

"Dakotah...like Sioux."

"I see. Well, I think it's a lovely name."

As she replaced the receiver and walked back to the bedroom, she felt a strange excitement. Spring was a mother...after all this time. A new life had entered this world...and Clarence was still asleep. She may as well let him sleep. He'd have trouble going back if she woke him. She climbed back into bed and settled in beside him, and lay there thinking about Dakotah. What would life have in store for her? She wondered if she would be like her mother? Suddenly, she thought about her trip out. Oh Goodness! She was gonna fly! She felt nervous again. She'd vowed she'd never put foot on one of those things! But Spring needed family now. She needed her, and she must not be thinking of herself and her own fears. That was selfish and foolish, but the little dark cloud just kept hovering there. God will take care of me, she told herself, and I'm not going anywhere until my time comes! She smiled in the dark. There!

As sleep ever so softly beckoned her, she whispered the name into the night..."Dakotah." Well, why not? Our second cousin in Charlottesville is named Virginia. I suppose if you can be named Virginia...you can be named Dakotah.

Spring lay in the firm hospital bed in Rapid City, and stared out the window as the early morning sky compelled the darkness to dissipate and firmly took charge of the oncoming day. A new day...the first day of her daughter's life. Yes, she'd had the daughter she'd expected, and somehow, she felt that this little piece of fragile flesh would make a difference! She would have to teach her...about the two worlds that would fill her days on earth. But especially her noble heritage. She would learn the language of her people, the old customs, the things that are important to them...and the land. She would help her to develop a deep love and respect for the land.

The door eased open, and Dean peeped in with a broad smile. He sauntered in behind an elaborate bouquet of deep red roses.

"For my love...."

"Why Dean, they're lovely...."

"Not as lovely as my two girls...." He placed them on the table beside her. "Have they brought her in yet?"

Spring smiled, "She should be here any minute."

"Oh, I called your sister...."

"Pru...what did she say?"

"She's coming out...and she said to tell you that she's glad it's a girl."

"I still can't believe she's coming."

"She must really want to see you...and the baby."

"Pru has always been there for me, although we are very different."

"You know, it's still hard for me to fathom that you have another family...and not an Indian family...."

"I can't wait for you to meet them all one day."

"Look who's coming!" called out the nurse as she wheeled the hospital crib into the room.

Dean jumped up awkwardly. The nurse lifted the

tiny infant and placed her in her mother's arms. She began to cry. The nurse left, and Spring proceeded to feed her with the naturalness of a seasoned mother. The crying ceased.

Dean marveled, "How do you know what to do?"

"Well, some of it comes naturally...the rest out of all those books I've been reading for nine months," she laughed.

"When you're finished feeding her, I have a surprise for you."

"Dean, what is it?"

"It's Dad. He's waiting downstairs."

"You mean he actually came!"

"This is a big day for him, too. His first grandchild!"

"I know...but he's always said he'd never cross the doorway of one of these places."

"Well, he changed his mind...as soon as he heard."

"What did he think of her name?"

"He likes it fine...but he said you should've named her Lakota."

"I'm not surprised. I know she's a Lakota Sioux... but Dakotah encompasses all the Sioux. And she must learn of all the Sioux...of all Indians...."

"You speak as though she has a mission," Dean kidded.

Spring looked up seriously. "She may."

When the old man shuffled into the room, Spring couldn't help but notice the contrast between his dark, weathered skin and the stark white hospital walls. She held the baby out to him, and his thin wrinkled face slowly spread into a smile...a deep proud smile.

PATRICK THOUGHT ABOUT HIS SISTER way out there in South Dakota just giving birth to her firstborn and here he was deeply concerned about his own firstborn and whether or not he would return home safely. Life was funny. He pulled into Pru's drive, wondering why he always showed up here whenever anything big happened in the family. Was it because they were twins, and therefore unusually close? Or was it because Pru partly filled the void that Mama had left? Whatever, here he was. He knocked on the door and entered. Pru insisted that family come on in without waiting.

"Pru...," he called as the screen door slammed shut.

"Be down in a minute," her welcoming voice drifted down the stairwell.

He pulled up a chair at the kitchen table and thought to himself...this big kitchen sure has a cozy feeling, more than most of the modern ones nowadays. Of course, he was proud of the new home he and Ellen had built a few years back, but there was just something about this old homeplace. He glanced at the two rockers sitting in the corner inviting any who might feel the urge to sit a spell. Between them was a sagging rack overflowing with colorful magazines, old newspapers and such. Next to the rockers was the Siegler oil heater that warmed that spot more than ample at times, and everyone was automatically drawn to it in the cold, winter months. And even now, in early spring, it was appreciated as it conveniently knocked the chill off, and created an inviting atmosphere. He looked over at the old enamel sink that shined and actually looked rather comely with its starched yellow and white skirt that

matched the kitchen curtains. Beside it was the tall
kitchen cupboard. He wondered how Pru got along so
well without those modern wall cabinets. She certainly
seemed to have no problem...just like Mama, he thought.
Suddenly he missed the old homeplace further up the
mountain...the cabin. How he wished he could enter its
familiar little kitchen again. This place...Pru's homeplace was the next thing to it...it too was old...very old
...and of course Pru was here....

"My, aren't we serious this morning?" she kidded.
"Oh hello, Sis. You caught me reminiscing."
"Reminiscing?"
"About old times...the homeplace...Mama...."

Pru poured them both coffee and sat down in front of
him. "I know what you mean. The older we get, the more
we remember the past...the good times...."

"I miss Mama...and Daddy...." Patrick almost
sounded like he did when he was just a boy.

Pru patted his hand, "We all do, Patrick." Her mood
quickly changed from solemnity to merriment. "Just
what do you think of this little addition to the family?"

"Dakotah...a very interesting name."
"Yes. It grows on you. Can you believe Spring... our
independent, stubborn, strong-willed Spring is a
mother?"

"Well, it will take some getting used to, that's for
sure. Are you really gonna fly out there, Pru?"

"I've already made the arrangements; I'm picking
the tickets up tomorrow."

Patrick searched her face, "And you're not afraid?"
"Patrick Barrett! 'Course, I'm afraid. I never planned
on getting on one of them things...but Spring needs me.

And, I'm trusting in the Lord to bring me back safely."

"I'm sure He will."

"You've said yourself that you're not gonna die 'till your time comes. I've heard you say that many times in your sermons."

Patrick nodded, and recited, "Hebrews 9:27 'And as it is appointed unto men once to die, but after this the judgment'."

"You see. And if God has my time already appointed, why then there's no need in worrying about this thing. I'm not going anywhere until it's His time."

Patrick smiled.

"So that's that!" She stood up to peer out the window, "Someone's coming."

"Who is it?"

"Looks like Jonathon."

Patrick gave a knowing look. He wasn't the only one who needed to touch base.

The screen door slammed again, and Jonathon burst into the kitchen. "Well, folks, do we celebrate or what?" His still young and boisterous voice was followed by one of his ready laughs.

"Another one is added to the circle."

"That's a nice way to put it, Preacher Brother. Wouldn't Mama and Daddy be excited if they were here?" He began pouring his own coffee.

"They sure would," Pru replied thoughtfully.

"Did you notice the Dogwoods coming up here today, Patrick?"

"I did, but they're a bit late this year it seems."

"You know," continued Jonathon, "I don't think I've ever seen them in such vibrant bloom...except for that summer so long ago."

"You mean the treasure time?" Prudence looked around.

"Yes. Do you remember how those Dogwoods were blooming? That was something!"

"I'll never forget...and I'll never forget Gertrude...." Pru smiled remembering the old woman of their childhood.

"None of us will, Pru," Patrick added, "But you know when you stop and think about it realistically... that old confederate money that we found...the treasure...well, it seems like a fairy tale now."

"You're right," Jonathon agreed.

"Not really," Pru quickly intercepted.

They both looked at their sister.

"Well, I mean fairy tales have happy endings...and that money led us to our new home down in the valley. If we'd stayed at the cabin, little Charity would be alive today."

"But Pru," Patrick challenged, "would that really be a happy ending?"

She pondered his words.

"I mean, do you really believe Charity, severely retarded as she was, would be happier down here than in heaven?"

Pru smiled, "Of course not, Reverend Barrett."

THE PLANE TAXIED down the runway and Pru held her breath and gripped her new purse. Jessica's words were wringing in her ears as the powerful motors roared, *'The takeoff is the most dangerous'*.

She prayed again, "Lord please let this plane take off

safely and carry me to South Dakota safely." She
quickly opened her eyes as if this would help the pilot,
and looked out the small window, watching the propeller zooming around. She noticed all those little clamps
and bolts, and wondered who put them together. She
remembered what Patrick had said in his sermon the
other week, "Whatever man does, there will be mistakes, but God makes no mistakes...." Oh my, she
thought to herself. I sure hope whoever put this thing
together didn't make any mistakes. Suddenly, the
engines roared and the plane sped down the runway.
Pru closed her eyes tightly. *What on earth am I doing on
this thing?*

As the flight attendant demonstrated the safety
devices, she silently prayed.

The Piedmont aircraft lifted off the ground, and
Pru's eyes flew open! She was acutely aware of a strange
sensation. I'm flying...imagine that! She even let a
slight smile escape her worried face. Once the plane
leveled off, and the fasten seatbelt sign disappeared, she
relaxed a little and leaned over, gazing out the window.
At 6:15 a.m., there was a thick haze, but she could see
the faint rays of the sun. Oh, what beautiful clouds they
are. How she wished Patrick were here to see this.
Wouldn't he simply marvel? She peered down on the
minute houses. It must seem like this to God...looking
down on multiplied millions of them...what a great God
we have!

The plane's roar was drowning out the talk of the
other passengers, and Pru felt almost alone, but she felt
God's presence. He was there just as He said He would
be...'I will never leave thee nor forsake thee'. She

glanced at the propeller again. It was still zooming around, and she was glad of that! She strained to read the tiny words printed on a sticker on the propeller...'*Caution, Support Cowl while lowering to Rest Position*'. Now what did that mean? Oh well, she reached for her book. Ellen had advised her to read — this was supposed to keep her mind off things. She opened up to the first page of *The House of the Seven Gables*...

> Half-way down a by-street of one of our New England towns, stands a rusty wooden house, with seven acutely, peaked gables, facing towards various points of the compass, and a huge, clustered chimney in the midst. The street is Pyncheon Street....

She looked up again, struggling to concentrate. Clarence would be amused. He said she shouldn't bother reading novels...that anything that wasn't true, wasn't worth reading. She knew Clarence was a smart man, a good provider and a very good husband...but Clarence didn't know everything! How could he know about novels when he'd never read one himself...and certainly Nathaniel Hawthorne was a smart man! Why, anyone who could paint a picture with words the way he could had to be more than smart...brilliant maybe. Clarence might even appreciate Nathaniel Hawthorne. At least he was a man! Not like Pearl Buck, one of her favorite authors, and one that Clarence had demeaned more than once. Of course, she understood that was mainly due to her particular sex. Why, my goodness, hadn't she won the Nobel Prize? And didn't she graduate from Randolph-Macon Woman's College right near home in Lynchburg, Virginia? That was one reason she liked her so well...she sort of felt a kinship to her.

She would read a paragraph or two of the famed *House of the Seven Gables* and then look out the window, only to repeat the scenario again and again. Finally, she closed the book and sat glued to the window, watching the misty clouds become transparent as the small plane glided through them, and she remembered how Mama had loved clouds...but she'd never seen them this way! Often Mama had spoken of the long trip they'd made to South Dakota when she and Patrick were just babies. That must have been something to travel all this way on a train with two babies. She wondered if she'd been as afraid on that train as *she* was now. Life is interesting with its twists and turns. If it hadn't been for Daddy injuring his arm, they never would have moved to South Dakota. There never would have been a 'Spring', and she wouldn't be on this plane going to see a little baby girl named Dakotah. All of a sudden, she felt excited and could hardly wait to see her!

"WE'RE ALMOST THERE!" Melony declared as she turned another mountain curve. Roxy stared out the open window at the vast hillsides covered with huge Oaks, Poplars, Maples...and the Dogwoods that graced the darkened forests with their intricate lace of fragile white blossoming flowers.

"I've never seen so many Dogwoods!"

Melony smiled. She was proud to show Roxy Oak Mountain. They would finally be spending the weekend here...just them and the girls. With Mama gone out to see Spring and Daddy on a fishing trip, it would be delightful having the place to themselves.

"Emily, give that back to Laurietta now," Melony scolded as Laurietta fussed over the fuzzy toy kitten that was just beyond her grasp. The girls were becoming restless with the long drive.

"Sure is a ways up here."

"Not when you're used to it. We're off the main road now, and after we go a few more miles, we'll be there."

"I knew we were off the main road. This here is a dirt road."

Melony laughed. "Not dirt, Roxy. It's a gravel road. Now, I can remember when I was a child, it was a dirt road...and when it rained, it was a mess."

"I can imagine."

As they jolted down the uneven, graveled road boarded on both sides with barbed wire fences, Roxy's observation skills were fine-tuned. She noticed some of the fence posts leaning from age with the barbed wire sadly sagging. She inhaled the keen freshness of the mountain air and watched the tall grass swaying ever so gently in the breezes.

"What's that I smell?"

Melony smiled. "I love it...don't you? It's just the pasture land. See the cows yonder?"

Roxy spotted the few black and white cows dotting the hillsides as they leisurely grazed. A few raised their expressionless faces to the passing car but nonchalantly went back to their pastime.

"It always reminds me of my childhood. I know I'm safe and secure in the country — on Oak Mountain — when I smell it."

She looked at Melony queerly.

"But now...what do you smell?"

Suddenly the car was filled with a pungent sweetness that was almost intoxicating. Melony pointed to the rambling fence that was covered with masses of honeysuckle, drooping with large clusters of the fragrant yellow and white blooms. "I just gotta have one." She stopped the car and jumped out.

"What're you doing?" Roxy called as Melony broke off one of the stems.

"Want one?"

"No thank you," she frowned at her.

"All you have to do is break off the bloom and catch the end of it between your fingernails and then pull this little stem out which brings out the honey juice with it...." She proceeded to put it into her mouth and suck out the juice.

"It's a good thing my mama can't see you sucking on weeds from a smelly pasture."

Melony laughed, "Shucks, we grew up on honeysuckle. Mary Tom and I would fight over them. I always liked the white blossoms better than the yellow ones. So did Mary Tom. It's a sweeter taste."

The girls began fretting for one, too. "Not yet, Girls. I'll teach you later." Melony hopped in, and they drove on.

Soon in the distance, Roxy could see a quaint farmhouse nestled among tall Oak Trees with a barn and several other buildings nearby.

"Is that it?"

"That's it."

"You don't have any neighbors, do you?"

"Not for a mile or so."

"I see."

She watched Roxy study the homeplace. "Sure are a lot of little buildings sitting about."

"Yeah, that's the smoke-house over yonder by that tallest tree, and the chicken house next to it, then the brooder house. The woodshed and corncrib you can see further out...and the outhouse off in the distance."

"Outhouse?"

Melony laughed again. "Don't worry. We don't use it anymore. In fact, it's all filled in, but for some reason, they left it standing."

"Thank you, Lord."

Melony smiled at her. This was going to be a fun weekend. "Over to your right is the barn and the pig-pen."

"Do you have any pigs?"

"A few, not as many as we used to. You'll meet them."

Roxy grinned. "Can't wait."

"Yeah, while we're here, it's our job to feed them and the chickens and the cats and Music...."

"Music?"

"Our dog. Music is part of the family. But we don't have to feed the cows. Whenever Dad goes fishing, Uncle Jonathon takes care of them."

"Good. I'm scared of cows."

"I'm going to pull over here for just a minute and put the flag back up on the mailbox. Mama told me to check it. It keeps falling back down."

While Melony fixed the bent red flag, Roxy surveyed the old farmhouse with its porch winding around two sides. Masses of Wisteria graced one end of the porch, and three white rockers sat side by side beckoning to all. On the other end of the porch was a long, narrow flower box standing on four spindly legs and holding an appealing spray of feathery green ferns. Everything was painted a glistening white, even the house itself. It was old, all right, and you could tell it had had many paintings. But it was beautiful to Roxy.

"What do you think?"

"I love it."

The main portion of the house was two-story with the kitchen and dining room jutting off the back of the house, and a screened-in porch went out from the kitchen. Two large rock chimneys supported the house on either side, and twisted, old Oaks with their new crop of bright green leaves shaded it from the already warm morning sun.

Suddenly, an old brown and black hound dog appeared from behind the house. He stopped short and stared apprehensively, then bounded toward them, half yelping, half barking.

"Music!" Melony called.

"Music," Roxy repeated.

Melony pulled the car up under one of the giant Oaks, and jumped out. The old hound came running toward her laboriously with his aged weight.

"Music, Ole Boy." She rubbed his head and his brown tipped tail wagged vigorously. It was apparent he was delighted to see them. Little Emily was now out of the car and running to pat him. Roxy followed with Laurietta on her hip.

"Interesting name for a dog," she remarked while backing off, somewhat leery of the unfamiliar animal.

"Not really. It just fits him. Music is a happy dog...he's music to us. Seriously, Daddy named him Music because he said when he heard him barking at night, it made him think of hunting...and hunting is music to Daddy's ears." The old hound nudged his large head toward her for more caressing while his drooling tongue hung out to one side. All the excitement was a little too much for him.

"What does he hunt?"

"Mostly squirrels.... Come on in." Melony led the way through the screened in back porch.

"Just leave the door open, Roxy. We do that for Music because he likes to come onto the porch where it's cool and nap."

Roxy obeyed, watching the old dog follow them in, staring at her all the time. She entered the house, escaping his searching eyes, and looked around at the large, sunny kitchen. Little Emily led Laurietta off in quest of toys stored in favorite places.

"This sure is a fine place."

"Thank you, Roxy. It's home. I was born here... both Mary Tom and I were born here. So was Daddy."

"I can see it's old. That's what makes it so special. You were mighty fortunate."

Melony looked at Roxy as she continued examining the cheerful kitchen. They walked into the dining room where the girls had already made themselves at home with blocks strewn everywhere.

"You're right, Roxy. We were mighty fortunate."

"I guess you miss your sister Mary Tom?"

"I do. But you know, you can't go back. At least, I have wonderful memories. Let's open the windows...

it's stuffy in here. My, that's better. Feel the nice breeze coming in. That's one thing about this place... there's always a breeze blowing in with all the trees."

They raised all the downstairs windows, and then proceeded upstairs to raise those, too.

"I'll show you my room...or your room, that is for the weekend. You and Laurietta can stay there, and Little Emily and I will be next door in Mary Tom's room."

They climbed the creaking stairs and faced the family trunk at the top.

"This is where Mama keeps all of our 'treasured items'." Above it hung an aged family picture, and Roxy stopped to examine the unfamiliar faces vaguely staring out at her through the discolored brownish photo.

"Who are all these people?"

Melony turned back and looked at the old picture with renewed interest. "Well, that's Mama right there." She pointed to a young girl with a demure poise standing in front of the group and dressed in a plain dark dress accented only with a simple white collar. "Uncle Patrick is there beside her...then that's Uncle Jonathon. Grandma and Grandpa Barrett are in the center. You know, I told you Little Emily is named after her. Her name was Emily Barrett. And next to Grandma is my Aunt Spring, the one in South Dakota who just had the baby...."

"So that's her!" Roxy leaned real close to get a better look. "My, she's pretty."

"She sure is...beautiful black hair and dark eyes...but I think it's mainly the way she carries herself that sets her apart...a certain regal aura seems to follow her... wherever...."

"Well, you said she was a Princess."

"That's right. Aunt Spring is different, and I can't wait to see her baby. I know she must be precious."

"Who's this?" Roxy pointed to the small frail child in the picture.

"That's Charity, Mama's baby sister. She's dead... died in the big flood years ago when Mama was just a girl."

"How old was she when she died?"

"Mama says about six...but she didn't look six. In fact, this picture was taken not long before she died."

"She only looks about three...not a day older...."

"That's right. You see, Charity was retarded."

"Oh, what a shame!"

"Yeah. That picture is really old. Mama and her brothers and Spring all look so young. Mama and Patrick looked more alike back then, I think."

"Twins, you say?"

"Right. Now here's your room, Roxy. You'll be comfortable here. It has one of the best breezes in the house."

Roxy still stood studying those faces as Melony moved off talking. She thought about how queer it seemed that their youth had been captured and hung on this wall for years and years to come.

"Roxy?"

She hurried after, coming up behind her friend as she stood in the doorway of her childhood room. It was packed with all the little memorabilia that fills every young girl's life. Obviously, they had been a part of this room for many years, and no one had the courage to remove them. Roxy gently picked up a tiny music box and slowly turned the key. She sat it down on the dresser as the minute ballerina gracefully began to turn to the chimes of *Danny Boy*.

"You can tell Mama doesn't believe in change. In fact, that music box was hers, and she gave it to me on my eighth birthday."

"It's lovely. Everything's lovely. Sort of like having your childhood to step back into...whenever you wish."

"Never thought about it like that. Guess you're right."

That night after the girls were fast asleep, Melony and Roxy sat at the kitchen table looking through old picture albums. Roxy found it fascinating to trace this large family through the pictures, although many of the photos were discolored. Melony explained that the box that contained many of them had survived the flood.

"You mean the same flood that killed your mother's little sister?"

"That's right. Would you like some milk and cookies?"

"Sounds good. Mel, I've gotta tell you something."

"What is it?" She strained to get the cookie jar, wondering why Mama always put it on the top shelf. There weren't any more little kids here from whom to hide it.

"Well, I didn't want to bring this subject up again... because I know what you're gonna say...but I've just gotta tell you...."

"Well, tell me." She tediously balanced the large round cookie jar in one hand while getting out the milk.

"It happened again...."

"What happened again?"

"The ghost...I mean the light...I saw it again."

Melony looked at her with raised eyebrows, "When?"

"Last Saturday night when you were out. And this time, Melony, I not only saw the light...but a shadow with it. I tell you, I saw a shadow moving around!"

"Roxy, are you sure?"

" 'Course I'm sure. You know I don't lie!"

"I just can't figure this out."

"Neither can I. Mel, do you believe in ghosts?"

"No...I mean...I don't know for sure."

Roxy's eyes grew larger. "What do you mean?"

"Well, my Uncle Patrick says there are such things as spirits that we can't see because we are humans, and we're not capable of seeing them."

"Great!"

"Uncle Patrick says there's a lot of things we don't know about."

"That's what I thought!"

"What?"

"There's a ghost in the little house, Melony. I know it!"

BANG! A loud noise from just outside the kitchen door startled them both.

"What's that?" Roxy whispered while turning white.

"Shh-h-h, I don't know." Melony moved slowly toward the door.

"Don't open it!" Roxy ordered.

She cautiously pulled the kitchen curtain slightly to one side and peered out into the moonlit night. She laughed aloud.

"What is it?" Roxy still whispered.

Melony motioned for her to look out the window. Roxy didn't move.

"Come here, Roxy. Look!"

Reluctantly, she moved toward the door and looked out. The young moon cast a silver glow on the darkened porch. She looked back at Melony and then leaned closer to the window.

"What is it?"

"Just an ole possum!" Melony laughed as the strange animal stared at them with its round, beady eyes.

"Why, bless my soul!" Roxy exclaimed.

The fat possum also appeared silver in the moonlight as he sat perched atop the banister with its rat-like tail curled up behind him. It didn't move, but continued to stare at them with its black pooled eyes framed by a white face and accentuated with a sharp pointed nose.

"What's it doing on the porch?"

"He just wants something to eat. Mama said she'd been seeing an ole possum for a few weeks now. I'd forgotten it. He sneaks up here to steal the cat's food that Mama puts on the banister so that Music won't get it."

"If that don't beat all!" Roxy laughed. And sure enough, the fat possum inched his way toward the remaining pieces of cat food.

Chapter VIII
The Lone Chimney

The next morning dawned clear with the promise of a beautiful day ahead, and Roxy awoke to the sweet scent of honeysuckle that drifted languidly in through the open windows. She stretched and turned over. Laurietta was still sleeping soundly beside her with her tiny thumb half in her mouth. Roxy kissed her brow and swelled with pride. What a beautiful little girl. She couldn't wait for Seth to see her. The soft, transparent curtains were ever so gently moving with the invisible mountain breeze. She lay there looking around the charming room. Laurietta will have a room like this! Yes, when Seth gets back...and they get their own place, she would fix up Laurietta a room just like this one. She smiled. 'Course she'd have to share it with her little sister. She planned to have another little girl just like Laurietta as soon as she could. 'Course, if it was a boy, Seth would be mighty proud. She hoped to have a big family...at least three or four. She thought she heard a creaking...a rhythmic creaking outside. Slowly, she eased out of the solid poster bed, trying not to awaken Laurietta, and looked out the window, but couldn't see anything. It sounded like someone rocking on the front porch. She remembered seeing those rockers. Hurriedly dressing, she stepped lightly down the hallway, down the stairs and noticed the front door was open, letting in the sun rays that fell criss-crossed into the foyer. She walked over and looked out.

"I don't believe it!"

Melony looked up and smiled. "The best part of the day...here on Oak Mountain."

"It must be, to get you up!" she kidded.

"Come on out, sit down...and listen...."

She sat down in the rocker beside her quietly, trying not to squeak her chair and listened. After a few seconds, she asked, "What're we listening for?"

"The stillness of morning."

"Oh."

Melony smiled, inhaling the dewy fresh air. There was just nothing like a fresh morning before the problems of the day had a chance to mar it. She wished life had that chance.

Roxy glanced around at the vast lawn and fields and hills that surrounded it. My, it must be something to own all this!

"How did your folks come by this place?"

"Oh, it goes back a long way. Daddy inherited it from his father, and his father inherited it from his mother. Originally, it was a land grant tract, Daddy says, from the Governor. You know, they did that back then to entice settlers to locate here in the Blue Ridge Mountains. He said my great-grandfather bought it for $3.00 an acre, Confederate money. Can you believe that?"

"My goodness! Why, this house ain't that old?"

"Oh no. The first house and buildings were replaced years ago with what you see here. 'Course these have been here a mighty long time, too. Did you hear Ole Mack this morning?"

"Who?"

"Ole Mack, our rooster. I love to hear him. It's probably the one thing I miss most in town."

"As a matter of fact, I did. Where is Ole Mack? I'd like to meet him."

"Come on." Melony jumped out of her rocker, leaving it tossing back and forth aimlessly. Roxy followed.

The chicken house was just around the corner. "How would you like to collect the eggs?"

"Could I? I've always wanted to do that." She stopped. "What's this?"

"I forgot. You'll love it. Come here." She pointed to a window in the building adjacent to the chicken house.

"Oh-h...just look at them little babies...."

"This is the brooder house...where the baby chicks are kept. It stays heated by that light...keeps the little chicks warm."

"We've gotta show this to Laurietta!"

"We will. She'll love it just the way Little Emily does. You ready to fetch some eggs?"

"I s'pose so. Will them chickens bite?"

Melony laughed, "Sometimes."

"NO!"

"They don't really hurt, though. Come on."

Roxy timidly followed her into the chicken lot as the chickens, reddish brown and snowy white, scattered midst excited flutterings and shrill hideous noises. Roxy jumped this way and that, not sure which way to go. "Hold up, Mel!"

"Come on in." Melony ducked her head while entering the chicken house. Roxy followed closely, holding her nose and adjusting her eyes to the darkened space. She witnessed a number of hens roosting and others perched placidly on their individual nests. Melony poked her hand up under some of them which brought on outraged cries of injustice. Just who did she think she was?

"See here?" She held up a couple of speckled eggs just like the ones she bought at the Ideal Market on Fifth Street. "Try it."

Roxy hesitated, and then cautiously extended her right arm toward a mild-looking hen. Suddenly the old hen let out a piercing sound and pecked frantically at her arm, causing her to jump backwards, knocking over a crate behind her. She caught herself, regained her composure and turned to Melony, "You get the eggs...I'll watch."

Melony laughed and continued gathering the few remaining eggs. She handed a couple to Roxy, who felt their warmth while rubbing their smoothness and enjoying this new experience, even from a distance.

"Catch!" Melony threw an egg high into the air toward her. Unconsciously, she dropped the other two eggs in her effort to retrieve the one sailing toward her. She caught it! Then looking down at the other two, broken and oozing around her feet, she yelled, "Melony

Hunter! Look what you did!" Melony only smiled. Roxy turned the egg around and around in her hand. Somehow it felt different. "What kind of egg is this?"

"A wooden egg." Melony laughed and laughed.

Roxy dropped it, too, on the dirt floor, and watched it roll around and come to rest next to a hen that stood looking at it curiously. The old hen shook herself and strutted off.

"For a fact...it is a wooden egg!" Roxy marveled. "Now just tell me why on earth you'd have a wooden egg in this here chicken house?"

"Dad uses it to fool the hens, makes them think they're gonna have more babies than they are, and causes them to stay put on their eggs. Works!"

Roxy shook her head.

As they left the chicken yard, Ole Mack appeared high upon the rooftop, flapping his wings proudly.

"He's King of the Courtyard."

Roxy laughed and bowed to him. She glanced at her watch. "We better check on the girls." They started back to the house.

"Guess you have to kill some of them chickens to eat?"

"Sometimes. You have to catch one first, chop off the head, boil her, pluck her...."

"Think I'd rather buy mine from the store."

"I know you would if you could see the poor chicken running around without a head...."

"No!"

"Sure does. An eerie sight for sure."

The morning was spent touring the place with the

girls, happily sharing their experiences. Roxy enjoyed the pigs mostly, sitting on the fence and scratching their leathery backs with a long stick. The girls peeped through the lower railing and watched the old hogs wallow in the mud and squeal with delight.

"I don't know who's enjoying this scratching more... you or the hogs," Melony kidded.

The morning flew by as the sun rose higher, reaching its peak.

"Roxy, how about lunch down by the pond? We can make some sandwiches, and the girls will love it."

"You got a pond...with fish in it?"

"Of course, Silly. You ever heard of a pond without fish?"

"Can we fish?"

"Suppose so, but who's gonna fix the bait and all that yucky stuff?"

Now Roxy laughed. "You mean you grew up here on this farm, and you don't know how to fish?"

"I didn't say that. I know how to fish...but Dad always baits it and takes the fish off. Who wants to do that?"

"Somebody has to. Got any poles?"

"I know where they are. Do you really want to go fishing?"

"That's one thing I know how to do. My grandpa and mama used to take us kids down to the river...the James River...to catch those big catfish. They're delicious."

"Well, we don't have any catfish that I know of... but we have plenty sunperch."

"Fishin' is fishin' all the same. Let's go."

Little beads of perspiration began to streamline down Roxy's forehead as she sat cross-legged on the sunny bank with bamboo pole in hand. The orange cork bobbed once, twice and dove under the still waters. She waited a second and jerked the line up with the empty hook. No fishing worm! She hollered over to Melony, "Shouldn't have thrown that other'n back. He's done told all the rest!"

Melony smiled as she and the girls enjoyed the shade of the massive old Willow that extended its protective limbs out over part of the pond. Its long, slender branches spanned the circumference of the aged tree with each willowy twig gracefully touching the ground, thus creating a fairy-like playground for the girls. Melony spread out the checkered tablecloth beneath the tree and set about preparing lunch. A honeybee buzzed by, and she swatted at it with the dishtowel. Little Emily and Laurietta were unsuccessfully trying to climb the tree.

"You girls be careful. Emily, bring Laurietta with you now. Time for lunch. Come on, Roxy." She reluctantly laid down her pole.

After lunch, while the girls played contentedly under the Willow tree, she and Roxy rested for a bit before continuing to fish.

"This sure is some tree."

"You're right about that. We always came here... Mary Tom and me...when we wanted to be alone. The branches shielded us from Mama's watchful eye, or Daddy's. We brought our corn dolls here to fix up...."

"Corn dolls?"

"You know, dolls made out of corn husks, but Daddy

didn't appreciate us pulling them off...."

"I think I know what you mean. I remember seeing one years ago when Grandpa took us over to my uncle's place. They lived sort of out, but not like this."

"Actually, ours were quite simple. We'd pull us each a corn husk and run down here under the tree. Couldn't let Daddy catch us...or he'd give us 'down in the country'. Mary Tom liked the red-headed ones... but I always picked the bright yellow silky ones like the summer sun. We'd take a stick or maybe a nail if we happened to have one in our pocket and punch holes in it for the eyes, nose and mouth. Sometimes, we'd even dress them up with odd pieces of scrap material left over from Mama's quilting. They were special, you know, because we'd made them ourselves...."

"Must have been fun...growing up here."

"It was."

"Emily," Melony scolded, "put Laurietta down! She wants to walk herself." She chuckled, "Emily loves to play mama with Laurietta."

"She does that. Melony, do you think we're different?"

"Different?"

"You know what I mean?"

"You mean because you're colored?"

She nodded.

" 'Course we're different. You're colored and I'm white."

"But do you feel like I'm different from you?"

Melony thought for a moment. "No."

"How come?"

"I don't know...because you're not...I guess."

"That's what I thought."

"Why're you thinking about this?"

"Don't know. Just do sometimes. Not everybody's like you."

Melony settled back against the old tree, "I remember years ago when I was about ten years old, and we were having part of the basement dug out. Daddy hired Jim Jennings, an old colored man from up the hollow. One day he brought his grandson, who was about my age...a real nice little boy. I was bored because Mary Tom was gone to Grandma Barrett's for a short while. So I began to play with him. Can't remember his name, but we played marbles. I remember he kept beating me...I never was very good with marbles, but we were having a good time when suddenly Daddy called me aside and asked me to go in the house. He told me I wasn't to play with the little boy anymore. I can vividly remember how hurt I was...and how I didn't understand."

"So what's he gonna say about us being here now?"

"Oh, Daddy's changed somewhat. He's glad you're here with me."

Roxy sighed. "Sometimes, it just bothers me...and I feel like talking."

Melony was silent.

"Should be used to it...but I don't think I'll ever be. The Good Lord just put too much feeling in me...I guess."

"I know how that is."

" 'Course things are a lot better'n they used to be. Laurietta won't have to go through some of the things I did...."

"Like what?"

"...things like riding the city bus and...."

"What about the bus? Remember, I'm from the country."

"Just having to ride in the back and get off by the back door and such...we couldn't get off by the front door even though we got on that way."

"Why not?"

"You just didn't. It was understood that the white folk used the front door and we used the back door... 'course we had to use the front door when we got on so that we could put the change in the box."

"That's ridiculous."

"I thought so, too...but that's the way things were back then."

"Suppose you had gotten off by the front door?"

"Nobody ever tried...that is until things began to change. Then sometimes, one of the young people would try it. I can still remember the first time it happened when I was on the bus. She must've been about eighteen I guess...and she marched right up that aisle like she was 'white'. At first, a hush fell over the bus...and then the whispers began. I remember an old lady sitting not too far up from me saying, 'The nerve of her...they're gettin' mighty uppity!' I was too scared to do anything but watch, but I wondered what she meant by 'uppity'."

"Well, it certainly wasn't fair," Melony concluded.

"Fair?" Roxy repeated absently.

"Well, things are changing for certain. Look at Martin Luther King and what he's doing."

"Yeah, I hope he'll be able to accomplish his dreams before...."

"Before what?"

"Look what happened to Abraham Lincoln."

"Yes, but this is the 'sixties'."

"You know what Seth wrote in his last letter?"

"What?"

"He says it's ironic...Seth likes to use big words... that he is there in Vietnam fighting for freedoms for another people...when his own people still don't have the freedoms they deserve...."

"I can see his point."

" 'Course Seth don't uphold all this racial fighting going on. He says he's got enough problems with fighting that war over there...he can't be worrying over what's going on back here. If they want to fight, he says, they ought to come over there...the black and the white."

"Why Roxy, that's the first time I ever heard you use the term 'black'."

"Well, it won't be the last. We're not colored folk. That's the term white folks gave us. Everybody's colored...some color! We're black. Cassius Clay even said so!"

"Cassius Clay?"

"Yeah, I read it in the paper. He said so when he was in Louisville, Kentucky. He said, 'I'm fighting for the black man, not the Negro. There ain't no such thing as a Negro. I am a black man, and I am fighting for the black man'."

"I heard the term recently...*black is beautiful*," Melony added.

"That's important for our young folk. Children need to have pride in their people. I plan to teach Laurietta to be proud of her ancestry. I'm gonna tell her that *she's not less than anyone else...but she's not more than anyone else.* That's what the Good Lord teaches!"

"You're right. I'm sure Laurietta will grow up to be quite special."

"If I have anything to do with it, she will."

"You know, I'm sure gonna miss you and Laurietta when Seth gets back."

Roxy smiled at her. "I can't hardly believe he'll be home soon...just a while longer." She wiped her eyes. "Can't wait for you to meet him, Mel. I'm so proud of him...always have been. Never have understood how I was lucky enough to get him! Shucks, half the girls in my class would've traded places with me. And me... never was pretty...never had any frilly dresses or such like the other girls. Always will be a mystery why he took to me."

"Oh Roxy, you sell yourself too short. You're a very special person. I'm sure you were just as pretty as the other girls, too."

Roxy laughed. "I know myself. But, now my Laurietta...she's gonna be mighty pretty...takes after her daddy. Look at her yonder. Already she's fine lookin'...nice skin color like Seth...got his bright eyes... his set jaw and his Roman nose...."

"Roman nose," Melony laughed, "she's too little for a Roman nose."

"Just the same...she's got one...just like my Seth. I'm glad she took after her daddy."

The next morning, Roxy awoke to the sound of pitter-patter on the tin roof over the farmhouse. Rain! A spring shower was more like it. She stretched out and reflected on the day before, and how much she'd enjoyed it, and hated to see the weekend come to a close. It was Sunday morning, of course, and Melony hadn't said a word about going to church. She wasn't surprised. Well, she'd have to have her own... she and the girls. If Mel wanted to join in, that would be fine.

A delicious country breakfast of scrambled eggs, gathered the day before, sausage and grits was enjoyed by all of them...well, almost all. Little Emily finally won out and happily exchanged hers for Puffed Wheat. They pushed back the chairs, and Melony watched Roxy reach for the family Bible lying on the buffet.

"We gonna have us a little reading and singing...me and the girls."

Melony nodded, while the girls gathered around ready to sing. Their little voices chimed in, both off key, but beautiful to Roxy and Melony.

'Jesus luv me' was followed by a medley of broken songs. They added another and another until Roxy had to coax them to stop and sit down quietly for the Bible reading. She opened the big, worn Bible...and the little ones rolled around on the warm, braided rug...and Melony watched.

"Gonna read about the Lord...in Isaiah...Isaiah 53.... 'Who hath believed our report? And to whom is the arm of the Lord revealed? For he shall grow up before him as a tender plant, and as a root out of a dry ground: he hath no form nor comeliness; and when we shall see him, there is no beauty that we should desire him.' "

"Who is he?" Melony asked.

"Our Lord, of course, when he was on the cross."
"Oh."

'He is despised and rejected of men; a man of sorrows, and acquainted with grief: and we hid as it were our faces from him; he was despised, and we esteemed him not.
'Surely he hath borne our griefs, and carried our sorrows: yet we did esteem him stricken, smitten of God, and afflicted.
'But he was wounded for our transgressions, he was bruised for our iniquities: the chastisement of our peace was upon him; and with his stripes we are healed.
'All we like sheep have gone astray; we have turned every one to his own way; and the Lord hath laid on him the iniquity of us all.'

Melony lowered her head.

'He was oppressed, and he was afflicted, yet he opened not his mouth: he is brought as a lamb to the slaughter, and as a sheep before his shearers is dumb, so he openeth not his mouth.'

"That's exactly right," Melony interjected, "I remember learning about that in Sunday School often."

Roxy smiled, and kept reading...'He was taken from prison and from judgment: and who shall declare his generation? For he was cut off out of the land of the living: for the transgression of my people was he stricken.

'And he made his grave with the wicked, and with the rich in his death; because he had done no violence, neither was any deceit in his mouth.

'Yet it pleased the Lord to bruise him; he hath put him to grief: when thou shalt make his soul an offering for sin, he shall see his seed, he shall prolong his days, and the pleasure of the Lord shall prosper in his hand.

'He shall see of the travail of his soul, and shall be satisfied: by his knowledge shall my righteous servant justify many; for he shall bear their iniquities.'

Roxy paused and Melony questioned, "How can all this be spoken of in Isaiah? The Old Testament and Isaiah were written hundreds of years before Jesus was even born."

"That's right, Mel, but they both have the same Author!"

She finished reading...'Therefore will I divide him a portion with the great, and he shall divide the spoil with the strong; because he hath poured out his soul unto death: and he was numbered with the transgressors; and he bare the sin of many, and made intercession for the transgressors.'

Melony stood up and walked over to the window and looked out to the mountains.

Roxy placed the Bible back on the buffet and went out to the kitchen to wash up the dishes. The girls followed after, asking for cookies. While she was satisfying their wants, Melony appeared in the doorway.

"How about a ride up the mountain?"

"I thought we *were* up the mountain!"

"There's a place I'd like to show you...further up... and I haven't been there myself in quite a while."

"Sure."

The ride up was delightful even though the morning sun was obscured by numerous clouds overhead, but the showers disappeared almost as soon as they appeared. However, a deep pungent and earthy fragrance hinted of future happenings underway as nature silently labored. Soon these mountains would burst forth with vibrant, emblazoning color. Roxy's eyes were glued to the window as they climbed higher up Oak Mountain.

"Did you come here often as a child?"

"Oh yeah. I've such fond memories. Guess that's why I yearn to return from time to time. Only I wish the homeplace was still here."

"What happened to it?"

"Right after Grandma died, the highway department bought the place...for a new road. It actually runs right through the old front yard...where we kids used to play."

"What a shame!"

"Yeah."

"Well, at least your grandma didn't live to see it. How about your granddaddy?"

"Oh no. He died just before Grandma. They're both buried up here."

"That so?" Roxy could still see those thoughtful faces staring out at her from the aging picture above the hall trunk. The mountain road curved around a sharp bend and a few loose stones were scattered over the pavement.

"S'pose one of them rocks fell on us?"

"Possible...never have so far," Melony kidded.

They rounded out of the curve and Melony sighed.

"This it?" Roxy looked around, but didn't see much.
She nodded and pulled over. It was then that Roxy
noticed the crumbling chimney that stood alone, slightly
leaning and reminiscent of bygone days. She pointed to
it.

"That's all that's left."

Roxy was quiet.

"I'm surprised they left it...except I'm told it wasn't
in the way. 'Course they like to leave obscure re-
membrances here and there in remote areas of the Blue
Ridge Mountains...you know...symbols of the vanishing past."

"What kind of house was it?"

Melony seemed lost in thought. "Oh...just an old log
cabin...very old. Granddaddy brought Grandma here
on their wedding day, and they lived here most of their
lives...raised their family here."

They stepped out of the car, holding onto Little
Emily and Laurietta, who were anxious to explore.
Melony slowly walked over to the chimney, pushing the
weeds aside. She gently rubbed the rough, crumbling
rock as Roxy watched.

"I remember Grandma putting wood on the fire in
this old fireplace. Her hands were worn and
calloused...but loving." She turned and looked up the
hillside. Roxy's gaze followed. The little group began to
ascend the hilly terrain that was overgrown and unkempt, but passable. Melony forged ahead with pur-

pose. Roxy tried to keep up, carrying Laurietta and pulling Little Emily along. Her eyes searched for what Melony saw, but the weeds succeeded in concealing its secret. Then she saw it...the black wrought iron fence that enclosed a tiny cemetery. Approaching the fence, she could now see several headstones. Melony gently pushed upon the stubborn gate, and its creaking sound lent an eerie mood to the already desolate scene. She began automatically pulling weeds from around the tombstones and Roxy followed suit. Soon Emily and Laurietta were down on their knees in proud imitation. As Roxy yanked the tangled masses from around a stone, she read...' 'Till Death us do Part'. She stood up and examined the tombstone beside it... 'But only for a Season — Together Again'.

"Oh how lovely!" she exclaimed.

Melony smiled and wiped a tear away, leaving a dirt-smeared streak down her cheek.

Roxy turned to the smaller graves and began clearing away the weeds.

"That one's Little David's. He was their firstborn... killed in an accident on Christmas Day...just a little lad. The other one belongs to Charity...."

"Your mother's little sister that died in the flood."

"That's right."

"How did they find her?"

"They didn't."

Roxy looked up suddenly.

"I mean...she isn't here...only her little Bible is buried here."

"Oh."

"The flood occurred right after Charity's birthday,

and Mama had given her a little white Bible for her birthday. Mama says she dearly loved it. Somehow it survived the flood, and when they found it, the sun had dried it all out, and it was Mama's idea to bury it. She said it made Grandma Emily happy to do that."

"I see."

"Guess we better get going. It's beginning to rain again." The increasing raindrops pelted down upon them, sending a shiver up Roxy's spine. They turned to see Little Emily still down on her knees and moving her tiny finger in the grooves that spelled out...*Emily Barrett.*

THAT EVENING AS they drove back toward Lynchburg, the car was quiet with only the rhythmic sound of the windshield wipers breaking the silence, but even so it was a dull and hypnotizing one. The girls were asleep, and Melony and Roxy were both busy with their own thoughts.

There must be some enormous invisible magnet hidden among these Pines and Oaks that invariably draws me back time and time again. Such were Melony's thoughts on that dark and rainy night as she held the car on the wet, slippery roads. But I can't go back. I must go forward. Even if I did go back, it could never be the same. She thought of Mary Tom off in that alien land of Africa. She envisioned the scene they'd just witnessed only hours before...the lonely cemetery that held those two people who had meant so much to her from the time she could stand alone...Grandma and Grandpa Barrett. Oh, if only she could experience a 'love' like they had. That's what life was all about! Suddenly she felt a bitterness sweep over her.

Roxy didn't notice the audible sigh as she recounted the events of the last couple of days. Country life is a good life she thought, as she watched the peaceful forests disappear and civilization increase with every mile. I'm gonna get Seth to move with me to the country. Laurietta needs this fresh air...and the wide open space to grow...to explore God's creation. Yes, that's what I'm gonna do. She felt a warm glow within just thinking about it.

"Thank you, Mel." Her words broke the spell.

"For what?"

"For this weekend."

"Oh, sure. It was kind of special, wasn't it?"

The rest of the trip was also quiet as they returned to their private thoughts.

Soon the lights of Lynchburg beckoned them from across the James River as they rounded the curve, descending toward its blackened waters. The amber twilight displayed the small town's Victorian outline, accentuating its varied church spires as they pierced the coming night.

They crossed the old viaduct with its concrete railing obscuring their view, and Melony envisioned those tiny raindrops pelting the darkened waters and creating minute circles in the otherwise placid waters. They began to climb the hill toward home.

"Mel, did you know Lynchburg is called the *City of Seven Hills?*"

"Seems I heard somebody speak of it not long ago. All I have to say is somebody didn't know how to count!"

Roxy laughed. "You're right about that. There sure are enough hills around here...especially if you try walking them. But they're speaking of the seven most distinct hills from the early days...they're downtown here."

"Maybe so. But I could do without some of them. Do we have any milk at home?"

"No. Don't think so. Better stop and get some."

"S'pose I let you and the girls off, and then I'll run down to the store."

"Good idea. I'll get supper started. It's getting rather late."

With that decision, both girls pitched in to go.

"Well, look who's suddenly awake," Melony kidded. "Okay, I'll take you two."

"How's leftover meatloaf sound?"

"Wonderful."

Melony pulled up to the curb in front of the house and Roxy jumped out. No sooner had the car pulled off, than she noticed the strange car parked up a ways in front of their house. She started up the sidewalk and heard a car door shut...and then another. She turned to see two men following her...and she quickened her pace. Upon reaching the porch, she saw them approaching her. Suddenly a sick feeling enveloped her, and she caught hold of the nearest pillar. The two men dressed in complete military uniform now stood below her. One was somewhat young, and the other nearest her was a bit older with greying hair. He took out an envelope from his coat pocket and started to speak...but Roxy spoke instead.

"He's dead...isn't he...my Seth...he's dead."

The officer nodded his head.

Chapter IX
Walk on Through the Rain

Prudence stood gazing out the window at the wide open plains comparing them to the Blue Ridge. She'd just hung up the phone from Melony.

"What a tragedy!" she voiced aloud to the empty room. Would it ever end...this ugly war? The baby's cries interrupted her depressing thoughts, and she rushed to the nursery, but Spring was already there.

"Spring, you should be resting. Don't you know I can take care of this little girl?"

Spring smiled at her as she lifted the tiny infant and sat down in the nearby rocker.

" 'Course I don't blame you. I was the same with my girls."

"Who was on the phone?"

"Melony. She's awfully upset. She called to tell me some very sad news. Remember her friend, Roxy? The colored girl. Well, they just got word that her husband was killed...in Vietnam."

"How terrible...don't they have a little girl?"

"Yes. Laurietta...and Little Emily adores her. You know, I hadn't thought about the colored boys getting killed over there...."

Spring looked at her sister thoughtfully.

"You know, Sis, there are Indians fighting over there, too."

"Really?"

"Most people aren't aware of that. Of course, most people aren't aware of a lot of things concerning the Indian."

"Spring, are you having problems here?" she asked with concern.

Spring smiled at first and then answered, "Sis, no matter where you go, it is there."

"Why surely...here in *Indian* territory...I wouldn't think so."

"For that very reason, it is much more prevalent. Only last week, I drove Grandpa Eli into town...to Rapid City to take care of some business. We stopped first at a bank for him to cash his check. Since he was ailing somewhat I offered to go in for him, but you know how stoic and independent he can be. He insisted on going in himself. So, I went along to assist in case he should fall or whatever. Well, he shuffled up to the cashier in his usual quiet, unobtrusive way, and this lady (and I use the term loosely) of about fifty, snatched the check out of his hand with a conspicuous audible sigh and proceeded to process it. She practically slammed the money down in front of him."

"Oh, Spring, what did he do?"

"The same he's done probably for years. Tucked his head and walked away."

"How sad."

"Needless to say, my blood was boiling."

"Oh no, Spring, what did you do?"

"You don't really want to know."

"Spring, did you make a scene?"

"No, I simply re-enacted the scenario."

"What do you mean?"

"I wrote a check...a very sizable check...and handed it to her. When she reached for it, I held onto it and my eyes locked hers. I let go, and she counted out the money. Then I spoke in a loud voice, 'Now I would like to withdraw my savings...all of it, please'. She looked at the sum and asked, 'All of it?' "

"I repeated 'All of it'. She began making the transaction and meekly placed the bills in front of me. I picked it up and said, 'I will find a bank that chooses to extend proper respect for the Sioux'."

"Oh no," Pru blushed. "What happened?"

"Well, the *lady's* mouth dropped as onlookers gawked in surprise, and a stout, bald-headed manager hastened over. 'Ma'am, can I help you'? he humbly asked. 'I don't believe so, Sir. Your bank has done just about all the damage it can do today'. With that, I walked out."

"Spring, you didn't!"

"Of course, I did."

"Well, I'm really proud of you, but I wouldn't have had the nerve to do it myself."

"You're not a Sioux."

"But why did the lady act that way?"

"You see, they...the white people...some of them...

look at these checks as welfare checks. But they are not! These checks are for the lease of lands and compensation suffered by the tribe. It is money *owed* to us!"

"I see. What did your father-in-law have to say about all this?"

"You know he is not a verbal person, usually. However, once in the car and headed for home, he said, 'Spring Leaf, I am proud you are my daughter'."

"Wasn't that touching? But how can people be so unkind?"

Spring looked at her sister, "The same way people all over the world are unkind to those around them that are different."

"But this is Sioux country, as you say."

"It was...and still is, in a sense. You know, I was passing through a little town a good ways from here a few weeks back. It was past lunch time, and I was quite hungry. So I stopped at a small restaurant on the side of the road. But as I reached for the door, a posted sign on the door caused me to stop short!"

"What did it say?"

"No dogs or Indians allowed."

"You're kidding!"

"I wish I were."

"You didn't go in?"

"No. I started to, but looking down at my bulging stomach, I decided not to. It wasn't worth it."

"That's one time you used your head."

"Frankly, Pru, it scares me to think of what I might do if I'm faced with that same situation again."

"Spring, maybe you and Dean and the baby should consider moving back home to Virginia?"

"I want to raise Dakotah with her own people, Pru. That's important to me."

"Because you weren't?"

"Maybe."

"I understand. But, we're sure gonna miss seeing this precious little one grow up."

Spring smiled up at her, and they both looked around to see Grandpa Eli standing in the doorway. He nodded silently and shuffled off.

A few days later, the early spring sun shot its piercing rays of warmth down across the wide open plains, caressing the tall, waving prairie grass, the hardened sands of the Badlands and miles and miles of highway that stretched across the Dakotas. It also warmed the upturned earth that Pru and Spring worked patiently over, carefully planting the minute seeds that would transform the barren yard into a flowering garden of beauty. Soon Spring rose and brushed the dirt off her hands.

"I'm going to check on Dakotah."

Pru continued to dig in the rich, black earth, enjoying the feeling of oneness with nature. Suddenly, she was aware of someone watching her, and she looked up into the dark, wrinkled face of Grandpa Eli, who stared at her with a grim expression. His thin hands were clasped in front of him, and his moccasin clad feet stood solidly on the freshly turned earth. She felt uneasy, and waited for him to speak.

"Isn't this a beautiful day?" She sought to break the uncomfortable silence.

He spoke in a deliberate and guarded tone, "What is reason for this?"

She looked down at the fresh earth. "Reason?"

Waving his hand out over the garden area, he questioned again silently.

"Sir, the reason is for beauty. Flowers give us beauty."

"Hummf," he uttered and shuffled off.

Mystified, she sat back on her heels and watched the old man, fragile but strong, walk off. Spring quietly closed the door.

"She's back asleep again...must have had a bad dream...I wonder what babies dream...." She looked at Pru, "What's the matter?"

"Is there...I mean...do your people have something against flowers...against beauty?"

"Why do you ask?"

"Well, your father-in-law was just out here, and he seemed to disagree with our efforts."

"Oh, I see. Beauty...of course not! Flowers...the way we see them...planting them in and around our homes is not something they do that much or have done in the past. They experience beauty in so many other ways...in ways that we do not appreciate. I guess they don't feel the need as much for planting flowers. Indians see the natural beauty of the land more profoundly than most."

All too soon, the two weeks were up and Pru reluctantly said her farewells to Spring, Dean and little Dakotah. As she waited for the large aircraft to taxi down the long runway, she said her good-byes to the state of South Dakota, as well, and all of its unique beauty. Never had she witnessed such variety in one place, such resplendent and miraculous beauty. She

recalled what Pearl Buck had to say about this unusual state in her own autobiography... *"If this state were anywhere else in the world, it would be such a wonder that people would be streaming here to see it by land and air and sea."*
She breathed a little easier on her return trip, excitedly anticipating her arrival back home, and as she approached the familiar Blue Ridge Mountains, she felt a tingling warmth encompass her.

THE PLANE SOARED over rows and rows of mountains that lay beneath in a darkened mass, and Pru leaned close to the window, trying to pick out Oak Mountain, although impossible in the passing twilight. She wondered what Clarence was doing? Melony was to pick her up...she and the girls. They were excited about seeing the plane land. Soon the lights of Lynchburg were shining in the distance.
As the plane passed over the small, sleepy town, down below a deep resonant voice filled the void of not only the empty rooms, but of an empty heart, as well. The words that echoed off the high-pitched ceiling flowed from inner depths and carried with them, the eternal hope....

When you walk through a storm, hold your head up high
And don't be afraid of the dark
At the end of the storm is a golden sky
And the sweet silver song of a lark

Walk on through the wind,
Walk on through the rain,
Tho' your dreams be tossed and blown

Walk on, walk on, with hope in your heart
And you'll never walk alone,
You'll never walk alone....*

Roxy wiped the lone tear from her cheek as she stared out into the darkened night...and sought his face...the face she'd never again behold on earth. It appeared for a second and then vanished again. Why couldn't she hold it? She turned away and walked over to the sofa, reached for his picture on the end table, and he smiled out at her, breaking her heart all over again.

She whispered..."*Tho' your dreams be tossed and blown...walk on, walk on, with a hope in your heart.*"

"You'd want me to do that, wouldn't you, Seth? I know you would. And I have a hope...thank the Lord! I'm gonna see you again one day...when I get there. You better be waiting for me!" She smiled at him through her tears.

Walk on through the wind...walk on through the rain....

Her thoughts drifted backwards, past the recent days so unreal, past months of waiting for him to return, past the years of happiness...back to a time...a special time...their high school graduation. They held hands as they waited for the word to march down that old high school aisle. She remembered how nervous she'd been, but how he'd helped her to relax. It was then...then that she'd first heard that beautiful song. They'd practiced it for days. But on that eventful night, she was afraid she'd lose her voice...so uptight was she. She could still hear his sweet voice as he sang those words behind her,

*(You'll Never Walk Alone, by Rodgers and Hammerstein)

standing there on the side steps of that stage in the old auditorium. He'd told her just before they entered...to listen for *his* voice and sing with him...and this she did...and beautifully they sang together midst the group that surrounded them.

However, it was that night...at that time...while singing their graduation song, *You'll Never Walk Alone*, that she'd felt it...a premonition of some sort...a foreboding. Never would she have guessed...never would she have dreamed that it would be this song that would ease her pain...and give her hope.

The plane touched down and approached the terminal. Pru strained to see in the dying light, but all that was visible was the orange cone-shaped wind sock blowing straight out toward the east...or was it south? Oh well, she never could get her directions straight. The plane slowed, circled and taxied up toward it. Now she could see people standing and waving. There they were! She could see them...Melony and the girls...Little Emily and Laurietta...standing there on the grassy bank that framed the airstrip. She could hardly wait to get home! She wondered if the Rhododendrons were blooming yet...and the strawberries. Would her patch be ready to pick? Suddenly she felt hungry. A big bowl of strawberries with a little milk and sugar would be delightful.

A happy reunion it was, and before long, they were approaching Oak Mountain. Pru hadn't stopped talking.

"I can tell you enjoyed the trip," Melony kidded.

"Did I tell you about the Badlands...the likes of which we've never seen back here. I can't say that I like them really...but a sight for the eyes. Wait 'till I get my film developed...."

"I can't wait."

"Oh, I guess I'm boring you. Don't mean to rattle on so...just keyed up. You say your daddy's okay?"

"He's fine. I'm sure he'll be extra fine when he sees you."

Pru smiled, "I've missed him, too. First time we've been apart like this, you know."

"I know."

"How thoughtless of me. How's Roxy doing?"

"She's holding up great. In fact, I'm amazed at how she's taking this. It's as if she has some mysterious secret that only she knows."

"Didn't you tell me that she has a lot of faith?"

"She sure does!"

"Well then, it's no secret. She has unseen strength — inner strength. The only kind to get you through such a thing."

"I guess so. I didn't tell you on the phone, but they're bringing him home now. It took this long."

"Oh goodness...it's gonna be hard."

"I know...I need to be there for her."

Pru looked at her daughter. "Certainly."

They climbed the mountain in the darkness with the silver glow of the half moon graciously lighting their way.

SEVERAL DAYS LATER, as the welcomed sun embraced the scanty hillside and with it, the aging tombstones, some leaning, some erect, Melony inhaled the pungent freshness. After two full days of hard rain, the earth seemed renewed as the warmth of the sun slowly dried it out...and just in time, too.

She looked at Roxy, sitting erect in front of the casket, draped with the red, white and blue. Her somber black dress created an illusion of one older than her years...or was it that? The blue awning blocked the warmth of the sun as it sheltered Seth's family, and the crowd flowed outward, onto sunken graves of past souls that awaited yet another. She watched Laurietta squirming in her grandmother's arms, beside Roxy...too little to comprehend the depth or even the surface of this eternal event.

Out beyond the crowd, a group of elderly men stood at attention with their rifles poised. A certain aura of reverence hung silently about them as their blue uniforms, trimmed in yellow, created a stark contrast with their pessimistic surroundings.

Two members of this group now approached the casket and quietly took their places at either end of it, facing each other. The Commander spoke in a deep bass voice concerning the role of soldiers, and he described the noble cause for which Seth had given his young life. Soft audible cries could be heard, but Roxy sat poised and quiet. Melony's attention was drawn upward to the blue, sunny skies, where a small flock of brown speckled wrens fluttered just overhead, creating an unusual spectacle...but one of touching serenity.

Suddenly a shot was fired...the wrens scattered... another shot...and another...twenty-one shots in all... followed by a deafening silence. Then the silence was broken by the mournful and pensive strain of a bugle that sent forth its melancholy but proud message. A chill ran up Melony's back.

The taps concluded; the Commander and his assistant proceeded to painstakingly fold up the flag, carefully moving in front of the family with bowed heads. The Commander approached Roxy with the folded flag held reverently in both hands. She looked up at him, and he placed it in her hands. She thought, 'I will not cry. My tears I'll be saving for when we're alone...the Lord, Seth and me. But now is the time for standing strong. My Seth was a soldier...and he'd be proud of me'.

She hugged the flag to her breast.

Chapter X
The Jim River

"Dakotah...you're two years old today! Blow out the candles, Sweetheart." Spring leaned down close, feeling the warmth of the candles.

"Blow...," Dakotah mimicked while smiling up at her mother. She clapped her small hands and blew with all her might, succeeding in the challenge before her. Everyone laughed and applauded...everyone that is except Grandpa Eli, who sat back in a corner taking in the whole affair without so much as a hint of what might be going on beneath that head of white.

Dean picked her up, holding her high into the air as she squealed with delight.

"My little Princess is growing up!"

"Be careful, Dean," Spring reminded him while clearing away the dishes.

"Listen to her...protective Mom for sure...," Mareen kidded. She spread out her arms for Dakotah, but Dean whisked her away playfully and then gently sat her down upon Grandpa Eli's thin legs. A slight smile appeared upon his wrinkled face. Grandpa Eli was often a mystery and difficult to understand, but one thing was certain — there was no mistaking how he felt about his one and only grandchild. He tenderly stroked her shiny black hair that Spring had tied back with a soft pink ribbon. She was content.

"Painted any pictures lately, Spring?" Mareen's latest escort asked.

"I'm working on one, Young Hawk...a very special one."

"Oh yeah?"

"She won't let you see it," Dean interjected. "She won't even let me see it."

Young Hawk's curiosity aroused, "Why the secrecy?"

"In time you will see it." She changed the subject, "What do you think about Johnson not seeking re-election?"

"I think it's great!" Mareen quickly answered. "I had high hopes for the peace talks in Paris, but guess that was only wishful thinking."

"Somebody better stop this bloody war!" Young Hawk added adamantly. "It's not worth what it's costing us. Look how many of our young men it's taken already. How many more will it take before somebody wakes up?"

"You're right about that, Young Hawk," Dean joined in. "I've been wondering whether or not blocking this Communist expansion in South Vietnam is worth it. I was at least glad to see the President cut back on the bombing of North Vietnam."

"He's also rejected Westmoreland's request for all those troops...how many was that?" Mareen asked.

"Something like 200,000 more," Young Hawk replied. "I just hope it ends soon. My nephew's over there, too. It would kill my sister if anything happened to him!"

"I had a nephew there, also — my brother Patrick's son, David. But he's back now...only not quite the same."

"There...see what I mean."

"What is the problem?" inquired Mareen.

"He suffers from depression and is rather nervous most of the time. My folks are very concerned."

"What a shame."

"Let's get off the war...enough of it!"

"I agree, Dean. Changing the subject, have you heard about AIM?"

"AIM?" Spring repeated.

"Yes," Mareen explained, "the American Indian Movement that was recently organized in Minneapolis. Its purpose is to help the city's Indians, protecting them from unfair police actions."

"Oh yeah?" Young Hawk's interest was peaked. "It's about time somebody got organized. That's been our problem."

"It's not easy to organize a bunch of Indians!" Dean kidded. They laughed...all but Spring. She sat thinking.

When she spoke, it was with her usual sense of urgency. "It is true. There is strength and power in unity. That is precisely why the black movement is successful."

"Successful?" Young Hawk challenged, "How can you say that when Martin Luther King was just killed?"

"They have lost a great leader, true, but they will continue on because they are unified in purpose."

"She's right," Dean agreed.

"But what about this fighting and rioting since he was killed?" Mareen questioned.

"It is only grief and anger," Spring continued, "It is natural to follow, and after a while, it will cease. But his cause — Dr. King's cause — will not die. He gave it birth, and now it is like a young child. It will grow and mature, hopefully blossoming into beauty and peace."

"Hopefully so," Mareen concluded.

"...and his dream that one day his children would be able to live in a nation where they would not be judged by the color of their skin...but by the content of their character...is our dream also," Spring concluded and then stood. "Where's Dakotah and Grandpa?"

She hastened to the door and saw them walking around outside. She stood there watching with Mareen beside her.

"Grandpa Eli looks more fragile than the last time I saw him," Mareen observed.

Dean nodded.

"What are they doing?" he asked, joining them at the door.

The old man was holding onto the tiny child's hand and showing her something with the other.

"My flowers!" Spring smiled.

"Your what?"

"My flowers, Dean...Grandpa is showing Dakotah the flowers. I don't believe it. Remember, he was not too impressed with them initially."

"Let them be." Dean herded them away from the door. "It is good that they be together on this birthday." Without saying more, they all knew that Grandpa Eli couldn't spend many more birthdays with her.

They sat down at the table around the cake. "Well, Spring, how's your work coming along at the schools?"

"Slow, Mareen...but it's coming along."

"What exactly is your work?" questioned Young Hawk with a hint of cynicism. Spring wondered what Mareen saw in him as she proceeded to explain.

"To raise the self-esteem of the children. To teach self-worth, to teach them who they are...the descendants of a great and noble race. I've been researching and analyzing a very prophetic thought...'*whatsoever a man thinketh, so is he*'."

"*Whatsoever a man thinketh, so is he,*" Young Hawk repeated.

"There's certainly depth in that," Mareen commented.

"More than any of us realize," Spring continued. "I really believe the reason I am what I am today is because of the self-worth and encouragement I received and was taught by my parents from the beginning. They encouraged me to paint. I began to believe I could paint from an early age. Then I believed I could be a painter."

"Interesting," Young Hawk remarked.

"Yes," Spring added. "This idea needs to penetrate the young minds of our children. They need to believe in themselves...believe that they can do...believe that they can be what they want to be...that they can rise above their circumstances and make a mark in this world."

"Sounds good," Dean encouraged.

"And why not? Why can't it be done? It's up to us!"

"True," Mareen agreed with a sigh, realizing that this was no small task. She wondered if there were enough "Springs" to do the job...she wondered if even *she* had the motivation that it would demand.

A couple of weeks later, the fragile spring flowers were struggling to stand as the sudden downpour of rain beat upon them, stinging their delicate leaves with the hard pellets of raindrops. The house was quiet within. Dakotah had gone on a little shopping excursion with Dean. The absence of her busy chatter left the house unusually still, and Spring relished this solitude to engage in her work. It had been difficult since Dakotah was born to find the time she yearned for to paint. She possessively grabbed every moment that presented itself, taking fierce advantage of it.

This day, she was so engrossed in her present work that she did not hear the soft step of Grandpa Eli as he quietly entered her studio room. He silently stood in the back of the room watching her paint...a look of concern on his aged face. After a while, Spring turned.

"Grandpa!"

He motioned to the painting. "What is this water on Fire Thunder?"

Spring's obvious surprise and embarrassment weren't concealed as she returned the old man's stare. His keen eyes questioned.

She fought for words to explain what she felt to be her masterpiece. But how could she make him understand? He shuffled closer to examine the work of art.

"Grandpa, I wanted this to be a surprise for you. I planned to show it to you when it was completed."

"Not finished?"

"Not exactly. Please sit down, Grandpa. I'd like to explain to you what you see."

He looked at her keenly, slowly moved over to a chair, and sat. Spring pulled up another chair in front of him, facing the unfinished painting.

"You see, Grandpa," she began awkwardly, "I want to show the world my feelings — our feelings — our people's feelings through my painting. As you know, I've been striving to do this since I came here...ever since Dean and I were married. By painting life here on the reservation, I've sought to capture the true 'spirit' of the American Indian today. And in this painting of you, I feel I've truly accomplished this."

"Waters?" he questioned.

"The waters, Grandpa, coming from both sides, are the Great Missouri River and our Jim River as they merge together...the Missouri representing the white man and the Jim River, our people. The shadowy figure within the Jim is you, of course. And the look on your face is concern...concern that your people will be lost in the Great Missouri."

His aged face changed with understanding.

"Is true," he uttered.

"I know."

He pulled his chair closer to the painting and studied it.

"Is good."

She smiled and reached out to clasp the old man's bony hand. He began to speak very slowly and deliberately.

"First...you must understand the spirit of our people in the old days."

"I'm trying, Grandpa."

"It was not as today."

She waited.

Suddenly a faint glow stole across the old man's face as he settled back in his chair.

"I was a boy then. I was proud to be Indian. My father taught me to be proud."

"Yes, Grandpa?"

"Didn't live in a big house like this. Didn't have cars...but had more...had pride. We were Sioux...great and mighty people."

Spring nodded.

"We live in tipis...."

"What was it like, Grandpa...living such as that?"

"Good, my Daughter. Good. I remember sleeping on cold and rainy nights when the rain beat against the tipi. I feel good...pleasant to sleep when storm rages and the ice and sleet hit sides of the buffalo hides. But so nice and warm in tipi."

"Sounds nice. I wish I could have experienced that."

"My father, Swift Antelope, was well fixed. We had very big tipi, and many spotted ponies. I wish to be like Father."

"I see."

"But not to be. Our world changed. I cannot be hunter that my father was." A slight smile appeared. "I don't know if I would be so good hunter as my father."

"Why?"

"Buffalo scare me...once I go on buffalo hunt when I

was but so small. Buffalo is so big and I am so small. I
was very much afraid the buffalo would kill me."
    She smiled.
    "But no matter. I never hunt buffalo. All buffalo
gone...and I go to reservation. That is end."
    "What do you mean, Grandpa? You were young.
That was just the beginning of your life."
    "Beginning and the end. Reservation life was not
good. In winter, there is little food for our families. The
white man did not keep his word. I wonder why we
expect this. All treaties, they break. My father
change...become very sad. No longer can he hunt, but
he does not know how to be a farmer. As young boy, I try
to help him, but is no use. His heart is not on reservation. It still roamed the wide open plains where the
buffalo once graze by thousands. We get food rations
from government to pay us for land...sometimes...some-
times we don't. Much food is wasted. Our people don't
understand about white man's food...."
    "What do you mean?"
    "Like flour. Our people do not know for what it is
used. We do not eat bread. Our women dump much
flour out on prairie...but they use the sacks. They are
good for making clothes. But no one teaches our women
about flour. Later our women learn to make fry bread
with flour, and we are glad."
    The old man was quiet for a bit. Then he continued,
"My older brother, Yellow Thunder, goes away to school
to learn how to be like white man. My father is more
sad."
    "What school?"
    "Carlisle in Pennsylvania. This is long ways from

the prairie. I never go, but Yellow Thunder say it took many days on train. He was very sick on train and scared. I still feel sadness for my brother, Yellow Thunder."

"Why?"

"He change. Come back to reservation wearing white man's clothes and white man's shoes...even though they very much hurt his feet. Our people laugh at him...poke fun. He did not want to live in tipi anymore or eat the way we always eat. He is not happy the way he was happy before. So he leaves reservation for new life. He goes to city, but he returns in the *'moon of the sore eyes'*."

"March?"

"Is so," he smiled at her, "I test you sometimes."

"I know. Do I pass?"

"Most times. Why is it *'moon of the sore eyes'*?"

"Because of the snow?"

He nodded.

"Did Yellow Thunder stay on the reservation after that?"

"Sometimes. He was not happy. He tell me once that he learn too much of the white man's ways to be happy as Indian...but he still too much Indian to be happy with white man's ways. Yellow Thunder was very much mixed up."

"Whatever happened to him?"

Grandpa Eli shook his white head. "He drink too much. Got in big fight and was killed...by his friend."

"Oh, I'm sorry, Grandpa. I didn't know."

"Much you don't know...but you learn."

She smiled at him again.

"So I decide to stay here with my people."

"On the reservation?"

"On the land...what is left."

"I see."

"I am old now...very old...but I never leave the land...all this time. Soon my cycle will end."

"Your cycle?"

"My Daughter, life is a cycle. We come from the earth...and we return to the earth. That is why one cannot own the land. How can we buy and sell the land? It cannot be owned."

"I agree, Grandpa, but in reality, the land is being bought and sold every day."

"What is reality? When we think we own it, we deceive ourselves."

"I see."

He pointed to the west. "The Black Hills — who owns the Black Hills? Can anyone own the Black Hills?"

Spring closed her eyes, seeing those dark majestic hills. And then she saw in her mind's eye the rolling slopes of the Blue Ridge. Who could own them?

The old man talked on. "The Black Hills are the 'heart of everything that is'. There our ancestors came to pray. It is a sacred place where our dead rest. Who can own this land?"

"Grandpa, the government owns it!"

He looked at her sadly. "This should not be so."

"I agree, Grandpa."

"Crazy Horse say, 'One does not sell the land upon which the people walk'."

"Grandpa, I've got to make a trip over to Keystone next week. How would you like to accompany me and see how the Crazy Horse Monument is coming along?"

"Maybe. I like to see one more time."

"Oh Grandpa, stop talking like that. You'll probably be around when it's finished."

His thin shoulders shook slightly, but his laugh was almost silent. "It will be a very long time, I think."

"That's true, but it's progressing. The last time I saw it, they had begun the tunneling into the mountain for the opening that will be under Crazy Horse's outstretched arm. I'm excited!"

"Korczak had heart attack."

"A slight one, I believe. They say he's better now."

"When he dies, who will finish the mountain?"

"I don't know...but I believe it will be finished."

"It is good. Korczak is good man."

Spring nodded in agreement.

"Chief Standing Bear have good idea...and he pick right man for the job."

"You see, there are good white men, Grandpa."

"I never say there are no good white men. I say white men break promises. I only say what I see. This world had harmony. We recognize this...and live in harmony with all things...before white man comes. But when he comes...there is no more harmony."

Spring silently digested his words.

"I know, Grandpa."

"My father tells me this many times."

"How did your father die?"

"Smallpox...brought up river by fur traders."

"I know you have missed him many times."

"I miss him *now*. I miss the old days...the old life... before the reservation. Now that I am old, I remember

the days of my youth...I remember all the time."
"But it's gone, Grandpa. What about our children...
like Dakotah? How are they to understand the spirit of
our people?"
"It is up to you, my Daughter."
Spring listened.
"While she is young and tender, like the slender
blades of the new prairie grass, tell her of the ways of the
past, of our people. Teach her to love the land...to be
part of it...to give to it...not to take from it."
Spring nodded.
"You have strange ways, my Daughter...coming from
the east...from the white man's world...ways I do not
understand. But still I see in you something that makes
my heart glad. It is the spirit...the spirit of our people."
She smiled.
"Keep this spirit, my Child...and I will rest in my
grave. For I know then that it will live on...in Dakotah."

THE NEXT DAY, SPRING stood in the classroom
before her attentive audience. How can I teach them
what I'm struggling with myself? she thought.
Slowly she repeated...*" 'whatsoever a man thinketh,
so is he'."*
The response was what she expected. Most heads
were down, barring eye contact. She studied them...
their worn and faded clothes revealing the lack of
monetary means within their homes. But it was the look
of resigned hopelessness that tore at her heartstrings.
Or was it contentment? They were a contented
people...and with so little to be content. Maybe it was
she that was in need? These children didn't need the

vast array of toys to be content. They simply had fun playing together. Especially baseball. What a fondness for baseball!

Little Agnes Whitefeather looked up at her and smiled demurely.

Affectionate they were...and how they craved affection. Sometimes she wished she could take them all home with her.

John Rushing Wind slowly lifted his hand.

"Yes, John?"

"It is from the holy people...what you say...I hear this from the holy people."

Spring understood what he meant. The children had great respect for the Church and ministers and missionaries of such. Their parents did also. They referred to them as "holy people."

"That is right, John."

Such a sweet boy. Such sweet children. Should she even attempt to change them? Would they become spoiled? But she had to give them the only thing that she had to offer...the pride of their heritage...the realization of their uniqueness.

Suddenly Rae Youngblood looked up at her and met her gaze as if waiting for an answer.

"It is what we think about inside, Children," she continued. "What we think about and long for every day and every night...that we will become. So, you see, we want to set our goals high...high as the stars in the sky. What is it you want to be? Think about it. Think about it way down deep in your heart. Think about it today and tomorrow and next week and tonight and tomorrow night and every night. Think about it until it becomes a part of you...*'Whatsoever a man thinketh, so is he'."*

Rae Youngblood spoke up rather timidly, "I want to be a doctor for the ponies and dogs and birds...and all the other animals."

"Wonderful, Rae."

She nodded her head proudly.

The next day, Spring drove to school full of anticipation. She was going to try and uncover the dreams and goals of the students through small group discussions. Little Rae Youngblood would help lead the way. But when she entered the classroom, she was taken back by a new student that had just moved from The Rosebud Reservation to Pine Ridge. It was a startling encounter!

The small child standing there in front of her erased twenty...thirty...forty years. Spring found herself speechless. It was like looking in a mirror — seeing herself again as a young child. She regained control.

"Hello and welcome! What is your name?"

"Thetis," she answered uncertainly.

"Thetis...what a beautiful name! We're so glad to have you. Come this way, and we'll find you a seat."

The morning wore on, and Spring found it hard to concentrate on her challenge, as her eyes and thoughts were drawn to Thetis.

Several days later, as she drove herself and Grandpa Eli to Keystone, her mind involuntarily drifted back to that little dark-haired girl...Thetis. The small child had pushed all those carefully hidden feelings to the surface She looked over at Grandpa Eli. He was napping again.

She was glad he'd come. Even though he slept most of the time, he was still company. It was time, she thought...time she went back to Rosebud.

She recalled her last visit there, brief though it was. She'd left feeling more mixed-up than ever. Probably because of that cantankerous old Chief she'd dealt with. How could he understand her concerns? No, she'd go back again...and be more patient. This time she'd find her answers!

She pulled into Keystone, noticing all the usual excitement on a Saturday in June. Tourists shielded their eyes from the sun beating down upon the small western town, while trying not to miss a thing. Grandpa awoke.

"I'll only be a short while, Grandpa. As soon as I take care of this matter, I'll be back. Then we'll head for Crazy Horse."

He nodded.

The door slammed behind her, and he pushed down the lock. He never felt quite safe with all these tourists running to and fro. Sinking down in the cushioned seat, he watched the parade of men, women, and children crossing back and forth the narrow street, dodging the hurried traffic. He wondered why all of them were in such a hurry? Suddenly he looked into the cold eyes of a woman who had appeared out of nowhere and stood staring at him curiously. Quickly, she snapped a camera at him. He flinched and sunk deeper into the seat. She took off with her prize.

He waited a while longer, noticing nature's signals. Yes, a storm was upon them. The sun was now partially hidden by one of the many clouds quickly filling the vast sky. She better hurry, he thought.

Spring tossed her packages into the back seat and jumped in as the first large raindrops hit. "Sorry, it took longer than I thought."
He nodded.
As she sped along the curvy roads, the rains increased.
"The sun is hot and the rains fall. This makes roads very evil," the old man admonished.
Spring slowed down.
Soon they were there. They could faintly see the image of the mountain in the distance somewhat obscured by the falling rain. As they drew nearer, it rose before them proudly.
"I see him," Grandpa Eli whispered.
Spring watched the old man lean forward, struggling to see through the rain swept windshield. She followed his gaze. The rock above the outstretched arm was all cleared now...and was it long! She stopped at the entrance gate, paid the entrance fee, plus more, and proceeded to the parking area. They pulled up facing the mountain. It was raining too hard to get out, so they sat in the car staring at the colossal mountain being carved in the round. There was silence except for the rain and the slight rhythmic motion of the windshield wipers as they dutifully performed their job.
"I am glad it will be in the Black Hills," his voice cracked with emotion.
"From what I understand, they insisted it be here."
"That is right."
"I'm glad too, Grandpa. It should be here."

"Did you know that Korczak was born on September the 6th?"

"No."

"Crazy Horse died thirty-one years before on September the 6th."

"An omen?"

"Maybe."

"I don't know whether it is the rain or the mountain...but I have chills."

He looked over at her. "It is the mountain."

"I think you're right. When I think that one day this will tell future generations our story, I get all tingly."

"You know the mountain is 600 feet high?"

"Yes, I know. What a feat to tackle!"

"It is a big job to carve a whole mountain."

"A big job...a big dream, but I believe this dream will one day be a reality."

The old man smiled at her. "I wish I could live so long."

"So do I, Grandpa. But this dream is bigger than both of us."

"Dakotah will see."

"Maybe."

The rain fell harder, blurring the vision before them.

"Can you see him in your mind, Grandpa...towering above the masses of Ponderosa Pines...above the crowds of tourists...with his arm outstretched... pointing with purpose? *'My lands are where my dead lie buried'*."

Grandpa looked at her with tired watery eyes. Was he happy or was he sad?

Chapter XI

A Time to Every Purpose...

A few days later, Spring awoke to a bright morning with the early sun bursting forth, reclaiming its territory after many days of dismal rain. She stretched and turned over, remembering that today was the day...the day she'd chosen to revisit Rosebud. She glanced at Dean, sound asleep beside her and wondered why Dakotah hadn't awakened. Climbing out of bed, she quietly crept into the sunny nursery. Still asleep...with her dark hair drawing a vivid contrast with the soft pink comforter that Ellen had sent her, she was simply precious. Her heart brimmed over with emotions...love ...pride...wonder...to be a mother! How she cherished this little bundle of flesh. Dakotah stirred and smiled in her sleep. Spring smiled back. Today was Dean's day with his daughter...and she would go to The Rosebud Reservation.

"Are you sure you want to go alone?" he asked later

at the breakfast table.

"I am sure," she replied. "Don't forget to give Dakotah her nap at 2:00."

"Don't worry. I'll make sure this time."

Spring swallowed the last of her orange juice and stood up. "Well, it's off with me." She gave Dakotah a big hug and kiss.

"What about me?" Dean stood waiting. They embraced, and again Spring felt warm and secure within his strong arms. She held on a little longer, and then sighed.

"For every morning we get up...and do something that we don't want to do, it builds character within us. I'm going to build character today, Dear."

He smiled. "Perhaps so."

SHE'D JUST PASSED LONG VALLEY and Buzzard Butte, heading southward toward Rosebud, when the image of little Thetis appeared again. She caught her breath and braced herself. She would not turn back today. Gusty breezes were causing the tall prairie grass to sway back and forth. A tumbleweed rolled awkwardly across the two-lane road up ahead of her. But it was a beautiful sunny day in spite of the winds, and the vast blue sky overhead seemed exaggerated as only the plains of the west could boast. Even Virginia could not equal this! A few puffy clouds dotted the awesome sky, throwing evasive shadows over the freshly plowed fields that lay waiting their fate as a young mother-to-be awaits her time. Soon they would ripen with seedlings of corn, wheat and the many grains that enrich the bountiful midwest. She noticed another pile of rocks stacked in the midst of a plowed field resembling an island surrounded by sea. This always amused her. You didn't see this in Virginia. Where were the rocks in Virginia? In the many folds and crevices that made up the hills of Virginia, she supposed. Not so here. Everything stood exposed to nature's command. She passed a few grain silos grouped together and a few cows grazing nearby. It was a lonely drive, and her mind wandered back to Thetis — but actually not Thetis — another little girl... a mysterious little girl.

Finally, she pulled onto the reservation, noticing the worsened conditions. She got out and inquired as to the whereabouts of Bear's Heart, having been instructed by one of Dean's friends to ask for him. He supposedly carried the memories of the old days. She stood waiting for him, and carefully studied the grounds...trying to remember something...anything. But her mind was blank. Then she saw him, an old man probably in his seventies or eighties, slowly hobbling toward her, supported by a crooked cane. He nodded a greeting.

"Bear's Heart?"

"I am he...and you are Spring Leaf...Granddaughter of Lost Son...Daughter of Bright Star?"

"That is right." She could feel the blood rushing to her face being described as such. "Can we talk somewhere? I was told that you could possibly tell me things about my childhood when I was here at Rosebud."

"I can tell little, but I know one who tells more."

"Really? I would very much like to meet with this person if possible."

He turned and shuffled off, expecting her to follow. She did. They weaved in and around the reservation grounds, and she noticed the curious stares from the people going about their daily chores. Did she stand out that much? They arrived at a small, shabby house with the paint peeling off in many places. The old man knocked on the fragile door. They waited.

"It takes some time," he uttered.

Soon the door opened, exposing a dark and veiled interior wherein strange and abstruse odors drifted outward and slowly evaporated in the fresh, sunny air.

An old woman that was barely a wisp of human life stood before them, squinting in the sun. Her dark, piercing eyes were sunk deep into her skeleton face that was wrinkled many times over by passing years. Her dingy clothes hung loosely on her bony frame. But her eyes were alive and penetrated her guest.

"Saunie, I have brought..." he nodded in Spring's direction. "She wishes to speak with you."

Still the old woman peered out at Spring without words.

"It is Spring Leaf...Granddaughter of Lost Son... Daughter of Bright Star."

Suddenly her expression changed, but Spring didn't know why.

She stepped back and motioned for them to enter. Spring followed Bear's Heart into the darkened room that smelled musty, mixed with unusual odors such as that of incense. The old woman waved her toward a well-worn, dilapidated chair that looked as if it had had its share of guests. She sat down and waited for them to do likewise. But Bear's Heart spoke, "I go now." With that, he left the two of them alone as the door closed behind him, shutting out the light.

Spring sat looking at the old woman in front of her as she proceeded to light up a pipe. Her aged face took on a sinister appearance as the flame ignited with her puffs. The oil lantern nearby cast shadows about the room, revealing odd and cluttered furnishings.

"Why are you here?"

Spring was startled by her words. "Bear's Heart told me that you may be able to tell me...about my childhood...many years ago when I lived here...."

"Many years indeed."

"I was very young when I left...."

"I remember."

"You do? I have no memory of it myself."

"Sometimes, it is best to leave things as they be."

"What do you mean?"

"One should not pull up old rocks. They hide many things."

Spring suddenly felt as if she were at the threshold of many unanswered questions. She almost wished she hadn't come.

"Are you a strong one?" the old woman asked.

"I am."

"I would think so. Your mother, so beautiful, was strong, also." She seemed to lapse into memory.

"You knew my mother?"

She leaned forward. "I did."

"What was she like?"

"She was like a warrior. She was not afraid. Not like other women in camp...and she was beautiful like the sun of dawn that kisses the day."

"I was told how she died...trying to stop the white men that day from taking my father away. They both died that day trying to save each other."

"You were told right. It was a tragedy...never should have happened. Those two...Bright Star and Son of Grey Fox...had special love. Too bad...too bad."

"Did you see it happen?"

"No. But I hear story over and over for many years. How men grab Son of Grey Fox to take him away...and Bright Star throw herself between him and white men. They hit her with barrel of gun. Son of Grey Fox attack them, and they kill him with loud blast. Then Bright Star go crazy and spring on white man with gun, and she stab him with own knife. But then Bright Star fall dead, also from gun's blast."

"Why were they trying to take my father away?"

"They say he's thief. He lead Sioux party to distant farm and take food...to feed our hungry people."

"I see."

"But Son of Grey Fox not thief. He is noble warrior. Our people go hungry. No food comes from government."

"What happened after their deaths?" Spring pried further.

The old woman puffed on her pipe leisurely. "After they die, there is much trouble in camp. Soon it die down, too. But then what to do with baby...baby is you, of course. No parents now, no grandparents for you. Chief Wild River call his brother to his tent as soon as it all happen. He take baby...you...to his wife, who had just had first child days before. She could nurse."

"Who was this woman?"

"She was my friend from childhood. Her name was Red Feather."

"Is she...?"

"She no longer lives."

"What was she like?"

The old woman peered at Spring as if trying to discern secrets.

"She was...well...she had been good friend to me from childhood as I say. She try to give birth many times. All babies die, but this one live. But it was scrawny, little thing. I did not think it would live long."

"And she nursed us both?"

"That is right...well...partly right."

"What do you mean?"

The old woman suddenly looked irritated. "Why do you come to me after all these years, Child? I forget all this for many moons. I remember only good things, and I remember how we play as children...much fun."

"Saunie, I need to know these things. All my life, I have avoided the unknown, shrinking from bits and pieces of memory that surfaced occasionally to raise mysterious questions. Now, I am ready to face the unknown and find the answers. Please do not keep me in the dark. I am Spring Leaf, strong as my father and my mother."

"You are. It was long time ago. Red Feather was... jealous of you...you were healthy...and her baby scrawny and weak. She would nurse her baby...but let you cry. I tell her not to do this. She get very angry with me. We stop being friends after the many years, though we live side by side. I still see much; she not treat you good."

"What did you see?"

The old woman continued puffing on her pipe. "Many things...I don't know I'm sure. I hear baby cry much in the tipi...cry many hours into the night. I want to go to

Chief Wild River, but my husband, he say no. He tell me
the Chief would take side of brother. So, I don't go.
Many times I am sorry for this. But one day, I see
something that make me brave and I go to Chief Wild
River."

Spring waited.

"I see Red Feather and her little one leave at dusk.
I wonder where other baby is. I want to go see, but
husband say stay away from other man's tipi. So I wait
for him to sleep. Then I steal away, creeping ever so
silently out of tipi, and I make my way to Red Feather's
tipi in the silvery light of the new moon. As I get close,
I hear sounds...."

She looked at Spring through the darkened room,
judging her strength and puffed again her worn pipe.

"...Sounds of muffled cries coming from tipi. I
enter...and I cannot believe eyes! Baby was tied to post
in center of tipi with cloth stuffed half in mouth. I never
forget this. I never forget look in baby's eyes...so
afraid...so sad...."

Spring dropped her head into her hands, and silently
shook. The old woman moved closer.

"It is good, Child. Get thoughts of darkness out of
you. Too long have you kept them hidden."

As Spring trembled, a clock could be heard ticking
very softly somewhere in the small house. Still the old
woman watched. The trembling subsided, and Spring
looked up.

"Then what happened?" she whispered.

The old woman forced a half smile. "I take you to
Chief Wild River. You don't go back to Red Feather's tipi
no more. You stay with others...and then one day, they

take you away from Rosebud forever."

Spring sat quietly in the dark. The clock ticked on.

"Thank you, Saunie, for what you did."

The old woman hung her head.

"How can I repay you?"

"I take no pay. I only do right thing. It is my sorrow I wait so long."

"We all make mistakes." Spring smiled at her through her misty eyes.

"Spring Leaf, go in peace."

The old woman waited for her to leave. As Spring closed the door gently behind her, she felt as if she were finally closing a chapter of her life...a very important chapter. On the return trip home, she did not notice the lonely drive or the wind or the tumbleweeds or even the vast blue sky. Instead, she pondered on all the old woman had said, and quietly laid to rest the past. A new sense of freedom filled her being. She didn't need to fear the past, the unknown, anymore. She no longer needed to wonder what was behind those closed doors. The secrets lay exposed...repulsive and foul though they were, just as the odors from the little darkened house. She was free at last!

The long narrow road stretched out before her as she thought of her parents...Bright Star and Son of Grey Fox. How she wished she could have known them. She thought of what Patrick said, 'You will see those that have passed on again when you get to Heaven'. But would her Indian parents be there? Would she be there? Now that her past was finally settled, the future seemed to pose more questions. Would she ever have peace? The haunting words that had followed her from Oak

Mountain, from that tiny cemetery, again echoed within her mind…'Seek and ye shall find'.

THAT NIGHT AFTER Dakotah slept, and after she and Dean talked, and he also slept, Spring got up, walked over to the dresser and pulled out the bottom drawer. There it was, tucked underneath…her mama's Bible. Pru had given it to her when she left. She didn't want to take it, but Pru said that Mama had wanted her to have it. She wondered why her…and not Pru or Patrick or Jonathon. But deep down she knew. Mama had known, too. Dear sweet Mama. She could still see her sitting there, with all of them gathered around her as children, and she would read from this Bible, by the faint candlelight. She turned it over, noticing its frayed and worn condition. She crawled back into bed, and silently turned the pages. What should she read? Again she thought of Mama. Mama would know if she were here. Suddenly, recalling the day's events, she missed her very much. What would have happened to her if it hadn't been for Mama. What an act of love when she took her in and adopted her…taking her back to Virginia, especially when she already had three babies…Pru and Patrick and Jonathon. But still Mama wanted her! It made her feel all warm inside just thinking about it. Mama loved her and Daddy loved her. But still she wondered about her real parents. She turned back to the concordance. Let's see. *Seek…Seek…Seek.* She would begin with those words spoken to her that day on Oak Mountain…spoken so audibly and yet not spoken at all.

She turned to Matthew, chapter seven, verse seven

and began to read... 'Ask, and it shall be given you; seek, and ye shall find; knock, and it shall be opened unto you: For every one that asketh receiveth; and he that seeketh findeth; and to him that knocketh it shall be opened. Or what man is there of you whom if his son ask bread, will he give him a stone? Or if he ask a fish, will he give him a serpent? If ye then, being evil, know how to give good gifts unto your children, how much more shall your Father, which is in heaven give good things to them that ask him? Therefore all things whatsoever ye would that men should do to you, do ye even so to them; for this is the law of the prophets.'

She pushed back against the softness of the pillow and thought on these words...these words of Jesus. They made sense to her. Why, she would never want to give anything to Dakotah but the best...the very best that she could get for her. If God is truly the Father, the God of all, He certainly would want to give good things to those that would ask him. She remembered her mama again. Mama always said that He gave the best of everything to her. But then Mama had suffered so much. What was the best of everything? Not material things, for sure. Not a life without problems. Poor Mama had had more problems than most. She wondered what Mama considered the *best of everything?*

Dean stirred in his sleep. She felt very tired. Such an eventful day! She must sleep. She reached over, laid the Bible on the night stand and switched off the light.

The following Sunday, she visited the Native American Church where Dean belonged but seldom attended.

Throughout the service, she sought to unscramble her thoughts. The Peyote...the Sacred Pipe...and the Cross. All three? The Peyote...the Sacred Pipe...these were part of her heritage, and she yearned to embrace them. But her eastern upbringing kept illuminating her mind with questions. She must find the truth.

That night, again she opened her mother's Bible... to the concordance. 'Way...way...way'. Which is the right way? She turned to the book of John, chapter fourteen....'Thomas saith unto him, Lord, we know not whither thou goest; and how can we know the way? Jesus saith unto him, "I am the way, the truth, and the life: no man cometh unto the Father, but by me." '

"I am the way...," she repeated as she closed the old Bible and closed her eyes. Dean sighed. What was going on with this troubled lady he'd married?

The next Sunday, she visited the Episcopal Church where Mareen belonged. She sat next to Mareen and studied the flowing white formal robe that the minister wore. She examined the elegant choir standing beyond him. The solemn organ melody infiltrated the sanctuary through its resonate pipes. Questions kept popping up. Who was right? Dean? Mareen? Mama?

Suddenly, she knew she couldn't find her answers from man...or man's denominations or religions. She had to seek elsewhere. Seek...seek...seek. As the choir sang out in harmonious unity, she picked up the Bible from the pew, leafing back to the concordance again. 'Seek...seek...seek....' She turned to the book of Hebrews, Chapter eleven, verse six...'He that cometh to God must believe that He is; and that He is a rewarder of them that diligently seek Him'.

The minister's monotone voice began the morning sermon, but Spring's mind was elsewhere. 'Must believe that He is....' She did believe in a supreme being...a great spirit...God even. Certainly she hadn't lived the past forty plus years not to realize that this great universe didn't just happen. It was planned by a master hand, for sure.

Mareen looked over at her and smiled as she held the Bible in her hands. She laid it back down.

IT WAS WEDNESDAY, and her class had let out early. Spring was happy to have this time alone. She'd driven into the Black Hills...for a purpose...to think...meditate...seek. She parked her little sports car in one of the park's parking lots, and walked out to a trail, noticing the grey mountain crags towering above the trees. She followed the trail that was quite abandoned by tourists. That's why she'd picked this particular one, not for its popularity but rather for its obscure setting. The further into the forest she walked, the more pensive she became, almost feeling the presence of others...her ancestors...her people all around her...somber souls reaching out to her...trying to make contact. A twig broke and she jumped.

Quickly surveying her surroundings, she caught her breath as she looked squarely into the eyes of the most beautiful creature she'd ever seen...an antelope... a Pronghorn Antelope. It stood camouflaged against the summer forest, and its sharp eyes held hers without flinching. Its branch-like horns lifted proudly into the air, and she could tell it was a buck because they were black. What an elegant, graceful creature! It reminded her much of the deer back home in the Blue Ridge, with its tan coloring, slender legs and large ears. She moved ever so softly toward him, but he began to back away. He then turned, displaying his white rump, and took a fantastic leap into the air, disappearing into the Pines.

She smiled, remembering the brief discussion she'd had with her class only recently on the antelope. After their study of this magnificent animal, they found that it really wasn't an antelope after all...but a Pronghorn. Oh well, she'd continue calling it an antelope. She thought of how the Black Hills were a haven to so many creatures...the antelope, the buffalo, the whitetail deer, elk, turkeys, prairie dogs and many others. It had also been a haven for her people many years ago, and in a sense, it still was. Not only to the bones that lay beneath her rich soil, but to the living that were drawn here again and again like herself.

She sat down on a fallen tree that was slowly rotting away, and looked around at the thickness of the Ponderosa Pines, so tall and so dark. She wiped her forehead. It was getting quite warm, even here in the forest. Where are my ancestors? Are their bones rotting away beneath me as I sit here? Where are they?

She thought about her real parents again. Somewhere in these hills, my parents lie buried...but where? No one seems to know. She had traced that to dead ends more than once. While sitting in the hushed silence, staring up through the tall Pines, she gazed into the clear blue sky beyond.

"Are you there?" she called out, and her voice echoed back to her in the stillness that prevailed.

Suddenly a bird flew into the green needles of a nearby Pine. It fluttered its wings and perched itself atop a swaying branch. Spring thought of the song she'd just heard sung in the Episcopal Church last Sunday...*His eye is on the sparrow, and I know He watches me....* Again she looked upward. Was He watching her? Could He see her way down here lost in the thickness of the Black Hills forest? Was He interested enough to look? *His eye is on the sparrow, and I know He watches me.* She wondered if that came out of the Bible.

Her leg had gone to sleep, and she shifted her weight on the tree. It didn't take long these days. Was she getting old or what?

She recalled how young she'd been when she'd first visited these hills. Now, it seemed so long ago. Would her bones lie rotting here also? Or back on Oak Mountain in the Blue Ridge? But then what? There had to be more! Man with all his intellect, knowledge, feeling...why it couldn't just be wasted...it couldn't just end with the grave...in the dirt! There had to be a hereafter. She would seek the hereafter...but how?

She inhaled the pungent earthy fragrance of the summer forest, and watched the tall Pines swaying ever so gently in the subtle breeze. Silently, she sat... listening...listening to the prevailing stillness. She lost track of time as she sat almost in a semi-daze waiting and watching and just enjoying being a part of the hills. Suddenly, an earth-shattering thunder reverberated from the tall canyon walls beyond, and she looked up to see the clear blue sky replaced with dark sinister clouds. Oh no! Another summer storm! How quickly they appeared.

The raindrops began pelting her with an increasing intensity, sending her for cover beneath the thick needled Pines. She crouched down and huddled as close as possible to a strong Ponderosa trunk as the rains increased the already vibrant Pine scent. She felt good! Was this what it was like for her ancestors... to be one with the earth and the sky? She closed her eyes, focusing on the present feeling, and tried to imagine what it was like then. She was soothed by the beating rain, but thrilled by the thunderous cracks. Why wasn't she afraid? There was a kinship here...to her people and to the Black Hills and to...the storm even.

Just as suddenly as it had come, the thunder storm spent itself, and the rains ceased. The clouds disappeared and the sun reappeared with a renewed brightness. She crawled out from under her Pine shelter, her wet clothes clinging to her, and stretched herself in the warmth of the welcomed sun. The shining raindrops on the millions of Pine needles glistened in the rich yellow light. And the evergreen Ponderosa Pines boasted of a richer green than before. She sat back down onto the soaked tree and smiled. The magic of the Black Hills!

That night, after Dean had fallen asleep, she lay thinking about her day in the forest. She recalled each minute detail of her stay in the Hills. It had been so peaceful...so quiet...so still. So still. She remembered something...something her mother used to say to them so often. She got back up and crept into the living room, reached for the Bible now on the table and turned to the concordance. She flipped the pages... Psalm 46:10...'Be *still, and know that I am God'*. Her hands began to tremble. She closed the Bible and placed it back on the table.

For the next few weeks, Spring did a lot of seeking... in the Bible...in the library records...and by talking to the aged and wise. She found it difficult to keep tuned in on current events as her mind sought for answers. One night after she'd closed the Bible and climbed back into bed, Dean reached out and pulled her close, wrapping his strong arms around her.

"Good to have you back! Is my troubled little wife still pursuing the deep answers of the great universe?"

She snuggled close to him. Her lips found his, and he had all the answer she needed. The next morning, she awakened still in his arms, and smiled to herself as he slept. How fortunate she was to have him. Too vividly, she remembered all the lonely years as she walked her path alone. Suddenly, she recalled it was Saturday...her favorite day of the week. Her day to do whatever she wished. She arose to prepare Dean breakfast.

The inviting aroma of fresh brewed coffee and frying ham filled the kitchen. Spring enjoyed the solitude of the morning...briefly. Dakotah toddled in.

"Mama?"

"Yes, Darling, good morning."

"Grandpa gone?"

"Grandpa? Oh no. He must be around somewhere." She leaned to look out the window. "There he is...sitting on the porch. Why don't you go out and see him?"

She took off. Again Spring thought how good it was...this relationship that was blossoming between

them. Age was certainly no barrier there. She popped
the bread in the oven. Just as she straightened herself,
Dean eased up behind her and kissed her head.

"Good morning with a kiss on your crown."

"My crown?" she laughed.

"Yes, every princess has a crown!"

She smiled at him affectionately.

"Well, you are *my* princess...and where is my other
little princess?"

"Guess?"

"Outside with Dad?"

She nodded.

"Is everything okay with you?"

"Okay?"

"I mean, since your trip to Rosebud and all. Everything okay?"

"Yes, I have come to terms with that. It is behind
me."

"That's good. What is troubling you then?"

She looked up.

"You seem to be lost in deep thought much of the
time...and not here within these walls."

"I see."

"Is it this hereafter thing?"

She nodded.

"Don't worry about those things now, Honey. We're
still young. Let's enjoy living. We'll worry about those
things when we get old. Hey, let's do something special
today?"

"Today? I thought you and Young Hawk were going
hunting for prairie dogs."

"Changed my mind. How about it?"

"Sounds good to me. Where are we going?"

"Suppose I surprise you?"

She looked at him with a quizzical expression.

"You do like surprises, don't you?" He grinned with pleasure.

"Of course."

About an hour later, they were on their way. Dean driving his fairly new Ford pick-up with Dakotah standing up beside him, her little arm entwined around his neck, and Spring staring straight ahead with her thick, dark hair blowing out the open window. The day promised to be another hot, cloudless day.

"Where Grandpa?" Dakotah repeated.

"Remember, I told you, Honey. Grandpa didn't feel like coming along. He wanted to stay home and rest." She winked at Dean, and he smiled. They were amused with Dakotah's constant concern for Grandpa.

After driving for quite a ways out into the farmlands, Dean turned off the main road and proceeded down a rural road that was certainly not traveled much. She wondered where he was going. Finally, he pulled over to the side of the road in front of a sprawling farm with large fields encircled by freshly painted white rail fences. Sitting in the midst of all this was a long red brick ranch house that appeared relatively new.

Spring looked at Dean.

"How would you like to live here?"

"Here?"

"That's right."

"You mean...instead of on the reservation?"

"That's right."

"But I thought...."

"I know...but I've been thinking. And, I think it would be best to raise Dakotah out here."

"What about your dad?"

"Well, you know how Dad is. I don't think he much cares where he is these days. At his age, he's more tuned in on internal happenings than external. Guess that's part of growing old."

"You're right, of course."

"So, what do you think?" He had a hard time concealing his excitement.

"I think it's beautiful, of course. It's just such a surprise."

"That's what I wanted."

Spring gazed at the vast fields, the rich soil, and the large modern house. A dream come true.

"I haven't signed any papers," Dean added. "I wanted to make sure you liked it first."

"Like it? I love it!"

They both laughed and embraced with Dakotah in the middle. She laughed along with them while clapping her pudgy hands.

The next morning, Spring awoke to bright sun rays streaming through the old window panes. She suddenly thought of that big, new ranch house. She was excited. This was going to be her first home...after all these years. It would be wonderful! Dakotah would have the luxury of all those fields to roam and explore...all that land. She felt so good thinking about it that she didn't want to wake Dean. She wanted to revel in her own private thoughts a little longer. She thought about all the things she would be able to do like planting flowers and trees and shrubs. She'd plant some shrubs from back home. She'd get Pru to send her some shoots. Yes, Pru would delight in doing that. And she and Dean would plant a large garden. They'd hire some help and have fields of gardens...and cows. Of course, they'd have cows and some horses. Dakotah would have her own spotted pony. It was going to be wonderful!

That Sunday, she and Dean made plans. They drove back out to the farm. This time, they took Grandpa Eli along. Just as Dean had said, he wasn't too interested. If he wasn't dozing, he was watching Dakotah. By the end of the day, the decision was made, and Dean was to start the paperwork the next day.

Monday morning, as Spring drove off to class, she experienced mixed feelings about the reservation. She knew she wanted to leave and make a home for them out there on that beautiful farm. But something seemed to tug at her about leaving the reservation. She felt as if she were deserting her people, but yet Dakotah would have so much more. She told herself that even though they wouldn't be living here, they would still be working here and spending much of their time here. The day itself overtook her thoughts and her mind was crowded with the tasks at hand in the classroom and out. Soon it was time to return home, and she couldn't wait to hear about Dean's progress.

All the way home, she silently made plans for her new home, even down to the color of kitchen curtains. They would be yellow like Pru's. She loved Pru's kitchen.

She noticed a certain stillness when she entered the house. She looked around for Dean and Dakotah.

"Dakotah?" she called while placing her briefcase on the hall table.

Still only a hushed silence prevailed.

She walked down the hallway, fighting off the foreboding feeling that was beginning to shake her usual calmness. She entered the kitchen and gasped!

Dean was slumped over the kitchen table in an awkward position. And even before she reached him, she knew he was dead. The coffee he'd been drinking was spilled over the table and down to the floor.

She rushed to him and placed her arms around him. His stiffened broad shoulders confirmed the worst. She cried out, "Why? Why Dean? He's not old enough! This isn't fair! It shouldn't be him...why not Grandpa Eli?" She looked around. Where were Grandpa and Dakotah?

She must call...she must get help! She grabbed the phone and dialed, hearing her own voice as though it was not hers. And then she knelt down beside Dean in the cold spilled coffee and wept. She talked to him like she'd done so often...but this time, he didn't answer.

"Dean...I loved you...you know. You were such a good husband to me...and I will always love you...."

Sirens approached the humble dwelling, and Spring stood silently by as the rescue workers proceeded with their methodical actions. She observed the scene as one far removed, not able to comprehend. But when they pulled the sheet over his head, she ran to him, grabbing at the sheet.

"NO!"

The workers gently pulled her away, and she allowed

them to do so. She felt helpless and defeated.

"Would you like to ride with us?"

Suddenly she remembered Dakotah! Where was she? Fear seized her again. And Grandpa? She ran out of the house calling, "Dakotah...Dakotah....Grandpa...Grandpa...."

As she turned the corner of the house, she looked off into the distance and thought she distinguished two figures. Yes! One large and one very small. It was Grandpa and Dakotah!

They were bringing him out now and proceeding to place him in the vehicle. She looked at the familiar form outlined beneath the thin sheet, and then she turned back to the two figures in the distance.

"Ma'am?" the kind gentleman urged.

She was torn, but she looked into the man's eyes and said, "It is life that needs me."

They closed the doors to the rescue vehicle and drove silently away. Spring turned and ran toward Grandpa and Dakotah. As she neared them, she slowed and listened, realizing they had not seen her. Grandpa Eli was very intense in what he was trying to relay to Dakotah. He was pointing to the west while Dakotah stood looking up at him questioningly.

"It is there, my Child...there," his aged voice cracked. "The Black Hills, the sacred land of your ancestors. It is there that my son's spirit roams...he has been joined to our people...cut off before his time. He has stepped out before his old father...but it will not be long...and I will join him." He stopped talking and looked down at the small serious child listening so intently, but not comprehending those deep words. He extended his lean, dark arm, and she reached up and clasped it.

"Don't forget, my Child, it is the Black Hills where your fathers are...even Dean Loud Thunder...son of Eli Fire Thunder."

Spring listened. So he knew. Still he brought Dakotah out here to tell her what was in his heart.

THE PHONE CONTINUED to ring on the other end. Maybe no one was home. Spring sat down with the phone to her ear, feeling very tired. It had been a long three days.

"Hello," Pru's voice called out.

"Pru."

"Spring!"

"Pru...I just buried Dean."

"Spring...No!"

"Yes, he died of a sudden heart attack three days ago."

"Spring, I'm so sorry. What can I do?"

"Nothing now."

"Why didn't you call sooner?"

"I wasn't ready."

"Do you need me to come out there?"

"No. We'll be okay. I have to take care of Dakotah and Grandpa now."

The following days were hard. Spring pushed herself to resume not only her former role, but Dean's also. She watched sadly as Dakotah looked through the house for him, and Grandpa withdrew into a shell not even Dakotah could penetrate.

She couldn't erase those questions that seemed to

echo off the walls around her...why...why...why...why?

"Mommy, where's Daddy?" Dakotah's question broke into her thoughts.

Once again caught off guard, she groped for the right words...but were there any?

"Daddy's gone away now, Honey. Mommy explained that to you."

"But I want him to come back." She stomped her little foot emphatically.

Spring reached out to her and hugged her tightly. "I understand, Sweetheart...Mommy does, too."

"Where's Grandpa?"

"I think he's out on the porch."

She watched her wander out to the porch and over to the old man, who sat either dozing or in one of his semi-conscious thinking modes. Dakotah gently tapped him on the knee, but he didn't respond. Finally, she walked away.

As life has a way of doing, crushing one down with a double portion of pain, Spring arrived home exactly three weeks later to find Grandpa Eli sitting outside on the porch facing the west, his spirit departed and now joined with Dean's and all the ancestors that he had spoken of so often.

Spring laid him to rest beside Dean.

She decided to leave the sadness of Pine Ridge and return to the Blue Ridge Mountains...to her people on Oak Mountain.

Chapter XII
Listen to The Wind...

It was September and the hint of autumn was casting its elusive spell upon the folds and crevices of the hazy Blue Ridge Mountains. Spring gripped the wrought iron gate to the little cemetery that held her once vibrant family. Death...she thought. It's like a rotting cancer robbing one of all that is important and precious.

She thought of Dean and Grandpa Eli lying beneath the already cold plains of South Dakota. She looked at the sunken graves before her...Emily Barrett...Heath Barrett...Little David Barrett and Charity Barrett. She fought back the tears and turned away from the cemetery, looking beyond and on up the hillside to the thicket of Oaks, Poplars and Pines. Yes, it is meant to be. She neared the thicket, surveying the breathtaking beauty of Oak Mountain.

I will build my home here...a home for Dakotah and

me...near the souls of my people. She recalled what Patrick had said earlier..."their souls are not there. They are in a far better place." Well, maybe so, but somehow, she felt closer to them here. And then there was the lone chimney that stood as an ever present reminder of the past...her happy childhood.

A couple of weeks later, Spring was studying the blueprint that lay before her when Pru walked into the kitchen.

"What's that?"

"A blueprint."

She leaned over her shoulder. "Interesting."

"It's going to be my little tipi here on Oak Mountain."

"Well, it does sort of resemble one. It's different, that's for sure."

"It's an A-Frame. My studio will be here," she pointed to the top window framed by the peaked roof. "Just below it, on the second floor, will be Dakotah's and my bedroom. We will be up high where we can view all the beauty of the mountainside."

"Aren't you afraid to live there all alone...I mean just you and little Dakotah?"

Spring looked up at her.

"No, I guess not. I forget how brave you are." Pru set about preparing a layered cake. "But, you sure it's what you want? You know you're welcome to stay here with us. We have plenty of room."

"It's what I want, Pru. I've never owned a home." She looked off. "I came close to it...with Dean. But now Dakotah and I...we will have our own place, and I can't wait to get started. I really appreciate you and Patrick and Jonathon selling me your part of the land."

"What could *we* do with it?" She lightly floured the pans. "You know, deep down inside, I'm really happy to know there will be life, a home and happiness again there on Oak Mountain. Ever since Mama died and the highway took the place, there has been a void. But I didn't think there was enough land left to do anything...especially with it being perched on that mountainside."

"Well, it's just perfect for us."

A car horn honked outside, and Pru looked out. "It's Jonathon."

He burst into the kitchen, bringing with him the crispness of the cool fall air. Rubbing his hands together, he laughed. "Fall is here, ladies!"

"It sure is," Pru agreed. "Where's Jessica?"

Suddenly his boyish smile vanished, "She's gone over to talk with Heath and Caroline."

He noticed Pru's look of concern.

"Oh, they're gonna work things out. You know how newlyweds are...have to get adjusted and all."

"Jessica says that Caroline is too demanding on Heath. That's not good," Pru remarked while sifting the flour into the mixing bowl.

"I don't know. 'Course you know Jessica has a hard time seeing any side but Heath's. Guess that's natural. Caroline's okay...maybe a little too crazy about Heath. But what's wrong with that!" he laughed. "And Heath is a bit ambitious, you know. Don't know where he gets it, but I think the boy wants to be president or something!"

"President?" Spring laughed.

"Well, maybe not president...but he *is* talking about running for public office later on when the time is right. Guess that's what that political science schooling did for him."

"Well, I'm certainly proud of him," Pru interjected, "but I do hope he and little Caroline can work out their differences."

"I'm sure they will. Where's Clarence?"

"Gone over to Peak's Orchard to see Ole Man Wright about something or other. You know I can't keep up with him."

Jonathon laughed, "How's Melony?"

"Haven't seen her for about three weeks now. Seems she's staying away more and more these days."

"And Roxy?" Spring asked.

"She's doing fine, I guess...but even Roxy seems to be getting discouraged with our wayward Melony."

"Just what seems to be the problem, Pru?"

"I wish I knew, Spring. She appears to be rebelling against all that we ever tried to teach her. It's so ironic, too, that when the girls were growing up, she was always the settled one...the well-behaved one. Why, you both remember how Mary Tom was the troublesome one...always into something." She smiled. "That Mary Tom...and here she is a missionary. Just shows you never know."

"Maybe she's like some people I know...takes her a long time finding herself."

"Well, I wish she'd hurry up and do so. I'm worried about Little Emily."

"I think it's just her way of dealing with her broken marriage," Jonathon added. "She'll come around sooner or later."

Just then the shrill ring of the telephone interrupted their conversation.

Pru answered quickly, "Oh hello, Melony." She raised her eyebrows at Spring and Jonathon. "Emily's sick...not too sick? What are you giving her?"

"Just aspirin right now." Melony rolled her eyes at Roxy. "She'll be okay. We were planning on coming up this weekend, but, of course, we can't now. Maybe next weekend."

"Well, I hope so. And you watch Little Emily carefully. You know how sometimes these viruses can go on and on...and sometimes go into other things...."

"I know, Mother. I'm taking good care of her. Tell Aunt Spring 'Hi' for me."

Melony placed the receiver back on the phone and turned to Roxy, who was staring at her.

"Well?" she asked.

"You gonna go out tonight?"

"I was thinking about it...but Emily seems to be feeling a bit worse."

"Well, if you ask me...I think she'd like to have her mommy with her tonight."

"Guess you're right." She proceeded to pull the curlers out of her hair, letting them drop half-curled.

The phone rang, and Roxy grabbed it before Melony.

"Hello. Yes, she is. Hold on." She reluctantly handed it to Melony.

"Oh hi, Eric. No, I'm afraid not. Emily's still sick. That will be fine. Talk to you later."

Roxy stared at her as she hung up, "Eric?"

"Yes, Eric."

"A new one?"

"That's right."

"He ain't married...is he?"

"No Roxy...he ain't married," she repeated while walking out the room.

She wished sometimes she hadn't kept this arrangement with Roxy. She was becoming even more of a nag than her mother. She looked in on Emily, who was sleeping soundly now...her little dimples smoothed out. Must be the aspirin, she thought. Poor little thing. She eased across the room to close the curtains, and noticed that it had begun to sprinkle a few drops of rain. It made her feel better. She wondered why? Probably because her mother liked rain...and her mother before her...Grandma Emily. Yes, Grandma Emily loved the rain.

That night, after Little Emily finally fell asleep for the night, and Roxy was occupied putting Laurietta down, Melony slipped downstairs and out to the porch steps. She often did so, enjoying the peacefulness of the night. The rain had increased to a steady drizzle. She sat down on the steps anyhow, letting the cool drops fall upon her. It was a warm rain, though, for this time of the year, and it felt good as its gentle sting caressed her upturned face, creating little rivulets that streamed down her cheeks and off her chin. She felt a part of it, and smiled into the darkened sky that was sending forth its bounties.

Rains of God...that's it...rains of God. She smiled again, blinking as the drops hit her eyes. She felt a strong urge to express her feelings. And after a long

while of sitting on those wet steps, she whispered into
the dark night...

> Within the midst of it, the midst of it
> Oh, such peace and tranquillity,
> As on these darkened steps I sit
> The rains, so gently, fall upon me
>
> A closeness it is, yes...a closeness it is
> To that something...that something great
> Which through the years I've seemed to cherish
> But could not reach...nor could not take
>
> It's You, I know, You above
> That's letting these rains so gently fall
> It's You, I know, You I love
> So, God, to thee I call

She blinked back the tears that were mildly mixed
with the warm rain.

THE DOOR closed softly behind him, and Caroline
watched the darkness fill the room, bringing with it the
same old fears. She'd thought tonight would be different
after his mom had talked with them. But then, the real
truths had not come out. It was a game they played,
each masking their individual secrets. But somehow,
she'd hoped that Heath would come to her, and they
would talk as they once had. Instead, he'd chosen to
read his papers, and she fought back the ever present
tears. They were growing further and further apart like
two ships that had passed in the night, and now were
fading into the fog with only a dim light that tracked
their distance. She sadly remembered when their lights
had burned brightly and intensely for each other. What

was happening? Was their love dying? No, she still loved Heath...and would never love another. And somehow, she believed he still loved her...but was his love strong enough?

Was there enough feeling left for her after he'd exerted all his forces into his ambitious goals? She heard him rustling paper, no doubt working on his research papers. At first she'd resented him going to night school, but now she realized that she was happier on those nights than when he was home. At least she had an excuse then for being alone. If only some of that driving force could be focused on her. Then the old guilt crept in. Poor Heath...working so hard, and she feeling sorry for herself again. But if she had...if she could have had...then she wouldn't be so lonely. The door opened again.

"You asleep?"

"No."

"Well, I'm just too tired tonight. Can't study anymore. Think I'll turn in, too."

He pulled his dark blue sweater over his head. It was a Christmas present from her, and he really liked it. He unbuttoned his Oxford shirt with one hand, while sitting down on the side of the bed to take off his loafers. He casually pitched his shirt onto the chair across the room, and Caroline looked at his broad, bare shoulders, admiring his strength. She was proud of his looks...always had been.

He turned out the hall light and climbed into bed. As he sank down into the soft mattress, she found herself rolling toward him. He laughed his old laugh, "Always works."

She snuggled up to his hairy chest that smelled of Old Spice, and they embraced.

"I love you," he whispered.

"I love you, too," she whispered back.

The next morning, Caroline awoke to a strange sound coming from outside her lace framed window. She knew Heath was gone already. He was putting in long hours these days. What was that sound?

Then it occurred to her that it was acorns falling with such force from the nearby tall Oaks that one would think they were actually being hurled by unseen hands within the trees. She smiled.

Last night had been beautiful...special...the way it used to be. They had given their all to each other, recapturing the magic of their youth. Of course, they were still young...but it seemed so long ago when they had felt those first joys of love. If she could have Heath ... all of Heath...like that forever...then she would be happy.

She threw her bare legs out of bed and yawned, and sat shivering on the side of the bed, feeling the coolness of the house. She reached for her chenille robe, pulling it around her bareness, and sighed within its warmth. She couldn't wait to talk to Clara. Clara would be so happy, too. Clara was always happy when she was happy. But then, Clara could be sad too, when she was sad.

OCTOBER WAS SHEDDING its last remnants of magic as Spring stood back assessing the end result of her labors — well, not quite the end result, but at least it was under roof for the winter, and that was saying a lot since the roof went from ground up to the sharp pitched top. The construction crew had worked miracles.

She admired the many windows that provided a sense of outdoors within doors…just what she wanted. Its overall appearance, predominantly its dark rustic exterior, created an impression that it had simply grown there with the rest of the mountain. It sat precariously perched upon the rugged mountainside with its back partly resting against the rocky earth and securely surrounded by White Pines and the many varieties of Oak Mountain trees. Although they stood half naked, these trees still boasted of remaining leaves that surpassed all former color. The vivid deep crimson reds of the Maples and the bright yellow Hickories, interspersed with the delicate Dogwoods that now displayed their clusters of deep red berries, drew a sharp contrast to the towering Oaks that could only offer their lifeless brown leaves. But proudly they stood as a reminder that once it was all over and the mountain turned bare, they alone would hold onto their covering throughout much of the oncoming winter.

Excitedly, Spring made her way up to her new home, pushing aside the brush that had not already been trampled down by the carpenters. She opened the unlocked door and walked in, looking around the spacious great room even though it was only half finished; that's the way she wanted it. She had cut off the workers in order to finish it herself. This way, it would be home to her. She glanced at the slanting side walls and smiled. She would find out how Michelangelo felt. Of course, this was no Sistine Ceiling, but it was the

nearest thing she'd ever paint. The Oak beams above
her were just what she'd envisioned, a country feeling.
And why not? She was about as far up in the country as
she could get. She began to climb the stairs to their
bedrooms. They, too, needed paint and wallpaper. She
walked over to the balcony...she preferred to call it a
porch. What a view!

She pushed open the glass doors and stood there,
leaning against the wall and feeling incognito, one with
the forest. Two little squirrels were hurriedly gathering
food for the winter, and a blackbird rested itself on an
extended branch of a nearby Oak. She listened to the
crispness of the leaves as they fell aimlessly to the
already covered earth, and she inhaled the earthy fragrance of nature's bounty. Oak Mountain was resplendent in its autumn foliage and caused an excitement to stir within her that overshadowed the deep
sadness that she'd brought with her from the Plains.

They moved into the unfinished cottage, or tipi as the
family now referred to it, a few days later. Melony, Roxy
and the girls came up to help.

"Aunt Spring, where do you want these spatulas to
go?" Melony called from the kitchen.

Spring's mind was elsewhere, and she answered
absently, "Oh, stick them anywhere."

Melony looked at Roxy and shrugged her shoulders.
"Some system," she remarked with a smile to Roxy as
they busily unpacked the boxes loaded down with kitchen
utensils, books and toys.

"Well, I guess she didn't have her mind much on
packing when she left."

Melony noticed the sudden sadness as Roxy retraced the time that took her back to that night...that dreadful night when her world fell apart. She could understand Spring's obsession with this place. It was medicine ... medicine for her illness.

A squeal echoed from upstairs where the girls were playing in Dakotah's new playroom. Both Roxy and Melony jumped up from the floor.

"I'll go." Roxy hastened upstairs and called back. "They're okay...just a little misunderstanding."

Melony took a break and stood with her hands on her hips, watching Spring begin her work of art on one of the side walls.

"You gonna paint the whole wall?"

"Sure am."

"How long will it take you?"

"Don't know. I'm in no hurry."

"What's it gonna be?"

"This side...the east side...will be a slice of the Blue Ridge Mountains...our very own Oak Mountain."

"Interesting. Can't wait to see it. What about the other side?"

"That...," Spring raised up and gazed at the blank wall opposite her, "that will be a slice of the Black Hills."

"No kidding. I wish you'd paint that first...since I've never seen it."

"No. I'm going to paint Oak Mountain while we're surrounded by autumn's richness. I can *feel* it now."

"Well, are you going to go back to the Black Hills to feel *it* before you start the other side?" Melony kidded.

"No. The Black Hills stay with me," she replied seriously.

Roxy bounced down the steps. "Back to the boxes, Miss Mel."

"What a slave driver," she joked as they returned to their task.

"Oh Mel," Spring called after her.

"Yeah?"

"Roxy tells me you're writing some poetry."

"Some."

"How about doing me a favor?"

"Sure. What is it?"

"I'd like you to write a poem about Oak Mountain."

"That shouldn't be too hard. With all this beauty, it writes its own."

"Not now, Melony. I want you to write a poem about the woods, the mountain woods...in the winter."

"The winter?"

"That's right."

"Hmmm...never thought about that," she began pulling toys out of the box at hand, "but I'll try, Spring, when winter comes."

Spring smiled to herself as she began applying her creative strokes to the barren wall, rising to meet the challenge of translating it to the majestic beauty of autumn on Oak Mountain.

That evening after supper with cornbread and pinto beans, they went out to the porch to sit. The little ones, exhausted from so much play and fresh mountain air, had already fallen asleep. Roxy plopped herself down on the porch swing while Spring and Melony began a rhythmic competition with the rockers.

"My, this swing looks a mite old," Roxy casually

remarked.

"It's more than a mite," Spring replied. "It belonged to Mama."

"Is that right? Sure seems sturdy and all."

"It's sturdy all right. Survived the flood when the rest of the house didn't...and Mama loved it."

Melony spoke up. "I'm surprised Mama gave it to you."

"Your mama didn't give it to me. It belongs to *us* — *all* of us. And it sure wasn't doing any good hanging up on that shed."

"You're right. How did you get it looking so good?"

"A little sanding...well, a whole lot of sanding and some stain to match the house."

"You sure did a good job."

"Thank you, Roxy."

"Well, Aunt Spring can do anything she sets her mind to. That's why she can live up here on this mountain all but alone. Mama would never dream of doing such a thing...neither would I. But Aunt Spring... she doesn't need anybody."

"I reckon I can understand that...being independent myself."

Melony laughed, "Roxy, what are you talking about? You need to get yourself a man."

"No lady, I'm not lookin' for no man. There was only one man for me...my Seth."

Melony shook her head. "Do you plan to spend the rest of your life alone?"

" 'Course not! I have Laurietta."

"But Laurietta will not be with you always."

"No. But God will be."

Melony didn't answer. All that could be heard for the
next few minutes were the acorns hitting the roof and
spinning off into space for a brief second before joining
their mates on the darkened ground. A gentle breeze
floated across the porch.

"Heaven's breath," Spring whispered.

"What did you say?" Roxy asked.

"Heaven's breath."

"Why, that's real pretty."

"It's an old Indian saying."

"My."

"What did you think about Martin Luther King?"
Spring asked suddenly.

"I still can't believe it."

"You know, you practically predicted it...that weekend up at Mama's."

Roxy looked at Melony. "You're right...but I guess I
really didn't believe it. How could anybody kill such a
good man that never hurt nobody?"

"It's life, Roxy. It's history," Spring answered. "At
least you had a great leader...one who made a difference...who made people listen...made people think. His
life was not wasted."

"You're certainly right about that. He made a difference!"

"That's what *we* need."

They both looked at her.

"A strong leader...a strong spokesman...to make a
difference."

"You're a strong leader, Miss Barrett."

"I am a woman...and it is too soon for that."

"I still think you could do it," Roxy stated.

"I agree," Melony added.

"Thanks girls. But I'm not getting any younger. It's strong young males that we need now. But maybe one day there will be a strong female leader...who knows. But we were talking about Martin Luther King...."

"I remember exactly what I was doing that day."

They looked at Roxy.

"I got up as usual, put the bacon on and went downstairs to get the paper. I was reading about the President...President Johnson going to fly to Hawaii that day to make contact with the North Vietnamese people. I still remember that. And I was thinking to myself, too bad these peace talks hadn't done any good so far. If they had, I'd still have my Seth. There was a time when I couldn't read the paper...couldn't read anything about Vietnam, but that changed. I'd taken to keeping up with the war news again...and I prayed every day for peace...I still do. I know Seth would want me to do that. Well, while I was reading the paper, Laurietta woke up crying. Now Laurietta seldom wakes up crying, but she did that day."

Melony raised her eyebrows.

Roxy ignored her and continued, "It was a nice enough morning, but the weather forecast called for a chance of rain, and I'd planned to take the girls to a movie. I decided to wait 'till the afternoon and see how it was. A few showers never hurt nobody, so we took off downtown after lunch along with Mel's umbrella. Both Laurietta and Emily kept taking turns carrying it, poking each other in the head with it." She laughed.

"We turned up Clay Street, my favorite way to go, even though Melony says it's longer. But I always enjoy

the shade of the big trees that line the uneven sidewalk.
I remember noticing that day their small leaves of a
bright green...just new for spring."

"We stopped and watched some pigeons pecking
away on the cobblestones, their black and grey coats
shining with the blue and purple around their necks. I
like pigeons. The girls loved them, too. They didn't pay
no mind to us either, went on about their business
pecking at something in the wet leaves from last year
that was blown down beside the curb. Then we passed
our favorite place...the reservoir."

Spring looked at Melony.

Melony rolled her eyes. "She likes plenty of detail in
her stories."

"Why the reservoir, Roxy?"

"Miss Barrett, you'd like it, too. There, standing atop
the reservoir, is an Indian statue just as pretty as you
please."

"Indian?" Melony challenged.

She looked at her. "Well, it *looks* like an Indian
anyway...an Indian girl."

"We're not certain what it is," Melony added. "Some
people say it's an Egyptian water boy; others say it's an
Indian girl."

"Well, it really don't matter," Roxy continued.
"Laurietta and I talk to her anyway...and we think she's
Indian."

"You talk to her?" Spring asked with interest.

"Sure do. We think she kinda looks lonely, standing
there all by herself all the time out there in the middle
of that reservoir."

"I presume the reservoir has a top on it?"

" 'Course it does, but it didn't used to when I was growing up."

"What did you say to her that day?"

"I don't rightly remember."

Melony looked amused.

"But we usually talk to her about how the sun is shining so bright or about how many clouds are in the sky or about where we are going. 'Course she stands there all stone-faced like always, but we feel better by talking to her."

Spring smiled.

"Well, we went on down the street, turned up Eighth Street so that we could walk down the Ninth Street steps...Monument steps. Laurietta and me... we especially like to walk down Monument steps. That day it was particularly nice walking down them because the Dogwoods had just begun blooming. You know they bloom all up and down the sides of the steps. Really something to see."

"I'd like to see that," Spring said with growing interest.

"Laurietta kept on trying to pick one, and I had to tell her that would be breaking the law. You can't pick a Dogwood...being the state tree and all! Well, we got downtown and went to Woolworth's first like we always do. It's our favorite store...so many cute little things that the girls like...me too. Afterwards, we went on to the Paramount Theater."

"What movie did you see?" Spring asked.

"Well, I'd been planning on seeing *Bonnie and Clyde*. That was playing at the Warner. But at the last minute, I changed my mind and went to the Paramount to see

Lord of the Flies. I really did want to see *Bonnie and Clyde.* But *Lord of the Flies* was recommended to me by my neighbor. 'Course the Paramount has always been my favorite anyhows...seems more elegant you know...more like a movie theater ought to look like. I'm not that big on movies anyhow. But I reckon I get a certain satisfaction out of going now that I'm able to sit anywheres I please. Wasn't like that when I was growing up. We always had to sit up in the back...the balcony. Couldn't sit in the good seats. Laurietta won't ever have to sit in the back."

"When exactly did you hear the news?"

"It was in the evening, Miss Barrett, after we'd gotten back from downtown. I'd just put Laurietta and Emily down to bed. Melony had gone out, you know. I went to the kitchen to tidy up and cut on the radio. They were talking about somebody that had been killed. I came in on the news in the middle of it. I wondered who it was, and then I heard...*Martin Luther King is dead!*"

She paused and wiped a tear from her eye.

"How did you feel?"

She thought a minute. "Sad...Miss Barrett...real sad...I didn't just feel sad for Dr. King and his family... but I felt sad for all of us."

Spring nodded with understanding. "I'm sure you felt the same way my people felt when Crazy Horse was killed and Sitting Bull and many other noble leaders."

"Hey, you two, you gonna blame me for all this?" Melony joked, and they laughed.

"It's humanity," Spring stated. "Unfortunately, prejudice is a human trait...not a good one...but a human trait just the same."

"That's right," Roxy agreed. "It's not right for sure, but it's the way people are sometimes. It goes back to Bible times even...like the Israelites and the Egyptians. 'Course the color was backwards then."

"What do you mean?"

"The Israelites were the slaves to the Egyptians, who were the dark people, Miss Barrett. Remember the story about little Moses?"

"Oh yes, of course. And it goes further back than that."

"I know. But if people were to follow Christ, they wouldn't act so."

"Christ?" Spring repeated.

"He said, 'Do unto others as you would have them do unto you'. Now that would solve it all."

"That says a lot," Melony added.

"But that's what He said." Roxy continued, "God says He is no respector of persons, and He don't want us to be either."

"Apparently, nobody talks much about it in church," Spring concluded.

They each looked at one another silently as the mountain darkness closed in upon them, and the dampness of the evening dew penetrated through their clothing.

Spring took a deep breath. "Don't know about you two, but I'm turning in." She rose.

"Good night," they said as Spring disappeared inside.

"It's so peaceful out here," Melony remarked.

"Sure is. I don't want it to end. Think I'll sit here a bit longer."

All that could be heard for the next few minutes was the rhythmic creaking of the old swing as Roxy pushed it to and fro. The full moon fought its way through the tree masses casting its silvery glow downward, outlining the two lone figures on the porch as they silently sat.

"You ever felt like nature was talking to you?" Melony's voice reached out into the darkness.

"Sometimes. Lotta times."

"It's been speaking to me now for quite some time."

"Oh?" Roxy replied.

"Yes, sometimes it speaks more clearly than people."

"That so?"

"Especially the rain. But the wind, too. Last winter, I was over at JoAnn's party, and the group was quite lively...all laughing, drinking...you know...having a party. And the wind was blowing something fierce that night. It was March, I believe, quite cold. It seemed to me that the voices all faded out, and the wind took over, throwing its high-pitched howl straight at me." She paused.

"What did you do?"

"I listened...I listened to the wind. It spoke to me without words." Again she paused.

"What did it say?"

"It didn't say anything. It warned."

"Warned?"

"...warned me of my ways."

"I see."

Again, there was silence as the two watched the silver moon disappear and reappear again and again as the fast moving clouds slipped by just over the tree tops.

"Just like the trees and the moon and Oak Mountain...seem to be reaching out to me...trying to tell me something."

"Like what?"

"The secret."

"The secret?"

Melony smiled into the darkness. *"The secret is purpose.* The rain has purpose. The wind has purpose. The bees have purpose. The dew that settles in the night has purpose. The trees and the sun and the moon have purpose. Oak Mountain has purpose. And people need purpose."

Roxy was quiet.

"It took me a long time, Roxy, to find that out. I guess I'm a bit stubborn."

"More'n a bit."

She smiled. "You know something else I found out."

"What?"

"It was God speaking to me...speaking to me through his creation all the time."

Roxy remained still, afraid to interrupt.

"He's been calling me for some time. Do you remember the week before last when you and the girls had gone downtown. I had a headache and was lying down."

"I believe so."

"That's when it happened!"

"What happened?"

"Well, after you all had gone, I got up, went downstairs and out to the backyard. My head was hurting from the night before. But I had a purpose in what I was doing."

Roxy strained to see her in the dark.

"I sat down on that big rock under the tall Poplar tree

and stared out toward these here mountains. It was a clear day and their dark ridges stood out against the blue sky."

Roxy leaned forward.

"I started singing real quietly...'Lord, I'm coming home'. I didn't really know what I was doing or what I meant...but I knew I was turning my life over to Him."

Roxy wiped her eyes.

"I just kept on singing...'Lord, I'm coming home'. By then, the tears were streaming down my face...because I was so happy."

"Oh Mel!" Roxy jumped out of the swing and gave her a big hug.

"I don't believe it...I just don't believe it. The Good Lord's answered my prayers."

They began to laugh.

"Why didn't you tell me before?"

"Because I wanted to be sure...now I'm sure."

Roxy sat back down in the old swing, and pushed it happily. "So it was God's creation that did it!"

"That...and other things, too, of course. I've been running and searching for a long time. God's been dealing with me for some time. But the turning point was probably the night...it happened...."

"What happened?"

Melony sighed. "I've never told this to anybody...but then you're not just anybody."

Roxy waited.

"It was this winter. I was at a party and JoAnn got sick and left early. I didn't want to leave, so I stayed on. A friend of mine — or at least I thought he was — offered me a ride home. He did...only he made a stop on the way.

Well, not actually on the way. He drove us way out into the country somewhere."

"No!"

"He started making advances. I tried to stop him... but he wouldn't take no for an answer. He threatened to leave me there alone in the dark and cold."

"What did you do?"

"I was afraid...really afraid of being left there. He already had the door open...and it was so dark. I didn't even know where I was...so I...well, you know the rest."

"The rotten animal! Why didn't you tell me?"

"I was so humiliated...I couldn't tell anyone...not even you."

"Oh Mel...."

"And I figured I had it coming anyway."

"No Mel! He had no right!"

"Roxy, it wasn't as if I was a virgin...I certainly was no little innocent girl."

"No matter. You might've been running around acting crazy and such. But still he had no right...the scoundrel!"

"It's behind me now, Roxy. Sometimes, we have to get way down low before we look up, you know. And when you're forced against your will to...well, something changes within. All sorts of mixed-up feelings begin tumbling around inside, and you begin to seek answers. I realize now that he was definitely wrong. But I was wrong, too. I should never have allowed myself to be in such a position."

Roxy shook her head.

Melony reached over and patted her arm. "Don't worry, little Mama. Things are different now."

Chapter XIII
Winter Woods

It was three days before Thanksgiving and a light feathery snow was falling over Oak Mountain, but the tiny flakes quickly disappeared as soon as they touched the frozen ground. A few flakes managed to hold on longer to the hard, leathery leaves of the Rhododendrons. Prudence sat at the window watching this unmatched work of art and sipped her coffee. She loved the snow, but hoped it wouldn't get too bad.

She was so much looking forward to this Thanksgiving Dinner. The whole family would be here like old times. She tried not to get too excited as she reached for Mary Tom's letter again. She read it over to confirm it in her mind. *Before Thanksgiving!* She said they'd be home before Thanksgiving! Every time the phone rang, she jumped up with anticipation. Oh, she hoped they'd make it! She couldn't wait to see Mary Tom and Melony back together again...her girls. A sharp horn sounded outside, and she saw Spring pull up in her sports car and jump out, followed by two little bundled up creatures. She rushed to the door.

"Come in!"

They entered, brushing the snow off. "Oooh, it feels so good in here." Spring began to unravel Dakotah and Little Emily.

"Grandma?"

"Yes, Emily?" Pru was struggling to assist her with her leggings.

"Can we make oatmeal cookies...me and Dakotah?"

"Emily, your grandmother's got a lot to do before Thanksgiving," Spring chided. "By the way, have you gotten the turkey yet?"

"Oh dear, yes. Got it over a week ago."

"I should have known. Winn-Dixie has turkeys for twenty-nine cents a pound. Thought I'd pick one up if you hadn't."

"It's taking up most of the freezer now. But thanks for the thought."

"Hey, what do we have here...two pouting little girls?"

"It's okay, Spring. I promised them. I think we can fit some cookie making in."

Both Dakotah and Emily squealed with delight.

"Well, guess it does go with the weather."

"That's right. Remember how Mama always made cookies when it snowed?"

"I sure do."

"They behaving themselves?"

"They've been wonderful. In fact, I believe two's

easier than one. They play so well together. I actually had some time for myself."

Pru laughed. "You're right. Melony and Mary Tom always played so well together when they were little. Of course, they had their squabbles, but then all children do."

"Have you heard yet?"

"Not a thing. But she did say they'd be home before Thanksgiving."

"Well, we have three more days. How about David? Did Patrick say whether or not he's coming?"

"He expects him to come. I think he's doing some better."

Spring shook her head. "Poor David. He should never have gone over there."

"None of them should have been there. But that's war, Spring."

"I know, but David was always so sensitive. Vietnam was no place for him. He couldn't deal with the atrocities of such a place."

"I know. But time heals."

"Maybe. For some things. It has certainly helped me with losing my Dean. But David...he seems to be drifting further and further away from us."

"Patrick is concerned, I know. But, as I said, maybe in time...."

Spring got up abruptly and walked over to the window. "Yes, time helps.... I'm glad to be here with all of you during these upcoming holidays...."

Pru looked at her sadly.

"Oh my gosh!"

"What is it, Spring?"

"What they're doing!"

About that time, a blood-curdling squeal sounded from outside, and the hair rose on Spring's arm, but she stood glued to the window, unable to turn away from the oppressive sight.

"Oh, you mean the hog-killing?"

"Yes."

"I forgot how much you despise seeing it. You're not the only one. Melony hates it, too, and she'll be arriving any minute."

No sooner than she'd said it, Melony drove up and slowly parked. She turned the motor off and stared at the fatted hog dangling from the old Cherry tree where he was hoisted up by ropes until he almost touched the top of the stout limb that stretched out from the tree. He twisted and turned and squealed a frightened cry, trying to escape his dreadful fate. Melony decided to make a run for it. She jumped out, pulling her belongings with her and ran toward the house. Suddenly, there was that dreaded sound as the powerful, wooden sledge hammer banged into the old hog's head. The squealing ceased and silence followed for a few seconds as the men stood there witnessing what they'd done.

Melony stopped in her tracks, and looked, too.

"I don't believe it...and right here at Thanksgiving, too!" she yelled out.

They waved her off, and laughed at her foolishness. Clarence handed the large butcher knife to his close friend and neighbor, and Melony ran into the house.

Spring still watched as they slit the hog's throat. The men sat down on the rail fence to drink their coffee and watch the blood drain out. A couple of them proceeded to stuff tobacco in their pipes, light them and puff heartily as the sweet smelling tobacco mixed with the cold air. Spring watched the smoke circle above their heads while the blood oozed out of the old hog.

"I don't believe it! Why does Dad have to kill the hog right here at Thanksgiving...I'll never understand!" Melony yanked off her coat, throwing it over a chair.

"Melony, you know your father has to wait for the weather to get cold enough. It has to be good and cold."

"I know. I just hate seeing it. Hello, Aunt Spring."

"Hello to you, and I must say, I empathize with you."

Melony smiled and sat down at the table.

"Well, I don't see either one of you turning down the platter of ham on Thanksgiving day."

They looked at each other and laughed.

"And you know, I always found it intriguing to sneak into the smoke house, too," Melony added. "All those hams hanging up there never bothered me either. It's just the reality of it that upsets me when I witness it. I forgot about Dad doing it, frankly."

"And I forgot to mention it. Would you like some hot chocolate to warm up?"

"Sounds wonderful. Where are the girls?"

"They're upstairs playing. They've certainly had a great time together," Spring replied.

"I'm glad they can be together. It's good for them."

"I like seeing them close...like sisters...since they don't have one...either one of them," Pru added.

"No. But Emily certainly has a little friend in Laurietta. She talks about her constantly...."

"You're right, Spring," she looked at her mother.

"I think it's fine, too," Pru smiled.

"She's come a long way," Melony kidded.

"Well, you can't grow up in the south without your feelings being a little overshadowed by color. But, as I said, I'm glad Emily and Dakotah are close. Why, they're first cousins!"

"Not really, Pru."

"Of course they are, Spring. Don't talk like that. You're a Barrett, remember?"

Spring was quiet, not wishing to discuss her identity at this time. Why, she hardly knew herself who she was.

Pru rattled on, "I do hope Heath and Caroline will both show up. Ellen said they've been having more troubles lately."

She shook her head while reaching high into the cupboard for the mixing bowl. She pulled it down and called, "Emily...Dakotah...come along."

"We'll have these cookies underway sooner than you can say 'scat'."

The girls ran in, giggling between themselves.

"I wonder who Heath takes after?" Spring thought aloud. "He's not really like Jonathon or Jessica. Certainly has a mind of his own...."

"Well, that much is like Jonathon and also like Daddy. You remember, Spring, how much Daddy was like that."

"That's true. But the ambition part...that's what I'm speaking of mostly. He seems driven."

"I know. The others can't hold a candle to him. Paul and Mark still seem to be floundering a bit like most young folk. Even Esther can't make up her mind what she wants to do."

Melony leaned over the turkey, examining it. "What

else are we having?"

"The usual. Giblet gravy, mashed potatoes, cranberry sauce, yams, string beans, homemade rolls from Mama's recipe, pumpkin pie, chocolate cake and other things...."

"It's the 'other things' I like," Spring kidded.

The phone rang and they all looked at each other. "Hello," Pru answered anxiously.

"Mom!"

"Mary Tom!"

Spring's face lit up as Pru fought back the tears. Her daughter was coming home at last.

THANKSGIVING DAY ARRIVED clear and cool ...a perfect Thanksgiving. There was a tangible stillness upon Oak Mountain that lent itself to the contemplative mood that drifted throughout the old farmhouse. Pru was up early making ready the varied preparations; she was keenly aware of the abundant blessings bestowed upon them...she and her large family.

Clarence was getting dressed upstairs. She could hear him knocking around occasionally, trying not to awaken Mary Tom and her husband, Dan, who were still sleeping in her old room. Pru was sure they needed rest after that long, trying journey. She lifted the bountiful turkey, plopped him into the roaster, and while lavishing him with the rich, yellow butter, she awaited the rest of the family.

"Aunt Pru, we're here!" Esther called out as Patrick's family made their way in, loaded down with baskets and dishes covered with foil and cloth. They burst in, single file with Patrick pulling the door behind him.

"Looks like a great day for praising the Lord for His many blessings!" he stated cheerfully.

"You're right about that!" Pru agreed, pulling the tray of yams out of the oven. "Where's David?"

"He'll be here directly."

It wasn't long before the old farmhouse buzzed with chatter and gleeful play. The tables were set and already laden with part of its bounty. In addition to the large dining room table that had been in Clarence's family for numerous years, the more sought after kitchen table, painted many layers of white and trimmed in yellow, boasted of its wares already. Its oil cloth matched with a spray of yellow and white daisies intricately painted upon it. The little smiling daisies peeped from under bowls of gravy, platters of hot rolls and long slender cut glass dishes filled to the brim with crimson cranberry sauce. Lastly, was the miniature table that had belonged to Melony and Mary Tom when they were the age of Emily and Dakotah. Scratched and worn in places, it still had the same magic effect on children as they fought over who was to sit where.

"Roxy, I'm so glad you could come." Spring lifted Laurietta into her chair. "These three have such fun."

"Wouldn't have missed it for the world!" There was a gleam in her dark eyes.

"David, you're gonna sit in here, aren't you?" Ellen called out from the dining room.

Soon they were all seated. Chairs stopped scooting, laughter ceased, and Patrick rose from his seat at the head of the table. He moved over to the doorway between the dining room and the kitchen. All was still with only the crackle of the Pine in the fireplace popping occasionally.

"Let us give thanks to the one from whom all blessings flow." He bowed his greying head and all others followed.

"Our Heavenly Father, we come to thee as a family lifting up our hearts with thanksgiving for all the bountiful gifts you have seen fit to bestow upon us. Again, it has been a good year, and our hearts are grateful! Thank you for bringing our family back together again! We praise thy name, Oh Holy God...and we love you...in Jesus name."

Amens went up in unison.

Patrick sat down...but Melony rose silently from her place beside Mary Tom and eased over to the doorway. She swallowed hard, and began to speak... "On this special Thanksgiving of 1968, I would also like to say 'thank you' to God publicly for drawing me to Him over the past months and years actually. He's been speaking to me in many ways...and through many of you." She looked at Roxy and Patrick and her mother, and paused for a moment.

An aura of suspense hung in the air like the morning fog over Oak Mountain. All eyes were riveted on her.

"I have given my life to *Him*."

Silence followed momentarily, and then applause from both the dining room and kitchen broke out.

"Praise the Lord!" Pru whispered.

"And Sunday, Uncle Patrick, I'm gonna walk that

aisle of yours."

She looked over at Mary Tom and they exchanged smiles. Roxy sat back proudly, grinning from ear to ear. She watched the different faces of the Barrett household as they individually digested this sudden announcement along with their dinner. There was joy upon most, surprise on some, skepticism on others, and confusion upon the regal face of Spring.

Everyone settled down to enjoy the feast before them, as the fine china, painted with delicate blue flowers, floated before them, steaming with the Thanksgiving Dinner.

"This reminds me of Thanksgiving when we were children," Jonathon reminisced, "except we didn't have turkey."

"What did you have?" Esther called from the kitchen.

"Why, Mama always had a nice hen...and we were just as happy with that hen as we are now with this here turkey," Pru replied.

"I think more so," Patrick added.

"Well, it does my heart good to see us all together here at this season. If Mama and Daddy are watching...I know they're happy," Pru declared softly.

Clarence and Patrick nodded in agreement. And so did Ellen, Jessica, and Jonathon. Heath and Caroline remained quiet while slowly eating their meal. Pru noticed David's hand shaking as he lifted his fork.

The kitchen group was a bit livelier.

"Well, Aunt Spring, how do you like your mountain house?" Paul asked nonchalantly.

"You mean our tipi?" she grinned.

He laughed. "Cool."

"It is my tipi and my mama's," Dakotah stated emphatically.

"Just like her mom," he winked at Spring.

"Have you seen it, Paul?" Melony asked.

"Not yet."

"He's too busy with his social life," Esther kidded.

"Come on, folks. My social life isn't nearly as lively as Mark's here."

"Leave me out'a this," Mark mumbled with his jaws filled with potatoes.

"Well, Paul, you should see it," Melony continued, "especially the living room...with its full size paintings."

"I might have guessed. What has she painted now?" he asked, prepared for the next ten minutes of painting discussions. Melony just couldn't brag enough about Aunt Spring's paintings. He grinned at Mark as she proceeded to do just that.

Spring concluded, "Well, they're not nearly finished. You might want to wait to see the finished product, Paul."

"Sounds good to me."

"Mary Tom, you're awfully quiet," Melony inquired. She'd noticed her contemplative mood for the last few minutes.

"I'm sorry. I've just been thinking about what I read in the morning paper...about that teenager that died in Germany. It was just so...so awful."

Roxy looked up suddenly. "I saw it, too. I just can't believe people could be so blind."

"Well, what happened?" Paul asked impatiently. "Who reads the paper on Thanksgiving Day?"

Mary Tom looked at Roxy...and Roxy began. "It

happened just Monday. The paper said for nearly four hours the border guards from East and West Germany stood by and watched a poor little teenage boy bleed to death in a piece of land called no-man's land. Seems it was filled with mines...and his legs were blown off when he tried to escape from communism. He was only˙ sixteen years old, too."

"How utterly horrible!" Melony gasped.

Mary Tom picked up the story, "And the guards said they heard his cries...agonizing cries from a boy. He was crying, 'Help...You East Germans...get me out of here...I've done nothing wrong...I'm just sixteen years old...I don't want to die'!"

"And they did nothing?" Paul asked in disbelief.

"That's right," Mary Tom continued. "He had stepped on mines and lost his two legs. The paper said the West German guard moved up to the fence and looked into the death trap. He saw East German guards with pistols standing at the other fence. The boy was pleading... 'Get me to a hospital...my legs are blown off!' Seems the poor boy pleaded first with the one side and then the other for help...but nobody helped him...and he died."

Everyone was quiet for a few seconds. Then Roxy summed it up in her calm, sad voice..."War is a cruel answer to man's greed." She wiped her eyes with her napkin.

Back in the dining room, the mood was also subdued.

"Caroline, do you feel okay today?" Ellen asked. "You look a mite peaked."

She looked up suddenly. "Fine, Mrs. Barrett, just fine," but the tremble in her soft voice suggested otherwise.

"Heath, my boy," Clarence boomed, "Understand you're getting into politics?"

"Well, Uncle Clarence, if you want to call it that. I'm considering a post in D.C."

"The big city of Washington D.C., huh? How do you feel about that, young lady?" he addressed Caroline.

"It's fine," she practically whispered.

Heath wiped his mouth. "I have some friends that are there, and I feel this might be the most opportune time for me."

"How is your mother going to get along without you?" Ellen kidded with a smile in Jessica's direction.

He smiled at her, too.

Jessica, still a beauty at middle age, spoke defiantly, "I'll just have to go along."

"None of that, My Dear." Jonathon patted her hand.

"Well, with Nixon in the White House, I don't know what to expect."

Everyone looked at Clarence.

"What do you mean by that, Dear?" Pru questioned while passing the rolls.

"I don't rightly know, but the man's got guts. He won't give up for sure."

"That's true. Look how many times he's lost...but he keeps coming back," Ellen added.

"Well, I for one am certainly glad that Humphrey didn't get in," Heath stated.

"Or Governor Wallace!" Jessica spoke up.

"It certainly was a narrow win...but a win...that's what counts." Clarence continued, "I hope he'll bring our boys back home and bring an end to this ridiculous war."

David looked up momentarily.

Pru quickly added, "But you know what I like about Nixon...he's worked hard in his life. I read he started working part-time as a bean picker when he was only ten. You can't find fault with that."

"Like I said, I hope he'll work as hard bringing peace," Clarence concluded.

As the conversation drifted from D.C. to Ellen's new kittens, Pru watched David eating quietly. What could she say to him?

"David, do you remember the Thanksgiving years ago when you grew all those pumpkins...and one of them weighed almost a hundred pounds?"

He smiled. "I do."

"Have you ever topped that one?"

"I don't grow pumpkins anymore," he answered flatly.

All eyes on him, his hand began to shake more rapidly and his face flushed a crimson red.

"We have pumpkin pie for dessert!" Ellen intercepted. "Made from my grandmother's recipe."

"We sure do...," Pru added, "and chocolate cake and jello and banana pudding."

Jonathon laid his fork down. "Better save room for that!"

Laughter echoed from the kitchen.

"Sounds like the young folks are enjoying themselves." Patrick pushed his chair back.

The half-eaten chocolate cake sat on the cupboard and the empty pumpkin pie dish signaled an end to the sumptuous meal as the hum of female voices filled the warm kitchen, and the clean up process began.

The little ones were put down for their much needed naps and the grown-ups were basking in the quiet aftermath.

"What a meal!" Clarence bragged, stretching out in his favorite living room chair, the dilapidated green vinyl recliner.

Jonathon joined the younger guys outside in a game of softball. The adjoining field to the farmhouse had long been an inviting place to run off an over abundant meal and to escape awaiting dishes.

"I think we've got more help than we need," Pru joked while maneuvering around Mary Tom and Ellen, who were bringing stacks of dishes in from the dining room. The fragile china cups teetered atop the mound of stacked dishes Ellen balanced with one hand.

"You don't have to convince me. I'm gone," Melony teased while tossing her dishcloth into the sink. Roxy followed her outside.

"If you don't mind, Roxy, I'm going for a walk... alone...in the woods." She pulled her heavy woolen sweater over her head.

"I like you, too," she kidded as Melony strode off toward the darkened Pines. Roxy didn't notice Caroline sitting alone on the porch at first.

"Why, hello Caroline...such a beautiful Thanksgiving!"

Caroline looked up surprised.

"Mind if I join you?"

"Help yourself."

She sat down in a rocker beside her and commenced

to slowly rock back and forth in silence. She figured
she'd give her a chance to talk if she had a mind to, for
it certainly looked as if she had something weighing
mighty heavy upon her.

"Life's funny." The soft voice broke the silence after
a while.

"Excuse me?"

"How things work out."

"You're right about that."

"What is happiness anyway?" The lovely young girl
tossed the profound question out to the universe.

Roxy didn't reply.

"Is it a new home...a new car...a prized husband...
who can define happiness?"

"Maybe a peace of mind," Roxy gently added.

Caroline turned to look at this dark stranger for the
first time and sensed a sincerity there.

"Maybe you're right."

"You know, the Good Book says, 'He will keep him in
perfect peace, whose mind is stayed on Him'."

"But how can you do that?"

"Now, I'm not gonna say it's easy. It's something you
have to work on. But when something's troubling us, we
need to turn to Him, talk to Him, think about Him...it
works. He gives a peace in the midst of the storm."

Caroline was quiet...sitting still in the rocker.

Roxy spoke softly..."You know I've had my troubles...and I'm a good listener."

"You think I have troubles...," she laughed aloud,
but the laugh was filled with bitterness.

"Maybe not...but sometimes it helps a body to talk
things out."

"You wouldn't understand...you couldn't. You with that beautiful little girl in there...to love...to cherish... how could you understand my feelings?"

"My goodness. You're young yet. The good Lord will give you a child in his own good time. We have to learn to wait on Him."

Tears welled up in her big blue eyes. "It's too late!" She got up and walked away.

THE WOODS WERE SILENT at first as Melony stepped down the worn path through the Pines, beneath the mighty Oaks, straight Poplars and slick-barked wild Cherries. The tall, barren trees swayed gently in the slight mountain breeze, creating an ever so soft humming and a slight rustle every now and then. She noticed the familiar decaying fence that must have been there a hundred years, and she reached out to touch its ruggedness.

She recalled how many times she'd run down this path as a child hiding from Mary Tom. She thought, too, of the times she'd escaped her teenage sorrows by coming to the woods to be alone...to think. She inhaled the cool November air and stretched out her arms. There was something special about this place. There was something special about Oak Mountain!

But there was something elusive about these woods in the winter time. She couldn't quite put her finger on it. The colorless forest that it became held a certain aura. What was it?

Oh, she loved the woods in the fall when the leaves made their heavenly descent, and she loved them in the spring when they burst forth with new life. And even the summer woods invited her often to bask in its coolness on a hot, torrid day. But winter?

What was it about winter? She kicked at the leaves already forming a new layer of earth and inhaled the pungent earthy fragrance. She sat down on a tree trunk to listen to the stillness, and the woods reached out to her....

Winter Woods

Tall skeletons of once vibrant trees
Reach for the overcast sky
Their branches shiver void of leaves
Their stark nakedness cries

The Evergreens' fullness now presides
And boasts of its bounty exalted
For winter is here, much to its pride
Each year, a time awaited

The earth is frozen, covered with remnants
Crisp and crushed is their fate
Silence prevails, its whisper haunts
Seeking life, it reigns and waits

Yet hope lingers midst winter woods
Through rains, snow and hail
And steals through ravines, up hilly woods
Casting its elusive spell

But inevitably, its spark will ignite
As if by an unseen hand
Creatures will waken, buds delight
And spring will return again!

That night, Spring looked out her upstairs bedroom window and watched the shadows in the half moon. She read again Melony's poem, *Winter Woods*, and sat down remembering Mama.

Mama loved to write down her feelings, too. She guessed Melony took after her. She got up and walked over to Dakotah's room and pushed the door ajar. She was sleeping soundly after such an eventful day. Spring leaned over and kissed her softly on her cheek. The small child never stirred. Spring's heart filled with love, and she tiptoed out. What was it about holidays that made one feel lonely? She missed Dean so. She missed Mama. She missed Daddy.

THE STATELY OLD HOUSE on Madison Street cast its over-powering shadows, complete with its circular turret, in the silver rays of the half moon. Melony and Roxy carried their sleeping charges up the wide sidewalk, the end of a full and joyous Thanksgiving Day. Suddenly Roxy stopped in her tracks.

"Mel!"

"What is it?"

"Sh-h-h," she hushed her while trying to point toward the little house out back. Her hands occupied, she motioned with her head, but Melony didn't grasp her meaning, and the shadows obscured her vision.

"What is it?" she repeated.

"The light...did you see it?"

Melony strained to see in the darkness.

"What light?"

"It's gone...but it was there."

"Roxy...."

"Now come on, Mel. I tell you I saw it." She followed her up the steps and into the house. "It's that ghost again!"

They laid the girls down with their clothes on, too tired to awaken from their exhausted sleep.

"I tell you, I saw it."

Melony turned and looked at her, "Okay, so you did. Come on. We're gonna find out once and for all." She pulled her coat back on.

Roxy stood planted to the floor, her large eyes growing larger.

"What you talking about?"

"We're going down there and take a look."

"Mel, you done lost your mind!"

"Nope. I'm tired of this ghost thing popping up every time I think it's gone. Are you coming or not?"

"No ma'am."

Melony started toward the door.

"Mel, you can't go down there alone!"

"Well then, come on."

Roxy just stood there, and Melony opened the door.

"Wait...I'm coming."

She grabbed her coat and followed Melony down the creaking stairs. Quietly closing the heavy front door behind them with its loose glass rattling, the cold night air met them. The two young women, wrapped in their winter garb, crept stealthily around the side of the imposing house.

The dew clad Iris stalks left over from summer felt wet against their legs. As they approached the cottage, or carriage house, as some called it, although Roxy knew it to be former slave quarters, all was dark. The glow of the moon lit their way before them, but unfortunately exposed their secret figures. A door closed silently.

A screech owl could be heard in the distance. Roxy hovered close behind Melony as they reached the ivy-covered brick wall. Melony strained to see in the high window. All was black within.

Roxy screamed!

Melony fell backwards upon her, knocking her to the ground. Quickly, they scrambled to their feet, and grabbing hands, half ran, half climbed the hill before them, trying to make it back to the house. The wet grass became a treacherous enemy, causing them to slip and fall more than once. Frightened and cold, they reached the side porch.

Melony gasped, "What was it?"

"I don't know. Something touched my leg!"

Quietly, they stood there staring down at the little house that had suddenly become sinister in the moonlight. All was still.

"Meow...meow."

They looked down at a scrawny stray cat.

"Don't tell me!"

Roxy looked at Melony in the dark. "How was I to know?"

They broke out in laughter, and the stray cat continued to rub against their wet legs.

But after the others were asleep that night, Roxy lay still in her bed, listening to the silence. She saw the *light* again in her mind, and a chill ran down her spine. Something was wrong...awfully wrong in the little house down the hill.

THE DAYS AND WEEKS AND MONTHS rolled down the path of time on Oak Mountain practically unnoticed, except for an occasional winter storm. The Barrett family quietly witnessed the changing world around them, voicing their opinions at the regular get-togethers. However, in the year 1969, there were two exceptions.

On that eventful day of July twentieth, there was much ado in the Barrett household along with most of the households in the great land of America. MAN HAD LANDED ON THE MOON!

The television set at Pru's homeplace was aimed at its riveted audience, and each face glowed with excitement. Intent on every move, their eyes followed the legendary Neil Armstrong as he took that historic step and said, "That's one small step for a man, one giant leap for mankind." A hushed reverence fell over the room. Only the coffee pot could be heard still perking.

Jonathon broke the silence, "I'm proud to be an American!"

Pru wiped her eyes with her apron, and Patrick spoke up, "Why don't we have a silent prayer to thank God."

All heads bowed, down to the youngest...even Dakotah.

A few weeks later, Hurricane Camille smashed into the states, violently hitting seven of them, including Virginia, and carrying with it a deadly force that claimed over two hundred fifty lives. Many of those who perished had lived their lives midst the Blue Ridge Mountains and the fertile valleys that wove around and about them. Oak Mountain was spared this time. But its neighboring ridges wept for its lost.

It was a time that brought haunting memories quickly to the surface for the Barrett household. Patrick, Prudence, Jonathon, and Spring reached out to the hurting with vivid memories of the dreadful flood that had swept them up in its monstrous arms many years before. They remembered little Charity. Rumblings could be heard on Oak Mountain for some time afterwards.

"...You go fooling around up there...and this is what you get...ought not to be trying to act like God...got no business up there...."

History was made that year in 1969. Those famous words spoken by Neil Armstrong were recorded in the history books and encyclopedias...and the last words of many loved ones were forever implanted in the minds of those that lived and lost.

Chapter XIV
Wounded Knee

Spring finished reading the newspaper and tossed it on the floor. What next? Things were coming to a head one way or the other. Ever since they'd marched on Washington, there had been trouble. She couldn't blame AIM. She could appreciate what they stood for, although they might be going about it a little too aggressively.

She recalled her conversation with Patrick last week. He was definitely against The American Indian Movement, claiming it to be a rebellious outfit and not to be encouraged. But what did he know? So it had grown out of the urban ghetto, it stood on principles that were right...principles she'd fought for all her life.

She got up, walked across her bedroom, and stood looking out over Oak Mountain, feeling that familiar unrest that had been overshadowing her lately. The windows were frosted with tiny ice particles as the cold mountain air met suddenly with the warmed window panes. Today was February the first, and Spring felt good that at least they were on a downhill slide now. She couldn't wait for winter to end.

She must get busy and awaken Dakotah for school, but still she paused, thinking of the turmoil going on out west. If only that Indian hadn't been murdered by the white man...maybe things would have settled down. But then, did she really want things to settle down? This was getting the attention of people, people all the way back here in the east even. Wasn't that enough? The wind increased and brushed the leaning Pine against the window. She better get going.

She pulled up to the old school.
"Give Mommy a kiss good-bye."
Dakotah leaned over and planted a big kiss on her cheek and then jumped out of the car, pulling her large book bag behind her. As she trudged through the week old snow that was now brown and dirty, Spring's heart went out to her. So tiny she seemed, walking up to the large red brick school house. When she reached the tall doors, she turned and waved back to her. Spring threw her a kiss, and then she disappeared behind those stone walls. Each day that she dropped her off, she felt a pang of sadness, remembering her own pain when she'd been in school so many years ago, and how the other kids had made fun of her. She wondered if Dakotah experienced any of the same thing. Of course, a lot had changed since then, but not everything. She'd tried tactfully to find out by her subtle questions, but Dakotah never revealed a

thing — if there *was* anything.

She sat there watching the other children as they filed into the old school house...some white, others black. But Dakotah was the only one of her kind here...and she knew all too well how people reacted to that. Was she making a mistake? Again her mind began to weave through the pros and cons of staying on Oak Mountain. Maybe it would be better to take Dakotah back to her own people now that she was older and in school. She wouldn't feel different...and she would benefit from the knowledge that she was one member of a big family...one member of the great Sioux nation. How would she ever know that here? Did she want her to grow up like *her*...balanced on a thin line between two peoples...never able to choose between them.

As she drove down the winding mountain road, her thoughts took another turn. There he was again! Toh-kah!

Her heart still raced when she thought of him. She'd decided to call him Toh-kah many years ago. It seemed to fit him. As he struggled for his hidden identity, she would confirm his position...eek-CHAY-we-CHOSH-tah, TOH-kah...American Indian...but TOH-kah for short.

In the five years since she'd been back on Oak Mountain, she'd only seen him once, and that had been over a year ago now...but it seemed like yesterday. She had been grocery shopping, and her hands were loaded down with items while standing in the cashier's line. She looked up and found herself staring once again into those deep set eyes. Caught off guard, she stood there like a school girl unable to speak. So they just stared at each other until a young girl grabbed hold of his arm and whisked him away.

"Come on, Daddy...we'll be late."

She'd placed the groceries on the counter absently and wrote out her check with difficulty, while her mind raced backwards in time. She walked out of the store in a daze. But the sudden rainstorm brought her back to reality, and she ran through the cool wet rain to her car. Straightening her dampened skirt, she settled back behind the wheel. Directly in front of her was a scene that would forever be indelibly imprinted upon her mind.

He was leaning over a lady in a wheelchair, his wife apparently. She was a fragile-looking creature, but very beautiful in an angelic sort of way. Though not so young anymore, her face still wore a girlish look, especially with that soft blonde hair framing it. She looked up at him with adoration as he maneuvered the chair toward the car door while trying to hold a large black umbrella over her at the same time. A young boy of about seven opened the door to the late model sedan while the teenaged girl she'd seen earlier jumped in the other side. Then she saw a third child, a girl somewhere between the other two, already in the car.

She watched him lift the lady out of the wheelchair and into the front seat of the car, dropping the umbrella in the process. The pretty lady reached up and wiped his wet forehead and gently kissed him on the cheek.

The family drove off in the rain, and Spring sat there feeling very alone. There was an emptiness within her. Many years ago, she had realized that she'd made a mistake. As the years rolled by and she couldn't shake that feeling, she knew. And now, seeing him had erased all those years, and the old stored away sentiments came tumbling out...filling her emptiness.

But what about Dean? She felt somewhat a traitor toward him as she experienced those old familiar feelings. But no...she had loved Dean...only differently. Her dear sweet Dean. But Toh-kah was her first love — a fleeting one for sure — but a lasting one. She could still feel his presence there on Oak Mountain as she painted *The Dogwoods*...even after all these years.

She turned the ignition and watched the wipers swing back and forth. Life was funny. But maybe it was fate...maybe it was meant to be. Certainly, he would be the one for such a wife...with his gentle ways. And Spring Barrett didn't need that! She was strong! She laughed out loud...and then a lone tear escaped her reservoir.

Pulling out onto the highway, a tractor trailer flew past, throwing muddy water all over her windshield, and for a split second, she was helpless...unable to see. But the faithful wipers did their job and once again, the highway appeared. Ironic as it was, this scenario revealed her plight. Seeing him once again had briefly caused her to lose sight of herself. But no, she wouldn't wallow in self pity. She had Dakotah; she had a purpose.

Now, as she drove through the wintry weather, recalling that day, it sealed her decision. Her life wasn't meant to be one of comfort and cherishing. She'd been born into hardships and most likely, she would leave this life still fighting...still alone. Those brief happy years with Dean had been an escape, a time of refuel...and

they had provided her with her legacy...Dakotah. But
her life must be one of purpose as it had always
been...even though sometimes she almost lost sight of
it. Her people were her purpose. She would go back to
South Dakota...to the Black Hills.

"BUT SPRING, I THOUGHT you were happy here!"
She looked at Pru, her dear sister. "I was, Pru. I was
as much as possible. But as I said, I believe Dakotah
needs to be with her own."
"We are her people, too."
"Of course you are."
"Little Emily will certainly be lost."
"I know...and that's the hardest part. But, Pru, I
have to do what I have to do."
"I know, Spring. You always have."
They smiled understandingly at each other.
"What about the tipi?"
"I will keep it, of course. I will always keep it."
"I surely hope so. Maybe you can rent it?"
"Not just yet, maybe later."
"Well, we'll look after it the best we can."
"Maybe Melony and Roxy can go up occasionally for
some rest and solitude."
"They'd love that for sure. And you're leaving when?"
"In a couple of weeks."
"Two weeks!"
"Two weeks what?" Clarence asked coming into the
kitchen for a cup of coffee.
Prudence hesitated..."Spring and Dakotah...are leav-
ing us in two weeks...going back to South Dakota."
"What kinda tom-foolery is this?"

Spring stood firmly, "It is something I feel I must do, Clarence."

"Wouldn't by any chance have anything to do with this fighting going on out there, would it?"

"Maybe."

"Well, you better think about Dakotah. You know fighting's no place for a little girl. Anyway, I wouldn't want to get mixed up with that group that's making all the fuss. I've wondered about them ever since they took over the headquarters of the Bureau of Indian Affairs in Washington last year. I don't hold for such doings."

Spring bit her tongue. "Well, Clarence, I didn't know you were such an authority on Indian affairs."

"Now you two. We might as well drop the subject," Pru intervened. "We know we don't agree on certain things. But the subject at hand is your departure. I at least thought you'd wait 'till school's out."

"We will be gone before the *Moon when the frost covers the prairie chickens' eyes.*"

"Now what kinda riddle is that supposed to be?" Clarence asked a bit irritated.

"No riddle, Clarence," Spring smiled. "It means the month of March."

True to her word, Spring and Dakotah were in South Dakota within two weeks.

FEBRUARY 28, 1973...the six o'clock news reported on Oak Mountain a new Indian War at Wounded Knee. Pru and Clarence listened in astonishment!

"I'm gonna call Spring!" She rose to her feet, pulling the afghan after her.

"Wait...let's hear the rest."

The news report went on to describe briefly that a large group of armed Indians, including AIM Members, had seized the village of Wounded Knee, South Dakota where the U.S. Cavalry had massacred more than two hundred Sioux over eighty years ago. They were barricaded against the police.

"What on earth! I'm calling Spring."

She listened to the shrill ring on the other end until it was vibrating in her head.

"Where could she be?"

Clarence looked up but remained silent.

She dialed again.

"Who're you calling now?"

"Patrick."

He shook his head.

"Patrick, did you hear the news? You did! What did you think?"

Patrick's voice seemed a bit tired on the other end. "What do you mean, Pru?"

"Well, I'm concerned...you know, about Spring and Dakotah. I called her but got no answer."

"I'm sure they'll be home directly. Why don't you wait 'till later and try again?"

"Well, I plan to. I'll talk to you later," she hung up and dialed Spring again. The phone still rang. Off and on throughout the evening, she called and always the phone rang. Spring didn't answer.

"Come on to bed, Hon. I'm sure there's a perfectly good reason why she's not answering. They've probably gone to a movie. Come on and get some sleep. You can call her first thing in the morning."

She carefully placed the receiver back on the phone,

and went to bed, but she couldn't shake that foreboding feeling. She knew they were not blood sisters, but there was something stronger between them...and she knew when her sister was in trouble. Where was she?

THOUSANDS OF MILES away from Oak Mountain, away from the Blue Ridge, across wide open plains, in the little village of Wounded Knee that was now surrounded by police, sat Spring huddled on the ground as the night air pierced through her heavy jacket. She pulled the earlaps of her cap down firmly over her cold ears and blew circles of hot air into the frosty night. Dakotah sat beside her and smiled up at her, enjoying every minute of it.

Had she done the right thing? Was it wise to bring Dakotah along? But she must learn soon of such things. She was not too young. And wasn't this just what she'd envisioned many times in her life...a chance to speak out to the nation? Listen America! We have something to say!

She witnessed the excitement among the mix of people that surrounded her...young Indians, old ones, mixed bloods, even white people...but they all shared the common spirit that flowed through the camp. A spirit of freedom...a spirit of control...a spirit that had been lost for many years. She reached over and pulled the scarf more tightly around Dakotah's neck. She must not catch cold. Suddenly there were gunshots.

"What do you suppose that is?" she asked the elderly man beside her.

"Coming from that road block the Marshal's got set up out there."

"I don't think so. It's not from the direction of the roadblock. I believe it's coming from our side."

"It is, Ma'am," a young, hippy-looking character affirmed as he eased over toward them. "They're just giving a little warning when them cars come too close to the village, that's all."

"I see. You don't look even a little bit Indian. What's your cause?"

"Same as your'n, Ma'am. Just got back from 'Nam ...and don't have much patience with injustice."

Spring half smiled at him and turned to Dakotah. "Come along, Honey; it's getting too cold out here."

The next morning, Pru anxiously grabbed the newspaper from the box and hurriedly read the headlines while stumbling back to the house.

'INDIANS, MARSHAL EXCHANGE GUNFIRE...'.

"Clarence," she called coming into the warm kitchen, "listen to this!"

He stopped in the doorway and commenced to blow his nose into the overlarge handkerchief.

"Oh Clarence, listen!"

"I'm listening." He continued to blow.

"It says here that the Indians are in charge of the town...and hostages are there...and roadblocks are up...oh my!"

"Did you get in touch with Spring?"

"No...still no answer. Clarence, I'm worried."

"Now, Pru. Your sister is a grown woman...a little strange perhaps...but she is a grown woman, and she can take care of herself." He smiled, "In fact, I'm sure of that."

"Says here that the hostages are all from one family...nine of them that is...and a Roman Catholic priest...if that don't beat all!"

She continued reading aloud, "They're demanding to see Senator Edward Kennedy and another fellow... they want to discuss the Indians' grievances. Oh my, sounds just like something Spring would be in the middle of!"

Later in the day, Patrick stopped by.

"Still haven't gotten in touch with her?"

"No, and I've been calling every hour on the hour. Patrick, something's wrong. I feel it in my bones."

"We don't want to jump to conclusions, Pru. Spring has a level head...most of the time."

"Yes, except when it comes to this Indian stuff."

He picked up the paper lying on the table. "Seems their demands are reasonable. They're just asking for an investigation of the Bureau of Indian Affairs...to see how they've been handling things...and they want to be able to elect their own officials. Seems fair to me."

"I know. But why go to such extremes to accomplish it?"

"Sis, there's a lot we don't understand about the Indian nation that Spring does. She more than understands it...her heart beats with its rhythm."

"I know that. They're saying that the government has two choices...either to attack them and wipe them out like they did in 1890...or they can negotiate their demands."

MEANWHILE, SPRING was being drawn deeper and deeper into the conflict. There was talk of the women and children leaving Wounded Knee without repercussions from the F.B.I. and Marshals waiting outside. But Spring's mind was made up. As she sat outside of the small bungalow that she and Dakotah shared with a number of other women and children, she listened to the intermittent firing and struggled with the internal fight going on within her. What about Dakotah's safety? But she wanted more than anything to take her stand here for what she believed...and if there were no cause...no purpose...then what did Dakotah have to look forward to?

"Ma'am, you're mighty brave to be here in a place like this."

She turned to a man who looked to be in his sixties, and he smiled his toothless smile at her.

"Sure is an eerie feeling in this place," he talked on. "Never thought I'd be held up here. I been struck with this place ever since I was a boy. My grandfather died here at the massacre. When I hear them guns a'firing, I wonder if I'm gonna join him in that grave yonder."

"I don't think so," Spring stared at him, "but I know what you mean by the feeling. I've been feeling it, too. Sort of like we're connected to the past in an elusive way...and if we leave here, we'll lose it. It's a oneness."

"You got a nice way with words, Ma'am. I been thinking, too. In all my sixty-odd years, I don't ever recollect seeing so many tribes together in one place and all seeming to get along so."

"*Unity*. That's the word." Spring's voice rose, "Why can't we have this spirit of unity outside of Wounded Knee? Just think what it could mean?"

"Don't know how it could ever be. Our people been fightin' among themselves ever since the beginning of time most likely." He rubbed his dry, parched hands together. "Gettin' colder. Think I'll turn in. Nice talking to you."

Spring extended her hand and clasped his cold, gnarled one. She rose to go back in, noticing the drop in temperature, also. She quickly closed the fragile door behind her to shut out the cold and walked over to Dakotah, who was rousing from her nap on the makeshift pallet on the floor. She picked up the spelling book beside her.

"Time for your studies."

Dakotah winced, "Do we have to, Mommy?"

"Of course we do. Can't get behind now, can we?"

She shoved the book in front of her, and Dakotah began reciting the words automatically. An old lady stood watching in the corner, and slowly limped over.

"What'ya doing?" she asked abruptly.

"Homework."

"Homework?"

"Yes, my daughter, Dakotah here, must not get behind in her work."

The old woman steadily held her gaze.

"So we're studying."

"What?"

"Right now, spelling."

"Where'd you get the book?"

"A friend...a relative...brought it last night. She is very brave...though she's a mixed blood."

"Lot of mixed bloods here now."

"You're right." Spring began to warm up to the old woman. "And it's good for them...and good for us. We will learn from each other."

The old woman smiled, "You're smart lady."

"Thank you."

"Look, I'm moving out'a here. Too crowded. I found an old tipi up in the attic today. Gonna put it up. If it works, you and the little one here can join me if you like."

Spring thought quickly. What an opportunity for Dakotah!

"We would love to. I'll help you. I know a little about tipis."

FIVE DAYS HAD PASSED since the siege occurred. Pru read the newspaper anxiously to Clarence.

"Says here...a team of lawyers met with the Indians on Saturday and tried to work out a compromise. Also says that the AIM leader is urging the Indians...about two hundred of them...not to waste their shots. They think they're running low on ammunition. Clarence, I don't think I can wait any longer. We've gotta do something. This here just sitting and waiting is getting to me. I'm gonna call again."

The phone rang as usual.

Pru was startled to hear a strange voice on the other end.

"Who is this?" she questioned.

"Mareen," a soft voice replied.

"Mareen?"

"Yes, who's calling?"

"Prudence...Prudence Barrett Moore...and I'm calling for my sister, Spring. Is she there?"

"Oh, you're Spring's sister in Virginia. Well, I'm sorry...but Spring isn't here."

"Where is she?" Pru could hear her own voice

shaking.

"She's...well, she's detained right at this time...."

"She's at that place called Wounded Knee...isn't she?"

"Yes Ma'am, she is. But she's okay...both she and Dakotah are fine."

"Oh my! Dakotah's with her?"

"Yes Ma'am, but as I said, they're both okay."

"How do you know?"

"Well, I have ways of knowing."

"Why are you there now?"

"Actually, I was collecting a few items for them. You see, there are those who steal quietly into the camp at night and carry supplies to them. That's how I know."

"I see. Can we stay in touch with you? We've known nothing until now."

"Of course. Give me your number, and I'll keep you updated. I'm sure Spring would like that...and don't worry. They will be fine."

Pru hung up repeating those words...*don't worry.* How can anybody not worry when their own kin are right smack in the middle of a civil war!

During Sunday dinner, the conversation, of course, centered on Spring and Dakotah and Wounded Knee as the winter winds beat at the windows.

"What can we do?" asked Jessica aloud.

"Pray...pray for their safety...that's all," Patrick replied.

"Poor little Dakotah...I can't believe she would actually take her into such a situation!" Ellen pronounced.

"I can," Jonathon retorted. "We fail to remember

that even though Spring was part of us, a part of her was never with us."

"We've gotta do something," Pru added with concern.

"I'm going to write a letter."

Every head turned to Patrick.

"Who to?" asked Jonathon.

"To the Senator...of South Dakota. I'll express our concerns."

"Just what good do you think that will do?" Clarence spoke up.

"Maybe none...maybe some."

SPRING LOADED THE RIFLE that had been given to her, and fought off the fears that plagued her. The situation was grave now, and she wondered what to do. She didn't want to leave...but she must protect Dakotah!

The negotiations were off, and the women of the village were having to decide whether or not to stay. She had never heard so much shooting from both sides. It was frightening!

The women were making their decisions...to lay down their lives for the cause. She was willing...oh... was she willing! But Dakotah?

"I've never been one for violence," the young man next to her said softly.

"We must be prepared," she answered a bit curtly.

"Now that the deadline has passed," he continued, "we can all be arrested...you know...when we surrender. Don't reckon they'll arrest all of us."

"Don't reckon," she repeated.

"You don't talk much like a Sioux." He eyed her curiously.

"You don't either."
"I'm Cheyenne."
"I see."

The fighting lifted once again. Negotiations re-opened, and Spring breathed a little easier. But howling snow storms hit the midwest on March fourteenth, piling drifts as high as ten feet and paralyzing parts of the Dakotas. The negotiations were stalled once again between the federal authorities and the Indians. Roads in the area were impassable with five inches of snow on the ground and very deep drifting. The cold, wet snow piled up against the tipi, creating a warmth inside that surprised Spring.

This was what it was like in the old days, she thought as Dakotah slept beside her. She'd never felt so *cozy* before. Truly the old woman knew her 'stuff' about tipis ...and Dakotah loved every minute of it.

Spring listened to the wind howling outside as it whipped at the sturdy old tipi. If only she could have a cup of hot chocolate and a large piece of Mama's home-made bread just now. She wrapped herself in her blanket and nostalgia. Mama always gave them hot chocolate and bread on those cold wintry nights. But no chance for that now. The supplies were quite low. Too low for comfort.

"Do you think we'll be getting supplies soon?" she asked the old woman who was busy working on some piece of beaded art.

"Wak-KON-ton-kah will not let us down."

Spring smiled. "You remind me of my mother. That's what she used to say...only she called Him God."

"You see, it is not such a big difference between us."

She nodded. "Each wants the same thing...to live in peace...but their ways conflict...."

"The white man feared our *Ghost Dance*...that it would prevent their peace...their progress."

"And the Indian feared the white man, of course...."

"The Ghost Dance was a hope...a hope of a fallen people...the hope that the white man would disappear and the buffalo return."

"But it was because of the Ghost Dance that there was a Wounded Knee."

"True," the old woman sighed. "You know I live here in this village for many years. I just move away a year ago when my brother died and left me his place."

"Why did you come back?"

"I don't know...I guess because I feel it is a part of me...Wounded Knee has always felt like a part of me... and I am now an old woman...not too many years left on this land. I believe in this cause. I believe the white man should honor our treaty...."

"The Treaty of 1868?"

"Yes, the treaty signed at Fort Laramie. They should honor it."

"You mean by returning the Black Hills?"

"The Black Hills belong to us, and have since our people first were."

"I couldn't agree more," she reached over and patted the old woman on her shoulder. "Guess we better get some sleep."

Soon all was quiet within the old tipi. Spring closed her eyes and listened to the wind howling outside, remembering Grandpa Eli's words.

The old woman spoke once more, "The Black Hills are the heart of everything...the most special place on earth." Then she slept.

The next morning, Spring and Dakotah ventured out in the blanket of snow for a brief playful act. While tossing the light, frozen snow up into the air, Dakotah stopped suddenly.

"Look Mommy, why is the flag upside down?"

Spring looked up at the flag that was blowing in the wind, while hanging upside down. "It is a sign of distress...Darling...a distress signal."

"What is distress, Mommy?"

"It means...well, it means in trouble...a people in trouble."

"Are we in trouble, Mommy?"

Spring struggled for an answer.

"No, Honey, we're not in trouble. We're going to be okay."

Dakotah smiled.

PRU SAT DOWN at the kitchen table with the paper in front of her, devouring every word of the Wounded Knee reporting as she had done each morning since it all began. Clarence was her willing or sometimes unwilling listener, depending on how he got out of bed.

"Listen to this, Clarence...."

"What is it now?" he answered abruptly after a night of fitful sleep.

"It says here that a Marshal's been shot...seriously injured. Says they just had the heaviest exchange of shooting since the siege began."

"It's a wonder the Marshals and the FBI don't just go in there and put an end to it."

"Clarence! Are you suggesting a second massacre?"

"No. But usually the FBI takes control, you know, and things come to an end."

She continued reading. "Oh my goodness!"

"What is it?"

"Says the tribal leaders are refusing to let a carload of food past the blockade...that they're intending to starve them out!"

"Now...now...," he sensed the fear in her voice.

"I can't bear to think that little Dakotah and Spring could...actually...."

"They're not gonna starve."

"How do you know?"

"I just know...that's all...I just know." He put his arms around her, and she drew from his strength, but inwardly, he, too, feared the outcome.

ROXY SHOOK HER HEAD as she read the same words.

"Mel, we need to pray for your Aunt Spring and Dakotah. Things are sounding mighty bad."

"I know. Mama and I talked about it yesterday."

"Poor little Dakotah."

Melony sat down beside her on the couch.

"Roxy, I know they're gonna be all right. I know God is going to answer our prayers."

"I believe so too, Mel."

Melony leaned over and read the headlines that Roxy had laid aside.

'FINAL U.S. GIs STARTING PULLOUT'.

She glanced at Roxy, and their eyes met.

"It's finally over." She whispered, "They're coming home."

Melony put her arm around her, knowing how hard it must be. Roxy smiled with teary eyes, "But he's already home, Mel. It's okay."

"I know, Roxy...I know. Goodness, it's been over a decade since our men first went over there. It's hard to believe it's finally over." She shook her head, "And over 50,000 soldiers gave up their lives...and for what?"

Roxy sat up. "Mel, don't ever say that again. We will not forget what they died for...the fight for freedom. That fight has been going on since the beginning of time. Freedom is a precious thing."

"Yes, I know. Guess that's got something to do with this thing going on in South Dakota...why Spring's got herself in such a mess."

Roxy settled back on the couch. "That's a complex one. They're free...the Indians...but yet they're not. They're prisoners of their fate."

The wind rattled the windows.

Mel eyed Roxy. "You haven't seen any more lights ...have you?"

"Nope."

APRIL BROUGHT WITH IT showers a plenty and Pru enjoyed each one...her legacy from Emily. She stared out the kitchen window as another shower sprinkled down upon the nearby Apple trees bursting forth with their white blossoms. She smiled. In times when all seemed to be going haywire, it does a body good to see the same old Apple trees budding again. Year after year, they continue to bud, blossom and bear fruit, while adorning the yard with their intricate beauty.

She turned to the Wisteria hanging from the porch, dripping with crystal clear raindrops. This year, the twisted vines that climbed their front porch, draping it gracefully, seemed particularly abundant with their heavy clusters of lacy, lavender flowers. What a joy to behold! Her eyes wandered across the bright green lawn, coming alive once again, to the rows of Maples and Poplar trees sporting their pea green embryonic leaves. Every spring, it was the same...the land produced...the land came through. One could take stock in it, feel a kindred to it, a sense of security. What with all the confusion and troubles that life was at times...take this trouble with Spring and Dakotah, and the problems brewing with Heath and Caroline, and then there was Watergate...only God knows how it all will turn out, she thought. The kitchen window was clouding up with steam from the pot of pinto beans on the stove, and the mountain ridges were barely visible now. She walked over to the sink, filled a glass brimming with water and dumped it in the pot. The bubbles popped, fizzled and settled down. Can't let them beans burn! Clarence would be awfully outdone.

She opened the back door to check the weather, and the cool dampness met her nostrils instantly, transmitting a sweet fragrance, that of the lilacs blooming just around the corner. There was a hint that the shower would soon end, giving way to the hiding sun. She would wait and then ride over to Patrick's later. He would be plowing the field today with Jonathon's help. Maybe they could have lunch together...maybe they could lift her spirits.

"Sis, did'ya bring some of your coconut cake with you?" Jonathon called from the tractor as she got out of the car with her bundle.

"No, but I've got something just as good."

He answered with his old military salute, and put the tractor in gear.

"Pru, come on in," Ellen motioned from the door.

"Looks like the men have done quite a bit already."

"Yes, we thought that little shower was gonna interfere...but it wasn't enough to dampen our spirits, much less the ground."

Pru laughed. "I brought a lemon pie over for lunch."

"Great, I know Patrick will be delighted, not to mention Jonathon."

"Are any of the kids around?"

"No, all are doing their thing. Just us old folks here."

"Where's David?"

"Patrick didn't tell you?"

"Well, I haven't spoken with him since Sunday."

"He rode over to Charlottesville for a few days. Spending some time with his old war buddy, James Ridgeway. He's gotten rather interested in history again. Says he's going to do some touring. You know, start with Monticello and go from there, I suppose. I think it will be great therapy for him."

"That's great, Ellen. He needs some interest."

"Well, I hope so. He certainly needs to get his mind on something besides the past...besides the war. Come on upstairs. I want to show you my new quilting design. Got it from Maggie Johnson, and she got it from a lady over in Charlottesville. I'm tickled pink with it."

Patrick plowed the last row for the day and hollered for Jonathon to quit also. It was half past noon, and he was downright hungry.

After washing up, the two tired but satisfied men pulled up chairs at the long, homemade table that was already laden with corn, beets, ham, hot rolls, and Pru's lemon meringue pie.

"No, Jonathon, that pie's last," Ellen kidded.

"I know, and I can hardly wait to get there. Nobody makes meringue like Sis."

Patrick looked up, "Mama used to."

"Where do you think I got the recipe?"

"You're more like Mama every day."

"Thanks, Patrick. I'm just glad she's not here to worry about Spring. Have you heard anything?"

"Nothing yet. We just need to continue holding them up in prayer. I'm sure they'll be okay."

"I wish I could feel as sure as you do, Patrick. I pray...day and night...I pray."

"Remember, Sis, the Bible says...'all things, what-soever ye shall ask in prayer, believing, ye shall receive'...Matthew, chapter twenty-one."

"I know, Patrick...but...."

"The key is believing."

"In other words, we gotta believe that we're gonna get what we pray for," Jonathon added.

"Oh ye, of little faith...," Pru smiled.

"I can't believe they haven't given up yet."

Pru looked at Jonathon. "Why not? If they're all as determined and stubborn as our Spring, it should not come as any surprise to us."

"Guess not," he laughed. "Pass the beets, please."

"How are things with the children, Jonathon?" Patrick asked a bit reluctantly.

He frowned. "I don't know. There's a real strain in that marriage for sure. Heath seems to be under a lot of stress lately."

"Maybe if they were to have a child...," Ellen suggested while passing the rolls.

"Maybe...," Jonathon repeated. "I just don't know. Changing the subject, how's Melony's new job situation coming along?"

"Well, I've hardly had time to think about it, but she tells me that she goes on the final interview this Friday. She's sure excited about it...but I don't know."

"What's this?"

"Jonathon, I know Melony stands a chance to get a good job...a move up...she'd be responsible for a number of stores in the piano line. You know, sort of sales, I guess. And, anything to do with piano, Melony is a whiz...but this traveling part...I don't know...."

"Just what do you mean, Pru?"

"Patrick, you know it's not right for a mother to leave her little ones and go off running around on business. What about Little Emily?"

"Just what does she intend to do with Emily?"

"I'm not totally sure. She tells me Roxy will be looking after her, and, of course, in the summer months, she can stay with us...but still...."

"How long will her trips be?" Jonathon questioned.

"Oh, she says most will only be day trips, but sometimes she'd be required to stay overnight. She'd be working mostly in Virginia, but some in North Carolina."

"That doesn't sound so bad, Sis," Jonathon concluded. "You know Melony's gonna take good care of Emily."

"I know. I guess I'm just old-fashioned."

"Hey, nothing wrong with that, but times are changing, Sis. Not like it used to be."

"You can say that again."

"Well, what do you all think about this Watergate thing?" Jonathon inquired while reaching for the lemon pie.

"Seems like a lot of corruption in the administration," Patrick responded somberly. "It's definitely a tragic thing."

"Yeah, sounds mighty fishy to me, too," Jonathon added.

"Do you think Nixon is involved?"

They all looked at Pru.

"Well?"

" 'Course he is!" Jonathon replied. "Would have to be."

"Well, Jonathon, maybe we shouldn't be so hasty to judge. Maybe he is and maybe he isn't."

"Aw, come on, Patrick."

He shook his head. "Well, it does look like somebody got caught with his hand in the pot. Frankly, I'm sick of hearing about it. There are more important things going on in the world, I'm sure."

"I think the whole thing is very distasteful," Pru said decisively. "And I'm embarrassed for our country."

"I agree," added Patrick.

THE GUNFIRE CEASED! All was quiet within the village of Wounded Knee as the inhabitants mourned the death of their own. Another casualty for the cause.

Spring closed the door quietly not to awaken Dakotah from her nap. They had been forced to move back into the cottage as the firing increased.

"It's true...he's dead?"

"It's true," Spring answered. "Bullet wound in the head."

"You know, he was from Cherokee...Cherokee, North Carolina."

"I know."

"Such a shame."

"Such a waste. They've asked for a cease-fire," Spring said while sitting down beside the old woman.

"Why do you look so sad, my pretty one?"

She sighed. "I don't know...guess I know it's coming to an end...and that means back to the way it was. No more dreams of the old ways...no more of this feeling of independence and strength that we've experienced these last couple of months...no more chance to be heard...."

"We will be heard," the old woman replied. "As the wind blows through the ridges and crevices of the Black Hills and speaks with many voices, so will we."

Spring smiled at her sadly.

Chapter XV
Caroline

While sands of strife sifted through the Dakota Plains, words of doom were being echoed from the heights of the Blue Ridge. Caroline stood straight with her hands on her hips and faced Heath with a look of despair.

"Why did we come up here?" he demanded impatiently.

"I thought...I thought we could...be like we used to be...."

"Caroline, we can't go back to when we were teenagers again. We've discussed this before. We're different people now...with different goals and different lives...."

"Heath, do you still love me?" The words spilled out softly, caressing the cool mountain air.

"Of course. Of course, I love you...."

"Then let's reconsider our talk the other night... about...about...Heath, I know you'd love...."

"I DON'T WANT ANY BABY!" Heath yelled, drowning out not only her pleas but the soothing mountain sounds around them.

"But Heath...."

She clutched at him frantically, but he pushed her away.

"I'm leaving."

She grasped for him in her hopelessness.

"NO, NO, NO," she screamed, "YOU CAN'T!"

The next day, Pru awakened before dawn, and lay for some time thinking about Spring and Dakotah. She couldn't go back to sleep. She tried thinking of how different all their lives would have been without Spring. It was difficult to even imagine...her big sister! Even though Spring had spent most of her life running back and forth to South Dakota, she always knew she was there...there for her. It didn't matter that their origins were as far removed as the east from the west...or that their personalities differed as night and day...they were sisters...they were part of one another.

The fiery sun rose, casting shadows about the darkened room, and her eyes focused on Little Emily's picture sitting on the bureau. How precious! How could Melony leave her for one minute? But then, Melony's life was so different from hers. She'd never had to leave the comforts of her home to make a living. Of course, she realized that this job was a good one, and that Melony had reason to be excited. But somehow, she just didn't think that God meant it this way. The men should be the bread-winners and the mothers should be at home raising the children. But, the single mothers? They had to work. But the children...what about the children?

The phone rang. She jumped up to get it, and Clarence groaned. The voice on the other end was tense.

"Pru, are you awake?" Jessica asked.

"I am. What is it?"

"Well...I don't know. I just got a call from Heath. You know, he had to be in D.C. today; he left yesterday. But he just called me to check on Caroline. I called her, but she's not home...and it's 6:00 a.m.! Where in the world do you think she'd be at this hour?"

"I don't know. Are you sure you called the right number?"

"Yes, I'm sure. I called it several times...and I don't understand why Heath would be calling me so early in the morning to check on her. I don't understand any of this."

"Where's Jonathon?"

"He's here, but just as baffled as me. He didn't want me to call you, but I'm sort of worried...and I knew you were an early riser."

"That's all right. Please let me know what you find out."

MILES AWAY FROM Oak Mountain, in another world, Heath fought the early morning traffic, his mind racing over the previous day. What had he done! The picture of her standing there atop the mountain with her long thick hair blowing in the cool breeze seemed imprinted on his windshield. He couldn't escape it!

His mind raced back to their school days...and how she'd captured his heart while so young. How sweet she was...how trusting...and how she'd loved him. What had happened? The car behind him honked and swerved past him. How would he perform today...could he perform today...and today of all days.

It was noon, and the sun had made its final ascent. The farmhouse soaked up its warm rays along with all other inhabitants and dwellings on Oak Mountain. There was a knock at the door, and Pru answered. Jonathon stood in the doorway looking dazed, with Jessica on his arm.

"Why didn't you come on in?"

They walked silently past her.

"Jonathon...what is it?"

"Caroline," he whispered.

"Yes?" she asked anxiously.

"She's dead."

"Caroline's dead!" She stepped back.

"They found her this morning...below Lover's Leap...she's dead."

Pru grabbed hold of him.

"Here...sit down. I'll get you something to drink. Sit there, Jessica."

Jessica obeyed without a word.

"What on earth!" Pru muttered while pouring the coffee. "How did it happen?"

"She fell...fell from...the top."

"What was she doing up there?"

"We don't know...but I need to leave Jessica here. I'm meeting with...the authorities shortly...to go with them...to get Heath."

"Yes...yes, of course."

"The authorities, Pru. Do you understand?"

She looked at him blankly.

"They think...they think Heath...did it," he finally blurted out.

"What?"

He stood there looking at her, suddenly seeming very old.

"You mean...killed her?"

"That's right."

"Why, that's the most absurd thing I've ever heard!"

"Pru, I've gotta go. Please take care of Jessica." He looked painfully in her direction. She stood staring into space.

The following days passed in a blur. The Barrett household had been rocked as a giant ship rocks in the turbulent waves of a raging storm. Caroline's somber funeral was a grave affair to be remembered on those cold dark nights of the Blue Ridge when one couldn't sleep. The wretched sobs of Heath, mingled with the softer cries of many and rising about the preacher's final words, sent prickly chills down spines. It was a cool, spring day, and those present pulled their wraps snugly about them in an attempt to shut out not only the cold, but the eerie sounds of grief.

Days later, Pru sat in her kitchen, trying to absorb it all. The morning paper lay in front of her exposing its headlines..."*CANDIDATE FOR POLITICAL SCENE ARRESTED FOR MURDER!*"

She shook her head sadly. It was so senseless. Anyone could see how distraught he was by her death. Why would he have taken her life? Heath could not take any life...much less Caroline's!

She remembered him as a little boy, always so sensitive...the compassionate one. Why, it had stood out often as he played with Mark and Paul and the others. Sure, he'd gotten on the fast track like so many other young folk, caught up with ambition, but that wasn't all bad. There were worse things. She thought of Mark and Paul and David — not knowing where they're going in life...or unable to live in the present even. No, Heath was to be admired for his drive. She'd been so proud of him. There had to be an answer to all this.

Poor Jessica! She certainly hoped it wouldn't create problems for her...old problems. They could never fully forget all the pain she'd gone through and put everyone else through so many years ago with her emotional problems. But, of course, that was a long time ago. And Jonathon...her poor baby brother. As if he hadn't suffered enough with Jessica's problems... now this.

She was so engrossed in her thoughts that she didn't hear Patrick drive up, and his entrance startled her.

"Oh, Patrick. Come on in."

"Good morning." He glanced down at the paper. "Have you heard from them this morning?"

"No. Don't expect to for a while. The past few days have been such a nightmare for them. I told them to try and get some rest...to sleep in this morning."

"It's gotta be terribly hard to get any sleep knowing Heath's in jail. I just don't understand it all."

"Neither do I, Patrick. How can they take the word of some kids playing around in the mountains? Why, you never know what kids will do!"

"Apparently, these two have a pretty good repu-
tation for telling the truth, I understand...and, of course,
there is the *tie*...."

"I know...that part gives me chills. When I saw the
casket there at the funeral, I kept wondering if she still
held his tie."

"Pru!"

"Oh, I didn't really think she did...I just kept seeing
it in my mind, you know."

"Yeah. That will definitely hurt him. I can't figure
out why she'd have his tie in her hand."

"What did Heath say?"

"Nothing. Jonathon says he just won't talk about it.
Seems stunned, in shock, I suppose."

"I can understand that. Patrick, do you think Jessica
will withstand all of this?"

"I think so. We all know Jessica isn't the strongest
person, but I believe her faith will sustain her. I really
do."

"I sure hope so...I sure hope so."

"The main reason I came over this morning was to
tell you about the autopsy report. Jonathon called last
night...late."

"Well?"

"It confirmed the cause of death as a blow to the head
that occurred apparently during the fall."

"Poor Caroline...."

"Pru, that wasn't all they found."

She looked up surprised. "What?"

He sighed, "Caroline was pregnant."

"NO!"

"Yes, not quite three months...but she was definitely

pregnant."

"Did Heath know?"

"We don't know."

She looked up. "Sounds like Melony and them are here."

"Up for the weekend?"

"Yes, actually they're gonna stay at Spring's place."

In walked Little Emily followed by Laurietta.

"Hi Grandma."

"Hello Emily...and Laurietta. My, don't you two look ready for a weekend." They were dressed in blue jeans, flannel shirts and had knapsacks flung on their backs.

"They should be," Melony laughed coming in the door. "They've had us running around all week putting their gear together."

"We're going hiking!" Laurietta announced proudly.

"Well, springtime's here and that's the best time for hiking," Patrick chuckled, "that is except for the fall."

"Hello Roxy, have a seat." Pru pulled out a chair. "Why don't you girls run along upstairs and play a while." They ran off giggling before she finished the sentence.

"Mama, it sure is nice that you've made a playroom for them. Roxy, I'll have to show it to you before we leave. My old doll house is even in it, the one Daddy made for us — Mary Tom and me — when we were about the same age as the girls."

"I remember that doll house well, and Clarence making it," Patrick chuckled. "I've never seen Clarence quite so frustrated."

They all laughed.

"My, it feels good to laugh," Pru sighed.

A moment of silence passed. "How's Heath, Mama?"

"You tell'em, Patrick."

"Jonathon says he's sort of in shock. I plan to go over to see him later today."

"I'd like to see him, too, especially since he's just down the street from us. But I've never been to a jail before...."

"I'll go with you, Mel," Roxy offered. "I've been there before with Mama to see Uncle Walter. You know...her brother that has the drinking problem."

"We'll do it then. He seemed so distraught at the funeral, and I feel so sorry for him. I just can't believe all this is happening."

"None of us can, Mel." Patrick patted her on the shoulder.

"Patrick was just telling me before you all got here about the autopsy report. They did confirm her death as caused by the fall...and striking her head...poor little thing. But that's not all. It seems Caroline was pregnant."

Roxy looked up quickly. "Pregnant?"

"Not very far, not much over two months apparently."

"Oh, what a shame...and she wanted a baby so much!" Melony cried.

As they talked, Roxy walked over to the window and looked out at the mountains, those sound majestic mountains...always the same no matter what. No matter if life came or life went, they seemed the same. She recalled the conversation on the porch that day with Caroline. She wished she'd done something then. She should have reached out to her more! A baby! How she wanted a baby...more than anything. It was obvious.

"Roxy, you care for some coffee?" Pru asked.

"No Ma'am. Thank you just the same."

"What is this thing with those kids, Uncle Patrick? What is it they're saying exactly?"

"Well, what I can gather from Jonathon plus the paper here...it's their evidence that's incriminating him."

"What are they saying?"

"They heard Heath and Caroline arguing. Evidently, Heath said, or they said he yelled out something about not wanting any baby."

"Oh no!"

"Yes, and then they said they heard Caroline screaming."

"Did they see anything?"

"No, they only heard voices."

"How old are these kids?" asked Roxy.

"Thirteen...fourteen. They're supposed to be pretty responsible young people. In fact, it was one of the boy's father that found her later...found Caroline. He was coon hunting that night."

"So that's how they came forward?"

"Seems so. Who knows. They may never have come forward otherwise...if it hadn't been for the coon hunt."

"If only they hadn't," Pru added.

"Well now, Sis, justice must be done. The truth must be known...no matter what."

"I know, Patrick, but...."

"I can't believe Heath wouldn't want the baby!" Melony pondered aloud.

"That's a strange one. But, on the other hand, I don't

see any cause for these young people to lie about such a thing."

"That's right," Roxy added.

"Well, Heath has been quite caught up lately in his career," Melony continued. "You don't suppose he may have thought it would dampen that or maybe hinder him in some way?"

"Who knows what another person may be thinking. Only God knows our thoughts," Patrick concluded.

"Maybe the boys didn't hear him correctly?"

"Maybe not, Pru," Patrick agreed.

"So what's gonna happen now?"

"Well, according to our criminal justice system, Mel, a man is innocent until proven guilty."

"Thank goodness. But how're they gonna do that?"

"I don't know, Melony."

"I just can't believe all this happening to our family...first Spring and Dakotah in some God-forsaken place...and now Heath!"

"Pru, you don't mean that," Patrick said soothingly, "you know, there is no such place as God-forsaken...not on earth anyway."

"I know...I'm just so turned around lately."

They all looked at her.

"What about Spring? Have we heard anything?" Melony questioned.

"Nothing. I just haven't been able to think much about Spring at this time. I guess it's all too much."

The door flew open, and in walked Clarence, his large stature filling the room. "What's this?"

"Oh, we're discussing the woes of the Barrett family," Pru replied.

"Well, we're certainly not alone. The whole darn world's gone crazy! Even the president!"

"What do you mean?" Patrick asked.

"He just said publicly that he accepts the blame."

"NO!"

"He said that the blame belongs at the top and that he accepts final responsibility. What a shame for this country!"

"I just couldn't believe all those officials resigning!" Pru said.

"They might as well," Roxy added, "according to the Gallup Poll, half the country thinks Mr. Nixon is guilty."

They shook their heads.

THAT NIGHT AS THE silvery moon slid over Oak Mountain, casting its shadows about, Roxy lay quietly in the bed that rested under the upstairs window of Spring's home. She liked the way Spring had designed the place, especially this bedroom with the bed directly under the window. She looked up into the star filled sky...and thought of Caroline...poor Caroline. She turned over on her stomach, resting her head upon her clasped hands and stared out the window. The mountain ridges were delicately silhouetted against the silver glow of the moon. This whole thing was puzzling. She could still see pretty Caroline sitting out there on that porch on Thanksgiving...seemingly so unhappy. She wished somehow she could relive that moment. Maybe there was something she could have done differently that would have helped her...prevented this. Who knows? But the baby? She didn't understand that at all. That day, she'd implied...or at least she understood it that way...that she couldn't have children. And as much as she'd wanted a baby...why, I can't believe that she would've taken her own life. Oh my! She thought of Heath. What was gonna happen? Just before she fell asleep, she decided to keep quiet about that conversation on the porch. What good could it do anyway?

Not too many miles away, Jessica woke up trembling from another nightmare, and Jonathon comforted her within his arms.

"It's gonna be all right, Honey...it's gonna be all right."

She lay back against his broad shoulder and silently thought the same thoughts that had been haunting her since Caroline's death. What was it people said about history repeating itself? She could hear her mother's whispery voice accompanied by the sweet smelling perfume she always wore, telling her *the story*...how many times she'd heard *the story*. Always, it was the same. Her father pushing her mother off the sharpest ridge of Oak Mountain...and she'd disappeared forever from Oak Mountain. And now...this...could it be possible ...could it be possible that her Heath...grandson of another Heath...could have done the same? There, she'd said it! Even if silently. NO! It could not be so! Not her Heath...he would not do such a thing! She must not think that way!

Jonathon stroked her thick dark hair in the night, and she soon fell into a fitful sleep.

THE NEXT MORNING, Roxy woke to the sounds of

Oak Mountain...the mingled songs of the mountain birds and the rustle of Pine branches against her window pane. The gentle breeze caressed the morning and sent forth subtle scents of mountain growth that surrounded the chalet. She sat up and gazed out the window. My...what beauty!

Later, as the small group pushed their way up the mountainside, again Roxy sighed in awe of spring's adornment there upon Oak Mountain. The girls hiked excitedly up ahead, and it was all she and Melony could do to keep up.

"Look, Mom, what kind of tree is this?" Laurietta called back.

Roxy looked at Melony.

She laughed. "That's a Coffee tree. There aren't many of them up here. Its wood is quite valuable as they make musical instruments out of it, and it's shipped all the way to China or some place."

"Wow!" Laurietta exclaimed.

"She is such an inquisitive child."

"I know," Roxy smiled proudly.

"Well, the Dogwoods are just about gone."

"Not the Dogwoods, Mel...just their beautiful white flowers."

"Right. But I always hate to see them leave. They bring such magic to the forest."

"Watch out, Girls. Don't get too close to that briar patch, or you'll get stuck for sure."

"Ouch!" Emily cried out.

"Told you so," Melony scolded.

"Just look at'em. Won't listen a bit."

"Oh well. They'll learn. They have to be kids, you

know, like we used to be. Didn't you ever get into a
blackberry patch?"

"Not too often. Not many downtown, you know."

"Look yonder. They're everywhere here. We'll have
to come back when the blackberries come in. You like
blackberry roll?"

"Sure do."

"My Grandma Emily used to always make blackberry roll when the blackberries came in. Oh...look!"
Melony bent over close to the ground.

"What is it?"

"Do these ever bring back memories."

Roxy leaned down close to her, examining the tiny,
bluish flowers that were growing snugly to the moist,
mossy earth.

"What are they?"

"Little Bluets...they're very tiny wild flowers that
fill these mountainsides in the spring. I loved to play
with them as a child."

"Mighty pretty...but a bit fragile."

"You're right. I always loved their bluish-lavender
color and especially the little yellow center. See. And
they're real easy to pull up...they hardly have any
roots." She pulled a cluster of the minute flowers up
from the mossy earth.

"Now Mel, why did you do that?"

"I always do, Roxy...to take them home and put them
into a little jar on the kitchen table or in the window."

"Oh. When do the blackberries come in?"

"In August. We'll come back then. The girls will love
it. I can still remember going blackberry picking with
Grandma. We'd set out real early in the morning with

those little tin pails she kept for such occasions; my hands would be purple before we finished." She laughed, "My face, too, from eating almost as many as I dropped into the pails. Before we left, Grandma not only had her pails full...but also her apron. Seemed she couldn't bare to leave any."

"Bet her apron was a mess."

"Didn't matter any. Grandma always wore her oldest so that she didn't mind ruining it."

"Sounds like your grandma was some lady."

"She was that. I wish you could've known her. I know you would've loved her, too."

"Is that what you call Mountain Laurel?" She pointed to large clusters of soft pink flowering shrubs growing out from the jagged cliffs of the mountainside.

"Sure is...one of the many beauties of the Blue Ridge, along with the Rhododendron, of course...but don't let that fool you; it's poisonous."

"You're kiddin'!"

"Its leaves are."

"Now, ain't that just like life. Many of the beautiful and tempting things in life have the bite of an adder."

"How right you are. You know, I can't make any sense out of this whole thing with Caroline."

Roxy struggled with herself, wondering whether or not to relate the porch conversation. Just as she opened her mouth to speak, Melony yelled out, "Come on girls...time to get back."

She sighed.

As they started down the mountainside, Roxy remarked how lovely the mountains were in the spring.

Melony agreed, "However, at night these mountains

can become dark and ominous at times."

"You mean *you've* been scared?"

"I have been...not much. There's a lot more to fear in the cities than here, you know."

"I know." She decided to tell her latest news. "Mel, speaking of fear...I saw it again...*the light*."

Melony looked at her quickly. "Again?"

"Again. I didn't mention it seeing all this going on with Heath and Caroline, but, Mel, I really think there's something strange down there. And, I think we ought to get to the bottom of it."

"And just how do you reckon we'll do that?"

"Well, I been thinking. Suppose somebody was to go in there and spend the night...somebody who's not afraid to."

"Like who?"

"I've got somebody in mind. I'll let you know if he agrees."

"How will he get in? The place is locked."

"No problem. *He* can get in."

"This ought'a be interesting," Mel smiled.

They arrived back at the chalet, and Roxy mentioned she sure missed her paper.

"Well, we could use some more rolls for lunch seeing as the girls want hot dogs again. Why don't we drive down to Bob's Store...and you can get your paper there, too."

The girls chattered away in the back seat as they returned from the little store, and Roxy opened the paper.

"Listen to this!" She suddenly burst out, "'*Wounded*

Knee Agreement Reached'. That's the headlines."

"You're kidding!"

"No. Says right here...*'An agreement for disarmament and further negotiations to end the 68-day occupation of historic Wounded Knee by militant Indians was announced Sunday'.*"

"Great!"

"An answer to prayer."

"That's right. What else does it say?"

Roxy continued reading...*" 'Further discussions are to involve representatives of the White House who will come to the Pine Ridge Reservation'.* It says the agreement will be effective on Wednesday, beginning at 9:00 a.m. and that the government will remove all armored personnel carriers...and that the occupants of Wounded Knee are to lay down their weapons, evacuate their bunkers and assemble at their tipi chapel in the village to surrender."

"Wow!"

"Listen...*'the Indians say that AIM's job is done there...that it must be understood that AIM was called on to aid these Oglala Sioux in their struggle against repressive government forces'.*"

"It all seems very complex to me."

"Me too. It goes on to say...*'the disarmament will clear the way for a meeting between White House representatives and Sioux elders on the Pine Ridge Reservation to discuss and explore the 1868 treaty'.*"

"What's with this 1868 Treaty?"

"It says that the 1868 Treaty gave all the land west of the Missouri River to the Sioux. Boy, that's a lot of land."

"And, of course, it was taken from them...except for what's left on the reservations. Spring's told me often enough about that."

"It's a shame, for sure, but I don't know what could be done about it now. It's too late."

"Seems so. I can't wait to call Mama."

When she reached Pru on the phone, she'd already heard.

"Patrick read it in the paper this morning...and called me right away. It's laying here on the kitchen table now. I'm so excited. I've been calling Spring, but still no answer. Clarence says to give her time...but I can hardly wait. In fact, I better get off the phone now. She might be trying to call."

"They should be okay, Mama. When's the last time you heard from Mareen?"

"About ten days ago. But you never know."

"Okay, I'll talk with you later."

THE FOLLOWING SUNDAY, Pru had just finished the family dinner when everyone arrived...Melony, Roxy and the girls, with Patrick and Ellen completing the group. Jonathon and Jessica had declined.

"None of the kids could make it today?" she asked Ellen.

"No, they all had plans. You know how it is."

"Of course."

Once seated, the conversation bounced from Jessica and Jonathon to President Nixon to the Treaty of 1868 and back again.

"Well, I'm sure sorry that Jonathon and Jessica

didn't come. Would've done them good to talk it out probably."

"Think you're right, Clarence, but I don't expect they're feeling much like talking these days," Patrick commented.

"Poor Heath...did you see him yesterday, Uncle Patrick?"

"I did, Mel...and he's been on my mind ever since. Seemed so utterly despondent."

"Do you believe he's innocent, Reverend Barrett?" Roxy asked suddenly.

All heads looked from her to Patrick.

He wiped his mouth and carefully placed the large napkin back in his lap. "I believe he is, Roxy. I can't explain away the events or the damaging evidence... but I believe the boy's innocent."

"Let's just hope there'll be those like you on the jury," Clarence added.

"Pray...we gotta pray. That's the only thing that will help him now," Pru spoke decisively.

"You're right, Sis."

"But if he's innocent, and, of course, I think he is...what really happened to Caroline?" Mel questioned.

They all shook their heads, each pondering the same question...each wondering about the striped tie...the argument...and most of all...that piercing scream that the boys heard.

"One thing for sure," Roxy spoke up, "there's plenty of trouble from here to the White House...but when you take a walk in these here woods on a beautiful spring day like we did a few days ago...why, you still gotta believe in the good, I say."

Pru smiled at her. "You're right, Roxy. These mountains keep us believing...they protect our faith."

The phone rang!

Pru jumped up to answer.

"SPRING!"

A hush fell over the dinner table.

"You're okay...and Dakotah's okay...you're sure? She says they're fine...both she and Dakotah. Spring, we've all been so worried about you. You just don't know how much...I know...I know...Spring...you've always had to do what you had to do...but this time...I don't know."

"Tell her about Caroline," Mel whispered.

Pru shook her head at Mel. "I understand, Spring. You take care of things...and call me back later...when you can talk longer. I'll be waiting."

She hung up and sighed.

"Why didn't you tell her about Caroline, Mom?"

"I will...the next time. Let her settle down."

Patrick raised his head from a silent prayer. "Thank God they're all right."

The next morning, Patrick stopped by on his way to the bank in town. Pru was washing dishes at the sink when she saw him drive up. She always felt a warmness when he arrived. Quickly, he came into the kitchen.

"Did Spring call back last night?"

"She did...and we had a nice long talk. I told her everything."

"What did she say?"

"Well, she was shocked, of course, and very saddened about Caroline...just as we are. She wanted to know how Heath was fairing, and I told her."

She dried her hands and grabbed a cup from the cupboard for Patrick.

"Have some coffee?"

"Thanks."

"She wanted to leave on the first plane coming home...but I told her that wasn't reasonable if she had things to take care of there. I told her there wasn't anything she could do here. She admitted that she has a lot to take care of since the Wounded Knee thing has ended. I don't exactly know what she meant, but I don't see any sense in her running back here. There's nothing she can do."

"You're right."

HALFWAY ACROSS the vast lands of America, Spring sat at her kitchen table in front of Mareen discussing the same thing.

"I just can't believe it!"

"But Spring, things like this happen every day unfortunately."

"Yeah, I know...but not on Oak Mountain."

"I'm sorry, of course, to hear of your family tragedy...but I'm sure glad to have you and Dakotah back, safe and sound."

Spring smiled at her. "It's all so puzzling, but I must not dwell on it. There's nothing I can do about it...but there is something I can be doing here."

"Like what?"

"It's not over, Mareen."

"What do you mean? Wounded Knee is over."

"Yes, that chapter is over...but our struggle is not. I

did a lot of thinking while waiting out those long weeks at Wounded Knee. I know we can never turn back time. A million Ghost Dances couldn't do that for us, but we can bring changes...good changes...we can make a difference."

Chapter XVI
The Guest

It was a warm summer evening, and the moon was climbing its way up the twilight sky ever so slowly. Roxy watched it silently. What if this turned out to be another uneventful night? She recalled Melony's words...'If nothing happens this time, we should just drop the whole thing'. Twice now her cousin Jake had spent the night in the cottage out back to no avail. In fact, she had to do some persuading in order for him to agree one more time...not that he was the least bit afraid, mind you. Not Jake Callahan, but the rats he fervently disliked.

Cautiously, he laid out his sleeping bag again in the darkest corner of the main room...the room in which supposedly a candle mysteriously burned from time to time. He snuggled down into the soft material of the bag without zipping it up, and lay quietly listening. He wished something would happen. This was for the birds! Or maybe the rats! He confidently patted the cold metal of his revolver and sighed, hoping he really wouldn't have to use it. 'Course, he'd heard that bullets didn't hurt ghosts anyhow. He chuckled to himself quietly.

The evening wore on, changing from twilight to dusk to dark; still the little house out back was silent. Jake Callahan watched the moon through the dusty window panes as it climbed higher and shrunk before his very eyes.

Roxy leaned on the window ledge in the darkened bedroom, trying hard to keep her eyes upon the cottage. But as the evening passed, they became heavier and heavier. She wished Melony was here. Unfortunately, she'd been sent out of town and would return the next day. The house was so quiet, it was almost uncomfortable, with the girls sound asleep...and everyone else in the large house...all the other occupants scattered throughout its vast rooms and floors.

The moon boasted of its sheer height in the now blackened sky, and Jake Callahan dozed in the cottage out back. A doorknob turned. Ever so softly, it turned. Still Jake Callahan dozed. Suddenly, the doorknob was released and all was quiet for a moment. There was the faint sound of keys rattling just outside the door. Again, the doorknob turned. A ray of silvery light appeared as it streamed through the slight crack in the door. Jake Callahan sat up! He was camouflaged in the darkened corner, and he silently watched as the crack widened. He could feel his heart beating wildly. Not you...Jake Callahan...he reproached himself!

Then to his utter surprise, a small frame, that of a child, stood in the doorway. Jake strained his eyes in the dark to see what appeared to be a small boy of very slight stature, who was closing the door behind him. He walked across the dark room just as if he knew where he was going, and pulled out a drawer in the table and was soon striking a match. The match moved toward a candle on the table, and suddenly the small room was illuminated with shadows as the child turned around and gasped!

"Hold on there, young fellow!" Jake pounced to his big feet.

The lad's eyes were filled with fear as he quickly analyzed the situation.

"It's okay, kid. I ain't gonna hurt you." He smiled his toothless smile, but the boy's eyes were riveted to the revolver still dangling in his hand.

Jake moved to the door, opened it and flashed his light up the hill toward the big house. The light fell into Roxy's bedroom just as planned. Her eyes flew open. Within seconds, she was on her way down the steps. While Jake continued flashing the light back and forth, he failed to notice the boy inching his way toward the door. Quick as lightening, he dashed by Jake...but not quick enough.

"You ain't going nowhere, boy. You gotta lot of explaining to do!" The lad looked up into his scraggly bearded face and trembled while being held firmly by his shirt collar.

Roxy was cautiously making her way down the slippery hill wet with dew. Even though she knew the flashlight sign meant 'everything's okay', she still carried a rolling pin in her right hand. She came into view, and Jake yelled out to her.

"Got your ghost here!" He laughed aloud.

Her keen eyes quickly assessed the scene before her. "Jake, let him go...don't hold him so!"

"You want him to run away...do you?"

She walked up to the lad and knelt down to him. He spoke not a word. His disheveled appearance was not lost on her, and she noticed the frayed and dirty clothing, the layers of dirt on his small wrists even in the darkness. He had an odor of uncleanliness that permeated his small being. But beneath all the dirt, unkempt curly hair and smell, there stood before her a child...a beautiful mixed child with large expressive eyes filled with fear now, which portrayed a life beyond its years. He only appeared to be about six, seven or eight years of age.

"What's your name?" she asked softly.

No reply.

"What are you doing here?" she asked even more gently.

"I ain't done nothing wrong!" he blurted out fearfully.

"It's okay...it's okay," she extended her hand to him.

He stepped back, looked at her, and then to Jake. He took her hand.

She led him up the hill from the little house.

"Don't forget to blow out the candle, Jake," she called back.

"Be glad to...a fellow might get some rest now...."

As they climbed the steps to the apartment, she thought, I wish Melony were here. She'd know what to do now.

Once in the apartment, she sat him down on the sofa and pulled up a hassock directly in front of him.

Smiling at him, she asked again, "What's your name?"

Hesitating a moment, he spoke hardly above a whisper, "Antonio."

"Antonio," Roxy repeated. "My, what a nice name. What's your last name?"

"Ain't got one."

"Oh...where do you live...where is your home?"

"Don't have one'a them either."

"How old are you?"

"Seven and a half."

"I see. Well, that's mighty young to be out so late at night by yourself, don't you think?"

He remained silent.

"Do your parents know where you are?"

Again silence.

Roxy looked puzzled. "You know we're gonna have to call your parents to come get you."

"Don't have none."

"Well, if you don't have parents, who do you live with?"

He looked away.

She stood up, "Would you like something to eat?"

Immediately, his dirty face brightened.

"Have you had supper?"

"No Ma'am."

She turned around with surprise at his manners. "Well, we'll fix that."

She proceeded to take out the leftovers from supper and lit the gas range. Once finished, she sat down across from him as he devoured the food and gulped down the milk. It was then that she realized the child very likely had gone some time without a good meal. She sat there watching him, and wondering what she was going to do

with him. If she couldn't find out his name, what was
she to do? She decided to test him.

"Antonio, if you won't tell me where you live or who
you live with...well...I'll probably have to call the police...."

"NO!" he yelled, a sudden fear overtaking him.

"Calm down. I didn't say I was gonna do it. I just
need for you to tell me some things!"

"Please Ma'am...can I stay here?"

Roxy sighed. "Well, I guess since it's so late and all,
you might as well to. We'll finish talking in the morning.
But first you gotta take a bath."

He looked up surprised.

"Looks to me like you need one."

After much coercing and resistance, finally the young
lad was immersed in hot water and suds, feeling rather
good, much to his own surprise. Roxy waited patiently
for him to finish, pondering this strange turn of affairs
and wondering what her next step would be. Then she
heard him step out.

"Okay, now hand out your clothes to me," she called
through the bathroom door, "so I can wash them...and
put on these pajamas."

Obediently, he handed out the pitiful bundle of
soiled clothing which Roxy held out from her and rushed
to the washing machine. Soon he came out, looking
rather sheepish in a pair of Laurietta's pajamas that
almost swallowed him. At least they were Superman,
even if they did have a touch of pink on them.

"Did you wash your head, too, like I told you?"

"Yes Ma'am."

"Well then, you're beginning to look like a fine young man. Come along. I fixed you a nice bed here on the sofa, plenty warm and plenty soft."

The lad climbed in reluctantly, gauging Roxy's behavior as he pulled the covers up close to his chin.

"Wait a minute." She got down on her knees by the sofa and bowed her head.

"Lord, thank you for your blessings today...even your unexpected ones. Give us thy wisdom tomorrow. Amen."

The little fellow watched her keenly. She looked up into his big green eyes and smiled.

The next evening, Melony arrived home later than usual and tired. She slowly climbed the steps and opened the door. She saw Roxy, Emily, Laurietta and a strange little lad sitting down for supper.

Emily jumped up, ran to her with a hug and the news.

"Guess what, Mama?"

"What is it?" Her eyes were still on the little lad.

"We have a new friend," she proudly pointed to Antonio.

"I see you do." She looked questioningly at Roxy, who shrugged her shoulders and continued eating.

"Roxy?"

"Come on and get some supper, Mel. We'll talk later after the kids here finish eating their supper...when they're watching the *Waltons!*"

Later as they sat glued to the television, Roxy took Melony aside and explained the last twenty-four hours.

"But what are we gonna do with him?" she asked in

disbelief.

"I don't know…if I did, I'd tell you."

"Well, we gotta do something?"

"I know that."

"I know how you feel, Roxy…but…."

"No, you don't! He needs us, Mel."

"But we have to report this. You know that."

"I know." She walked away.

"Tomorrow…tomorrow we'll do it," Mel decided, "but tonight, we'll just enjoy…tonight."

Roxy looked around with a smile. "He's a beautiful child, Mel…ain't he?"

"He is. Biracial…isn't he?"

Roxy nodded.

IT WAS JUNE EIGHTH and school was out for the summer. Dakotah bounced into the living room, tossing her books on the floor.

"Mama!"

"Yes Dear," Spring called from her studio room.

"No more school!" she exclaimed with joy.

"For the summer, Dear…but, you remember we'll be doing some tutoring to catch up."

Dakotah ignored the remark. "Can I go to camp, Mama?"

"Camp?"

"Yes. Maria Alljoy is going and so is Betty Jo Lansing. I want to go, too, Mama…please?"

"Well, how long is it…this camp?"

"Two weeks…maybe three…."

Spring couldn't imagine spending two to three weeks

without her. She tried to be evasive.

"Well, we'll talk about it. Now go wash up for supper...and pick those books up, too."

She grabbed up her books and raced upstairs just as the phone rang.

"Pru, how are you?"

"Fine, Spring...and you and Dakotah?"

"We're okay. Dakotah just informed me that she wants to go to camp...imagine that?"

"Goodness, how time flies. She hardly seems old enough. Are you gonna let her?"

"I don't know. But you know how determined Dakotah is...."

"My, my. I wonder where she gets that from?"

"Well, I guess it would be good for her."

"That's right. Both Melony and Mary Tom had their time with summer camp. And it would probably be good for you, too, Spring."

"I know. Any news on Heath?"

"Nothing. His trial comes up soon, you know. He seems so depressed; I can't blame him."

"Is that lawyer doing anything?"

"I guess he's doing all he can do."

"Has he turned up anything?"

"I don't think so."

"How's Jessica?"

"Seems to be holding up fairly well. Of course, I don't know how she'll handle the trial. Melony went to see Heath a few days ago, and he asked about you."

"He did? Poor boy. How's Melony's job working out?"

"Fine. She likes it. Oh, guess what?"

"What?"

"Remember I told you about that boy...that little boy they found down in the cottage below their house?"

"Yes."

"Well, they're keeping him. I mean Roxy's keeping him. Got him as a foster child."

"He was an orphan?"

"Seems so. The poor little fellow had actually been living on the streets with an older boy for some time."

"No parents?"

"No, don't think there was a father in the picture, and his mother's gone. Apparently, she was mixed up in a lot of wrong doing with the wrong crowd. They say she half way took care of him in between jail time and other problems until one day she took off and never came back. He was tossed from one family to another...nobody really taking care of him or wanting him. Can you imagine? He was afraid he'd be picked up by the police and put in jail. Poor little fellow. So, he'd been hiding out...first one place and then another...including the cottage."

"What a sad story, but sounds like he's in good hands now."

"Oh, you can count on that. They brought him up here last week, and Roxy dotes on him...just like she does Laurietta. You know, he's an unusual looking child, being mixed like he is...a very handsome child with real pretty skin, sort of coppertone and his hair is a thick, silky reddish color, but his eyes are what really stand out. They're a beautiful faint green. He just looks different, but you can tell he's half and half. Ellen says it's a blessing that Roxy took pity on him because most folk don't want to adopt a mixed child."

"She's right. But you know, all of us are mixed to some degree. I'm anxious to meet the little fellow."

"Decided when you're coming?"

"Not yet. Got to get the dates all scheduled for Dakotah's tutoring plus now this camp thing, but I'm getting anxious to see all of you...especially Heath."

IT WAS HOT THAT SUMMER in Virginia and it was hotter still in the hills of the quaint town of Lynchburg. The city jail was discreetly hidden among those hills, and Heath stared out the barred window, watching a small bird fluttering in a nearby tree. It finally rested on a fragile branch that matched its own fragility. Was it a Sparrow? He remembered hearing Uncle Patrick speak of the Sparrow in his sermons, and how God's eye is on the Sparrow. He looked up into the twilight sky and wondered if His eye was on him, too.

Some blocks away, Roxy and Antonio sat out on the front steps of the old house on Madison Street, watching the lightening bugs tease them while darting this way and that, turning on their bright little lights just long enough for you to see where they were. It was just the time of day when it decides to succumb to stronger forces and give way to dusk.

"You ever caught lightening bugs?"

Antonio shook his curly head.

"My, my. When we were kids, we used to always catch'em, put'em in a jar and watch their lights. My granddaddy used to call'em fireflies because of their lights, you know."

"Can we get a jar?"

"I've got just the thing. Let's get it."

The two of them spent the next hour chasing those fleeting little bugs until the mason jar was glowing. They placed it upon the porch and returned to the steps.

"Not as young as I used to be," Roxy laughed, out of breath.

He smiled up at her.

"You happy?"

"Yes Ma'am."

"What do you think about our new apartment? We're gonna be moving in next week...that is...as soon as the Browns move out. And you gonna have your own room."

"Ain't you gonna miss Melony and Emily?" he asked thoughtfully.

"Certainly...but it's not like we're really moving. We'll still be in the same house. They'll just be upstairs, and we'll be downstairs."

"Is it because of me?"

"Yes...I mean no...well, not exactly. We've been talking about this for some time now, and we finally decided it was the right time. You know we gotta pick out some material for some curtains for your room... and maybe a new bedspread to match. I saw some the other day in Sears and it had stars and stripes. It was red, white and blue...patriotic you know. Think you'd like that?"

He nodded, "And it's gonna be all my room...by myself?"

"Sure is."

"I never had a room."

"Well, you gonna have one now."

"Miss Roxy?"

"Yes."

"Which room's gonna be mine?"

"I was thinking of the back room...the one beside mine, and that way I'd be between you and Laurietta. How about that?"

"Yes Ma'am. I like that one. That's the one I wanted."

"Really?"

"Yes Ma'am. I can look out the window...and I can see the little house down the hill."

"Oh...and you like that?"

"Yes Ma'am. The little house was like my house," he declared proudly. "Nobody knew about it but me."

"And how was that?"

"Well, almost nobody but me. Jebo...my friend. He told me about it."

Roxy proceeded cautiously, remembering only too well how long it had taken to get him to speak of his past at all, particularly of anyone he had known.

"Jebo was your friend?"

"Yes Ma'am. He gave me the key."

"Where did he get it?"

"Don't know."

"Did he stay with you in the little house?"

"First he did. Then Jebo left and didn't come back no more...and it was all mine."

"And you liked that?"

"Yes Ma'am. When I didn't have no place to stay, I'd come to the little house. It was like a hotel and I was the guest," he smiled proudly.

"I see. Antonio, do you remember much about your

mother?"

He paused. "No Ma'am."

"Was there anybody you really liked...and felt close to?"

"I felt kind'a close to Jebo...before he left. And there used to be a long time ago...an old white-headed man we called Pops. He was real nice, and we stayed with him some. I felt close to Pops."

"Why did you leave?"

"I didn't. Pops left."

"He did?"

"Yes Ma'am...he died."

Roxy sat very still trying to conceal her tears. Antonio stared into the darkness for a moment, and then jumped up. "Can I go tell Laurietta which room's gonna be mine?"

"Certainly...go ahead." She smiled up at him as he turned back around.

"But what about the lightening bugs?"

"Guess we better let'em go."

He picked up the jar and carefully removed the lid, watching the fortunate creatures climb to the top of the jar, perch precariously atop it for a brief moment and then fly off to freedom.

Roxy continued to sit on the porch a while longer reflecting on what had been said. How could one little fellow fall through the cracks of the system of humanity? How could no one seem to care that he existed? But then she looked up into the darkened sky and smiled. Somebody did! That's why he was here. Her thoughts turned to Seth. Somehow she just knew he was happy about all this. The son they never had. She clasped her hands in front of her and rocked back and forth on those cool steps.

"Seth," she whispered into the night, "what do you think of him, Seth?"

SUMMER HEAT sifted through the windows and doors of the aging, but still stately homes that lined Madison Street. It was hot and uncomfortably humid that summer in Lynchburg...and in all of Virginia. Melony and Emily found themselves spending more time in Roxy's apartment than their own as it was much cooler on the first floor. Of course, that wasn't the only reason. Even though they were just floors away, they missed each other's company. Often though, Melony and Emily escaped to Oak Mountain on the weekends to 'cool off'.

It was on such a weekend that Roxy decided to get Laurietta and Antonio's picture taken. They spent an enjoyable time at Pittman Plaza, eating lunch at the counter of Murphy's and leisurely watching the birds and fish in the pet department. Antonio smiled proudly for the photographer as he snapped the picture, and then he jumped down quickly to avoid being seen sitting so close to a girl, even if it was Laurietta. She frowned at him and Roxy was amused.

They finally stepped up on the bus to head home. Laurietta and Antonio once again delighted in the stuffy old city bus, and bounced up and down on the seats while peering out the dusty windows. What was it about buses? Children always loved them. It wheezed and jolted and started up again after depositing an old man that limped off with a cane. They passed along a couple

of streets and then slowed down again at the entrance
of Miller Park with its lofty, old Oak trees spreading
forth their massive arms to shade the many squirrels
that scampered beneath them, plus anyone else that
might happen by. The gentle, sloping hills of the park
seemed to beckon, to invite one to partake of its bounties
flowing with coolness, tranquillity and peace midst the
busyness of the surrounding town.

Roxy's eyes were drawn to the pool — or what used
to be the pool — now filled in with dirt. She could
remember the cool, green water that would splash
against its sides while children screamed with delight,
jumping in and out. She could still see herself pulling
her mama toward the desirable scene, but her mama
resisted, saying that ain't for colored folk. And she'd
wondered again, confused and perplexed...why not?

The bus lurched forward, leaving the park, trees and
forgotten pool behind. Soon it stopped at Fifth and
Madison, and the three of them, tired but happy, got off
and marched up the tree-lined cobblestoned street to
home. She loved this street with its ancient sidewalks,
cracked and crooked from the stubborn persistent roots
of the tall proud trees that pushed their way through the
massive stone as if to prove their strength. She began
to hum a tune while swinging their packages.

Antonio looked up at her.

"*Just a Closer Walk With Thee,*" she replied.

He smiled, and she continued to hum.

The next morning, Melony was up at daybreak. She
rose quietly and dressed with a purpose in her heart.
Not often did she have the chance to do what she wanted

to do...alone. Emily had stayed on with her folks for a few days, and she wanted to go walking early in the morning...before church. It was simply something she'd wanted to do for a long time, and she dressed excitedly. Roxy would think she was crazy if she saw her leaving this early on a Sunday morning, she smiled to herself.

She quietly descended the steps, crept past Roxy's door and noiselessly opened the big door. She stepped out into the beautiful summer morning, inhaling the fresh dewy air. Aimlessly, she sauntered off, simply enjoying every little pleasure...the sweet fragrance of dew frosted leaves, the uplifting melodious song of a nearby Robin, the stillness of morning...the calm that soothes the spirit. As she meandered down the old streets toward the reservoir on Clay Street, she found herself putting together the fragments of thought that floated through her mind as matter floats in space...

A hazy mist hangs in the air
As I trod these vacant streets
The moisture of dew is everywhere
Upon the stones beneath my feet

A pureness exists about this time
Not yet corrupted by the coming day
As yesterday's sorrows are now behind
And those of today still on their way

With souls asleep midst their dreams
The morning belongs to that of nature
As leaves rustle and birds sing
All seems to rejoice in God, their maker

But all of a sudden, the sun appears

And sleepy eyes slowly open
A baby's cry...I do hear
The calmness of morning has been broken!

She filed away these thoughts for later and leaned against the fence to the reservoir, staring at the supposed Indian maiden, remembering Roxy's words. She glanced around at the empty street and back at the mysterious statue.

"Good Morning," she called out softly. "It's a beautiful morning! 'Course I guess you've seen many a beautiful morning standing their atop of the city." She smiled and looked around at the many church steeples that graced the surrounding hills. And then she heard them...piercing the still morning as bells peeled out their glorious chimes. It was awesome! It was humbling! She felt as if she were being serenaded by God himself as she stood there alone in the midst of such beauty. She walked slowly through the streets, letting the magic of the moment...the magic of the morning fill her soul.

The church bells ceased and Melony continued to walk the quiet downtown streets for much longer than she realized, absorbing each and every minute detail of the early morning mood. She glanced at her watch. It was time. She came to a stop on Clay Street and looked up at the stone building with barred windows. She climbed the steps and rang the bell, announcing herself. Then she found herself waiting at the window inside, and she wiped the perspiration from her forehead with the palm of her hand, wondering whether it had gotten that hot that fast or was it just her? Even though she'd been there several times before, as always, it was an intimidating experience. Suddenly the massive steel door opened, and she walked through it, following the jailer's robust frame as he wobbled through the darkened corridor with his large key ring dangling. The door slammed behind them, causing her to jump. There was another door facing them more threatening than the first. The jailer inserted one of his many keys, and they repeated the process all over again. It, too, slammed shut behind them, echoing off the stone walls with that cold, hollow sound.

She began to feel the first signs of claustrophobia... a stifling feeling of being shut in! How did Heath stand it? She was led into a cramped waiting room with a bare table and two chairs.

"Have a seat, Ma'am," the jailer spoke in his businesslike manner, "He'll be out in a minute."

She sat down in the chair and waited...feeling quite alone. Suddenly, another officer appeared with Heath, looking very thin and pale. When his eyes met hers, he smiled weakly.

The indifferent officer stepped to one side and posted himself there for the remainder of the visit as their silent witness. What did they think she'd do? For goodness sake! Free him? She wished she could.

As he sat down before her, she couldn't help but notice his nails, bitten to the quick. Oh Heath...you poor thing...she wanted to cry out, but instead, she heard her own chirpy voice asking, "How are you?"

"I'm okay."

"I know this heat must be getting to you."

"It's hot everywhere, I'm sure."

But Melony didn't think the heat behind those bars was comparable to the outside world. It seemed ten degrees cooler outside.

"How's Little Emily?"

"Not so little anymore, you know. She's nine, going on sixteen."

He smiled again.

"We were at Mama's yesterday, and I saw your dad. He's looking good."

He looked down at the concrete floor. Was it too painful for him to think of his parents, and what this was doing to them?

Abruptly, he spoke, "Mel, could you possibly do me a favor?"

She wondered what on earth. "Well, of course, Heath."

"Wednesday is...this Wednesday is...Caroline's birthday...."

She could feel the silence in the room. Her eyes briefly caught sight of the statue-like figure in the corner. He never moved.

She waited.

"Could you...would you...please put some flowers on her grave?"

"Certainly, I'd be glad to," she replied awkwardly.

Suddenly, he seemed to distance himself, lost in thought perhaps. She wondered if he was not back on Oak Mountain.

"She liked...she liked Daisies. She always liked Daisies."

Melony reached across the roughhewn table, and patted his clammy hand. "I'll take care of it, Heath."

Walking back home, up the tree-lined street, trying to stay in the shade, she wondered again. What *did* happen on Oak Mountain? A Robin swooped down in a nearby rosebush that bordered the neatly kept grounds of St. Paul's Episcopal Church. She watched it turn its tiny head this way and that as if it, too, wondered.

She walked on past the churchyard, listening to her own footsteps on the unlevel sidewalk. Her heart ached for Heath...a prisoner behind those cruel bars...unable to enjoy a beautiful day like this! But soon his trial would be...and then...she must pray much for him this morning in church. She turned up Madison Street, more solemn than she'd left, carrying her cousin's burden with her.

Heath sat back down in his cell to face another long day. His thoughts were the same as every other day since he'd arrived. If only he hadn't gone up to Lover's Leap that day! If he hadn't said what he said! If they hadn't argued? If he hadn't lost his temper? She might be alive today! If only he could turn back the clock and undo what had been done! But time doesn't allow us but one chance...no repeats. He looked up at the high window and saw a small patch of blue sky. He recalled an old western he'd watched often where the prisoner gazed up at the window listening to the dull thud of the hammer preparing his gallows. He wondered what *his* destiny was?

But as the sweltering heat lay low over Lynchburg, Oak Mountain thrived in the summer's climax. Pru walked through the cool evergreens with Emily tagging behind, swinging her slightly bent tin pail. She laughed, feeling like a kid again herself.

"Emily, my mama used to take us blackberry pickin', too."

"I know, Grandma...you told me...."

She smiled to herself wondering if there was anything you could tell kids nowadays that they didn't already know. But then, maybe she was repeating herself.

"How much further, Grandma?"

"Oh, not far. Just a bit up the way there and around that bend."

"Can we have blackberry roll tonight?"

"Sure can." She pushed the brush away, coming upon the spot she'd picked from for the past few years. She was disappointed.

"Oh my, looks like the pickin's gonna be light."

"Why, Grandma?"

"Don't know. Just happens that way sometimes. But when I was a girl at the homeplace, we had more blackberries than you could shake a stick at."

"Grandma, can we go there?"

"Where? You mean the homeplace sight? Why, I haven't been in a while myself...certainly not at blackberry season. I don't know whether there are any blackberries there anymore."

"But, I'd like to go. Grandma, please?"

Later in the day, as they drove up the mountain, Pru wondered what Emily found so fascinating about the old ruins of the place. Melony had told her how she'd reacted to it the last time.

"Are we there yet, Grandma?"

"Almost. Guess we should check Spring's chalet

while we're up here. She'd appreciate that."

Once there, they walked up to Spring's place, noticing how neat the grounds were. Spring would be glad to hear that. She was quite fortunate to have found someone so reliable, particularly with him being so young, too. They pushed through the underbrush that had grown up so thickly surrounding the site of the old homeplace, picking their steps carefully so as not to disturb any unexpecting rattler that might be sunning himself on such a nice day.

"Stay behind me, Emily...and watch out for snakes."

Emily obeyed.

Suddenly they stood before the old chimney again, a silent reminder of the past. Pru studied the crumbling fixture with childhood memories flooding back as always. Those ever-present thoughts were like a basket interwoven with happy memories and those not so happy, but they all made up her childhood and those of her family. And that was it...no matter what...they were family. She glanced back at Emily, the new generation. Too bad that she and the other young'uns would never know what lies hidden here on Oak Mountain.

"This is where you grew up. Right, Grandma?"

"That's right."

"Why did they tear it down?"

"Progress, Dear...they call it progress."

"Oh. Can we go to the cemetery before we pick blackberries?"

"Of course...just be careful where you step."

As they turned to leave, Emily looked back. "Wasn't

a very big house, was it?"

"No. It was quite small...but big enough for us. Kept us close together, I suppose. Perhaps that isn't such a bad idea after all," she answered thoughtfully.

They made their way cautiously up the hillside, arriving at the small cemetery somewhat out of breath. Pru pushed the creaking gate aside and stepped in. Emily followed. She went straight to the stone just as Pru expected.

"This is my Great Grandmother Emily."

Pru nodded, full of emotion. They were silent for a moment.

"Am I like her?"

"Well, now let me see. Somehow, I think you may have a very strong likeness. Not so much in appearance...but inside...you know."

"Inside?"

"Yes. Mama had a quiet strength...a soft power... you might say. I see that in you sometimes."

"You do?" She smiled with satisfaction.

Chapter XVII
History Repeats

The summer heat was kinder in the Plains without the sweltering humidity of the south. Spring was thankful for that, but still she missed those summers on Oak Mountain. She was quietly reflecting on this difference as she drove Dakotah out to camp.

Once there, unloaded and settled in, Spring turned to Dakotah, "Now, you're sure you'll be fine?"

"Of course, Mom." She looked around at the large tent she'd be sharing with three other little girls. "Isn't this the greatest tent, Mom? Better than the one at Wounded Knee...it even has a floor!"

The other mothers looked up curiously. She smiled at them. "It is that, Dear. I know you'll enjoy it."

"And look at my bed, Mom. I'm going to put my pocket knife that Grandpa gave me here under my pillow." She pushed it under the pillow and patted it gently.

"I beg your pardon, Ma'am," one of the mothers

quickly interjected, "She can't possibly do that!"

Spring looked straight at the lady and refrained from saying what was on her mind. "You're right, Ma'am. Dakotah, please give me the knife. It's probably not a good idea to keep it here. I'll take good care of it while you're gone...."

Dakotah looked up at the other mothers and then back to Spring, who wore that firm, proud look to which she was accustomed. Quickly assessing the situation, she retrieved the knife and reluctantly handed it to Spring.

As Spring sped away from the camp, she felt an overwhelming loneliness. How was she going to make it for two whole weeks? She rehearsed the episode with the knife over again in her mind, and hoped Dakotah would enjoy her stay with her roommates. She knew that this could be an everlasting fond memory or an everlasting painful one. Growing up was hard. But then, her own childhood was quite different, only surrounded by white children. This camp was mixed with white and Indian, of course. She felt it very important to provide Dakotah with a well rounded upbringing with exposure to all kinds of people.

She neared the reservation, and felt more lonely still. Ever since Dean and Grandpa had died, she and Dakotah had drawn even closer. But then, she had a full schedule planned ahead. Time would surely fly. And once Dakotah returned, they'd be flying back to Virginia to spend time with the family before school started again. She couldn't wait! So much had happened since she'd last been there. She really wanted to see Heath and Jonathon, of course. What a grievous thing for him to go through.

The time didn't fly, though. Each day seemed to drag, and she felt like she was living her life in slow motion. By the fourth day, she wondered if she could wait for the weekend to check on her. She pulled herself out of bed, feeling the sultriness already promising another hot, humid day. This oppressive weather was difficult. What had happened to the usual hot dryness? She supposed she'd have to break down and put in central air in spite of the fact that she preferred fresh air. While brushing her teeth, she thought of the meeting first on her agenda...a very important one at that. After much wheeling and dealing, they'd managed to get several of the local politicians to meet with them this morning concerning needs on the reservation.

The conference room was getting warmer and fans were swaying rapidly. Spring sat down after concluding her convincing talk, which was followed by a welcomed applause. She watched the last official rise and proceed to the podium with a seemingly hesitant stride. The temperatures were not only rising from the heat, but also from stored up emotions. She looked at her watch. 11:45 a.m. The meeting was moving slowly.

The speaker introduced himself, sipped at the glass of water placed strategically in front of him and began his orientation in a low, monotone voice. Suddenly, there was a loud knock at the door. It opened and the secretary appeared with a look of concern.

"Excuse me for interrupting...but we just received warning over the intercom of an approaching tornado!"

Everyone quickly rose to their feet.

"Where is it now?" several voices asked in unison.

"Just passed by the Badlands, heading this way, they say."

Spring felt a cold shiver pass over her. No, it can't be! The camp...the camp was in its path. She stumbled out the room, away from the confused crowd. She must get there! She must get to Dakotah!

She pulled open the door and looked out. Though it was midday, it looked like dusk. The sunshine was gone, replaced by an ominous darkening sky. She ran to the car, jumped in and sped off.

It began to rain, first large pelting drops that splattered her windshield, making it difficult to see. It changed to a spitting rain which quickly turned to hail...small marble sized pieces...then larger chunks that beat on the rooftop...reverberating throughout the small sports car...and throughout her brain. Dakotah! Dakotah! She must get to her. She should never have let her go, she thought frantically. I should have kept her with me. It's all my fault! First Daddy, then Mama, then Dean...NO! Not Dakotah!

"Calm down, Spring...calm down," she coached herself aloud. It's just a tornado. How many tornadoes have you witnessed throughout the years? Why, it's part of the plains. They can turn up anywhere and end up anywhere. Who can tell? It's probably headed in the opposite direction right now. But somehow, that foreboding feeling was pressing down upon her and her hands trembled on the steering wheel. She pressed down harder on the accelerator, speeding down the wet highway. Dakotah would be okay! Dakotah would be fine! But what Spring couldn't see or know was that the threatening funnel was headed straight for the camp.

They had been alerted. The staff were frantically herding the confused children into the cellar beneath the main building. However, there was mass hysteria as the children had been scattered at the time enjoying a "free time." It was nearly impossible to know the whereabouts of them all, and the counselors ran to and fro in search of them, discovering them either still playing, oblivious to the impending danger or crouched in a corner in fear, not understanding the sudden changes taking place. The wind was wildly ripping at the tents, exposing the once neatly made beds with teddy bears and dolls adorning them. Loose boxes and articles blew across the grounds, up against buildings or whoever was in the path. All eyes were riveted to the sky as they hurried, and they cringed as the lightening darted and danced over the camp.

As a thief appears suddenly in the night, often as such, the tornado appears on the plains catching its victims unaware. It was so for Dakotah, who had wandered off into the nearby fields much earlier in pursuit of butterflies, a favorite pastime. As she had a way of doing, totally absorbing herself in her own world, she had lost track of time and wandered further than planned. She knelt on the warm tall grass to watch a fragile butterfly light on a slender blade of grass, and shadows suddenly fell upon her as the sun disappeared. The butterfly flew off. The grass began rapidly moving in different directions. She clutched at it, looking upward into the darkened sky. What was happening? Then she saw it!

In the distance, hanging from the greenish black
base of a large cloud was a tornado. She knew it was a
tornado. She'd seen them in pictures at school. She
gasped, jumped up and began to run toward the camp.
Stumbling over the uneven clumps of wild grass, she ran
wildly with the wind now whipping at her skirt and
blowing her dark braids into her face, stinging her
tender skin. She looked back. It was getting larger...
coming after her. She tried to run faster, panting for
breath. Strange objects were flying around her in the
air...paper...sticks...debris. Suddenly, she felt a blow
to her back and fell forward. She struggled upward and
saw that it was actually a tree limb that had hit her, and
though her back ached, she pulled herself up and continued to run. She must get to the camp! She'd be safe
there.

Squinting in the wind, she ran on, panting with each
breath. Again she looked back at the monster that was
chasing her, and saw it dangling and writhing from the
sky. It looked like a giant snake coming after her. She
wanted to cry...but she must be brave!

She ran on...a tiny, frail object in the path of the
massive black wall of debris that was burrowing downward, plowing a path several yards wide, and then
lifting itself back up into the air to leave undamaged
areas for blocks. As the winds strengthened their
maddening force, she thought of her mother...her strong
fierce mother. What would *she* do? She would be
brave...and she wouldn't give up. Although her legs
were weak and wobbly beneath her, she ran a little
harder. She fought back the tears...she would be brave.

But though she ran, she felt like she was losing

ground...like somebody was pulling her backwards. I'm going to die, she thought. I'm going to die! She looked back, and saw to her amazement, a swirling mass of darkened debris...the monster funnel appeared to be alive! Her squinted eyes filled with tears...but, no, she wouldn't cry! Flying and sundry objects were hitting her as she continued to run, and she felt herself slowing down. She couldn't distinguish whether it was her own lack of strength or the magnetic power behind her, but whatever, she was losing the battle. There was a peculiar hissing, whistling noise now all around her. It sounded like a million bees buzzing. She looked back...it was bearing down upon her! The shrill high-pitched shriek changed to a terrible deafening roar encompassing her. She stopped and stood still, awaiting her fate, watching the monstrous funnel as it rose above her and hung directly over. Suddenly, there was the stillness of death and the strong odor of gas. She faintly whispered..."I can't breathe!" She looked up into the monstrous funnel with swirling walls that were lit up brilliantly with constant flashes of lightening which zigzagged from side to side. It screamed and hissed...and sucked her up into its raging force.

Spring drove on frantically. The radio cracked and sputtered its dreadful warnings..."*Tornado still doing a lot of damage...still moving toward Pine Ridge...there are power lines down everywhere...a number of houses and trailers are reported destroyed...we encourage you to stay off Route 44 and all areas close by...there is debris all over the road...please take cover if you're in its path.*" Spring's fear heightened as she continued to lis-

ten..."*We're here in the area just above Cedar Butte...
you may be able to hear some of the sirens...there's quite
a bit of damage in and around this area.*" She tried to
shut out the eerie sound of the sirens in the background,
but the shrill blaring continued. Her heart beat faster.
Her mouth was dry. She snapped off the radio! She
would be there soon. Everything would be okay, of
course.

As she struggled to calm herself, the deadly funnel
reached the children's camp and hovered over it for a
second as if looking for its prey. All was quiet except for
the horrendous winds. There was no sign of children...no sign of life. As if maddened by the sight, the
raging funnel smashed into the center of camp, ripping
off roofs, crashing walls in, toppling aged trees as if they
were spindly match sticks...and then suddenly...the
walls of the main house expanded as if blown outward
by a giant within. The crash was terrifying. And then
all was still again as the swirling grey mass departed
and moved onward.

Again, Spring reached for the radio dial, but withdrew her trembling hand. She was almost there. Everything would be fine, of course. She was dramatizing
as usual. Didn't everyone say that it was one of her
weaknesses or strengths...whichever? She did drama-
tize. And even if...if it did pass by the camp...why, the
camp had cellars for protection. Good safe cellars! She
remembered her own insistence of having a cellar in-
stalled in their house after she'd first moved in. Who
could be without one?

She had run out of the rain now. There was no sign
of a tornado, and she was just about there. Suddenly,

she heard sirens again. She checked the radio. It was off. Oh No! They were coming from up ahead...in the direction of the camp. Her knees went watery as she pressed the accelerator harder. She rounded the bend in the road; the scene before her testified all.

Strewn wreckage of shattered glass, broken boards, cars rolled over and trees torn up by their roots...the path of the tornado was obvious as if a large bulldozer had plowed through. She slammed on her brakes just in time to miss a trashed doghouse in the middle of the road. Slowly, she weaved in and out and through the debris...but soon gave up, jumped out of the car, and began running toward the camp. What was that noise? She looked up to see a helicopter approaching. It passed over and was now hovering above the camp. The camp! She stopped suddenly. It lay before her...a heap of ruins.

"NO, NO, NO!" she cried, running as fast as she could. The helicopter was landing in the distance just outside of the camp. Uniformed men were jumping out and running from it. She could see the blinking lights of rescue vehicles and people moving around. Where were the children? Oh God...let them be okay! "Dakotah ...Dakotah!" she called!

Dodging the debris, she ran into the camp. Jumping over boxes and rubble, she anxiously looked from face to face. There were children...a number of children, crying and dirty from their plight.

"Dakotah!" she screamed.

The rescue workers were carrying a stretcher toward the ambulance. She stumbled toward it only to see a mass of red hair protruding from under the sheet. The child looked up at her with frightened blue eyes.

"There's a child trapped below! We need to radio for help...," the large fellow reported to the other. Suddenly Spring heard a cry.

"Dakotah! Dakotah!" She ran toward the partially collapsed building wherein several men were quickly pulling away smashed boards.

"Take it easy, Mack. This place could go anytime."

"Stand back, Lady!"

Again she heard the cry and pushed past the workers, climbing in.

"Get that woman!" someone yelled, but not in time. The building rumbled, shook, and completely collapsed along with Spring. Downward, she fell through the boards, down the broken steps, glass and debris, coming to rest on the cold concrete. She didn't move.

THE NEXT DAY, the newspapers of the Plains reported..."*Tornado kills! Five fatalities reported as a result of the tornado on Wednesday. Coming up out of nowhere as these cruel monsters do, it appeared suddenly. The vicious funnel all but bypassed Rapid City, turned and targeted the rural area to the east. Shaving the Badlands, it caused tremendous damage on its route eastward. St. Francis' Children's Camp also lay in its path and was destroyed. Extensive damage is concentrated in and around the areas of Cedar Butte and Kadoka....*"

The newspaper, with its tragic headlines, lay on the chair beside Spring's hospital bed. She slept a troubled sleep that took her back many years to Oak Mountain. It was snowing. She could hear Mama calling them in for supper. They didn't want to leave the steep hill adjacent to the cabin...she and Patrick and Jonathon.

"Come on, Spring...one more time...," Jonathon hollered.

"But Mama's calling," she retorted. "We gotta go in."

"Naw...come on...one more time, Spring...," he pleaded, as his chubby little legs sank down into the deep snow.

"Jonathon, let's go!" Patrick ordered as he headed toward the house pulling his sled behind him. Reluctantly, Jonathon followed. Spring trudged behind the two, admiring Patrick's new sled. He'd made it himself, and she was proud of him, although a little jealous. But he'd promised to make her one next. The back door opened. Prudence stood with her hands on her hips. Miss Bossy, as usual. Then she caught the familiar aroma of hot vegetable soup drifting out the door and into the snowy landscape. She suddenly felt very hungry. She thought she could see Mama through the doorway in the background, but then she disappeared. She strained to see her.

Mareen, standing by her side, watched her lovely face frown, and wondered why. Was she in pain? Her head was wrapped in folds of white bandages, although they had assured her that it was not serious. Badly bruised and cut was supposed to be the extent of it. How fortunate she was! She sighed and left the room, walking down the corridor to another room.

Quietly, she pushed the door ajar and looked in on the tiny replica of Spring. Dakotah, too, slept...but her sleep was the sleep of death. Her fine Indian features seemed more prominent than usual. Her black eyelashes curled upward and her dark braids lay beside her, a stark contrast on the crisp white pillow case. The machine hooked up to her with small colored wires was systematically tallying the required data. Mareen turned away from the intimidating presence and stared out the window. What on earth would she say? How could she tell Spring? If only her family were here, but they wouldn't arrive for a couple of days. Imagine driving all that ways! Of course, flying would be expensive, or was it Clarence's fear?

How she dreaded facing Spring with the news. Footsteps coming into the room interrupted her thoughts.

"Oh, Dr. Henry."

The short Asian doctor smiled at her and began checking his patient.

"Doctor, is she going to be all right?" her voice sounded shaky.

He looked up at her again.

"I'm her cousin. Her next of kin besides her mother."

"It's difficult to say."

"How long will she be in this coma?"

"I'm sorry, Ma'am, but we have no way of knowing that. Right now, we're just trying to stabilize her and her blood pressure."

Suddenly, a piercing scream filled the hospital corridors. Mareen and the doctor rushed out. It was Spring! She stood in the hallway looking crazed while two nurses grabbed at her arms. She held the crumpled newspaper in her hand.

"Oh No!" Mareen exclaimed, "Spring, Spring... Dakotah is alive! She's...she's not dead."

Spring stopped and stared at her. "Alive?" she

whispered while going limp. The nurses caught her.

"Yes. She's here...in the hospital...."

"Where?" she demanded, pulling away from the nurses.

Dr. Henry was now standing beside her. "Come this way. Your daughter is in here." He led her to Dakotah's room. "She sustained extensive injury," he slowly explained, gauging her reaction, "and she's in a coma right now."

"Coma?" Spring repeated while staring down at her. "Dakotah...Dakotah...," she called out. Falling across the child's bed, she hugged her frail body.

THE LARGE DODGE crossed the Virginia line into West Virginia as the family again rehashed the conversation they'd had with Mareen prior to leaving.

"But why on earth did she leave the newspaper lying beside her bed?" Melony asked aloud.

"People make mistakes, Mel," Clarence answered flatly.

"I'm sure she was devastated, thinking poor little Dakotah dead," Pru added.

"Grandma, is Dakotah gonna be okay?" Emily asked from the back seat.

The car was silent for a moment.

"We certainly hope so, Honey. We'll have to pray a lot for her."

"I already prayed," she declared.

"Just what did Mareen say about the coma, Pru?" Clarence asked, while beating his pipe on the ashtray with one hand and steering with the other.

"Well...at this point, it seems that Dakotah's situation...the coma could be of long duration. There is that possibility, the doctor says."

"What do they mean...long duration?"

"Mel, I really don't know. I don't think *they* know. But I *do* know that if she stays in this state very long, I can't imagine what it will do to Spring."

"But Spring is strong, Mama. You've said that many times."

"That's true, but even the strongest have their breaking points."

Emily spoke up again, "Grandpa, do you think a tornado might come to Oak Mountain?"

"Not likely, Honey. Our mountains protect us. Seems they pick on the plains most of the time...and flat land. We don't have to worry much about them."

Emily settled back in her seat, snuggling up close to her mother and opened up her library copy of *Little Women*.

"What about the painting, Mom? Did Mareen say anything more about it...whether or not it has been found?"

"No. Nothing has turned up yet."

"Did she say how Spring feels about it?"

"Frankly, Spring hasn't mentioned it since they told her. I'm sure it's irrelevant to her right now. All her energies are consumed with Dakotah...and rightly so."

"That's the strangest thing, though," Clarence mused, "The tornado hits the museum...a number of paintings are destroyed...but only Spring's is missing."

"Mareen said they have determined it to be theft."

"But who would even think of stealing a painting in the middle of a tornado?"

"Mel, it's hard to comprehend, but historically, whenever such a crisis occurs...theft usually accompanies it."

"Oh, I almost forgot," Melony began rummaging through her large bag, "I picked this up yesterday when I was in Charlottesville." She held up the Charlottesville paper. "There's an article here on Spring... and the lost painting. Here it is." She handed it to her mother.

Down in the lower left hand corner, the headlines read..."*LOCAL VIRGINIA ARTIST SUFFERS DOUBLE BLOW...Young daughter and prized painting of Spring Barrett, Virginia Artist originally from Oak Mountain, are both hit by midwest tornado! Daughter is still in coma in Rapid City Hospital, and painting* The Dogwoods, *which won honors for Miss Barrett, is mysteriously missing from the museum in Rapid City that was also damaged by the tornado.*"

Pru laid the paper down. "Poor Spring."

"It's a shame," Melony declared. "Of all her paintings, that was her favorite. She told us so a long time ago...Mary Tom and me."

THAT NIGHT AS THE Dodge continued westward, Spring sat quietly in the cramped hospital room watching the faint ray of light that spilled under the closed door. She raised her tired eyes to the bed beside her and the small still form beneath the cover. For the first time in her life, she...Spring Barrett...was totally helpless. Now her strength, her determination, her persistence was to no avail. She was dependent upon what ... circumstances? Or was it fate? She reached out and smoothed the cool brow...her precious Dakotah.

But where was she? Where was her tiny spirit

soaring? She choked back a sob..."Dakotah...please come back...please come back to Mommy...don't leave me...."

She slumped back in her chair, giving way to despondency, wishing there was someone to lean on... someone stronger now...somebody bigger than herself.

Somebody bigger? Where had she heard that? Drifting backwards again to Oak Mountain...a little girl that looked a lot like Dakotah stood in the simple kitchen beside a wood stove watching her mother stirring supper in a big pot. Her mother wiped the perspiration from her forehead and onto her faded apron and smiled down at the child. Then she heard it ...the melodious voice singing....

> Who made the mountain, who made the tree
> Who made the river flow to the sea
> And who hung the moon in the starry sky
> Somebody bigger than you and I

The comforting words came tumbling out of the recesses of her mind...in that familiar and beautiful voice...

> Who makes the flowers bloom in the spring
> Who writes the song for the robin to sing
> And who sends the rain when the earth is dry
> Somebody bigger than you and I...

> He lights the way when the road is long
> Keeps you company
> With love to guide you, He walks beside you
> Just like he walks with me...

Tears rolled down her high cheek bones. She felt her mama reaching out to her. Suddenly a peace fell over her and all the years of confusion and doubt seemed to vanish as the morning dew in the sun. She knew there were no people on earth with a stronger faith than her people...except maybe for her mother. But whether in the words of her people...Wak-Kon-ton-kah...The Great Spirit or the words of the folk on Oak Mountain...Our Father in Heaven...He was real...He was there....

> When I am weary, filled with despair
> Who gives me courage to go on from there
> And who gives me faith that will never die
> Somebody bigger than you and I*

She knelt beside her chair there in the dark of that hospital room with the one faint ray of light spilling under the doorway...and wept for faith. A gentle rain began to fall upon the wide hospital window, and it continued throughout the night as she kept her vigil and reached out beyond those walls, beyond the hospital, beyond mankind...to somebody bigger.

ON THE AFTERNOON of the third day, Pru, Clarence, Melony and Emily rushed into the hospital corridor although exhausted from the trip. Spring stood before them.

"Spring...Dear...," Pru ran to her, embracing her midst tears, while the others stood close by.

"It's okay, Sis...it's okay."

"Dakotah...how is she?" she blurted out.

"She is the same," Spring answered calmly.

*(Somebody Bigger Than You and I, by Johnny Lange, Hy Heath and Sonny Burke)

"No change?" Clarence added.

"No change."

"She's still in the coma?" Emily asked.

Spring looked down at Emily and showed the first sign of breaking, but held her emotions in check. "Yes, Emily, she is...but I know she'd want you to still come and see her." She reached for her hand.

Emily looked around at the others and grasped Spring's hand. They started down the long corridor, passing by busy nurses, doctors and other hospital workers. Melony was concerned about Emily's reaction, and followed closely. Pru looked at Clarence and marveled at how well Spring was holding up.

But the long drive and Spring's words had not prepared them for the pitiful sight that was before them. Dakotah lay as still as death and almost as white. The medical machinery surrounding her, and reaching out to her with its wiry fingers, lent an aura of apprehension as its digital numbers and signs bounced around. What did it all mean? Melony wondered. She watched Emily step back.

"Dakotah, darling...," Spring leaned over her. "Guess who's here? Your cousin, Emily. She's come all the way from Oak Mountain to see you. How about that?"

Emily watched.

Spring turned, motioning for her to come closer. "Come, Emily. She's only sleeping...but she would like for you to say hello. You know how much she loves you...."

Emily slowly moved toward the bed.

"Dakotah," she began gradually. "It's me...Emily. I...I wish you'd wake up...." She gently patted the covers.

The room was silent...and so was Dakotah.

That night, as Melony sat with Dakotah, Pru and Spring talked in the hospital chapel. It came as a shock to Pru when Spring led her into the small, dark room. "Pru, I want you to pray for Dakotah," she'd asked with a tremble in her voice.

"Of course."

They had knelt and Pru prayed long and earnestly while squeezing her sister's hand. Afterwards, they'd sat in silence for a while. Then Spring spoke.

"Sis, everything's gonna be all right."

Pru looked at her mysterious sister intently.

"I'm okay, Pru."

"What's happened, Spring?"

"I believe."

"In the Lord?"

She nodded. "A few nights ago when I was alone in Dakotah's room, something special happened...and I prayed...I prayed for faith. Afterwards, I opened up the Gideon Bible and found a verse. It said...'he that cometh to God must believe that He is, and that He is a rewarder of them that diligently seek him'."

"...and you did that?"

"I did."

Tears rolled down Pru's cheeks as a wide smile appeared. "I know Mama's happy."

"I found another verse that night that completed my search and my questioning. Of course, I'm sure I'd heard it before, but never *really* heard it, you know."

Pru waited.

"In the Book of John, chapter ten and verse thirty ...Jesus was talking and He said...'I and my Father are one'."

Pru smiled.

"It's so profound...but so simple."

"Simplicity is God's way. Remember, I think, in the Book of Matthew, when Jesus called a little child to Him, and set him in the middle of them. He said, 'Verily I say unto you, Except ye be converted, and become as little children, ye shall not enter into the kingdom of heaven'."

Spring nodded. "We try to make it so difficult sometimes. I know I did. Children accept by faith and we try to analyze everything."

"That's right."

"Pru, I have a peace about Dakotah."

"You know, sometimes it takes a deep valley to cause us to look upward...like this. I cannot help but think how history repeats itself."

"What do you mean?"

"Well, remember when the flood came when we were kids. It was then that Daddy made peace with God."

Spring nodded. "God took Charity, Pru...but...I hope He doesn't take Dakotah...."

TWO WEEKS HAD passed since the fatal tornado ripped its way through the plains of South Dakota, creating havoc and leaving the stench of death. The monster's path could eerily be traced through the country side by shattered, twisted trees that had been stripped of limbs, foliage and very often uprooted. Fields of wheat and corn looked as if a bulldozer had plowed through. Vehicles lay overturned and crushed, and skeletons of former houses were sadly on display in the hot shining sun. And if one were to pause and look closely within the skeletons, they would see the former power of its destroyer as broken glass protruded from the plaster where it had been hurled as spears and stuck. They would witness the disruption of life as tea kettles remained on stoves and teddy bears lay forlornly on trash strewn floors, and families tried to rebuild and reshape their distorted lives.

The Barrett family sat around the kitchen table discussing their departure from the plains.

"Well," Clarence drawled, "as much as we hate to do it, guess tomorrow, we'll have to head back east. Can't afford to be away any longer."

Pru nodded.

"Hon, looks like you gonna be flying on one'a those flying machines again."

She smiled at him.

"Do we have to go, Mom?" Emily pleaded, "I want to see Dakotah when she wakes up!"

"I know, Dear," Melony replied, "but I have to get back to work...and you have to help Grandpa with the farm while Grandma's here."

"And what about Music?" Clarence tugged at her pigtail. "He's gotta be mighty lonesome."

Emily smiled up at him, and reached into her pocket, pulling out a worn rabbit foot.

"Grandma, will you give this to Dakotah when she wakes up?"

"Certainly, Dear." She took hold of the prized possession.

"Come along, Emily. We've got to get our baths and get ready for the big trip tomorrow."

Melony and Emily headed to the bathroom, as the others watched. Spring was quiet.

"I figure Jonathon might be needing some moral support right about now," Clarence added as he got up stretching.

"How long will the trial last?"

"Hon, that's hard to say, but it shouldn't last too long."

"Pru, you don't have to stay here," Spring repeated again. "If the verdict isn't good, Jonathon and Jessica will need you."

"I know, but they will have Patrick...and I feel my place is here with you until...."

"Until Dakotah wakes up," Spring finished.

Chapter XVIII
The Old Courthouse Witnesses...

The telephone party lines on Oak Mountain buzzed like a nest of hornets on a hot summer day. The scandal was cresting its peak. Heath Barrett, son of Jonathon Barrett, grandson of old Heath Barrett, was on trial ...trial for murder...murder of his own wife no less... and she being with child...oh horror of horrors! Those that knew of the skeletons carefully hidden away in the closet of the Barrett household, whispered among themselves...*"and you know what the Good Book says about how the sins of the father will be visited upon the third and fourth generation...."* Knowingly, they would shake their heads.

The judge pounded his gavel, calling a recess.
A grueling two days already, and the situation looked grave for Heath. He was led from the courtroom while returning a weak smile to his tense parents. Jonathon

squeezed Jessica's hand tightly. It had surely been an exhausting two days for everybody concerned, but especially for them as every bit and shred of evidence introduced tore at their heartstrings. The prosecuting attorney had chiseled away hour after hour watching with pride as the chips fell, and Heath's spirit sank deeper and deeper. Patrick struggled to encourage him every chance he got, but even he was beginning to feel the inevitable gloom of the courtroom.

Melony walked outside, squinting in the glaring sun, and looked across the street to the old courthouse that had been replaced by the one they were using. It sat perched atop its very own hill, proudly displaying its stately Greek Revival presence in the blazing morning sun. The sultry heat that lifted from the serene James below and floated upward, enveloping its prey on the way, now surrounded the old courthouse as a mirage. Interested folk, mostly from Oak Mountain, milled around beneath the shade of the tall and aged trees lining the sidewalks on either side of the street. Some had sauntered over to the other side to examine the old courthouse closely and express their own views of the trial more privately. In the distance, a mournful train whistle could be heard approaching the downtown lines.

An elderly gentleman standing in front of her pointed upward to the deteriorating courthouse, at a large clock that sat recessed beneath the main eave of the roof. It looked somewhat out of place as its giant Roman numerals stared outward while its timeless hands seemed to speak audibly...*eleven fifteen*....

He shouted, "You know, they tell me that somebody

has to go up there and wind that thing up every day or
so."

"You don't say," his counterpart, bearing a strong
resemblance to him, replied as they ambled off.

Melony found herself standing alone. She looked to
her right. A young soldier was standing atop a stone
monument, poised as if ready for action, with musket
and bayonet in hand. He was gazing off into the distance
as if awaiting his fate. She walked over to get a closer
look, and observed his fine features chiseled for eternity, but his wavy hair and common hat seemingly let
him live on. He wore no grey or blue now...but tarnished
green.

"A Confederate soldier."

"Roxy, I wondered where you were."

"Just talking to some folk about Antonio."

"Anything wrong?"

"No. That boy's all right. Nothing wrong with him."

Melony turned back to the soldier. "He looks so
young."

"Sure does. Reminds me of Heath...waiting his
fate."

Melony nodded. "Yes, but the soldier dies for a
purpose. There is no purpose in this."

A somber silence followed, and Roxy decided to
change the mood.

"There's a story that goes with this here soldier."

"Really?" Melony never ceased to be amazed at
Roxy's repertoire of stories.

"Well, Mama tells it this way. She used to do some
cleaning for a family nearby...a real nice white family.
They had this little boy that evidently was taken with

the soldier's bayonet. Seems that every night the little
fellow would climb clear up to the top of that statue and
unscrew the bayonet off the gun, take it home with him
and sleep with it."

"You're kidding!"

"Nope. Mama said so. But every morning, he'd bring
it back. Climb back up there and screw it back on.
Nobody ever knew the difference."

"Can't imagine sleeping with that thing!"

Roxy laughed, "Me either!"

The crowd began filing back across the street and
into the courtroom again. Melony and Roxy followed,
but turned for one last look at the old courthouse. Its
massive white pillars gleamed in the midday sun de-
spite its aging signs of chipping and wear. It proudly
radiated an aura of authority much like that of an aged
man in the autumn of his years, demanding respect for
his longevity. And thus it should, as certainly it had
altered the lives of many throughout its past.

"If walls could talk!" Roxy whispered as they left.

And right she was. The Lynchburg courthouse had
held its prominent place for over a hundred years,
gazing down upon the hustle and bustle of downtown
Lynchburg. It had silently witnessed its youth, and
amusedly looked on during its heyday when the small
city ranked as one of the wealthiest in the nation due to
its abundant tobacco crops. And now, a somewhat
saddened spectator, it kept its constant vigil in its
aftermath. Downtown Lynchburg had followed the well
worn path of numerous cities before, and a mad exit had
left its once beaming stores vacant and listless.

Melony and Roxy sat down among the rest of the family that had elected to stay inside out of the heat. The doors were shut. Judge Tyler stood. He looked like most judges, white-haired, robust in frame underneath his black robe that enhanced his stern looking face. The echo of his gavel resounded throughout the courtroom. Judge Tyler ran his court with a rod of iron...most folks said.

"Court is now in session."

"Would Dr. Harris please take the stand."

The doctor, stooped and limping from arthritis, made his way reluctantly to the stand. How he wished he didn't have to testify. He'd been seeing to the Barrett family all his life and his father before him. Why, it was his father that had tended to the boy's grandfather and grandmother when they'd lost their young son in that terrible accident on Christmas Day.

"Would you hold up your right hand, Dr. Harris?"

After he was solemnly sworn in, he sat down slowly.

"Dr. Harris," the prosecuting attorney, Mr. Bonheim spoke loudly, "can you tell us whether or not the deceased, Caroline Barrett, was in fact pregnant at the time of her death?"

Dr. Harris looked into the stone face of the attorney, "Yes Sir, she was."

"Exactly how far along was she, Dr. Harris?"

"Right about ten weeks, Sir...possibly eleven."

"Dr. Harris," the attorney moved from one side of the witness stand to the other, "in your professional opinion, would a young lady ten weeks...possibly eleven weeks pregnant...know she was pregnant?"

Dr. Harris squirmed uncomfortably, "Quite possibly, Sir."

"Quite possibly? Dr. Harris, isn't it highly unlikely that she would not know?"

"Generally speaking, Sir."

Mr. Bonheim turned to Heath, waving his hand in his direction, "The defendant here claims he was not aware of his wife's pregnancy. Caroline Barrett was approximately three months pregnant. Surely, she must have known she was pregnant. Therefore, Heath Barrett would also have known of his wife's condition."

"Objection, Your Honor!" Mr. Walker, Heath's attorney arose.

"Objection sustained."

"Thank you, Dr. Harris." Mr. Bonheim sat down.

Heath sat there motionless. Mr. Walker approached the doctor.

"Dr. Harris, we're not going to waste time wondering whether or not Caroline Barrett knew she was pregnant. That we will never know. But I would like to ask you a few simple questions." He smiled warmly at the old doctor, allowing him to relax.

"Just how long have you known the defendant?"

"Oh my, Mr. Walker, I've known Heath Barrett and his family all my life." He laughed a bit uncomfortably. "I don't mean I've known Heath all my life. He's not quite as old as myself." There was a murmur of laughter in the courtroom. "But I've known the family all my life...and a fine family, too."

"Dr. Harris, would you conclude that you could believe Heath Barrett in what he says?"

"That I would!"

"Thank you, Dr. Harris. You may step down."

The next witness was called and sworn in.

"Billy Franklin," Mr. Bonheim questioned, "how old are you?"

"Fourteen, Sir," the young football star answered proudly. He was feeling particularly important, and he'd noticed Sheila Williams in the courtroom. She must be taking note of all this, too, he gladly thought.

"Billy, where were you on the day of Caroline Barrett's death?"

"Well Sir, my friend Lynwood and me," he pointed to his friend sitting up front, "we decided to take a hike up the mountain...up to Lover's Leap."

"Just the two of you?"

"That's right, Sir."

"Billy, can you tell me in your words what happened up there on Lover's Leap that day?"

"Well Sir, Lynwood and me...we were just walking about...kind of quiet like...kind'a hoping to see a squirrel or something. We'd taken our gravel-shooters with us, you see. We do this now and again. We've caught a squirrel or two that way. Once we even hit at a bobcat. Didn't get'm though. We might have if...."

"Billy, could you please tell me just what happened *that* day?"

"Yes Sir...of course...well, like I said...me and Lynwood were walking along kind'a quiet like...when all of a sudden, we heard this here yelling. It was pretty close to us. Sounded like a lady yelling...kind'a awful."

"...and did you hear what she was yelling?"

"No Sir...I mean it was all kind'a mixed up, you know, with crying and all. Then we heard a man's voice. We could hear him all right...."

"...and what did he say?"

"He hollered...'*I don't want any baby!*' That's what he hollered all right."

"...then what Billy?"

"Well Sir, we heard some more yelling and crying... and then it got real still...real quiet like for a while."

"What did you two do?"

"We just sat there and listened."

"Then what?"

"Well Sir, after a while...we heard this here awful scream...like somebody falling...."

"What did you do then?"

"We went looking to see what was going on, but we didn't see nothing or nobody. So we went back home."

"Did you come back later?"

"Yes Sir, we did...with my Pa. That's because it was Pa who found her. He was coon hunting that night when he found her."

"Thank you, Billy. Mr. Franklin will take the stand in the morning. He is ailing today and couldn't make it," Mr. Bonheim explained to the judge.

"Mr. Walker?"

Mr. Walker stood up. "No questions, Your Honor."

The next couple of days passed much the same. Character witnesses gave glowing reports on Heath and the Barrett Family, but their words fell with little impact on a courtroom and jury that had been overwhelmed by cold hard facts. The evidence was mounting, leaving little recourse for alternatives. A heaviness hung over Oak Mountain, not only from the summer humidity, but also from hearts burdened with troubles.

The Barrett family laid their heads down at night and prayed for their young...Heath behind bars and Dakotah beyond reach.

The last day of the trial arrived. Again, it was a hot muggy day that forecasted a storm brewing for the evening. The jury, weary and anxious to wrap up this whole affair, took their designated seats. Even the crowd had dwindled, losing steam from mother nature's summer breath that drained energies and wilted hope. But interest aroused as the prosecuting attorney called Heath Barrett to the stand.

Judge Tyler spoke, "Mr. Barrett, are you aware that you have the constitutional right not to take the stand?"

"Yes Sir, but I wish to take the stand...to tell the truth...."

"Heath Barrett, will you please raise your right hand? Do you solemnly swear to tell the whole truth and nothing but the truth?"

"I do."

Every eye followed him as he sat down with his dark head bowed. Melony's heart went out to him. He didn't even look like the same Heath Barrett that had always been so sure of himself. His appearance was neat enough with his thick, wavy hair in place and light blue striped shirt and khaki pants completing the picture of a strikingly handsome young man, but his young face revealed the pain and stress that was obviously crushing him.

"Mr. Barrett," the gloating and confident Mr. Bonheim began, "you have heard Billy Franklin testify that he overheard two people near Lover's Leap that day...was that you and Caroline Barrett?"

"Yes Sir, it was."

"On that day, up at Lover's Leap...did you, in fact, tell your wife that you did not want any baby?"

"No...I mean yes...yes I did...but I didn't mean it that way...."

"Mr. Barrett, did you and your wife, Caroline, argue that day?"

Heath looked up sadly. "Yes."

"...and did you yell and holler at times?"

He nodded with his head down.

"...will you speak up for the record, Mr. Barrett."

"...yes...yes...we did!"

"...and in the crest of this heated argument, did you not push your wife, Caroline Barrett, off the cliff, Mr. Barrett?" Mr. Bonheim blasted.

"NO...NO...I did not!" Heath stood facing the courtroom.

Mr. Bonheim deliberately walked away from him and turned to the jury, still addressing him. "You may sit down, Mr. Barrett...and could you please tell the jury what event was to occur the week after the death of your wife?"

Heath looked stunned. He hesitated. "...it was to be our anniversary."

"...and it was a happy marriage, Mr. Barrett?"

Again he paused, looking first to the jury and then to the courtroom. "It was...at times...."

"...I see. Mr. Barrett, how do you explain the fact that your wife was holding onto your tie when her body was discovered sixty feet below Lover's leap?"

"...I don't know exactly. I didn't have it tied...it was just hanging loosely around my neck...and she must've grabbed it when we were arguing. I don't remember."

"Could it be, Mr. Barrett, that she grabbed it when you pushed her off Lover's Leap?"

"Objection, Your Honor!" Mr. Walker interrupted. "Mr. Bonheim is voicing his opinion again."

"Objection sustained. Mr. Bonheim, stick to the facts," Judge Tyler admonished.

"Yes Sir. Mr. Barrett, did you love your wife?"

He lowered his head and spoke hardly above a whisper, "I did."

"STOP...STOP...STOP IT ALL!" Clara Wilkerson yelled out as she stood up pointing her finger at Heath. "Heath Barrett...you're guilty...you're guilty of MURDER...maybe not as we think...but you're still guilty...and may your soul rot in HELL!"

The courtroom buzzed.

Judge Tyler hammered his gavel. "ORDER...OR-DER IN THE COURT! Another outburst from you, young lady...and I will find you in contempt of court!"

"Yes Sir, Judge...but Heath Barrett is not guilty in this court...and this letter will prove it...." She waved a small envelope in the air.

Judge Tyler immediately had the jury removed from the courtroom, and then requested Officer Brown to retrieve the letter.

Clara calmly placed the letter in the officer's hand and sat down. The big burly officer laid it before the judge, who proceeded to put his spectacles on. He began to read as a hush fell over the courtroom. He looked up and read some more.

"This court will adjourn for a recess. We will meet back in one hour," he declared. Clara was asked to accompany the officer to the back.

Heath was led out.

"What do you suppose that's all about?" Ellen asked aloud.

"I have no idea!" Patrick answered, looking rather puzzled.

"I sure would like to speak to her!" Jessica fumed, "the nerve of her, talking that way to Heath! Just who does she think she is?"

"Calm down, Honey. We'll find out soon. I can't imagine what's in that letter...but if it's anything that'll help Heath, we'll forever be grateful to her."

"That's right, Jonathon. This could be wonderful news...but my curiosity is killing me." Melony looked at Roxy, "What do you think?"

She hesitated, "I don't know."

The hour dragged by as anticipation rose minute by minute. The courtroom was literally buzzing with excitement, and most didn't venture far.

Finally, Judge Tyler reentered the courtroom and took his position. He informed the court that the letter in question had been verified and would be admissible as evidence.

Clara Wilkerson was called to the stand, and went through the preliminaries with a staid countenance, one of resigned but planned action.

"Clara Wilkerson, how long were you and Caroline Barrett friends?"

She looked up at Mr. Walker with her vacant grey

eyes and pushed a few strands of wispy blond hair from her forehead. Her pale face wrinkled with a frown.

"...all of our lives. We were childhood friends from third grade on."

"I see. Then you must have known Caroline quite well?"

"Yes Sir, I did...better than anyone, in fact," she exchanged looks with Heath.

"...did you know Caroline Barrett was pregnant at the time of her death?"

"No...I did not."

"As best friends, did you and Caroline share secrets?"

"We shared everything."

"Why do you suppose she did not tell you she was pregnant?"

Clara looked up suddenly. "Because she didn't know...she didn't know herself. Caroline would have told me if she had known! I knew everything about Caroline and she knew everything about me...that's how I knew how unhappy she was because of...," she looked at Heath with vibrant hatred.

"Because of what, Clara...why do you think Caroline was so unhappy?"

"...because she wanted a baby so badly and she couldn't have one...or at least we thought she couldn't have one." Again she looked at Heath with contempt, "...and he...he was too busy for her."

Mr. Walker held up the letter.

"Clara, how did you get this letter?"

Her eyes became watery, filling with tears. "It was sent to me...sent to my post office box. Caroline knew I had a post office box. She sent it to me just before she died...but I didn't get it until last week."

"Why is that, Clara? Why did you not get it until last week?"

Clara looked embarrassed. "Because I didn't check it until last week...."

There was muffled laughter in the courtroom.

"Can you explain, Clara?"

"Yes Sir. You see, I'd gotten the post office box because I had planned on using it for a little business I was starting. Well, it didn't quite pan out...so I just dropped it. But not the post office box. I kept it... actually I just forgot about it. That is, until last week when I received a notice from the post office that my rent was due...and that I still had mail in the box. I went down to the post office...and that's when I found it...."

The attorney turned to Judge Tyler, "At this time, Judge Tyler, I would like to ask Clara Wilkerson to read the letter."

The judge nodded.

Mr. Walker handed the letter still in its envelope to Clara, who slowly opened it and began reading hardly above a whisper.

"Clara, we will have to ask you to speak up...so the court can hear."

"Yes Sir." She raised her voice...

My Dearest Friend, Clara
    Today is the last...day of my life. The last day to see the sun rise...to smell the spring flowers or touch the new budding leaves. For all of this has become worthless to me. The task is too difficult...the path too lonely. There is nothing left. Rather than to continue this charade at life, I choose to

face the unknown in hopes of being reunited with the little
one that...I sent on before. Remember, Clara, the many
times we climbed up to Lover's Leap. Isn't it ironic, today will
be my last climb. Thank you for being my friend...and tell
Heath...I love him.

Signed, Caroline.

A hush had fallen over the courtroom.

Heath's silent questions reached across the courtroom, groping for answers, as tears flowed down his
face.

Clara stared at him icily. All eyes were fixed upon
the two of them, but she spoke only to him.

"Yes, Heath Barrett...the truth is finally known.
Caroline went to Lover's Leap to take her own life. She
didn't know about the baby she carried...but she could
never forget the baby she'd aborted years ago... because
of her fear of losing *you*. But its silent cries haunted her
to her death. Yes, Heath...it was your baby, too...and
now you've lost two...." She laughed out loud and its
eerie sound echoed within the courtroom before she
broke down crying, her sobs growing louder as they led
her out.

When she walked past him, his head dropped, and
the silence of the courtroom accentuated the cries of the
two people who had loved Caroline Barrett the most!

THE NEXT DAY, the newspaper read...*'Heath
Barrett Exonerated!'*

"Glory be!" Roxy exclaimed, "our prayers are answered."

"You're so right. I still can't believe it all," Melony
added.

"What do'ya suppose he'll do now?"

"I don't know. Guess he'll try to get his life back together...what's left of it."

"I do feel so sorry for him. But I feel even sadder about poor little Caroline. I can't imagine feeling that down to actually...take your own life!"

"Mama always said...guilt and loneliness are two very real enemies. I guess they won this time."

"But Melony...God's grace is sufficient! If only she'd known this. If only she'd known His forgiveness...His love that tops all love. If only I'd told her so...."

"I know, Roxy. I feel the same...like we let her down...but we didn't know...."

"Poor Caroline...poor Heath...."

"At least, he's innocent and free. You know, she must have been so distraught when he walked away from her and left, that she jumped not even realizing she still had the tie in her hand."

"I think you're right...I don't think she would have held onto it if she'd realized what it could cost him. I believe she truly loved him."

"Love does strange things," Melony concluded.

The melancholy mood prevailed for days, for weeks on Oak Mountain. A heaviness hung over the hills and valleys like the morning fog...obstructing the warm rays of sun. The gossip ceased, the speculation silenced. The truth was known and such a truth to bear, and the aftermath caught them unaware. The preceding weeks of anticipation and excitement had melted like the morning dew into a soberness that existed in silence.

Until that bright Sunday morning when the phone

rang!

"Pru, it's Spring."

"Spring!"

"Dakotah's back!"

"You mean out of the coma?"

"Yes...last night...it happened last night!"

"What happened?"

"She just woke up...like she had been sleeping for a long while. She was hungry. Imagine that! She was hungry, Pru," Spring was laughing on the other end.

Pru laughed with her, and then they cried tears of joy.

Clarence walked in. "What is it?"

"Dakotah's back. She's awake...and she's hungry!" Pru began to laugh again.

He smiled. "Praise God. That was a long nap."

"Pru, when she gets really well, we're coming back home to Oak Mountain for a while. I feel we need it."

"Wonderful. We'll be waiting."

THE LONG HOT SUMMER ENDED, and with it, all of its woes. Dakotah fully recovered and returned with Spring to Oak Mountain as it raised its curtain for all beholders to witness the Greatest Show on Earth. Autumn on Oak Mountain!

The brilliant array of fall color transformed the deciduous woodlands and mountainsides into a scenery so acute in its beauty that one had to blink one's eyes to realize its reality. The illuminated, shimmering atmosphere created a fairyland as entire mountainsides were swept ablaze with golds, crimsons, orange and red interspersed with deep green Pines. Even the Oaks outdid themselves competing with one another. The bronze-yellow leaves of the Chestnut Oak contrasted sharply with the deep red of its sister Red Oak, along with the yellow-brown of the Black Oak. Even the usual dullness of the White Oak seemed to stretch beyond its limits and add its tribute of richness.

It was on such a day that Spring wandered deep into the woods of Oak Mountain seeking solace after what had been the greatest test she'd faced upon earth. Her soul sought rejuvenation, and she knew instinctively where to find it. She smiled to herself. Indian Summer! No other time on earth could compare. She sat down upon the moist earth already covered with a bed of crisp colorful leaves gradually turning brown, and slowly inhaled the mixed scents, a combined essence of nature at work. The rich earthy scent peaked from the early morning showers, and the gentle breezes caressed her bare arms. She leaned against an aged Oak and closed her eyes, feeling the warmth of the morning sun. She was thankful for the healthful rays and tried to soak up as much of its energy as possible. It was good to be back!

Dakotah was happy. Emily, Laurietta and Antonio were spending the day with her, and they were building a treehouse at Pru's. Pru, herself, was busy baking for tomorrow when the family would gather for Sunday dinner. Heath would be there too, and Patrick hoped to spend some special time with him. Spring had offered to help, but Pru had insisted she take this walk. Somehow, Pru always knew just what she needed.

She ran her fingers over the moss covered ground beside her. It was quite spongy from the rain showers. The velvety green carpet glistened in the sunlight that

peeped through the tree tops into the quiet forest. Tiny,
minute mushrooms, or toadstools she called them, were
scattered intermittently around her. She remembered
how she'd loved to find them as a child, and always
sought to find a toad beneath one, but never did. Who
told her that, anyway? She laughed aloud and her
laughter echoed throughout the folds of Oak Mountain.

The forest suddenly lit up brilliantly with clusters of
colorful foliage as the sun beat its way down through the
masses of trees. The deep red Maples and bright yellow
Hickorys, the dark red Dogwoods and light yellow Poplars challenged each other's glory. Spring found herself
drawn to an iridescent yellow Maple that was gloriously
adorned with the rich red vine of Virginia Creeper. The
contrast was absolutely breathtaking, as the deep, red
vine wound itself up and around the translucent yellow
Maple.

"Only God can paint this picture!" she whispered
into the gentle mountain winds that blew up to the tree
tops and over the valleys.

She remembered that first time she'd sat alone in the
woods. It was in the Black Hills when she was seeking
purpose and answers. A large Poplar leaf gracefully
parachuted to the ground, making a crisp crackling
sound as it met mother earth. She smiled. She loved the
innocent beauty of nature and its pristine character.
She loved the mountains...she loved the land. It gave
her strength. Recalling the autumns of the Black Hills
with its acute and resplendent beauty, the brilliant
quivering Aspens would be contrasting with the dark
Ponderosa Pines about now. But there was something
about autumn in the Blue Ridge that drew her back

again and again. Warmth! Friendliness! That was it!
The Blue Ridge was her friend...her childhood friend.

'1990'

"TIME"

Oh time...Oh precious time
Why must you hurry on?
Endless hours cry out in chimes
First, you're here, now you're gone

My pace is quickened by your hands
Which continue round and round
My eyes are blurred by sifting sands
Which never cease flowing down

I beg of you...Oh precious time
To pause for a little while
If not, my youth will fall behind
And I will tread that last mile

Chapter XIX
Another Thanksgiving

Seventeen years had passed! Seventeen years of wind, rain and sunshine on Oak Mountain, but still one could not see the wearing down of those aging mountains...so subtle...so discreet is the passing of time upon God's creation...except that is...for man.

But changes were taking place beyond those comforting old mountains. The world was changing at a momentum unwitnessed in the past. The last seventeen years had headlined newspapers with often startling news...President Nixon resigned...the Vietnam War officially ended...a boy from the deep south by the name of Jimmy Carter was elected President of the United States...the King of Rock-n-Roll, Elvis Presley died... the Panama Canal was given away...900 followers of Jim Jones committed mass suicide in Jonestown...crime escalated and the drug culture erupted and spread over the country and over the world like a 'cancer'...Martin Luther King received his own holiday...John Lennon was shot and killed outside his own apartment in New York...the world watched a fairy tale on T.V. as Prince Charles and Lady Di said 'I do'...Miss Liberty received a facelift...John Hinckley, Jr. was found guilty of shooting President Reagan...the Berlin Wall was finally opened up...the 'Challenger' exploded 74 seconds after lift-off...the computer age was revolutionizing the world...the first black governor in the United States was elected...Governor L. Douglas Wilder...and in Virginia no less....

But all of these changes did little to affect life on Oak Mountain. The sun still came up at the same spot every morning, rising ever so gracefully over the mountain crest, while chasing away the early morning fog, and it set every evening in the same spot, dipping suddenly without sufficient warning, bringing with its departure the awaited twilight...a time for rest. In between, life moved slowly...and even more slowly for the Barrett Family.

It was autumn again in 1990, and it was Sunday morning. The little Baptist Church glistened in the early sunlight as it proudly displayed its fresh paint job. A harmonious melody flowed outward from its open windows...*just a closer walk with thee, grant it, Jesus, if You please, daily walking close to Thee, let it be, dear Lord, let it be....*

The singing ended, and the elderly preacher made his way wearily to the pulpit. He opened his large, black Bible and proceeded to expound the scriptures as he'd done for so long, and the small congregation listened intently as they had for years, for they loved their pastor...Reverend Patrick Barrett. He was preaching on 'changing times' as he seemed to be doing a lot these days.

"Why just the other day, I stopped by my nephew Heath's place. You know he's got that computer business down in the valley. Built a new building, prospering right nicely because everybody needs computers now! When I was a boy, like some of you, we never dreamed of such things!" He continued to relate other changes he'd picked up from the newspapers or television, not much from his own experience as he seldom left the security of the mountain. He concluded his message as expected, "If all this change has your head spinning like mine, you can just rest assured...*God never changes!*"

A chorus of Amens lifted up to the exposed rafters of the little church, followed by a solemn prayer. And after the last member shook his hand and departed, Patrick stepped carefully down the church steps with his cane. He was alone today as Ellen had taken a fall and sprained her ankle only the week before. He walked slowly across the church lawn, climbed into his '74 Ford sedan and headed for Pru's. As he descended the mountain, he contentedly watched the delicate dancing leaves skip across the smooth road ahead of him. He remembered when the road wasn't so smooth, but rough and rutted and a challenge in the winter. The crisp fall leaves fluttered, floated and some fell upon his windshield before blowing off into the autumn winds. A beautiful sight to behold...but a sign of what lies ahead...winter and death to the land. Just like life! One's autumn in life points to death up ahead. He sighed, and then spoke aloud, "For to me to live is Christ, and to die is gain...For I am in a strait betwixt two...."

And certainly that was the case with Reverend Patrick Barrett as it had been with Paul of old. For he was ready for the other side, but still felt very much needed on this side...needed by his congregation and needed more by his family. A deep crimson Maple leaf blew in the window and landed gracefully on the seat beside him. He smiled and reached out and touched its crisp cool texture. He thought of his children, his grandchildren...they were coming along. Still there were problems. Of course, there were problems...life was problems. God had said it would be so! The road wound around a bend and suddenly came out at a serene clearing. He was there. Nestled among a grove of Maples, mingled with a few young Oaks, sat the low cinderblock building painted a soft, dull green that fused with the foliage surrounding it, creating an aura of incognito.

Patrick pulled up front and got out. He could hear the creaking of the rocking chairs on the porch as he approached. Tipping his hat at the two aged ladies occupying them, he walked past, noticing their gaze never diverted from their fixed stares ahead. The storm door closed behind him and the coolness of the air-conditioned interior was welcomed. He passed on by the front sitting room with but a glance and a smile. The folk therein resembled actors in a play...waiting patiently for their parts. They silently sat in a semi-circle, but did not interact. Instead their wrinkled faces wore vacant expressions. Sadly, their parts would not come again...at least not on this earth.

Patrick walked down the recently waxed corridor that smelled of Pine-Sol struggling to conceal other odors not so pleasant. Old age was sad!

He came to the familiar door with the needlepoint hanging that spelled 'Shalom'. He smiled and peeked around the door.

Pru was sitting up in her wheelchair with her eyes closed as she very gently rocked herself to and fro. He moved toward her softly, and patted her hand that rested limply on the chair arm.

"Hi Sis."

She opened her eyes and looked up at him blankly.

"Today's not one'a her good days, Reverend," a small wiry lady declared authoritatively as she sat perched on the adjoining bed.

"Thank you, Mrs. Dudley, I can see that. How are you today?"

"Oh, fair to middlin'...can't complain. No use anyhow...nobody listens."

"You're right, Mrs. Dudley. Nobody wants to hear complaining...especially God. That's why He admonishes us not to."

"That'a fact, Reverend?"

"Yes Ma'am, it is. In the Old Testament, God lost patience with the Israelites more than once due to their complaining."

"Now, I know about them Israelites. Miss Pru, here, was telling me about them the other day."

"She was?"

"Yes Sir. It was one'a her good days, and she did right smart talkin'. Told me all about Mrs. Israelson. You know, she was Miss Pru's roomie before me. Miss

Pru can't speak high enough of her. Must'a been a fine Jewish lady. She left that hanging on the door there, you know. 'Course she couldn't take it with her where she went, and she didn't have hardly no family. So it just got left…but Miss Pru won't let nobody bother it. She's taken a right smart fancy to it, I'd say. 'Course I kind'a like it myself. Miss Pru says it means 'hello' or maybe it means 'good-bye'…depends on which way you going, I s'pose…but that ain't all it means. Miss Pru said it means 'peace', too. And that's what we need more of, ain't it, Reverend?"

He smiled, "Yes Ma'am. You understand who the Israelites are?"

"Why certainly, Reverend. Miss Pru said they're for sure *the apple of God's eye*…and we ain't to offend them either. I don't reckon I've ever offended one… since I ain't never known any."

"Did you go up to the services this morning?"

"No Sir, Reverend. My arthritis was actin' up again. Couldn't nigh get out'a bed. How was your service this morning, Reverend?" she asked while noticeably pulling out her jar of BEN GAY from the drawer.

"Had a good crowd. Thank you." He leaned down in front of Pru, but her eyes were closed again. "Did she eat her lunch?"

"Right smart. I made sure of that, Reverend. Wouldn't let'em take it out 'till she did."

"Thank you, Mrs. Dudley. I don't know what we'd do without you."

She beamed, "Always willing to help a body out, Reverend. And, Miss Pru here…well, she's a fine lady, and I'm proud to be her roomie."

"Well, guess I'll be going. If she...she gets better, please tell her I stopped by...and that I'll be back tomorrow."

"I sho will...like I always do, Reverend. You take care now."

Patrick smiled at the spunky little silver-haired lady.

"Good day, Mrs. Dudley."

Spring sat on the small porch of her 'tipi' that was now safely hidden from civilization, much to her pleasure. Throughout the past couple of decades, the forest had subtly wrapped its lush entwining arms around the small chalet, creating a sense of harmony as if the two had grown there together on the side of Oak Mountain. She'd never regretted keeping it, as it was truly home to her and Dakotah whenever they returned to Oak Mountain. This was one of those times, but this time she'd come back alone. Dakotah was busy with her own life. She felt a flash of joy just thinking about her...following in her own footsteps... seeking ways to help her people. How proud she was of her! Of course, she'd never cared for art, but her talents and strengths were many. She was a real business person, more like Dean in that manner, and communication? Why, she was a natural communicator, not like herself. It had always been a struggle for her. She pulled her shawl closely around her shoulders and sipped her tea. It was beginning to feel like fall.

A rainbow of leaves whipped up by a mild breeze fluttered and fell to the ground in front of her. Another autumn! Living is for the young, she thought. The old

must be content in walking the corridors of memory...
and I have such memories! She relaxed, inhaled deeply the autumn flavor and decided to take a leisurely
stroll down one of those corridors. Her breathing slowed,
and she slipped into a semi-sleep. She had sat there for
some time with a slight smile on her face when the car
door slammed. She jumped.

"Aunt Spring! It's me...don't get up. I'm coming up,"
called Emily as she climbed the hillside, pushing aside
the Rhododendron and Mountain Laurel that were
gradually taking over the place.

"Why Emily. You did come. I thought maybe you'd
found something better to do than visit an old woman."

"Shame on you, Aunt Spring. I can't think of anything better to do!"

"Thank you, Dear. Here, pull up a chair. That
rocker's a good one."

"Thanks."

"How's your mom?"

"She's fine. Busy fixing up the new house."

Spring looked at her keenly. "Is all this okay with
you, Emily?"

"What do you mean?"

"I mean your mom and Nelson and the new home...
and everything?"

Emily pushed the rocker. "Of course. I'm glad for
Mom. She's spent her whole life alone...with just me.
It's time she had somebody...especially now that I've
grown up. And Nelson? He's fine. He's good to her...
buying her that nice home and all. She's really happy
about that, and she certainly deserves it."

"And why am I sensing a certain mood of melancholy?"

"Aunt Spring, you're so perceptive. It's just that all of it comes as such a big change for me. You know, I've had Mom all to myself all these years. What really makes me the saddest is when I ride down Madison Street and see our old house. It looks sort of lonely."

"Oh?"

"Yeah. It has people living in it and all, but somehow it still looks lonely. But maybe it's just me that's lonely. Who knows?"

"Maybe a part of growing up, do you think?"

She smiled a knowing smile at Spring. "Perhaps so. But sometimes I just feel like there are too many feelings swirling around inside of me, and I just need to do something about it."

"Like what?"

"Like express myself somehow. Do you understand?"

She nodded with a smile, "How well I do."

Emily waited while Spring finished her tea.

"You sure you don't care for some?"

"No, thank you."

She placed the cup on the porch railing carefully. "That is why I paint, Emily."

"To express yourself?"

"Partly."

"Well, I could never be a painter, that's for sure."

"What's on you mind, Emily?"

"You'll most likely think I'm crazy."

"Hardly."

Emily leaned over closer. "I want to be a writer."

"A writer?" Spring's face lit up.

"Yeah, I know. I went to school all this time to

become a teacher...and Mom wants me to be a teacher. She's always wanted me to be a teacher...and she spent all that money on my education. But, Aunt Spring, I don't want to teach...I want to write."

Spring smiled at her serious young niece. "Was that so hard?"

"No."

They laughed.

"How long have you wanted to be a writer?"

"For quite some time. But I was afraid to mention it to anyone. Aunt Spring, I have this compelling urge to create something...something of beauty...something of my own...that will live on its own...with beautiful flowing words that evoke the same feelings in others that are bursting forth within me. Oh, I'm rattling on."

"You have a dream, Miss Emily."

"Yes, but I want more than a dream!"

"That will come."

"What do you mean?"

"The dream has to be first...the rest will follow...if you believe in your dream."

"I do, Aunt Spring. I do."

She smiled, "You know your mother writes poetry. She wrote one for me once on the beauty of the woods in winter."

"Yes. I know, but I don't know if she'd understand me wanting to do it full time...all my life."

"Well, I think it's wonderful!"

"You do?"

"Of course, and I think it's inevitable. It's been brewing for a long time...for this family to have a writer. Your grandmother also loved to write."

"Grandmother?"

"Your Great Grandmother Emily."

"She did?"

"She sure did, and even won a contest with one of her poems. I can still remember that day like it was yesterday...."

"Imagine that. How come nobody ever told me?"

"I don't know. Guess it never came up. Yes, Mama wrote lots of poems, I understand."

"Where are they?"

"Well, your grandmother had some of them put away for a long time. I don't know where exactly."

"They may be difficult to find now."

"However, I have one she gave especially to me, and I've kept it all these years." She rose from her rocker slowly. "I'll be right back."

Emily waited thoughtfully.

Spring returned with a wrinkled piece of yellow paper in her hand.

"Here it is," she handed it to Emily, and she read...

DIVINE PRESENCE

When the wind is blowing swiftly by
Is it not His out-stretched arm
Coming down from way up high
To warn all evil...not to harm

When rains are gently pouring down
Is it not His merciful tears
Shed upon sea and ground
For all sadness through the years

And suddenly when the thunders roar

Is it not His voice in anger
For sins committed more and more
By His children who fear no danger

Finally when the sun shines bright
Is it not His smiling face
Beckoning us to see the light
Before old Satan wins the race

"Grandma Emily had a lot of faith, didn't she?"

"She sure did."

Emily stood up and walked over to the porch railing. "Oh, I don't know, Aunt Spring, if I can even write or not!"

"What do you mean?"

"Sometimes I think I can...and then sometimes I think I'm just dreaming big. But I really want to...I really do!"

"Then you will, Miss Emily."

She looked at her questioningly.

"You have to feel it, Emily. Don't go looking for it in books. Find it in your heart."

"Find it in my heart?"

"It's there. Just dig way down deep for it. When I paint, I must feel it first. It has to be a part of me."

"I think I know what you mean...."

"And don't forget your Great Grandma Emily. She felt the same thing even way back then...with no means or time to fulfill her dream...and a part of her lives in you."

Emily smiled, "I would like to think that...if I can write, I will fulfill both of our dreams."

"Miss Emily, you're gonna be a writer!"

"You think so?"

"I think so. Promise me one thing?"

"Yes?"

"To write my story some day."

"Your story?"

"If you can figure it out...write my story one day, Miss Emily."

IT WAS THE DAY before Thanksgiving and Patrick felt the cool mountain winds through his light jacket as he walked up the walkway to The Shady Rest Home. Pru *must* be able to come tomorrow! It was Thanksgiving, and they'd never had a Thanksgiving without Pru! He entered the warm front room, and taking off his hat, he headed for her room.

As he neared, he heard that familiar laughter. It was gonna be one of her good days! He stepped in the doorway.

"Patrick! Come in. Look who's here. You remember ...oh me...I forgot again," Pru looked worried.

"Abigail Woodson. Hello, Reverend Barrett. It's been a long time." The tall, thin lady extended her bony hand. Patrick struggled for remembrance as he shook her hand.

"Let me see. Didn't you go to class with us way back in grade school? Yes, I remember now. My, it has been a long time. How are you?"

"Fine, Reverend. I'm visiting some relatives for the holidays and decided to look up Prudence. We used to be such girlfriends in school," she looked tenderly at Pru, who was basking in this unexpected day.

"Where is your home now?"

"Maryland, and has been since I was a teenager when my folks moved away, but Oak Mountain hasn't changed much."

"No Ma'am. We like to keep things kind'a the same around here."

"I don't blame you. Prudence is still as pretty as ever."

Pru shook her head in contradiction, but reached out and patted Abigail's arm.

"Prudence was my best friend from day one."

"That gets me smack-dab right here!" Mrs. Dudley pounded her chest.

"Good Morning, Mrs. Dudley. I didn't see you sitting back there."

"Good Morning to you, Reverend."

Abigail Woodson moved over and sat on the bed to be closer to Pru. "Prudence, do you remember taking me *snipe hunting?*"

"Snipe hunting?" Pru looked confused.

"Yes Dear, you took me snipe hunting."

"I did?"

"Yes...you left me holding the bag."

Pru laughed aloud. Abigail joined her, but Mrs. Dudley's wiry frame was in jerks of hysteria.

"You okay, Mrs. Dudley?"

"Yes...Reverend...," she answered between jerks.

"Who else was in the conspiracy?" Pru asked with an old twinkle in her eye.

"It was you...and your Indian sister...what was her name?"

"Spring."

"That's right. It was you and Spring."

"Just Spring and me?"

"That's right."

"And we left you holding the bag?"

"Yes, and I never told anyone about it. I went home and didn't tell anybody. I was too embarrassed."

They all laughed again.

The visit was a pleasant one, and after tears and good-byes, Abigail Woodson left. Pru sat quietly somewhat subdued. Patrick was quiet also, reminiscing bygone days. He'd remembered during the visit that he'd actually been sweet on Abigail Woodson in grade school. How could he have forgotten? It brought reality to him candidly clear and the distance between it and those far away school days. Mrs. Dudley decided enough was enough. She would talk if nobody else would!

"Did I ever tell you, Reverend, why I requested to be Miss Pru's roomie?"

"No Ma'am, don't believe you did...."

"Well Sir, my last roomie...her name was Ruthie... was mentally confused. And more'n one time, she confused my things with her'n."

"I see."

"No Sir, you don't. Not jest yet anyways. But, I'm gonna tell you. Like that day when I went down to get my hair fixed. You know, you can do that here if you take a mind to. 'Course Miss Pru don't see fit to do so. Well'sa, while I was gone, she...Ruthie, I mean...must'a been busy. When I got back, I couldn't find my T.V. remote anywheres. I asked Ruthie...'you seen my remote?' 'Course she didn't know what a remote was...never

watched T.V., you know. So I commenced to describe it
to her, but she just looked more confused. So, I said to
her... 'let's look.' You see, she wasn't no thief... she just
didn't know. We began looking in all her drawers. When
we got down to the last drawer, I opened it, and lo and
behold...there was *my* pocketbook and inside my pocketbook was *her* billfolder. Can you believe that? And I
didn't find my remote 'till the next day."

"Where was it?" Patrick was amused.

"In my tissue box. My nose was'a running, and I
went to get a tissue...and found my remote! You see,
she'd sleep in the day and roam at night. That's what
finally drove me out'a there. One night, I woke up and
saw her at the sink. She had my little blue box in her
hand...."

"Your little blue box?"

"Yes Sir, you see I keep my dentures in that little
blue box." She pointed to a small round blue box sitting
by the sink. "And she kept her'n in a little pink box.
Well'sa, that night she was standin' there with my little
blue box. I said, 'Ruthie, what you doing with my
teeth'?"

"She never answered. I asked again. She never
answered. Just stood there in the dim light with my
little blue box. So I got up and took the box out of her
hand...it was empty! My teeth were gone!"

Patrick chuckled.

"I asked...'Ruthie, do you know where my teeth are?'
She commenced to walk over to her bed. 'Yes,' she
said...'I got'em right here with me'. My teeth were all
but hidden, except for a slight rise in the covers."

"You got them back?"

" 'Course I got'em back. But I decided right then and there, I best be findin' me another roomie," she smiled at Pru, and Pru smiled back.

THANKSGIVING DAY promised to be unseasonably warm as the coffee aroma filled the kitchen at the homeplace. The women folk were already stirring around with Mary Tom and Melony in charge. Smoothly, they prepared the forthcoming feast as if they'd never left this old kitchen. Jessica was basting the turkey as if it was the first turkey she'd ever basted.

"This big bird is gonna be the best we've ever had!" she boasted.

"You think so?" Mary Tom kidded.

"It better be!" she laughed.

"What time do you expect the men folk back from hunting?" Mary Tom inquired.

"Oh, they usually get here around ten, maybe earlier. Depends on how their luck is, of course," Melony explained. "Did Heath go along, Aunt Jessica?"

"No, Heath isn't much for hunting. Jonathon tried to get him to go, but he declined as usual."

"Do you think he'll be alone?"

"Heath?"

"Yes, I mean...I heard he'd been seen out with some attractive lady."

"He'll be alone."

"Why are you so sure, Aunt Jessica?" Mary Tom questioned while greasing the sweet potatoes.

"I think Heath will remain alone. I don't think he'll allow himself a serious relationship."

"It certainly looks that way after all these years.

What a shame."

"Maybe...maybe not, Mary Tom. We all have to deal with our own lives the best we see fit. And Heath seems okay. He enjoys his business among other things, especially the rescue squad work...and he seems to be getting more involved with church work lately."

"He belongs to that new Methodist Church down in the valley, doesn't he?"

"Yes. I think Patrick was a bit disappointed that he didn't join his, but this church seems to have more to offer in a lot of ways."

"Isn't that where the attractive lady goes to church also?" Melony kidded.

"Yes. Apparently so."

Melony winked at Mary Tom.

Jessica continued talking, "You know, those first years were awfully hard on Heath, but he seems to have come to terms with everything in the last few."

"We certainly prayed a lot for him...Dan and I while in Africa. We couldn't be here to share the burden with you, but we tried to in holding you up in prayer."

"Thank you, Mary Tom. I knew you were, and it was a comfort. By the way, how does Mr. Dan Ray like living here in the old farmhouse?"

"He loves it just as I do...but I think he's restless."

"Restless?"

"Well, after spending your life in missions, going and doing for others, it seems like we're at a standstill now. It's all so different."

"We're so glad you're here," Melony spoke up. "After Dad died last year, we wondered what would become of the place. It was too much for Mama alone, but she tried

until she had the stroke. I know she'd be awfully hurt
if we were to sell the place…and, of course, I'd hate to see
it sold, too."

"So would I! This is our home. Aunt Jessica, you
should've seen us girls when we were growing up here.
We were a riot!"

"Now wait a minute, Mary Tom. You speak for
yourself. You were the riot!" Melony teased, "I was the
sweet little lady, remember?"

"How well I remember!" she retorted with a laugh. "I
could never live up to you!"

"Hey, you never tried. You were too busy being a
tomboy, getting stuck up in trees and tearing your
Sunday dresses and such!"

The two giggled as they'd done years ago.

"You two! Give me a hand with this bird. He's ready
for the oven."

They slid the large Butterball into Pru's old white
range and shut the door, peeping through the little glass
window at him.

Jessica wiped her hands. "Pru will be proud of us."

"How do you think Mama will do today?" Melony
asked reluctantly.

They were quiet for a moment.

"According to Patrick, she was fine yesterday."

"But that was yesterday, Aunt Jessica."

"I know, but she will *be* here. That's what's important."

"You're right. Let's get those pies going."

Thirty minutes later, Spring arrived with Dakotah,
bringing in more bags for the feast. Emily pulled up at

the same time that Roxy and Laurietta did. Roxy
carefully balanced her four layer chocolate cake while
coming up the drive. The menfolk returned from hunting early, with Jonathon being the lucky one, getting the
first deer...an eight pointer, although Mark insisted
he'd seen it first. Mark and Paul's families arrived amid
much ado. Heath followed alone, and finally Patrick
and Ellen with Pru.

The old farmhouse was alive with excitement, laughter and music as Melony sat down at the piano by
request and began to peel out the tune of *Will The Circle
Be Unbroken*, one of Pru's favorites. The appetizing
aromas sifted throughout the house, into every room,
reaching upstairs to the bedrooms.

Mary Tom had quietly gone up, and now sat gazing
out the window as she'd done so many times as a child.
She was painting a mental picture of the beloved mountains, trees, the old Willow in particular...a picture she
could keep forever and carry with her, for she had a
feeling that this was only temporary. She didn't know
what might be the future of the old homeplace, but she
suspected that their place, hers and Dan's, would be far,
far away.

Andrew and Anna, Mark's six year old twins, were
busily engaged in entertaining the family in the living
room, pantomiming *'Twas the Night Before Christmas*.
Their lively audience urged them on, while Spring sat in
a corner watching the two young children and remembering another time...another set of twins that she'd
mothered. Patrick and Prudence. How time moves on!
She glanced across the room at Pru, sitting in her
wheelchair, eyes closed to all around her. A tear slid

down Spring's high cheekbone.

"And how's David?" Roxy asked Ellen.

"Doing better. He's been at the Salem Veterans' Hospital for about three weeks now, and we're seeing significant improvement."

"Still the same thing?"

"Yes, he carries Vietnam with him daily...never left it behind."

"What a shame. I'm still praying for him."

"Thank you, Roxy."

"I hear Esther and her family couldn't make it because her youngest daughter has the flu?"

"That's right. Elizabeth is quite ill. They hated missing."

"It must be that time...flu time."

"Guess you're right. Roxy, I just can't get over Laurietta. She's turned out to be a beautiful girl!"

Roxy beamed, "Thank you...smart, too."

"Well, I should think so...working on her Masters now?"

"She is that. Gonna have enough education for both of us!"

Ellen laughed, "I know you're mighty proud of her."

"I sure am! 'Course you've got a lot to be proud of yourself with all these children and grandchildren and all. Always wished I could've had a passel of'em."

"What about Antonio? I understand he's in the service now."

"Yes Ma'am. He's in the United States Air Force and stationed in England."

"Does he like it?"

"He likes it. Seems to fit in real well over there. At least that's the way his letters read. 'Course he misses home just like we miss him, but Antonio's a man now. He's gotta be looking out for his own life. It's hard to say where he'll settle down."

"Oh, I expect he'll return to Lynchburg when he gets out of the Air Force, don't you?"

"He might. He might not. But, the way I see it is the good Lord gave him to us for the years we had him. He surely blessed my heart...that little fellow. Now, if he chooses to settle down someplace else, I'll understand. 'Course, I'll still have Laurietta, but who knows where she'll end up once she finishes getting all them degrees!" Roxy laughed a happy laugh.

Soon the Thanksgiving Dinner was ready, and everybody crowded into the dining room with the overflow spilling out on both sides toward the living room and kitchen. Patrick stood up to pray. He waited a moment for all to get quiet, and then he lifted his voice.

"Our Heavenly Father...we come here together to magnify thy name and lift up our hearts in thanks giving for all thy blessings you have so graciously seen fit to bestow upon us...not because we deserve them... but because you love us!

This is not new to us. We have gathered together this way for many years. Some of our members are not with us this year...but still we give you praise! When we meet again next year...there may be others missing as well. Help us, Lord, to keep our faith...and every day be thankful for thy blessings. We praise thy holy name! Amen."

Everyone followed in unison..."Amen!"

The food, the hearty conversation and the simple feeling of belonging enriched the Barrett family once again.

"Pass me the gravy, Tommy."

Mary Tom looked up in surprise. It had been a long time since she'd been called that!

"Why, Uncle Jonathon, I thought you'd forgotten," she kidded while passing the steaming gravy.

"Just because you're middle-aged and such, I haven't forgotten!"

"Whoa...look who's talking," Paul joked.

"That's right, Uncle Jonathon," Melony joined in. "We might be middle-aged, but we can still give you a hard time."

Everyone laughed.

"I bet you can. You young folks don't know that these two proper ladies here were the two greatest pests on Oak Mountain when growing up!"

"Now, Uncle Jonathon, you can't be serious?" Mary Tom winked at Melony. "But we did have fun when you were courting!"

"I remember that quite well myself," Jessica joined in, "in fact, our first meeting at that...that church social was one I'll never forget."

"Oh, Aunt Jessica, you were so beautiful! I can still see you in that lovely white dress, trimmed in yellow lace, and the little yellow ribbon in your dark hair. You were a sight to behold. No wonder Uncle Jonathon flipped!"

"Flipped?"

"You sure did, Mr. Barrett!" Jessica leaned over and kissed him on the cheek, and he smiled at her lovingly, thinking how beautiful she still looked.

"Miss Roxy," Mark spoke suddenly, "do you think Governor Wilder might run for president?"

"Can't ever tell! I can remember the day nobody would've believed we'd have a black governor...and in Virginia, too!"

"That's true," Ellen agreed.

"Some still don't believe it," Paul laughed. "But lots of things are changing. These are changing times, and I for one am glad for it."

"What about Margaret Thatcher stepping down... can you believe that?" Nelson asked, and everyone looked up as the newest member of the clan joined in.

"The Iron Lady herself. Well, I always had respect for her," Heath added. "She's certainly done a good job!"

"For a lady," Mark added.

"For a lady?" Laurietta repeated.

Mark grinned, and his wife, Sheila, smiled. Laurietta waited.

"Well, you know what I mean?"

Laurietta spoke calmly, "Mark Barrett, I'm surprised at you."

"Come on now, Laurietta, you know I'm not ma-cho...but the head of a country?"

"Yes?"

"Maybe we better change the subject."

Laurietta smiled knowingly, "That would be wise... however, I'll invite you to my inauguration!"

Roxy choked on her tea, "Laurietta!"

"Just kidding, Mom."

Mark chuckled, "If anybody could do it, Laurietta, you probably could!"

"Amen to that!" Roxy added. "That reminds me. I gotta write Antonio when I get back home, and ask him about Mrs. Thatcher."

"Roxy, I know you miss him terribly," Jessica sympathized.

"I do that...and I've been kind'a worried here lately about all the goings on over there in the Persian Gulf."

"Do you think we're gonna have war?" Paul asked.

"Lord, have mercy on us! I hope not."

"What do you think, Uncle Jonathon?"

"Who knows. I think we ought'a go in there and take care of Mr. Hussein!"

"Sounds like an old military man talking to me," Patrick kidded.

"Don't you agree, Brother Patrick?"

"Certainly. I'm just kidding with you. The crazy man needs to be stopped. I just hope we don't see another war. We've had too many wars in this family."

Jonathon decided to change the subject, "Can you believe this weather we're having! Most uncomfortable Thanksgiving morning I've hunted in a long time."

"I was just thinking about that," Melony added. "If Dad were here, he wouldn't have been able to have the hog-killing probably."

"Somehow, Thanksgiving seemed to be missing something. It's the hog-killing! Can't say that I mind," Paul joked.

"I do!" grinned Mark. "Always enjoyed that spectacle even though it did send goose chills up my spine."

Heath shook his head with a chuckle.

"Paper said it might even get up to the seventies today!"

"You're kidding, Roxy?"

"Nope...that's what it said, Mel."

"Sounds like weather for a good ball game after dinner."

"We'll take you up on it, Heath, my boy."

"Dad, are you up to it?"

"We'll see who's up to it. Mary Tom, why don't you and Melony join in like old times?"

She looked at Dan, and he smiled.

"Aunt Spring, you're in a mighty pensive mood today."

"I'm sorry, Melony. I guess you're right."

"Aunt Spring," Mark posed while reaching for the leftover rolls, "is it true that the local Monacan Tribe now has official Tribe Status?"

"That's right. We finally won state recognition last year...long overdue."

"What exactly does that mean, Aunt Spring?" asked Mary Tom.

Spring was thoughtfully quiet for a second. "It means, Mary Tom, that a gentle people that have lived in the shadow of the Blue Ridge for many generations can now stand up and be counted."

"Isn't it true that these people have been ridiculed and treated unfairly just because they were different?"

"That's right, Emily."

Dakotah sat quietly listening.

"It is mankind's sin," Patrick spoke up softly. "A lack of understanding of others...a lack of love for others. We are all guilty."

Spring smiled at him.

He added... " 'And now abideth faith, hope, charity, these three; but the greatest of these is charity' so saith the Lord."

After dinner, Spring, Melony and Mary Tom took a walk outside, while pushing Pru for a bit of fresh air, such a balmy inviting day that it was.

"I miss Music!" Melony spoke suddenly.

"He was a good old dog," Spring empathized.

"I miss Dad...and...," Melony stopped...realizing what she was about to say.

They looked at Pru as her head bobbed along while the wheelchair bumped its way over the lawn.

Spring spoke, "I understand. I still miss Mama and Daddy...I still miss them like it was yesterday. But the wonderful thing is that now I have a hope...a hope of seeing them again one day."

Mary Tom smiled, "That's right."

The sun did set on another Thanksgiving Day and the family dispersed, going their respective ways. Darkness fell on Oak Mountain. Mary Tom switched off the last light and crawled into bed beside Dan, who was already asleep. The old farmhouse was unusually quiet.

Chapter XX
Spring's Return

Dakotah left for the Plains two days after Thanksgiving. The last hours of November approached while Spring sat still at her bedroom window witnessing God's power and providence.

Relentlessly, the cold rains beat down upon Oak Mountain and its furry inhabitants as they sought shelter midst holes, trees and caves. Already, many had found solace and warmth in their winter homes. The skeletons of trees stood nakedly in nature's frenzy as the pounding rain beat off the remaining stubborn leaves. It lashed at the window panes, making it difficult for Spring to see out into the darkened night. She had sat there for almost an hour recounting the past few days and all the excitement of Thanksgiving, when suddenly there was a knock at the door!

Who could that be at this hour? She stood up, feeling the old ache in her knees, and walked across the room and down the stairs. The knocking grew louder!

She tried looking out the front window, but could see nothing in the blinding rain. Going to the door, she opened it cautiously.

It was him!

She stood there speechless as he braced himself against the pounding rain.

"May I come in?"

She opened the storm door, and the cold rain suddenly thrust its fury upon her, causing her to jump back to reality. How foolish of me! He's young enough to be my son!

She stood back, letting the young man, soaking wet, walk past her, and slowly shut the door behind him.

"Miss Barrett, my name is Nathan Branham. I came to bring you something," he explained awkwardly.

For the first time, she noticed the large, flat box covered in plastic that he was holding close to his side.

"Here, please excuse my manners. Have a seat." She waved him to the sofa. Carefully, he placed the box against the wall, wiped the water from his brow and started across the room.

"Goodness, you're soaked! I'll get you a towel." She rushed to the linen hall closet, while he stood dripping in the middle of the living room. Quickly returning, she handed him a large striped towel.

"Thank you, Ma'am." While drying off, he began to explain his mission, "You see, I heard you were back... and I was afraid you might leave again...before I brought it to you...."

She looked puzzled.

"Sit down, Nathan. Let me fix you some hot chocolate...you do like hot chocolate?"

"Yes Ma'am."

As she heated up the milk, her heart raced. He looked so like him! The same tall, erect stature, the same thick, dark hair, the same serious Indian spirit vaguely hidden behind that handsome face...but those eyes...those piercing deep-set eyes...they were his.

"I believe you knew my father...Nathan Branham, Sr.?"

"I did."

"He never told me. But, while remodeling our old home, I came across that." He looked across the room at the large brown box propped against the wall.

Spring stood up and slowly moved toward the strange box. The young man followed. She began to remove the plastic.

"Would you like me to open it for you? I've taped it pretty good."

"Please."

He took out a pocket knife from his jean jacket and proceeded to carefully open the large box. Spring stood by silently, knowing what was going to be in the box, and as the flaps opened, her thoughts were confirmed.

"*The Dogwoods!*" she whispered almost reverently.

"Ma'am?"

Kneeling down on the floor, she faced her beloved painting and gazed at it silently. He stood waiting.

Finally looking up at him, she questioned, "Please tell me the story?"

He sat down beside her. "As I said before, we were remodeling the house when I came across this box. I opened it...and discovered this beautiful picture...and also this...," he handed her an unsealed envelope.

"It was taped to the box. Apparently, my dad had intended on sending it to you."

She took hold of the faded brown envelope that was addressed to her and slowly opened it.

My Dearest Spring,

Please forgive me for my absurd actions, but allow me to explain.

I came to South Dakota. My purpose was to see you once more as I have never forgotten you. After my wife died, I decided to renew our friendship if you would have me. While trying to get up my nerve, I decided to visit the museum and see 'our painting'. Being from Virginia, I heeded not the tornado warnings.

When that monster crashed into the museum, I was there. I grabbed the painting and ran, barely escaping. Remarkably, there was no damage to this prized possession. Afterwards, I tried contacting you by phone over and over again, but I got no answer. Then the newspaper headlined the mysterious disappearance of the painting and concluded theft! Not knowing how to reach you or exactly what to do, I returned to Virginia. I continued to call, but to no avail. Therefore, I'm sending this to you by a friend, who I can trust whole-heartedly. He is a brother, and a Sioux, in fact, that has been visiting our community. He leaves for South Dakota this Sunday.

Please forgive me for the worry I must have caused you these past few days. When you receive the painting and this letter, if you care to speak with me, please call. I will be waiting!

Your special friend from Oak Mountain
where the Dogwoods bloom...

Spring sat very still, while tears began to slowly trickle down her high cheek bones that now were somewhat wrinkled.

"Miss Barrett, did you notice the date?"

She nodded and repeated softly..."July 11, 1973."

"Yes Ma'am...and the day after, my dad died."

Her aging face could not hide the shock, nor the pain. "Dad had cancer. He'd had it for some time. Mother had died about two years prior with muscular dystrophy. She'd been sick for years. But then, we were told Dad had cancer. It was a shock to all of us, both my sisters and myself, but most of all to him. We were used to Mother being ill. She had always been. But Dad was the strong one...the one we all depended on."

She smiled through her tears, and whispered... "Toh-kah...."

Not noticing, he continued his story, "He went through chemotherapy and the whole bit. He lost his thick dark hair. But then, the cancer went into remission, and he became his old self again. In fact, he seemed younger and more full of vitality than we could remember. His thick dark hair returned. It was then that he announced to us kids that he was going to South Dakota. We thought this very odd, and of course asked why. He'd only smile and say, 'To take care of some unfinished business'."

Spring wiped her cheeks with her hand.

"I'm sorry, Miss Barrett, that the picture here has been lost to you for all these years. But after Dad's death, we closed up the place for a good while. The box with the picture was not found. Dad's sister later moved into the house and lived there a number of years. I suppose it was Aunt Sally that stashed it away upstairs with a lot of other boxes and storage items. There it remained all these years. It was just a few weeks ago, in fact, when we began remodeling the house...that we found it."

Spring sat up straight and tall, regained her composure and gave the young man a warm smile.

"Son, you have made me very happy today. Do not feel bad about what has been done. We all have our regrets."

That night as the rain eased but continued to fall lightly upon the roof with a rhythmic pattern, Spring lay very still upon her bed. Every time she closed her eyes, his face was there, looking at her with those deep set, piercing eyes. All those years, she'd thought per chance their paths might meet...and he'd been dead! It was difficult for her to accept. So long she'd lived with that little hope hidden in the corners of her mind. She fell asleep at last. It was a peaceful sleep midst a mountain forest of Dogwoods. And she painted their fragile beauty while feeling warm and loved...in the presence of one nearby.

DECEMBER BROUGHT with it the north winds and even a snowstorm near its end. Christmas came and went. Old Man Winter delivered three frigid months that caused the residents of Oak Mountain to hibernate like their furry neighbors. But soon, as time mandated, the snows began to melt and water trickled out from the thawing mountainsides, down the rock bouldered cliffs, watering the first shoots of tiny wild flowers.

April arrived midst its gentle showers, bringing to life sundries of plants, flowers and seedlings. Oak

Mountain was once more a vibrant, pulsating forest intermingled with sunny meadows inviting the mountain creatures out to partake of its bountiful supply.

Though not so lush and breathtaking, the small park nestled in the center of Lynchburg offered an escape to those fenced in by streets, buildings and concrete. Roxy relaxed upon the park bench and watched the young squirrels scamper to and fro in search of lunch, she supposed.

"Little city squirrels," she rhymed, "this park is *your* world."

Her thoughts turned to the mountains in the distance, full of forests and squirrels that enjoyed a haven so vast and so private. A brazen young squirrel approached her, stopped short of her shoe and cocking his tiny head, watched her intently. She smiled.

"But then, you do bring us joy...and maybe to you, we bring some too."

She looked up at the tall, aging trees that graced the sloping hills of the small park. So long had they stood. She always remembered them this way...grand and reaching out...so friendly. A horn beeped!

"Melony!"

She waved at Roxy and parked the car, grabbed her lunch basket and ran toward her.

"What a gorgeous day!" she gasped out of breath.

"It is that!"

"What did you bring, Roxy?"

"Leftover fried chicken and fixin's. A picnic ain't a picnic without chicken."

"You're right. I've got some ham biscuits and potato chips, too. Did you bring dessert?"

Roxy smiled, "What do you think?"

Melony leaned over her basket, lifted the cloth. "I knew it! Chocolate layered cake. I just knew you'd bring it."

They laughed together as they'd done so many times before. But this meeting was special, sort of a renewal of friendship. Melony's busy life with her expanded job and new marriage had taken most of her days. She didn't have the luxury of time anymore, but she'd missed Roxy. She missed the old times!

They enjoyed their picnic immensely, their time together and the peacefulness of the park.

"You happy, Mel?"

"Yes Roxy, I am."

"That's good. I'm glad."

"I miss you, though."

"Don't need to. I'm always here."

"I know," she smiled at her, "You lonely, Roxy?"

"Lonely? Now Mel, you know I'm not alone. Oh, I know Laurietta's gone away still schooling and Antonio's way over there somewhere in England...but my Seth's still with me...and waiting," she smiled up at the broad blue sky that boasted of feathery white clouds slowly gliding by, "and God's with me...He said He'd never leave me nor forsake me...and He never has."

"I know."

They sat quietly sharing the peacefulness.

"Did you hear the latest news, Mel?"

"What?"

"They just approved a permanent cease-fire in the Gulf. Praise the Lord! I won't have to worry about Antonio no more."

"Wonderful!"

A bright orange truck pulled up, and two men in matching orange shirts got out and headed for the pool. They began to poke around at the heavy green canvas that covered it.

"They're looking the pool over. Guess summer's coming."

Roxy watched them with a smile. "Yes, in a few weeks, this place will be brimming over with kids...all kinds of kids...enjoying themselves."

Melony looked at her sadly, "You remember another pool, don't you?"

"Oh sometimes...but the Good Lord's let me live to see this. It does my heart good to come here on hot summer days and watch the young folk...both black and white...getting along so fine. 'Course, I don't get in myself. Kind'a lost the desire with the years, I guess," she laughed.

"What do you mean...with the years?" Melony kidded, "I don't see any grey hairs in your head."

"Takes longer. See you got'a few."

Melony laughed, "Won't next week. Going to the beauty parlour."

Roxy began to reluctantly pack up their leftovers.

"Went by the old house on Madison Street last week."

"You did?"

"Saw a couple of kids playing on the porch. Reminded me of Emily and Laurietta."

"Time flies."

"Does that."

"It's so good being together, Roxy. What're you doing tomorrow? How would you like to meet me and go to see

Mama?"

"That sounds real nice. I'd like to see your mama."

The next day dawned bright and beautiful, and the drive up Oak Mountain was exhilarating! The tree lined mountainsides had turned 'pea green' with tender young leaves. Occasional full white blossoms of wild Cherry Trees graced the picture.

"Look yonder!" Roxy pointed up ahead.

A tall gaunt Gum Tree was elegantly adorned with rich purple Wisteria. It draped the ordinary Gum, creating a masterpiece of art, as its clusters of full lilac flowers hung suspended in the mountain air that smelled of buds and blossoms exploding everywhere.

"Lovely," Melony sighed.

"Look at the Dogwoods! They don't look so good!"

Melony saw that the Dogwoods were only partially budding. The spindly trees looked sickly.

"What is it?"

"Dogwood Anthracrose."

"What on earth?"

"It's a fungus that's attacking the Dogwoods. The worst disease in Dogwoods ever...a vicious cancer."

"Oh No!"

"I read about it this month in *Southern Living,* but I'd heard about it before actually. In fact, I sent the article to Spring. Seems it's already killed thousands of trees...millions...in other places, particularly Tennessee. Now, it's hitting Virginia."

"What a shame! Could the same thing happen to our lovely Dogwoods that happened to the Chestnut...I wonder?"

"I sure hope not. What would spring be without Dogwoods?"

"Look, there's some more."

They arrived at the nursing home just after lunch. The corridors were clogged with wheelchairs and trays of dirty dishes standing outside the rooms. Melony and Roxy dodged all of this until they came to a full-fledged traffic jam! A shriveled little lady, with wispy grey hair pulled back into one thin plait down her back, was struggling to free her chair from the chair of another little lady, who was bent on going in the opposite direction. Concentrating on their goal of moving forward, neither seemed aware of the problem. Sadly, they didn't even seem to be aware of each other. One would inch forward, pulling the other along...only to be pulled back again as the other inched forward.

Roxy looked at Melony...and Melony looked at Roxy.

Simultaneously, they each grabbed a chair and set them free, then stood watching as the two elderly ladies slowly rolled up the opposite corridors.

Melony didn't seem in any apparent hurry to get to her mother's room for the expectancy wasn't there anymore. All of Pru's days were the same now. She sat contentedly in her wheelchair, silently watching her hands smooth out the wrinkles of the delicate blue handkerchief.

"Good Morning, Mama. It's a lovely day today." Melony patted her on the head, while moving her chair a little closer to the large window where the warm sun rays were oozing through.

Roxy watched.

"Good Morning, Miss Mel!"

"Good Morning to you, Mrs. Dudley. Didn't see you."

"Jest hidin' behind this here curtain, that's all. Howdy to you, Ma'am," she smiled her warm smile in Roxy's direction.

"Good Morning." Roxy gladly returned the smile.

"Mrs. Dudley. This is my best friend, Roxy. Roxy, meet Mrs. Dudley. She's a blessing to us. Looks after Mama better than anyone."

"You don't say," Roxy pulled up a chair.

Melony got busy straightening a few things on the nightstand, and Roxy chatted with Mrs. Dudley about the weather. Soon an old man shuffled very slowly into the room and peered around with a blank stare as if searching for someone. He looked from one to the other.

"Now Pete!" Mrs. Dudley quickly spoke up, "get on out'a here now. You know I done told you this ain't your room. Go along now!" She waved him off with her hand.

The old man just stood there looking at her vacantly.

"Pete, you heard me. Menfolks don't come in ladies' rooms. I done told you that. Now get on out'a here!"

He slowly turned with a sway and shuffled back out into the corridor to repeat the process down the hallway most likely.

Melony winked at Roxy, "Mrs. Dudley runs a tight ship."

"I aim to look after Miss Pru here."

Roxy smiled at her while at the same time, feeling sorry for the poor little man.

"Does Mary Tom come often?" she asked Melony.

"Oh yes. Mary Tom is here regularly, but I don't know what's gonna happen yet. I think they're seriously considering returning to the mission field soon."

"I see."

Prudence looked up with a distant smile.

THE SOULFUL INDIAN chants began, accompanied by the rhythmic beat of the drums. The young Indian dancers fell into step as if by second nature. Their feathers, plumage and jingles filled the large museum room as onlookers were caught up in the spirit of it all, mentally cresting the pinnacle along with the proud young dancers.

Suddenly the beat ceased, the dancers stopped, and Dakotah moved to the front and picked up the microphone.

"Ladies and Gentlemen. We our proud to present to you today...The Black Hills Indian Dancers! We will begin with the 'Lord's Prayer done in Indian sign language by Tance Raincloud'."

A young girl of about fifteen approached the center front with a solemn aura about her. Mature for her age, her bright yellow dress accentuated her coal black hair that was severely pulled back and tied with one single feather. As she walked, the ornamental dress jingled with its many shells and beads as she was later to perform in the jingle dance. The dress, falling just below her knees, revealed beautiful handcrafted white moccasin boots intricately designed with colorful beads. Beauty that she was, defiance was written on her stubborn young face. She wasn't happy being there. Spring watched her intently from her corner spot, feeling as if she were looking in a mirror...back in time. Not so much the actual countenance of the lovely young girl, but her bold, proud and rebellious bearing. More than likely, this was her last year with the group as she was obviously the oldest of the young group. She was ready to fly her own wings...test her own ideas...resist the 'status quo'. Ah...she'd been there. Dakotah had been there, as well. She smiled to herself, recalling Dakotah's opposing views not so long ago, and how she'd also resisted the continuance of this very group. But she had not yielded to her defiance, and their strong spirits struggled. And now look! She was so proud to see her Dakotah now leading this talented performing arts group.

Ah...Tance Raincloud...you, too, will look back one day on this scene. I wonder what your feelings will be?

The familiar music began...'Our Father which art in heaven...'. The proud young girl was transformed into silent praise to the Holy of Holies. Artistically, her hands and arms moved in perfect harmony with the reverent prayerful music, her whole being thrust into a oneness with the moment.

'Hallowed be thy name...thy kingdom come...thy will be done...in earth as it is in Heaven...'.

The audience witnessed a true worship scene as the young Indian maid looked upward to Heaven, pointing reverently....

'Give us this Day our daily bread...and forgive us our debts...as we forgive our debtors...and lead us not into temptation...but deliver us from evil...'.

Her head leaned back, gazing upward, she lifted her arms in full worship...'For thine is the kingdom and the Power and the Glory...Forever...'.

Clasping her hands prayerfully, she lowered her

head and closed her eyes. *'Amen'*.

Silence filled the large museum room at Crazy Horse.

Dakotah came forward to introduce a group of young boys ranging from six to ten years old. They were to perform a 'war dance', and dressed in full regalia, buffalo headdresses and all, they stepped up, anxious to begin.

The beat of the drums sounded; immediately, they fell into step, one behind the other in bent forward positions. Their heavy plumage, strapped to their backsides, bounced to the rhythmic beat as they moved in unison with the live tempo that rose and fell.

Dakotah felt every movement. So many times, she'd drilled them...to be exact...to be solemn, a thing not easy for little boys their age...to be proud!

She winked at Spring as they now proudly raised their tomahawks and shields intermittently with the signaled chant and excitedly shouted their war whoops, certainly their favorite parts. Round and round, they continued in a circle, keeping almost perfect time. Ben became a little bored and began looking around amusedly at the surrounding crowd; Dakotah wanted to poke him. But then, she was reminded of how far he'd come...a product of a broken home and alcoholism...he was a little trooper. And she was bound and determined to help him make it!

The drums ceased, and the young fellows happily scurried off the floor. There was a roar of applause, and Dakotah swelled with pride. She picked up the microphone.

"Now...it's time for our Fancy Dancers."

Three young girls, ranging in ages seven to twelve, advanced forward with their colorful shawls draping their slender arms. Their heads were adorned with beaded headbands, and their long, dark braids were woven with feathered native ornamental pieces. Once more, the drums sounded and chants rang out causing the young girls to fall into rhythm to its subdued beat.

Their relaxed movement complimented the pensive music in a peaceful sort of way as they gracefully moved across the glossy hardwood floor, while yielding their knees ever so gently to the soft beat. Femininity was delicately manifested in this beautiful and inspiring dance. The young girls held onto their feathered fans while keeping one hand resting on their hips. The tempo picked up, and they draped their long shawls around their slender shoulders, while moving across the spacious floor, whirling around and around, and picking their feet up higher to the beat. Barely gliding, but never losing step, the girls were seemingly enjoying themselves, lost in the art of their ancestral heritage.

The performance concluded with the Jingle Dance, a fascinating and inspiring creation. Tance Raincloud again held the audience in rapture with her mystical movements and proud defiant presence that Spring recognized so well. Later, as she and Dakotah began to leave, she asked, "Tell me about this Tance Raincloud?"

"Oh...Tance...Tance is unique. Beautiful and very talented, but occupied with analyzing life right now."

"That's not so unique, you know?" she smiled a knowing smile at Dakotah, who missed the gesture.

"Her folks are extremely concerned with her keeping

the traditions...but Tance is exploring on her own, and she highly resents the tourists gawking at her, you might say."

"I can understand, but that's going to be a bit difficult under the circumstances. One cannot help but stare at her...one is mesmerized with her performance... especially *The Lord's Prayer*. She seemed almost one with the prayer. Was that real...or just part of her professional performance?"

"Oh, I think that is real...but Tance is really seeking...seeking answers."

"Then, she has a good start. I think Tance will be okay, although it may take some time."

"I know. She's considering leaving us after the season, but I'm trying to convince her to stay one more year."

"That may not be easy."

Suddenly, Dakotah stopped and gazed up and over the large doorway. Spring stopped beside her, and they both silently read the engraved words...spoken by Red Cloud so many years before....

They made us many promises, more than I can remember. They never kept but one. They promised to take our land, and they took it.

Silently they stood for a while.

Dakotah broke the silence, "You know, when you used to bring me here as a child, I couldn't understand this."

Spring waited.

"Now I do."

They held hands and walked through the doorway, on out to the warm sunshine.

"Mother, I feel an urge to do something...something really meaningful and with great purpose for our people. Do you understand?"

Spring smiled, "I do."

"But this land thing has me confused. I've been reading about the Bradley Bill of 1987."

"I see."

"Do you think this Federal land in the Black Hills should be given back to us?"

"I would like to think this would be so. But, Dakotah, as you seek ways to help, remember one thing...no one really owns the land...no one can. It belongs to God."

Dakotah looked at her mother as she stood staring out into the distance at the colossal monument being etched out of the granite mountain....

Suddenly, it thundered on the other side and a cloud of white smoke billowed up from it...yet another blast.

"I'm glad I was able to see this."

"Excuse me?"

"He's opened his eyes...now he can see the Black Hills."

She followed her mother's gaze back to the emerging face of Crazy Horse. She was right. Both eye-openings had been completed, giving life to the famous Chief, whose proud profile from forehead to chin was blocked out against the soft blue sky.

"Now we have a fifth granite face in the Black Hills."

"That's right, Dakotah. Makes me feel all tingly."

"Me too. I wonder what Crazy Horse himself would think...considering what he said...*'would you imprison my shadow, too...you've taken everything else'.*"

Spring smiled and sat down facing the mountain,

"Oh, I think he'd be mighty proud!"

"I used to wonder why they picked Crazy Horse and not one of the more famous Chiefs."

"It was his spirit, Dear. He would not bend. He never signed a treaty or touched a pen."

"I know that now. It's a noble memorial for sure."

" '*Where are your lands now*'?" Spring whispered those words once asked of Crazy Horse.

" '*My lands are where my dead lie buried*'," Dakotah whispered back his famed answer.

They smiled at one another, and rose to go.

The warm sun penetrated through their sweaters as they walked to the car.

"I wonder, Dakotah, as time continues, and you find yourself as old as me...what he will look like?"

"I hope he'll be finished!"

"Korczak had a dream, a bigger than life dream, and we're witnessing his dream in progress even though he's been dead now for almost ten years. I had a dream once to be a great painter and to paint life as I see it."

"And your dream came true."

"Yes. Find your dream, Dakotah...and follow it."

"Like Carl Sandburg said, Mother, '*Nothing happens unless first we dream*'!"

Spring smiled.

They drove out through the Black Hills, and Spring noticed the new growth on the Ponderosa Pines, their thickness and their beauty, as they climbed the hills. She beheld the rushing mountain streams that spilled over with the cold clear water inviting the many tourists that flocked the winding roads.

"I love the Hills."

"So do I, Mom."

"Dakotah, I'll be flying to Virginia soon."

"Oh?"

"Ever since I read Melony's letter about the Dogwoods, I've felt a need to go...to see what's happening."

"But what can you do about it?"

"I don't know. Probably nothing. But the Dogwoods ...well...they are part of my childhood...part of Mama...a part of...a lot of things. I cannot think of Oak Mountain without...Dogwoods. They must not die out...."

"Just like us, Mom...all of us...we must not die out...."

"That's right, Dakotah, and it can happen. There is a people of the Great Sioux Nation...a ·distant remnant...that lives in the hills of the Blue Ridge...."

"The Monacans?"

She nodded, "These gentle people were persecuted for who they were...or for who they were not...whichever...they did not know themselves even. They were almost a lost people. But now they struggle for survival...to find their past...to find themselves."

"A fragile, gentle, beautiful people...like the Dogwood...," Dakotah said aloud, "So are you going back to help the Dogwoods...or the Monacans?"

Her mother was quiet for a moment, driving around the curvy roads of the Black Hills. She thought she saw a face shrouded by the thick Ponderosa Pines...a face with piercing black eyes.

"I don't know," she answered.

THE LARGE AIRCRAFT began descending the grey skies, coming in for a landing in Pittsburgh. Why does it always seem so grey and dismal here, Spring thought while collecting her book, purse and other things. Quickly glancing at her watch, she only had fifteen minutes to make the connection. Stepping off the plane, she hurried up the chute and out into the hustling expanded corridors of U.S. Air. She must not miss that plane. Surely, it would be the last one destined for Lynchburg. Rushing along, hanging onto her belongings, she thought of Melony. How nice of her to meet her at the airport. Sweet little Melony. She certainly hoped she'd be happy with Nelson. He was a quiet type, and she hadn't figured him out yet. But, she was happy that Melony had found someone. It was good for everybody to have somebody.

She rushed through Gate One and down the ramp, on outside to the small commuter. Oh me, she thought, another puddle-jumper! My ears will be buzzing all night. Entering the cramped plane with a bent-over posture, she flopped tiredly into the first available seat and looked around. Empty? Just then, a tall handsome business man filed past her with his chin touching his tie-clasp. She smiled to herself.

The engine started with a roaring that reverberated the entire plane. She grabbed her bag, pulled out an old musty book entitled *The Vanishing Virginian* and while holding it with one hand, she pressed the other up against her right ear and began to read...

Father lived in Virginia. I suppose he was what is called a small-town politician, for he was Commonwealth's Attorney of Lynchburg for thirty-five years, and Lynchburg, having only forty-thousand inhabitants, is certainly a small town. Moreover, Lynchburg is a typical Virginia small town, since it has never had very much influx from the outside world. Almost every family that lives there now has lived thereabout for at least a hundred and fifty years. One can't keep skeletons locked away in such a place, and this fact emboldens me to write Father's unconventional story.

She smiled to herself again. Even little Lynchburg was changing. The author, Rebecca Yancey Williams, a native Lynchburger, had written this little book in 1940. A lot had happened since that time...in the world, in Virginia and even in Lynchburg. She settled back to enjoy a trip back in time in spite of her uncomfortable conditions. Melony had picked the book up at a yard sale and mailed it to her some time ago, and finally she'd have time to read it.

Soon they were soaring through the vast sky and the words on the yellowed pages jumped with the constant jerks of the little plane. She hoped she wouldn't get a headache. She struggled to read the moving words, and finally gave up. Closing her eyes, she focused on the upcoming days. It would be good to see the family again, although it depressed her to see Pru...poor Pru. She would ask Patrick to go walking with her through the woods, the woods that would be coming alive just now, and up the mountain, way up high like they used to do when they were kids. She laughed, well, not quite the same. They'd have to take it slowly, stopping to rest ever so often, but that was all right. They'd be able to talk...really talk...maybe like they'd never talked before. In their youth, they'd had their differences, but now those differences were gone. In spite of the noise and jerks, she almost fell asleep, but suddenly sat up straight as if she knew. She looked out the tiny window and there they were!

The magnificent Blue Ridge Mountains lay rolling below looking vast and sprawling and blue...so blue. She felt good all over just seeing them again. How many times had she left them...and how many times had she returned...only to witness their lovely beauty as if for the first time all over again. She smiled. It was like coming home to see an old friend...one that never changes though life was full of changes...and the biggest change of all was life itself. When youth vanished, leaving one spinning in its dust, only to recoup with maturity in its aftermath, and once comfortably in tune with it, one wakes to find it too has gone, and only the twilight of life remains...a twilight in which to reminisce. She sighed, closed her eyes and rested her head against the seat.

Suddenly, there was a lurch...and another...and another. The pilot's voice was cracking over the intercom, but she couldn't hear what he was saying. Something was wrong! It felt like...like the plane was descending! Then she was thrown forward with a violent lurch. She looked around at the business man. His face was white! She looked out the window...and she could see the mountains...her beloved mountains fast approaching. She sat glued to the window and she knew.

"Lord," she whispered, "take me home...with you...."

The mountains loomed largely before her now, and in their blue folds, she could see the face of a little girl... crying...a long train ride was before her...the soft touch of her mama...school bells were ringing...dreaded school bells...the child was older...but crying again...ah, now she was painting...beautiful pictures...there was a picture...a lovely picture of Dogwoods...beautiful delicate Dogwoods...in full bloom...they were not dying... and there was a face with piercing black eyes...there was another time, another place...the Black Hills...a gentle Full-blood...a happy time...a baby was birthed... with beautiful coal black hair...Dakotah...her heart... then there was a darkness...a tornado...fear...but then there was God...He touched her...and she smiled....

The tiny plane crashed into the side of the mountain and burst into flames!

Chapter XXI
'To Every Thing There Is A Season'

The night was still with its ebony sky. Even the bullfrogs had at last quieted down by the rippling mountain stream as the four young teenagers sat patiently beneath the old wooden bridge, fishing poles in hand...waiting. Already the rope stringer was three-fourths full with wiggling, frightened trout, struggling to escape their destiny.

"Hey Joe, when you gonna catch any fish?"

The slim, sandy-haired teenager ignored him, while the others laughed.

"Cut it out, y'all. I been here fishin' for a whole hour just like y'all, and I ain't caught nothin' yet!"

"Done lost your touch, Joe...I do believe."

"Sam, give me your flashlight!"

Sam pulled the flashlight out of his back pocket and handed it over to him. Joe shined the light out to the end of his long bamboo pole, and suddenly the quiet night was pierced with howls of laughter.

Joe's line was going straight up in the air! He followed the line with the beam of light as it draped over a wide Oak limb that reached out and hung over the creek bank...and the end of the line, fishhook, fishing worm and all, dangled about two feet above the black water.

"Well, I be danged!"

"What're you fishin' for, Joe...a Bluejay?" Tucker asked between gasps of laughter.

About an hour later as the sun peeped over the nearby mountain, casting its fiery rays of light upward, the young fellows were still fishing, working on their second rope stringer. They were oblivious to the fact that the morning was waning, and they had chores awaiting them back home.

At 9:30 a.m., they reluctantly packed up their gear, and throwing the strings of flapping fish over their shoulders, they climbed up the slippery bank. As they reached the top, they were halted by a long procession of cars traveling slowly with headlights on. They stood waiting to cross the road...but the cars kept coming.

"Man, sure is a lot'a cars! Look't that, would'ya?"

Four long, sleek Lincoln Town Cars passed by, one black and three white.

"That ain't the family cars. They were up front. Who are they, do you reckon?"

"The way them windows were all blackened, must be somebody special."

"Dignities," Tucker explained.

"Dignities?" The others repeated in unison.

"You know," Tucker answered impatiently, "important people."

They all laughed.

"You mean dignitaries!" Ashby chided.

"Whatever," Tucker replied nonchalantly.

"Well, what do you s'pose would bring such folk way up here in these mountains?" Joe questioned.

"Some old Indian woman," Tucker answered again.

"Now, why would all these important folk...and dignitaries too, be making such a fuss over some old Indian woman?" Ashby asked.

"Don't know. Pa said he couldn't figure it out either."

Several yellow jackets swarmed around the fish dangling down Ashby's back. He angrily swatted at them.

"We gotta get out'a here before these crazy bees eat the fish and me, too!"

But the cars kept coming. Finally, the last one passed by, leaving a cloud of dust, and the young boys headed home.

The procession moved along the curves and bends, over the hills and down the hollows and back up the long stretch of Oak Mountain. It finally came to a stop beside an old crumbling chimney, and they began to file out of their shiny late model cars. They walked silently up the hillside, through the new undergrowth, upward past the mountain chalet or 'tipi' as it was known locally. The women's heels sought footing on the rugged hillside as they came to a clearing and a small cemetery enclosed with a rusting wrought iron fence.

The rich Oak casket was carried to its final resting

place.

"It's fitting that it should be Oak," Jonathon whispered to Jessica, and she clutched his arm tightly.

Patrick moved to the front of the crowd with his big black Bible in hand. The people crowded closely to hear the words of Reverend Barrett. There was a serenity that pervaded the mountainside that morning and all in attendance were acutely aware of it.

Patrick seemed to be waiting for something. Then two men laboriously pushed the wheelchair up and into place beside him. He reached out and patted Pru's shoulder. She looked up at him confused, and he smiled down at her.

A moment of silence followed, and then Reverend Patrick Barrett began in a subdued voice..."Spring is home at last!"

'To every thing there is a season, and a time to every purpose under the Heaven: A time to be born, and a time to die; a time to plant, and a time to pluck up that which is planted; a time to kill, and a time to heal; a time to break down, and a time to build up; a time to weep, and a time to laugh; a time to mourn, and a time to dance; a time to cast away stones, and a time to gather stones together; a time to embrace, and a time to refrain from embracing; a time to get, and a time to lose; a time to keep, and a time to cast away; a time to rend, and a time to sew; a time to keep silence, and a time to speak; a time to love, and a time to hate; a time of war, and a time of peace'.

Patrick looked up and repeated, "Yes, 'to everything there is a season, and a time to every purpose under the Heaven'. And isn't it fitting that our Spring...our Spring Leaf...would find her time...at this season...the most beautiful of all...to leave us...for a far better place. And friends, we know it is a far better place where Spring has gone...for the Lord says so in His word. 'But as it is written, eye hath not seen, nor ear heard, neither have entered into the heart of man, the things which God hath prepared for them that love Him'."

"Looking around us on this lovely day, seeing the newness of life, its richness and beauty and hearing the gentle rustle of the new leaves on the old trees and the soft melody of our feathered friends, we wonder how God could top this!"

"We wonder...but Spring knows...for in the autumn of her life, she trusted in the Lord. I kind'a think that Sis might be busy up there throughout eternity... painting all that beauty."

Reverend Barrett smiled up into the heavens through his tears and then read from his big Bible....

" 'And ye shall know the truth, and the truth shall make you free'. John 8:32. Spring found that truth. She found it in the Black Hills out west and she found it in our beloved Blue Ridge. When she found the truth, she found that He is everywhere."

The last car descended Oak Mountain. Dakotah stood tall and proud, holding back the tears. Emily and Laurietta hovered close by as a gentle mountain breeze caressed the nearby Dogwoods and the delicate white flowers quivered.

Emily broke the silence, "Life must go on." She gently wrapped her thin arm around Dakotah's firm shoulders. Laurietta grabbed her hand. The three girls began walking down the mountainside.

Dakotah paused and looked back, "There is no word in Sioux for good-bye."

Emily and Laurietta nodded, and they continued down the mountain.

"Well," Laurietta declared, "the next time you two see me, you must address me as Dr. Laurietta Banks. I guess it's time for us to make our mark."

Dakotah smiled weakly, "Mom always taught me...to learn the white man's ways...that it's a white man's world, but to hold onto my roots...for that's where my strength lies. Girls, I have my work cut out for me."

They both looked at her.

She smiled again, "I'm going to take up Mom's torch."

"We knew you would," Laurietta kidded.

They turned to Emily, "What about you?"

She looked at them with a twinkle in her eye, "I have a book to write."

"What book?" they asked in unison.

She turned and looked back up the hillside at the small cemetery with the fresh mound of dirt.

"*Spring's Return*," she replied.

Carolyn Tyree Feagans grew up in Amherst
County, adjacent to Lynchburg, at the foot
of the Blue Ridge Mountains.
(P.O. Box 10811, Lynchburg, Virginia 24506)